ROCKETS LIT UP THE NIGHT

Flashes of light and thunder rained cordite brimstone into the forest. An infernal chain-saw roar of .50-caliber guns droned beneath the blasts. The barrage sheared off treetops and turned them to sawdust before they hit the ground. Sharp reports from a dozen grenades were barely pops in the nightmarish din that swelled around Logan.

A blast hurled him forward, a leaf in a firestorm. Heavy bullets raked his back as he fell, ripping away large chunks of his flesh. Another explosion scoured him with burning shrapnel. He struck the ground in agony, his body torn and seared, his skin flayed. Screams of rage lay trapped inside his chest, unable to escape his bloody, shredded throat. His fingers clawed the carpet of dried pine needles, dug at the cold black dirt underneath. Instinct told him to get up, keep moving, but his leg muscles were still knitting themselves back together, magnifying his suffering.

The hum of engines and servos counterpointed a regular cadence of deafening booms, the thunderous herald of several tons of metal striding at a quickstep. Determined not to meet Death with his back turned, Logan fought against his ravaged body, forced himself to roll over onto his back. The metal colossus came to a halt towering above him, an iron god gazing with contempt at a mere insect.

Logan gathered the phlegm from his throat and spat it at the weathered, gray foot of th

he said in a voice like a couga

A ruby-red flash of laser li

The machine's targeting syste

WOLVERINE®

ROAD OF BONES

a novel by
David Alan Mack

based on the
Marvel Comic Book

POCKET STAR BOOKS
NEW YORK LONDON TORONTO SYDNEY

An *Original* Publication of POCKET BOOKS

 A Pocket Star Book published by
POCKET BOOKS, a division of Simon & Schuster, Inc.
1230 Avenue of the Americas, New York, NY 10020

ISBN-13:   978-1-4165-1069-7
ISBN-10:   1-4165-1069-9

This Pocket Star Books paperback edition November 2006

10 9 8 7 6 5 4 3 2 1

POCKET STAR BOOKS and colophon are registered trademarks of Simon & Schuster, Inc.

Cover art by David W. Mack

Manufactured in the United States of America

For information regarding special discounts for bulk purchases, please contact Simon & Schuster Special Sales at 1-800-456-6798 or business@simonandschuster.com.

For Kara, who makes my own road
a better one on which to walk.

"[History is] a record of unjustified suffering, irreparable loss, tragedy without catharsis. It's a gorgon: stare at it too long and it turns you to stone."

—BARRY GEWEN,
The New York Times,
June 4, 2005

1

A SINGLE LEAP AND MIYOKO TAKAGI WAS OVER the electrified fence. She landed, silent as a flake of snow falling on water, behind a patrolling security guard who had just turned his back.

Her gloved hand covered his mouth as her *kusarigama* found his heart. He twitched in her lethal embrace for a moment, then his body went limp. She pulled her blade from his chest, wiped it clean on his leg, and lowered his corpse into the shadows.

Ahead of her, two more of her fellow ninjas neutralized two more perimeter guards—one with a poison blow dart, the other with a throwing star. Both guards fell without a sound in the darkness, out of view of the security cameras that ringed the exterior of Tanaka Biotechnology's world headquarters.

Miyoko plucked three *shaken* from inside her black uniform and hurled them all with a single flick of her wrist. The throwing stars sailed apart on precise but subtle angles. Each one severed the data line of a different security camera. The path to the rear loading dock was now clear for the second team to move up. The loss of video signal would be certain to provoke an alert inside the building's security center, but if all was proceeding as planned, two of her ninjas were already there.

She traversed the underside of the loading dock's overhang in an inverted climb and stopped above the door to the building's main shipping office. Through the slats of the door's top ventilation grating, she saw inside the main freight-handling area. Its workers and managers lay unconscious on the floor. *Good,* she thought. *Sumotomo released the gas already. That should take care of all but the secured floors upstairs.*

Two more security guards turned the far corner and walked toward her. Pressed against the ceiling overhang, Miyoko remained absolutely still. Another trio of *shaken* was ready in the fingers of her right hand. This part of the dock was well lit and monitored by the cameras; she would have to wait until the security cameras deactivated before neutralizing the two men below. Killing them now could compromise the entire mission.

All this effort for the benefit of fools. Miyoko resented the daimyo for burdening her with two gaijin on this mission. *My ninjas could have acquired the daimyo's prize without help from these amateurs. Maybe not tonight, but eventually.*

Unfortunately, for some reason, the daimyo was not willing to be patient this time. She blamed Alexei Pritikin, the Russian to whom the daimyo had given her as a consort. Though the daimyo had told her that her assignment was to defend Pritikin, she'd understood that her presence had been requested by the Russian for a purpose entirely different from protection.

The fact that Pritikin was undeniably in love with her only slightly ameliorated her contempt at having been offered up like a geisha. Quiet fury coiled her muscles as the guards walked closer. If they glanced up even for a moment, she would be revealed. Like so many full-time security personnel, however, they had grown bored and performed their tasks by rote.

Above the main door to the freight area, the security cameras' red power indicators dimmed. Her ninjas inside the skyscraper had prevailed; its security system was offline.

Miyoko unleashed two of her *shaken* at the guards, struck each in the carotid artery. They fell dead before they had time to know that they'd been killed. Then she flung her third throwing star toward the main gate along the rear alley, cutting its lock in a flash of sparks.

Now we get to see what the gaijin can do, she mused darkly.

Surge and Slake—a.k.a. Gregor and Oskar Golovanov—waited in the shadows near the T-shaped intersection of two narrow alleys.

"*Chort vozmi,* juice me up," Gregor said. "I can fry the grid and frag the fence, and we can walk in."

"No," said his twin brother, a fellow mutant. "The daimyo said to let the ninjas clear the way."

"Whatever," Gregor said, shaking his head in disgust. He could unleash enough different types of energy to burn, disrupt, disintegrate, stun, or kill just about anything on earth—but only if his brother first drained the power from something else and transferred it to him. A "symbiotic link"—that's what it had been called by the Soviet researchers who had poked and prodded and measured and tested the brothers since they were old enough to remember . . . and until they became old enough—and powerful enough—to escape.

He looked at Oskar and brooded. *Same blond hair, same blue eyes, same cleft chin—and not a damned thing in common.* "This is ridiculous, Oskar," he said in an irritated whisper. "We could be inside by now. Charge me!"

"From what, Gregor? The electric fence?" Oskar rolled his eyes. "There's not enough amperage to get us inside, never mind take out the security grid. . . . Just wait for the signal."

Several dozen meters beyond the electric fence, past a perimeter patrolled by armed guards and ferocious dogs, the imposing glass-and-steel façade of the Tanaka Biotechnology Corporation's world headquarters loomed high and mighty into the night, a new fixture on the skyline of Osaka, Japan. Somewhere inside this tightly defended fortress of science was the prize that the brothers had been sent to acquire and deliver.

They were near the building's rear loading docks, which were secured by a fifteen-foot-tall electric fence topped with barbed wire. Every fourth fence post was topped by a slowly swiveling video camera, of a kind that Gregor knew had been made to detect everything from infrared radiation to tachyon interactions, a feature that revealed most "invisible" interlopers. Whoever had designed this building's security systems had done so with mutants in mind. Gregor wasn't sure he wanted to know what was waiting for them inside the building, but he knew that if it relied on energy to work, then it would be no match for his brother's power-siphoning touch.

He looked at his watch. "We've been standing here for over an hour," he grumbled.

Oskar arched one eyebrow, an expression of his contempt for Gregor's impatience. "What, are you in a hurry? Got a hot date?"

"Maybe I do," Gregor said, trying not to sound defensive.

"No, you don't," Oskar said, just a touch too confident in his tone for Gregor's liking.

"And how would you know?"

"We won't be here long enough," Oskar said, his eyes fixed on the building across the alley. "And Miyoko would kill you."

"Mm-hm," Gregor mumbled dismissively. "I can handle her."

"Sure you can," Oskar said.

"Give me enough juice, I can fry anybody."

"You have to *see* them to fry them, Gregor. She's a fucking ninja. You'd be dead before you knew what hit you."

Gregor looked at his watch again and sighed. "What'd she say the signal would be?"

"That we'll know it when we see it."

No sooner had he said it when, on the other side of the electric fence, two security guards stopped in the middle of their rounds and collapsed silently to the ground. At the same moment, the cameras on the fence posts halted in mid-swivel, and their red indicator lights dimmed and went dark. An evanescent flurry of sparks spat from the gate's lock as it was bifurcated by a *shaken* moving faster than the human eye could see. With a long, whining creak of dry hinges, the rear gates of the Tanaka Biotechnology Corporation's headquarters lolled open.

"I guess that's our signal," Gregor said.

Oskar grimaced with disdain. "You think?"

The brothers moved quickly across the dark alley, toward the loading docks. They passed two unconscious dogs and approached a door that was sandwiched between two of the platform's tall metal-slat gates. Before they were halfway there, the door opened, spilling dim light onto the dock outside.

Gregor still found it odd to observe the effects of the ninjas' actions without ever seeing the hooded assassins themselves. Oskar moved ahead of him and preceded him up a short but steep flight of stairs and then through the door.

Half a dozen TBC workers in gray coveralls lay sprawled on the concrete floor. Inside a nearby office, their balding, slightly overweight night-shift supervisor was splayed across his own desk, facedown on a pile of papers. There was no blood in sight anywhere, just the faintly medicinal odor of expired chloroform gas. True to form, the ninjas had chosen the path of least resistance and least effort; the workers had been unarmed and had posed no threat, so it had been deemed sufficient simply to knock them unconscious. Gregor knew that the guards waiting upstairs would not receive such mercy. *At least, not from me,* he promised himself, unable to suppress a sadistic smirk of anticipation.

On the left was a door that led to a fireproofed stairwell; on the right was an open freight elevator.

The brothers faced each other and shook hands.

"Good luck," Gregor said to his twin.

"Good hunting," Oskar replied. He jogged away from Gregor and opened the door to the stairwell, then bounded down the steps toward the subbasement.

Gregor walked briskly into the freight elevator and shut its safety cage, which closed from the top and bottom, like a set of metal-mesh jaws. Seemingly of its own volition, the elevator jerked and lurched into motion, then rattled upward on steel cables that vibrated with an almost musical resonance.

If their accomplices had done their jobs properly, Gregor knew, Oskar would have an unimpeded path to the building's primary power center. From there, he could drain the building's dedicated generators and tap into an almost limitless supply of raw power from its connection to the municipal electrical grid. With all the unbridled electromagnetic forces that Oskar's efforts would unleash in the subbasement, there had been no point in equipping him with any kind of radio-frequency transmitter; the signal would be garbled by all the EM interference, and it likely would be unable to penetrate the steel and concrete shell of the skyscraper's foundation.

Not that Gregor needed any such link to Oskar to know when it would be time to attack. When his brother tapped into the juice, Gregor would know. He'd feel the tingling in his fingers, the heat on the back of his neck, the trembling adrenaline rush.

Soon enough, he'd have more raw power than

he'd know what to do with—but he was certain he'd think of something.

It had been a quiet evening on the sixty-eighth floor until the wall behind the elevator bank exploded.

Private security guard Yoshi Tamura dived to the floor behind the soda machine and covered his face. A hundred thousand needlelike splinters of wood were airborne, dancing on a plume of fire. Then the lights went out. Dust settled in the darkness. Yoshi's ears throbbed, his hearing dulled by the blast.

From the far end of the corridor, narrow flashlight beams cut through the stygian haze. As they sliced past one another, he barely glimpsed blurs of movement along the walls, floor, and ceiling, like dark phantoms or shadows unchained from substance. *Ninjas,* Yoshi realized. Most of his own training had been in a more noble vein of the martial arts, but he'd learned enough of the ways of *ninjutsu* to recognize it in action.

A lone figure emerged from the elevator shaft and swung on a rope into the corridor. The guards who were aiming the flashlights from the other end of the hallway fixed their beams on the intruder. He lifted his arm in their direction and showed them his empty palm.

"Freeze!" shouted one of the guards. "Get down on the—"

A blinding flash and a thunder crack. The flashlight beams went dark, and the charnel odor of burnt meat filled the passageway. The intruders walked away from Yoshi's position.

He activated his two-way radio to call for help. Static, loud and constant, dominated every channel in his earpiece. *Scrambled,* he realized. *So much for backup.*

Moving with well-rehearsed grace, Yoshi stripped off his uniform shirt, revealing his long-sleeved black turtleneck . . . and the dark scabbard that was strapped diagonally across his back. He pushed off his shoes, under which he wore black-canvas *tabi*— one of the few practices he had adopted from *ninjutsu.* After taking a moment to reassure himself that he was alone and undetected, he donned a black balaclava to maximize his harmony with the shadows. Steady in his hand, his *wakizashi* glided free of its scabbard without making a sound. Brandishing the short sword, he set out in pursuit of the intruder he had seen—while remaining mindful of all the others that he couldn't see but nonetheless knew were there.

Darkness suited him. It was familiar, comfortable. He put on a pair of snug-fitting night-vision spectacles and skulked to the corner, stealthily navigating the obstacle course of broken concrete, pulverized brick and drywall, and fractured wooden debris. The air was thick with the cordite stench of overheated metal and broken stone. From the ragged gap in the wall behind him, he heard the snap and crackle of severed electrical wires.

Beyond the corner, there was only more darkness, dim even with the benefit of his UV glasses. Distant voices, panicked and plaintive, could have been only more security guards. One by one their voices were silenced—a whisper of steel through the air, the heavy *thump* of bodies falling to the dusty floor. Yoshi prowled forward, following the faint trail of sound.

A vibration in the air was all the warning he had. It was enough. He dodged, and the ninja's blade lunged past him. One cut across the ninja's throat ended the battle. Yoshi caught the man's corpse and lowered it quietly to the floor, wary of alerting any of the other assassins lurking about.

The intruders were moving quickly. He had assumed that they would be after the stockpiles of rare pathogens that were used at TBC for top-secret research. As he passed the storage areas, however, he saw that they were untouched. The ninjas and their human cannon were after something else.

Yoshi stepped onto the syrupy slickness of spilled blood. To his left lay another guard. *No sign of respiration,* Yoshi noted. *No point checking his pulse, he's gone.* He moved toward the next intersection, which led into a heavily barricaded central corridor. Then the darkness turned to golden sunrise: a fiery blast erupted beyond the next corner, momentarily overwhelming his UV glasses. Squinting against the glare, he saw four ninjas perched along the corner or dangling in the nook between the wall and the drop-tile ceiling. They were silhouetted in the red-orange light. As surely as the blast had revealed their presence to him, it had announced his own to them. Subtlety immediately lost its value.

The explosive glow faded like dying hope, and the ninjas rushed toward Yoshi, as if they were one with the encroaching shadows. Still half blind, he felt their approach, read the patter of footfalls and the hushing song of arcing steel.

A block, a parry, and an uppercut. One of the ninjas fell.

Yoshi ducked and turned, swung his blade to make another block, closer than before. He feinted right, lunged left, drew the closest ninja forward into a careless thrust. Yoshi's *wakizashi* pierced the other man's throat, through muscle and cartilage, then flicked out, severing the carotid artery.

Weighted chains snared his ankles before he could dance free. A hard upward tug landed him on his back. Rather than struggle to escape, he pulled forward on the chains by tucking his knees to his chest. As the ninja holding the chains was pulled forward and down, Yoshi's *wakizashi* jabbed up and twisted, impaling the man as he landed against Yoshi's feet. Then Yoshi pushed back and launched the man at his last remaining comrade.

The fourth ninja ducked clear. Though it was a

risk, Yoshi expended half a second to untangle his feet from the chain of the *kusari-gama*. Then he sprang back to his feet—and realized that the last ninja had either fled or hidden himself beyond discovery.

Another explosion rumbled, again from the hallway that led to the top-secret laboratory. Forced to choose between seeking out the vanished ninja and going after the cannon, Yoshi decided that the man with the firepower seemed to be the one for whom the ninjas were running interference. That made him the higher-priority target.

Yoshi turned the corner and halted. A fiery tunnel of demolished metal and reinforced concrete stretched out ahead of him. He had expected to find the cannon man working his way through the multiple reinforced barricades; the blast that had cleared this path, however, had been singular and focused. As a further testament to the control of its creator, the devastation stopped shy of the final wall, which would have rent a smoking scar in the façade of the building, drawing all kinds of attention from the outside world. That wall was pristine, its paint unblistered and its "No Smoking" sign respectfully unburned, despite being illuminated by the firelight of all that had been laid waste in the dozen or so meters between there and the intersection where Yoshi stood.

Footsteps crunched across crumbled cement and

broken glass at the far end of the hallway. Then a short, unimposing man was prodded forward, toward the smoldering impromptu passage. The man was one of the scientists Yoshi had often seen there, working late into the night, for the past several months. Fair-haired and bespectacled, he was in his late forties, and he wore a classic white lab coat over his wrinkled and coffee-stained dress shirt and rumpled trousers. Clutched in his folded arms was a metallic case. Behind him was the walking cannon.

Yoshi ducked behind the corner before either of the men saw him. *Hostage situation.* He abandoned all the strategies he had considered up until that moment and sheathed his sword. *Changes all the rules. Can't risk getting our guy killed.*

Using equipment left in place by the now-dead ninjas, Yoshi pulled himself above the drop-tile ceiling, then reeled in the rope and softly lowered the displaced tile back onto its square in the aluminum grid. Moments later, he heard the cannon say to the scientist in Russian-accented English, "Turn left."

The two men passed directly beneath Yoshi . . . then their footsteps stopped. Yoshi lifted the corner of the drop tile to see what was going on. Below, the cannon inspected the bodies of the three dead ninjas. He looked at the scientist. "Take a few steps back," he said. The scientist did so, and then the cannon pointed at the ninjas—and disintegrated them, one by one.

"Keep moving," the cannon said as he gave his

hostage a shove, and the two of them continued their quick-step march back toward the breach in the elevator shaft's wall.

Yoshi dropped back down, landed gently, and went into a crouch. *Have to follow them,* he decided, stealing forward in a hunched run. *Trail them, get past this interference, and call for backup. Maybe slow their getaway.* He was careful to remain far enough back to avoid being detected but close enough not to lose sight of the intruder and his hostage.

In less than a minute the pair was back at the breach in the wall. The cannon man took the briefcase from the scientist, then he knotted a rope harness around the smaller man's torso and pushed him into the elevator shaft. Reaching in, he grabbed a second, more professional-looking harness, stepped into it, and passed through the breach into the elevator shaft.

Rushing forward to the breach, Yoshi peeked upward first, to see if the intruders were heading toward the roof for extraction by helicopter. There was no sign of activity up there, except for the turning of the elevator's winches and the trembling of its cables. He edged forward and looked down to gauge the intruder's descent toward his escape.

A four-pointed *shaken* bit into Yoshi's throat.

Reflexively, his hand reached toward the wound, but he knew already that it was too late. The *hira shuriken* had severed his carotid artery and his larynx.

Death would be swift and silent. He pitched forward and plunged headfirst into the elevator shaft. Falling was heavenly, like freedom. Then he was snared in a tangle of metal cables, jerked to a hard and sudden stop, trapped in a suddenly constricting noose of steel.

Yoshi Tamura, honored *bushi* of the Tanaka clan, offered a final heartfelt prayer to his ancestors, then surrendered as darkness took him into its silken embrace.

Alone in the subbasement, Oskar felt Gregor's appetite for power subside. When Gregor's need was at its greatest level, Oskar felt it like a hunger, a gulf of desperate emptiness in his gut. He had learned early in his career with Gregor that he couldn't store much energy; his body wasn't designed to act as a battery. He was more like a capacitor, a circuit through which vast reservoirs of raw power could be channeled to his brother.

One thing that Oskar could not do was take power from living things: plants, animals, people, fire—all were immune to the effects of his energy-siphoning talent. Any nonliving power source would do, though: a live wire, a microwave beam, even sunlight, though it was too diffuse to be of any practical value to Gregor. The more concentrated the energy supply, the better. Car engines could pack a quick punch; a city's electrical grid was more reliable. Lately, Oskar had begun to wonder if he could absorb the normally lethal radiation of a nuclear reactor while siphoning its power. It was an experiment that so far he'd lacked the courage to attempt.

He withdrew his hands from the electrical junction. Immediately, he missed the rush of connection, the warm glow of conductance that accompanied his transmissions of power to Gregor. His symbiotic connection faded slightly as the bond of energy diminished and returned to its normal level.

Steam hissed and ventilator systems throbbed in the sparsely lit, drab gray sublevel. Oskar stepped quickly, slipped through narrow passages between tall banks of machinery and generators and phone-switching clusters. In less than a minute, he was springing back up the stairs, climbing the three switchback flights to the loading bay.

The timing was perfect. He walked through the door just as the safety cage of the freight elevator parted to reveal Gregor and the man they'd come to get. "Dr. Falco," Oskar said to the pallid, trembling scientist. "So good of you to join us." Falco glanced suspiciously at Oskar and said nothing in reply.

Gregor grabbed the slim, bookish man by the cuff of his lab coat and pulled him toward the exit. "Keep moving, Herr Doktor," he said. "We're on a schedule." It had always troubled Oskar to see how his brother's personality changed immediately after one of their missions. Flush from the infusion of raw power, Gregor became edgy, aggressive, hostile. It brought out a cruel streak in him, one that had grown darker and more pronounced during the years that they had worked together as mercenaries.

Oskar followed his brother through the door to the loading platform, down the short, steep stairs, and back out the open gate toward the alley. From the darkness, a black van pulled up in front of the gate and skidded to a halt. Its side door slid open as the brothers and Dr. Falco approached. Gregor pushed the scientist forward; the man banged his shin roughly against the edge of the van's doorway and yelped in pain.

"Nice manners, Gregor," Oskar scolded, while helping the hobbled Dr. Falco into the van.

Shrugging his shoulders, Gregor defensively shot back, "What do I look like? His valet?"

"You don't dress well enough to be a valet."

A female voice from inside the van rebuked them sharply: "Both of you, shut up and get in." They did as they were told.

Gregor waited for Oskar to get in, then pulled the door closed behind them. The van accelerated smoothly and quietly as it hurtled headlong into the urban nightscape of Osaka.

"That place was wide open," Gregor boasted. He cracked his knuckles. "I shoulda got in some target practice, fried a few more walls just for fun. Coulda burned the whole place down."

"With us inside it," Oskar chided him. "Brilliant."

"I told you two to shut up," said the woman driving the van. The threat in her tone was as implicit as her instruction.

You'll get us both killed one of these days, Oskar brooded, unwilling to look at his brother while silently cursing him. *Never thinking, never planning ahead. Foolish. Careless. Reckless.* But that had always been the way with the two of them. Oskar had always been the thinker, the planner, the strategist; he'd had to be. Gregor had always been able, by instinct, to wield the power given to him by Oskar. But it had always been Oskar's responsibility to guarantee that there would be enough energy to get a job done and that he could get to it without putting himself in jeopardy.

Unlike Gregor's talent, Oskar's skills hadn't come naturally. Caution, foresight, contingency planning— these were all vital contributions that Gregor mocked, but Oskar's penchant for overpreparation had saved them both on numerous occasions.

One of these days, he knew, *it won't be enough.*

With Gregor, nothing was *ever* enough. All his appetites were equally insatiable: gourmet food, luxury sports cars, vintage wines and liquors, designer clothes, five-star hotels, exclusive call girls . . . Gregor's philosophy was that with his great power had also come great entitlement.

Eventually, of course, all of Gregor's desires came to ruin. He would eat and drink himself sick, then vomit half the night and wake up the next day too hoarse to speak. Priceless bottles of wine often became targets for his demented variety of pulse-blast skeet shooting. All his cars ended up wrapped around trees or telephone poles, or smashed into other cars, or submerged beyond recovery in a lake or a river. Every suit he wore was reduced to tatters inside of a week. Hotel rooms were transmogrified, seemingly overnight, into boxes of rubble. And Oskar had yet to see one of Gregor's achingly beautiful, thousand-dollar-an-hour prostitutes depart his company without a black eye or a bloody, broken nose to remember him by.

The only commodity that Gregor coveted more than all those others put together, of course, was power itself.

It did not, in Oskar's opinion, bode well for their future.

2

LOGAN KNEELED ON THE WHITE STONE SLAB, rested his empty palms on his thighs, and bowed his head. A breeze, sweet with the promise of rain and the scent of new cherry blossoms, rustled the leaves of drooping boughs overhead, dappling the grave-yard with pale dawn light. Around him, generations of the dead lay in close company beneath ancient trees, honored by legions of leaning stones whose surfaces were thick with deep green lichen. Decades of acid rain had washed the markers white as albinos and worn down their inscriptions until they were all but illegible, beyond understanding, like a conversation cut short.

A million blades of grass trembled in silent unison. From somewhere close by came a sparrow's lonely song.

Mariko Yashida's gravestone towered in front of Logan, backlit by the rising sun. Its smooth, pale marble was as hard as his own heart, which still sank into despair when reminded of Mariko's absence. He had brought her a single red rose as a tribute; it rested at his feet—one perfect bloom for the one true love of his life, gone now all these years.

Her portrait was set into the face of the stone monument and protected by a transparent plate of Plexiglas. It hurt to look upon her as she had been. His guilt pursued him like an inquisitor; it reminded him of the pain and terror he had seen in her eyes when the blowfish toxin began to wreak its hideous effects on her nervous system. In the theater of his memory he relived her fateful request, the moment when she'd asked him to give her a merciful death. To let her die by his hand.

Honoring her request had been the right thing to do. That hadn't made it any less horrific. To see her impaled on his claws, on those shining blades of adamantium, had sickened him. He'd felt the fluttering tremors of her dying heart as death took her. When at last he'd pulled his claws free and realized that they were slicked with her blood, he'd had to fight a momentary temptation to use them to commit seppuku.

Killing her had cost him a part of his soul, the part that had known how to trust. How to hope. How to forgive. It lay buried now beside the memory of the one woman who had been able to look past his feral countenance and believe in the man he had struggled—and was still struggling—to be.

Some of his wiser friends had suggested that he focus on better memories during his visit today. *As if I could ever forget,* Logan told himself. This already grim anniversary was one that, with good reason, Logan had learned to dread. His foes had made a habit of visiting chaos and tragedy upon him, and on those close to him, at this time of year. Once, he'd nearly lost his foster daughter, Amiko, to Sabretooth and his accomplices, who had decided that the anniversary of Mariko's death should mark the opening day of Wolverine Hunting Season. Logan had become increasingly wary of this date ever since.

He reached up and rested one hand on the cold stone. *I miss you, darlin'. Every single day.*

The sun rose higher, spilling golden light and endless shadows across the countryside. Another billow of cool air snaked under Logan's loose, bomber-style leather jacket and rust-colored canvas shirt. He was traveling incognito, without his costume, whose insulation he had grown accustomed to. He didn't mind the cold, really; it simply had been a while since he'd last noticed it.

He considered reaching back to his weathered

brown rucksack and digging out a scarf that Rogue had badgered him into packing before he'd left the Xavier Institute. . . . How long had it been since they'd parted company? He couldn't remember off-hand. Months, at least. He hadn't kept track of the days. Hadn't needed to. Hadn't wanted to.

All he'd really wanted was to get away for a while—from everyone, from everything. But no matter where he went, his troubles always seemed a step ahead of him. In every town, on every lonely stretch of road, in every sprawl of ostensibly untamed wilderness, it was *something*. An old friend in need of help. An old adversary with a score to set-tle. An innocent person in danger, who would live or die by the grace of Logan's intervention, or lack thereof.

He'd heard the footsteps from nearly a hundred meters away. Whoever it was moved decisively, with-out any attempt at silence; the footfalls were marked by the distinctive *click* of high heels on stone. The brief intervals between steps suggested a person of medium height. A subtle, delicately floral essence of perfume was borne ahead of the visitor on a hush of morning air.

This better be a dame, Logan thought, *or this is gonna be weird.* Withdrawing his hand from Mariko's grave monument, he stood and turned to face the only other person in the graveyard.

She was Chinese; he saw that on first glance. Slender and innocently beautiful, she moved with a balletic grace, and her pace didn't falter as he gave her his full attention. Her long black hair was wind-tossed. It moved as though it were dancing in time with the tempo of her ivory-hued, spike-heeled pumps clacking against the paving stones. She looked young, barely out of her teens, but she carried herself with elegance and poise.

Her sense of fashion was distinctly Western and modern; she wore a white business suit, cut by a professional to flatter her figure. Its jacket was of the two-button variety and slightly longer than a man's suit jacket would have been. Beneath the long, narrow V of its notched lapels, a shimmering band of white silk was all that showed of her chemise. As she moved closer, Logan noticed a subtle, off-white, narrow-vertical-stripe pattern in her jacket and her trousers.

She clearly wasn't armed, but she also moved with the confidence of someone who didn't need to put her trust in weapons.

Several meters away from Logan, she stopped. "Mr. Logan," she said with a slight bow of her head. "My apologies for disturbing you here."

"You can't be that sorry," he said. "After all, you're here." After a few seconds, when it became clear to Logan that the young woman wasn't going to be baited into an argument, he added, "So, you know my name. . . . What's yours, kid?"

"Tse Wai Ying," she said. "And I would prefer that you not address me as 'kid.' "

"Suit yourself, doll," Logan said, intentionally defying the spirit of her request. He fished a box-cut Punch Rare Corojo from an inside pocket of his jacket, extended a single claw from between the first and second knuckles of his right hand, and expertly sliced off the tip of the cigar. He retracted the claw back into his forearm with a twinge of pain and a barely audible *snikt*. Fishing in another pocket for his Zippo, he asked, "What can I do for you?"

"My employer humbly requests the honor of your visit this morning. She is in need of your aid."

He clutched the cigar between his teeth as he opened and lit his Zippo with a snap of his fingers. The Corojo lit easily and evenly. He savored a mouthful of its smooth, rich smoke, then expelled it with a gentle puff. "And your boss would be—?"

"Lady Setsuko Tanaka," Wai Ying said.

Logan's jaw slackened. He almost dropped his cigar. "What's happened? Is she all right?"

"She is unharmed, Mr. Logan," Wai Ying said. "But a terrible crime has been committed against her, and she asks for your assistance—and your . . . *discretion.*"

Setsuko was the daughter of Masao Tanaka, a man who had befriended Logan in the 1950s during his years of training in isolation at Jasmine Falls, in the high mountains of Japan. Logan had been forced to leave Jasmine Falls after accidentally cutting his sparring partner, Miyagi, while training with swords beneath the falls. Later, when Logan had sought permission to return and resume his studies, the sensei had initially been of a mind to turn him away. Tanaka, however, had spoken on Logan's behalf, vouchsafing his own word of honor that Logan could be trusted. It was one of the most selfless things that anyone had ever done for Logan up to that point; he'd pledged an honor debt to Tanaka and his kin that day.

Now, decades later, that debt had finally come due.

He curled an index finger around the cigar and took it from his mouth. "I'm guessing you have a car?"

"It's waiting for us at the cemetery gate, yes."

Logan nodded. "Fine." He stuck the cigar between his teeth and turned back toward Mariko's grave marker. Once more he pressed his palm against the glass-smooth, icy stone surface. *Duty calls, darlin'. Like always.* He leaned down, picked up his rucksack, and slung it casually over his shoulder. It didn't weigh much; he hadn't planned on staying long, and he always traveled light anyway. He took a few steps toward Wai Ying and gestured to the gate. "Let's go."

The moment Logan saw the "car" that was waiting for them at the cemetery gate, he realized that Wai Ying possessed a peculiar gift for understatement.

The vehicle that had sat idling while she'd gone in to collect him was a black stretch Mercedes limousine, its entire elongated body cleaned and buffed to a perfect mirror brilliance.

The driver, a gray-haired Japanese man, opened the rear passenger-side door and dipped the visor of his hat politely in Logan's direction. "Excuse me, sir," he said with a mild accent, then pointed at the lit cigar in Logan's left hand. A moment later, the chauffeur recoiled from Logan's withering glare.

"*Daijyoubu-desu,* Hattoro," Wai Ying said. The driver nodded curtly and stepped aside. Logan tossed his rucksack through the open door, then climbed in and settled into the limo's luxurious leather rear seat. The interior of the car smelled brand new.

"Back to the tower," Wai Ying said as she climbed in and sat down next to Logan. The chauffeur closed the door behind her, then walked back to the front of the car. Wai Ying gestured toward the bar, which was recessed into the walls of the rear passenger compartment. "Would you care for a drink?"

"It's six-fifteen in the morning," Logan replied.

"We have espresso," she said.

"Maybe later." Up front, the chauffeur settled into his seat. Gravel crunched under the tires as the limousine pulled away from the gate and accelerated quickly downhill, back to the main road. The rural countryside blurred past outside the dark-tinted windows. Logan noted, from Wai Ying's spectral reflection on the car window, that she was watching him. Her expression was one of intense curiosity.

"Go ahead," he said. "Ask."

She accepted his invitation without embarrassment. "You're the one they call Wolverine, aren't you?"

Smirking slightly, he puffed once on his cigar and exhaled a small cloud of smoke. "I been called lots of things."

"Which name do you prefer?"

"Logan'll do just fine."

She leaned forward and took a thermos and a small porcelain sipping cup from the bar. As soon as she twisted open the thermos's lid, Logan's acute sense of smell was flooded with the rich, sweet aroma of freshly brewed espresso. A second whiff convinced him that the brand was Perla Nera. Wai Ying poured a double shot into her cup. Catching his stare out of the corner of her eye, she offered him the cup. "Care for some?"

"Why not?" He accepted the drink. She reached forward and poured another double for herself. She set it down in a drink nook on the door and put away the thermos. Then she lifted her espresso and turned back toward Logan. "*Salute,*" she said.

"Bottoms up," Logan replied. They downed their espressos in unison. He let out a satisfied breath as he savored its lingering flavor. "Thick as mud and strong as the devil," he said. "Just the way I like it."

The limo made the turn toward the highway and

continued to pick up speed. Wai Ying and Logan rode together in silence for what felt to him like a long while. Watching the signs, he noted that they were headed toward Osaka.

"So," he said, breaking the silence, "how long have you worked for Setsuko?"

"The details of my employment are confidential," she said.

"Of course they are."

"I'm sure you understand," she added.

"Not really."

Wai Ying appeared to consider her response carefully—or perhaps she was pondering whether she should respond at all. After several seconds, she said, "The Japanese government has not been as *openly* hostile as those of many Western countries, but it remains . . . *suspicious.* Secrecy is a virtue here."

Logan nodded his understanding: she was a mutant. So far, Japan had been spared a lot of the political strife that folks like Senator Kelley and his ilk had stirred up in the United States, but the Japanese government was undoubtedly wary of the potential threat to its authority that mutants represented. *New and different* was always something to be feared, no matter the time or place; experience had taught Logan that bitter lesson many times. He asked, "Do you have an alias that you go by?"

"I've never seen the need for one," she said. "And I don't wear a costume."

"Good choice." He exhaled another puff of smoke. "Truth is, they all start to look alike after a while."

"You wear a costume, though, don't you?"

He looked out the window and frowned at his own haggard reflection. "Not at the moment," he said. "Not for a while now."

"Why? Did something happen?"

Logan stifled a grim chuckle until all that was left was a muffled grunt of disillusionment. "Somethin' always does, doll," he said. "Somethin' always does."

The last time Logan had seen Setsuko Tanaka, she had been only a child, wide-eyed and vivacious. As the cherrywood double doors of her corner office swung open ahead of him, he beheld her as she was today: a trim and striking woman in her late forties, attired in a charcoal-gray blazer, plum-colored blouse, black skirt, sheer stockings, and spike-heeled black Manolo Blahniks. Where once her eyes had radiated trust and optimism, she now wore the steely gaze of a seasoned corporate chief executive.

She strode forward to greet Logan. Several paces apart they halted; he bowed to her, and she reciprocated the gesture. He was careful to hold his bow just a fraction of a second longer than hers. With that formality out of the way, she stepped forward, closing the distance between them, and reached out to shake his hand. "Thank you for coming, Logan-san."

Shaking her hand, he nodded politely. "It's my honor to be of service, Tanaka-sama."

She motioned with a wave of her arm toward a pair of chairs in front of her enormous mahogany desk. "Please, have a seat."

"I'd rather stand," he said as he followed her toward her desk. "It was a long ride in."

"Whichever you prefer," Setsuko said, moving behind her desk. Wai Ying followed Logan into the office and shut the double doors behind her. Taking a moment to look around, Logan noted that, like the rest of the building's interior spaces he had seen so far, it seemed to have been deliberately stripped of personality.

Setsuko waited until Logan joined her at the desk before she spoke. "I'll get straight to business," she said. "A few hours ago, this building was invaded and burglarized by a combined force of ninjas and mutants. They absconded with three things: our only sample of an experimental new drug that we've nicknamed Panacea, a set of flash memory cards containing all our research on how to synthesize the drug, and our chief Panacea researcher, Dr. Nikolai Falco."

Logan sighed. "This is gonna get complicated, isn't it?"

"I'm afraid so," Setsuko replied.

"In that case, I guess I'll sit down."

He sagged into the chair behind him, and the two

women settled into their own seats. Setsuko folded her hands in front of her on the desk and continued. "Panacea is a drug derived from a plant that our researchers discovered in Brazil more than a decade ago. Since then, the original plant has been rendered extinct by clear-cut logging in the Amazon basin. We've been trying to synthesize it artificially for years, and we were on the verge of a breakthrough when this happened."

"All right," Logan said. "I'll bite. What's the big deal about your new drug?"

"It can cure anything," Setsuko said.

"What do you mean, 'anything'?"

"Exactly that, Logan-san," she said. *Anything. Everything.* Illness, infection, injury . . . cancer, tuberculosis, the common cold—it can cure them all, and any other affliction you'd care to name. Viral, bacterial, congenital, it doesn't matter. We call it Panacea for a reason."

"The perfect drug," Logan muttered.

"Well," Setsuko demurred, "I wouldn't call it perfect. It does have one serious, unfortunate flaw."

He leaned forward. "And that would be—?"

"From the first dose," Setsuko said, "it obliterates the patient's immune system forever. Unfortunately, while the damage it does to the patient is permanent, its curative properties are temporary. The patient's health—and life—depend from that point forward on frequent booster injections."

"How frequent?"

"A person who receives it once will have to be dosed again every twenty-four hours for the rest of his life."

The more Logan heard, the more he hated what he was being told. "And if the patient doesn't get his dose?"

"Patients who stop taking Panacea die within seventy-two hours of their last injection. *Every time.*"

"Jesus Christ," Logan whispered, horrified. "And you wanted to mass-produce this stuff?"

Anger hardened Setsuko's expression. "Of course not," she said, her offense at his implication sharp in her voice. "For years I've forbidden my people even to discuss it outside the lab. We've all been aware since the beginning of how this drug could be abused if it fell into the wrong hands. Our goal has been to separate its healing properties from its toxic ones. I vowed from the start that we would never reveal this drug to the world until we'd made it safe."

Logan bowed his head with shame. "My apologies, Tanaka-sama. Please forgive my presumption."

"It's already forgotten," she said, then she picked up where she'd left off. "Dr. Falco was preparing to synthesize a safe version of the drug when he was kidnapped and the sample was stolen." She got up from her chair and paced toward the south-facing panoramic window to Logan's left. "The drug, its synthesis formula, and the one man who knows more about it than anyone else on earth are now all in the hands of some unknown third party, whose intentions for it are at best unknown."

"Let me guess," Logan said, his inner cynic rising to the fore. "You want me to save your scientist and steal back your missing wonder drug, right?"

"And we'd like you to do it without alerting the public—or attracting any . . . *official* attention."

"I get it," he grumbled. "Confiscation with prejudice."

Perhaps sensing his distaste for the nature of her request, Setsuko said, "This isn't some petty theft I'm asking of you. A man's life is at stake—and possibly the fate of all humanity."

Logan folded his arms across his chest. "If you ask me, you oughtta destroy it, not bring it back. As long as you have it, it'll be a target." Then he added ominously, "*You'll* be a target."

"I'm sure your pessimism is well founded, Logan-san," Setsuko said. "But I've devoted the past decade of my life, the future of my company, and my entire fortune to the perfection of Panacea. I can't—*won't*—give up on it now, not when it's so close to becoming a reality."

"And when you're so close to becoming Japan's newest billionaire," Logan added.

"Funny thing about philanthropy," Setsuko replied. "You have to *have* money before you can give it away."

It was probably a white lie, Logan figured. At the very least a distortion. He'd heard of more than a few wealthy people who liked to write thousand-dollar checks and call themselves philanthropists. As much as he wanted to believe that Setsuko wasn't just exaggerating her charitable intentions, she had too sharp an edge to her demeanor for him to believe that she was just a saint in sinner's clothing.

Before he could call her bluff, she added, "At the very least, please help rescue Dr. Falco."

With a heavy sigh, he unfolded his arms and nodded. "All right, you have my word: I'll do my best to save him." Reacting to Setsuko's inquisitively raised eyebrow, he continued, "And I'll see if I can get your wonder drug back."

Setsuko lowered her head in a courteous nod. "Thank you, Logan-san. You honor us." She picked up a slim, brown cardboard file folder and handed it to Logan. He flipped idly through the few pages inside—a biographical one-sheet about the missing Dr. Falco and a few digital photos of the metal carrying case used to transport the Panacea sample. "I'll be making available all my best resources to assist you," she said. "A TBC private jet, an unlimited expense account, our communications and security intelligence network, and the aid of my personal bodyguard."

Personal bodyguard? "You ain't gonna tell me it's—"

"I'm sure you and Ms. Tse will make an excellent team."

"No offense," Logan protested, "but I work better alone."

"It's not negotiable," Setsuko insisted. "She'll be your pilot, your gal Friday—and your sole link to our resources."

Wai Ying lowered her chin and fixed Logan with a sly smirk. "Don't worry," she teased. "You're in good hands. I won't let anything bad happen to you."

Logan had no words that adequately conveyed his contempt for this turn of events, so he rolled his eyes and frowned instead. "Let's get this show on the road," he said, rising from his chair. "Take me down to the break-in."

A rush of alarming odors overwhelmed Logan's senses the moment he, Setsuko, and Wai Ying got off the elevator at the sixty-eighth floor. The hallway that they stepped into looked untouched, but the smells alone told him to expect to find a killing field around the next corner: charred wood and bitter ash, cooked flesh, fresh blood.

It wouldn't have taken his enhanced hearing to note the dozen or so voices talking about one piece of evidence or another. The camera flashes reflecting off the walls ahead were also a dead giveaway that a forensic team was hard at work.

He strode quickly ahead of his two companions and turned the corner. A squad of men and women all wearing identical dark blue windbreakers lined the

hallway. Most of them were working inside the seg-
ment near the end, where a scorch-edged tunnel had
been blasted through multiple redundant security
barricades. Some of the technicians kneeled beside
the bodies of slain security guards. Others busied
themselves collecting bits of debris or snapping photographs or measuring things. Regardless of the job
each person was doing, Logan noted that all their
equipment was brand-new and state of the art.

Passing several of the investigators as he stepped
through the violently crafted breaches, Logan noted
a curious absence of insignia anywhere on any of the
technicians' matching garments. His knack for suspicion asserted itself.

"These aren't the cops," he said over his shoulder
to Setsuko. "These are *your* people."

"Yes," she replied.

"You haven't called the authorities?" He was
appalled. "These people are dead. How're you gonna
spin *that?*"

"Carefully." Off his accusatory glance, she added,
"We don't want to alarm the public."

"Or risk losing your happy little monopoly," he
said. Then he turned the corner and saw the lab that
the barricades had been meant to protect. Outside of
the Xavier Institute and a few other cutting-edge
facilities, he had never seen anything like it. Equipment and computers were piled high in the dimly lit
space, reaching toward a distant ceiling and encircled

with an endless serpent of power cables and data lines. Forks of electrical power snaked between arcane-looking components, and bright blue flames danced inside chromatographic analyzers. Banks of plasma screens scrolled with sequences of genetic code, flickered with electron microscope images, or rearranged themselves in a never-ending digital simulation of a complex-looking molecule that Logan could only presume was the reason for all this carnage: Panacea.

He turned back toward Setsuko. "I'm betting the folks over at SHIELD don't know you've got a copy of their genetic sequencer," he said, jabbing backward over his shoulder with his thumb. "And I don't think the NSA planned on sharing its new parallel mainframe design, either."

"Angels don't succeed in the tech sector, Mr. Logan," Setsuko said. "Innovation is the key to advantage."

"Gee, that's catchy," Logan said. "Too bad I forgot my notebook, I'd jot that one down." Walking back past her and Wai Ying, he said in a low, irritated tone, "Try to keep up."

They followed him as he stepped carefully back through the blasted tunnel. He pointed at bodies or bits of evidence along the way while he narrated, a tour guide of the morbid and grotesque. "Uniform dimensions and stress patterns on all the breached barricades," he said, running a fingertip along the scorched edge. "This was all done with one shot." Pointing down at one of the dead guards, he observed, "Minimal blood spray on the floors, walls, or victims. Each of your guards was killed with a single strike that severed the carotid artery, larynx, and spinal cord. Narrow blade, probably a *ninja-to*." He kept walking while he pointed straight up. "The ninjas moved freely by staying above the drop-tile ceiling. Whoever installed that here oughtta be shot."

His boot scuffed a thin layer of dust on the linoleum. He kneeled down and dragged his fingertips through it, feeling its grit. As he lifted his fingers to his nose, the telltale odor of a crematorium was unmistakable. "Are all your people accounted for? Living and dead?"

Setsuko sounded surprised at the question. "Yes."

Logan stayed in a low crouch for half a minute, surveying the distribution of fine powder on the floor. "Then someone killed three of the ninjas, right here. Looks like the same guy who opened a hole in your lab dusted his accomplices on the way out." Pointing past the corner ahead, he asked, "That leads behind the elevator bank?"

Wai Ying nodded and answered for her boss. "That's right."

He stood and continued following the trail of destruction. Setsuko and Wai Ying remained close behind him. Stepping over two gruesomely charred bodies that had fallen one on top of the other, he remarked, "They were the first ones to die." Pointing ahead, toward the haphazard gap in the concrete wall on the right, he said, "Your friendly neighborhood fireballer came in through there. Probably gained access to your freight elevator." Once again, Wai Ying nodded to confirm his deduction. "Textbook entry," he said.

Peering through the gap and down into the abyssal darkness of the elevator shaft, he saw the beams of helmet lamps and a cluster of bright orange safety lines. Several rescue workers and a pair of elevator engineers freed a twisted, bloody corpse from a tangle of steel cables. They began hoisting it back up toward the breach, where a black body bag waited on the floor.

He looked sidelong at Setsuko. "Whose body is that?"

"Yoshi Tamura, our *bushi*," she said. "If you're right, and someone killed three of the ninjas, it was probably him. He was the ace up the sleeve of our security division."

Logan scowled. "An ace up your sleeve don't mean much when the other guy's got a royal flush."

He looked back down at the broken body of Yoshi Tamura. The rescue team lifted the *bushi*'s corpse level with the breach. As the cadaver swung over the edge, Logan saw the glint of something metallic in Tamura's savaged neck. He guided the body softly to rest on the floor, on top of the black bag. Fishing through the mangled meat of the dead man's neck and throat, he grasped the metal object embedded between the corpse's cervical vertebrae. It came free with a wet noise and pulled a ragged tail of muscle and tissue behind it. Logan shook bits of bone from the ninja *shaken* and wiped the four-pointed throwing star mostly clean on Tamura's torn clothing. Engraved on the center of the *shaken* was a peculiar emblem that Logan had never seen before:

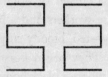

He tried rotating it ninety degrees. It didn't become any more familiar. He showed it to the two women behind him.

"Recognize it?" They shook their heads no. He tucked the *shaken* into his jacket pocket. "Neither do I," he said. "But I know a clue when I see one."

3

MIYOKO STEERED THE VAN OFF THE ROAD, through an ungated entrance into the dockyard. The sprawling expanse of weed-cracked asphalt and rusted, abandoned cargo machinery was like a forgotten piece of Osaka's industrial past, tucked behind some ram-shackle buildings on the far western edge of the city's bay. She guided the van through the slalom of derelict equipment and empty shipping containers, then hooked a hard right around the corner of one of the dock houses and stepped on the brake. The vehicle came to an abrupt, gravel-crunching halt.

The smell of the sea greeted Miyoko as she opened her door and got out of the idling van. She stepped toward the vehicle's rear, then pulled open its broad side door. It glided open with a low, smooth echo of weighty metal. Inside the rear compartment of the van, Oskar and Gregor sat on either side of the comically overrestrained Dr. Falco, who lay on the floor between them. Miyoko pointed at the identical mutants. "You two. Out."

The brothers traded quizzical expressions, then did as she had instructed. She stepped back and gave them room to climb out. They stood side by side in front of her, openly suspicious of her intentions.

She reached inside the folds of her black uniform jacket and pulled out a pair of travel-agency envelopes. She handed one to each of them, then waited while they opened them and inspected their contents. Oskar made sense of the situation first, and he looked and sounded annoyed. "Airline tickets?"

"There are two cars inside the dock-house garage," Miyoko said. "Leave separately, ten minutes apart. One of you departs from Yao Airport, the other from Osaka International. New passports are inside the envelopes."

"This wasn't the plan," Gregor said, mirroring his brother's irritated state. "We were supposed to deliver the scientist to the daimyo himself."

"That will be my responsibility now," she said. "Yours is to leave the country without attracting any more attention than you already have."

Oskar held up his boarding pass. "But separate flights? Separate *airports?* Was that really necessary?"

"Bad enough the daimyo sent me gaijin for this mission," she said, narrowing her eyes with contempt, "but he sent me *twins*." She pulled the van's side door shut. "Wait until I'm gone, then get out of here. And try to be forgettable."

She got back in the van, shifted it into gear, and accelerated away before the blasting brothers realized that, in addition to flying separately, they both would be flying coach.

Content to bide his time in silence and not provoke his captor, Dr. Nikolai Falco had made himself moderately comfortable after the twin brothers were evicted from the vehicle. He'd sat up and stretched his legs out in front of him. Roughly an hour after the van had departed the dockyard, the driver had pulled over and removed his bonds. She hadn't said anything, not an apology or a warning. One moment his hands had been bound behind him and his mouth gagged; the next he was free of constraints. He'd considered saying thank you, but under the circumstances it seemed inappropriate.

Hours had passed since then. The van's journey had continued uninterrupted. Peeking out the windshield, Falco saw that the sky was dimming with the advent of dusk. He was uncertain what direction they had been traveling. If the woman had driven south, they could be near the tip of Kyushu by now. If her path had been northward, they might be somewhere near Yamagata. Or they might be simply driving in circles around Osaka; Falco had absolutely no way of knowing for certain.

If the woman up front found his sangfroid unusual, she did not remark on it. Falco wasn't particularly worried about what would happen to him. Unlike several of his peers, he had no spouse or children to concern himself over. Most of his friends had fallen away over the years, as he had submerged ever more deeply into his research. As he'd gotten older and begun to see the true potential of his work, his isolation had become less of a burden. He was happy to live for his work; his destiny was greater than anything he had sacrificed in its name.

Of course, his captors likely had their own plans for his research and his inventions, so for the moment his life was in their hands. If his scientific vision was to have any hope of being fulfilled, he would have to comply with their orders.

For now.

There was nothing Logan liked better than a good workout.

He hurled a burly bald thug who was twice his size and had a face like a boiled ham. Baldy had already proved that he could take a punch. Now Logan wanted to see how the guy took a fall.

Not so well. The guy dropped onto a bar table like a sack of wet cement, splintered it on impact. Then he slid across the beer-slicked concrete floor and collided noggin-first with the wall.

Two of baldy's buddies tried to grab Logan from behind—one with an arm around Logan's throat, the other seizing the slack in his leather jacket. A simple hip throw landed Logan's would-be strangler on the floor at his feet. A back kick sent the second man stumbling backward; he landed on his ass in the corner and started dry-heaving. Meanwhile, his friend on the floor did the sensible thing: he covered his face.

Logan picked up the guy who was choosing to see no evil and unceremoniously heaved him through the bar's grimy front window, into the rain-slicked and neon-lit Tokyo gutter.

Clapping his hands clean, Logan walked back to the bar and sat down next to Wai Ying, who sipped her vodka straight up with an air of droll boredom. He nodded to the bartender. "Sorry 'bout the mess," he said. "Tack on a Sapporo, will ya?" Angling a thumb in Wai Ying's direction, he added, "She'll pay for it."

She nodded her weary assent to the bartender, then glanced sidelong at Logan. "Did they know anything?"

"About what?"

"The symbol on the *shaken*," she said. "That *is* why we're here, right?"

"Yeah, but not to talk to those clowns."

"Then what was that about?"

He shrugged. "About thirty seconds of exercise."

"If you want exercise, we have a gym at the Osaka office."

"Show me a gym that lets you throw people through

windows." The bartender delivered Logan's beer with a less than perfectly clean pilsner glass, which he set aside. Logan downed a healthy swig straight from the bottle, then allowed himself a moment to appraise Wai Ying's charms. "Of course, there are other kinds of exercise."

"I'm sure you'd find it most demanding," she replied with mocking faux sweetness. "But I doubt I'd break a sweat."

"Cold," he said, then swallowed another mouthful of beer.

She took a sip of her vodka, then set down the glass, dead center on her square napkin. "What are we hoping to learn here, Mr. Logan?" The bartender started to refill her half-empty glass, then paused as the phone behind the bar rang. He turned away to answer it as Wai Ying continued, "So far, this excursion seems to have been a waste of our—"

"Phone for you, Mr. Logan," the bartender said, handing him the cordless receiver.

Lifting it to his ear, Logan deadpanned, "I thought I told you never to call me here."

"And I thought the *yakuza* told you not to go in there anymore," replied National Police Agency organized-crime inspector Raiken Watanabe.

Logan took a quick sip of his Sapporo. "Since when do I listen to them?"

"Since when do you listen to anybody?" It was late, and Watanabe sounded tired. "I put that symbol through the computer. No links to any groups or people we know of."

"'Course not," Logan said. "That'd be too easy. Can you tell me *anything* about it?"

"It's ancient, a Chinese symbol called Fu."

"What is it? Occult? A tong sign? What's it for?"

"A bunch of different things. Depends who you ask."

"Boil it down for me."

Watanabe yawned. "The more benign reading is that it stands for collaboration or partnership. But in some circles it stands for authority, divine power, and the right to judge."

"Knowing my luck, the second one sounds about right."

"Maybe they're both right, and you're outnumbered."

"And on that happy note," Logan said, "I owe you a beer."

"Are you kidding? You owe me a whole bar by now."

"Go back to bed." Logan turned off the cordless receiver and put it back down on the bar. Then he picked up his bottle of Sapporo and drank with his head tilted back, emptying it in a steady stream down his throat.

Wai Ying watched him drink. "Who was that on the phone?"

He put the empty bottle down on the bar. "No one."

"What's happened?" She followed him as he got up from his stool and walked toward the door. "What are we doing?"

"'We'?" He was already out the door onto the teeming sidewalks of Yamanote, one of the sleazier neighborhoods of Tokyo. Block after block was lined with sex shops, nightclubs blaring music geared toward drunken foreigners, and dive bars whose attempts to seem "edgy" were, in Logan's opinion, undermined by their proclivity for featuring karaoke machines. "*We* aren't doing anything. Go home."

He ignored the blaring of horns and a slew of Japanese epithets as he jaywalked through a street choked with some of the weirdest cars he'd ever seen, all jockeying for position. Tiny shoeboxes with wheels cutting off hulking SUVs. Crafted-plastic show-off cars adorned with black-light neon trim and photo-realistic murals. The one thing they all had in common was the hideous, homogenized technopop music that thumped inside their fragile shells.

Pushing his way through the sidewalk pedestrian traffic on the opposite side of the street, he glanced left and saw Wai Ying weaving with him through the obstacle course of moving bodies. "You're not ditching me," she said without looking at him. "I can help you."

"What are you gonna do? Tuck me in? I'm calling it a night." He bounded up the stairs to the elevated train platform, hoping to catch the Yamanote line back to his hotel. She remained behind, at the bottom of the stairs. "Get some sleep, ace," he shouted to her over the street noise. "Today's a bust. Tomorrow we start over."

4

SWATHED IN A WEB OF MOSQUITO NETTING, trapped in a blanket of her own sweat, Nishan awoke in fear. It was routine now; it happened several times a night. Even in the deep hours of darkness, the African heat and humidity pressed down on her chest. The air reeked of stale sweat and infected flesh.

She rolled over and felt her way through the netting. Her eight-year-old son, Nadif, lay sleeping beside her, his arms wrapped protectively around his younger sister, Kanika. Despite the sweltering weather, both were shivering. Nishan pressed her palm against Nadif's emaciated chest, felt the heaving of his protruding ribs as he struggled for every breath. In his arms, Kanika trembled as well. Both had been ill on and off for a few weeks now. They had seemed to recover the day before yesterday, but now their symptoms had returned, worse than before.

Nishan shook the children awake. Their eyes opened, glazed and heavy-lidded. Neither moved or made a sound. She looked into her son's eyes. "Nadif? Can you hear me?" His chin dipped slightly, indicating that he did. "You're shaking," she said to him. "So is your sister. You have fevers. You both need the doctor. Can you carry her?"

His head lolled toward the floor, all the response he could give. He wouldn't be able to carry Kanika. Nishan was too weak from hunger and prolonged illness to carry both her children, or to make two trips to bring them both to the clinic. Her only hope would be to bring the clinic to them. Crawling, she fumbled through the layers of diaphanous mosquito nets and dragged herself out from under them. She found one of the support beams that held up the roof and pulled herself to her feet. Then she padded out of the communal hut and ventured alone into the night.

The rest of the village was deathly quiet beneath the ghostly light of a waxing half-moon. Inky darkness was washed with dark shadows; there were no lights at night. Partly it was to preserve the fuel in the clinic's two small diesel generators; it also helped avoid drawing the attention of nocturnal, roving squads of Tanjawar militia, who were always, it seemed, on the prowl for supplies or for blood sport.

Nishan's bare feet faltered upon sharp rocks that littered the village's central dirt road. The dust underfoot was still warm, gritty, and damp; the rains had been heavy for several weeks, spawning vast clouds of hungry mosquitoes. Even after three days of clear weather, the ground still did not feel dry.

Most of the huts along the road were empty now, burned by the Tanjawar during one of their countless raids. They were charcoal shells, collapsed in upon their own ashes, funeral pyres for the hopes and dreams of people who once had called this place home. The government had pledged to stop the Tanjawar's rampages and then had done nothing. The United Nations had sent a few dozen unarmed "peacekeepers" to quell the violence; very soon, they, too, had done nothing.

The only people who had ever kept their promises in Zibara were the doctors; they had come with more than just good intentions. They had brought medicine, machines, and full suitcases, which had implied that they planned to stay. The hand-painted sign they had hung from a stake in front of the village's largest enclosed building—now the clinic—bore three simple letters: *MSF,* which stood for *Médecins sans Frontières.* The healers had come from parts of the world that Nishan could only imagine: rich Western countries, newly stabilized Asian nations, other parts of Africa and the Middle East. They spoke numerous languages, though the ones that most of them had in common were French and English. During the past two years, Nishan had learned a fair amount of both tongues from a teacher who traveled with one of the doctors. In turn, the doctors had made an effort to learn to speak the local Zibarese dialect.

Nishan climbed the wide but rickety steps to the doctors' dormitory. She slipped through the drapery of mosquito netting that blocked the door, then found herself inside. Stepping softly on her thickly callused feet, she moved down the row of cots, which were cocooned in more netting, in groups of three and four. It was like trespassing in a spider's web.

She found the pediatrician, Dr. Rachanee Charoenying, fast asleep. Taking care not to snag any of the delicate netting around the doctor's cot, Nishan navigated through its overlapping folds.

Dr. Charoenying was a Thai woman in her late twenties. According to the male doctors who worked with her, she was quite beautiful; they admired her golden skin and lustrous black hair. None of them had ever won her affections, however; she was the kind of woman who held herself tantalizingly out of reach. With her patients, though, she was as warm and compassionate as she was meticulous and thorough. And when it came to procuring needed medicine or supplies from the distant patrons on the other end of the doctors' shortwave radio, Charoenying was by far the most passionate; she never took no for an answer.

Nishan gently rested her hand on Charoenying's shoulder.

Groggy and disoriented, Charoenying blinked open her eyes. "Nishan? *Quel* . . . ?"

She spoke to the doctor in French, the language they best had in common. "Doctor? Please wake up. My children are sick."

"Where are they?"

"They were too weak to move, and I can't carry them."

Charoenying rubbed her eyes with the back of her hand. "What are their symptoms?"

"The same as before, but worse."

The doctor nodded. She extended her foot and shook the cot next to hers. The older, white-haired man sleeping on it, an Irish doctor named Dannell Maguire, woke up and rolled over, looking very annoyed at Charoenying. "What?"

"Get up and bring your bag," Charoenying snapped as she got off her cot. She was already mostly dressed, in lightweight clothes suited to the sub-Saharan locale. Only her feet were bare; she slipped them into a pair of rubber sandals. Then she reached under her cot and grabbed a heavily scuffed, black leather medical bag with a broad, padded shoulder strap.

Beside her, Maguire forced himself to a sitting position. He slipped on his mud-caked loafers, then found his own satchel at the foot of his cot. When he stood, he looked like an angry pile of unwashed laundry.

Charoenying said to Nishan, "Take us to them."

Nishan led the two doctors out of their dormitory and down the main road, back to her own hut. Weaving adroitly through the netting, they soon were all kneeling beside Nishan's children. The doctors listened with their stethoscopes, took temperatures, drew blood with slender syringes, shone tiny lights into the children's eyes and ears and throats.

Speaking softly, Charoenying asked Nadif, in Zibarese, "Does it hurt?" The boy nodded. "Tell me where."

"My stomach," he said. "And my head."

"You have a headache?" Nadif nodded. "How does your stomach hurt? Sharp, like a knife? Or sick?"

"Sick," Nadif whispered. "Dizzy-sick." He coughed.

Behind Nadif and Charoenying, Maguire had been coaching Kanika through the same series of questions, with all but identical results. The two doctors turned their backs and conducted their whispered conference in English. In the stillness of the hour, Nishan heard every word, but, though she spoke English, half of what they said made no sense to her.

"Looks like falciparum," Maguire said.

"I know, but there might still be time," Charoenying said.

"If it's cerebral—"

"We don't know that," Charoenying interrupted. "We don't know anything until the blood work comes back."

"But if it is," he continued, "they need mefloquine."

"We haven't had any for weeks. All we have left is doxycycline."

"But we can't give that to—"

"Children under eight, I know." She glanced over her shoulder at Nishan, as if to say, *Please give us room.* Looking back at Maguire, she said, "Maybe we can get an airdrop from—"

"Unless it's an epidemic, we're not getting an airdrop," Maguire said.

"Please," Charoenying replied bitterly. "The whole damn continent's an epidemic. Christ, it's practically a *pandemic*. We are *one* viral change away from—"

"Preaching to the choir won't get you any mefloquine."

"No, but yelling at those clods in Cairo until they get off their asses just might." She blinked away her frustration, then looked back at Maguire. "Are there any free beds in the clinic?"

"Not yet," Maguire said. "But the mamba-bite victims won't last much longer. We'll have beds by tomorrow."

"I want them marked for these two," Charoenying said. "Don't let that *connard* Yang poach them like he did last time."

Maguire nodded. "I'll take care of it." He pushed aside the netting and slipped free, then walked away, stepping gingerly over the sleeping bodies that littered the slatted floors.

Charoenying removed the stethoscope that was draped over her shoulders and around her neck and put it back in her bag. "There's not much we can do right now," she told Nishan, once again in French. "We don't have the right medicine for your children, and there aren't any open beds in the clinic."

Helplessness made Nishan feel paralyzed even as panic made her want to do anything, even a million things at once, to help her children. "What am I supposed to do?"

"Make them drink a lot of water. Use a damp cloth to cool their heads and keep the fevers down. If they have new symptoms, especially vomiting or diarrhea, find me or Dr. Maguire immediately." Nishan nodded, numb with fear. Charoenying gently clasped Nishan's shoulder. "I'll be right back with some water and clean rags. Wait here."

Nishan watched Dr. Charoenying slip away into the night. Despite her certainty that the pediatrician would return, she began to cry without making a sound, not a sob or a whimper, for fear of waking her hut mates or frightening her children. *No medicine? No beds? Wet rags is the best we can do for my babies?*

She tried to tell herself to be thankful that her children were still fighting for life. Across Zibara, millions of other mothers wept tonight for children who were forever lost—to disease, to the genocidal rampages of the Tanjawar, to thirst or starvation. In a land of savage horrors, her children still drew breath, and it was her motherly duty to cling to hope, for their sake if not for her own.

But she knew, in her heart, that there was no point in hoping anymore. Death, that insatiable beast, had come in force to Zibara—and by fire, famine, or sword, it would devour them all.

5

LOGAN WAITED UNTIL HE HEARD THE BLADE swinging down toward his face before extending one set of his claws to block it. The *katana* never made impact; as he had expected, its wielder had checked her swing, halting it millimeters shy of contact. He extended his second trio of claws from beneath the crisp white bedsheets and twisted, trapping the sword flat against his bed. Then the pointed tip of a *wakizashi* tickled the underside of his densely whiskered chin.

"Hello, Yukio," he said. He had heard her slip into his hotel room more than a minute earlier. She was skilled, but not enough to elude his preternatural senses. Air disturbed by her passing had fluttered the curtains ever so slightly, and her scent was as familiar to him as that of his foster daughter, Amiko, whom he had left in Yukio's care many years ago.

Yukio crouched above him, perched nimbly on his queen-sized bed. She smiled. "*Konnichiwa,* Logan-san." He retracted his claws. She sheathed her swords across her back, then stepped off his bed and threw open the curtains, revealing a broad view of the Tokyo cityscape far below. The distant lights were reflected on her spiky black hair. "Not your usual hovel," she said.

"Not my idea," he replied, pushing aside his sheets. "What are you doing here?"

"I could ask you the same thing," she said, pacing around the foot of the bed. "Quite a ruckus you kicked up. How many *yakuza* dens did you toss tonight? Five? Six?"

"Something like that." He sat up and scratched the back of his neck. "What's it to you?"

"Starting a war?" She smirked and added, "Without me?"

"No," he said. He plodded across the room in his boxer shorts and retrieved his robe from the chair near the window. "Just looking for a few honest men."

Watching him intensely, she asked, "To tell you what?"

He lifted an empty beer bottle from the end table

next to the chair and picked up the *shaken,* which he had been using as a coaster. With a flick of his wrist, he tossed the throwing star in a slow arc to Yukio, who snatched it from the air with her thumb and forefinger. As she eyed it up close, Logan said, "To tell me where that came from."

"Then you were wasting your time," she said. "The *kobun* won't know about this."

"You've seen it before?"

"A few times, lately. Mostly as it's flying past my head."

"So it *is* a *yakuza* sign?"

"Not exactly," she said, tumbling the *shaken* over the backs of her knuckles. "It represents an alliance with the *yakuza,* but it's never them throwing it."

"An alliance," Logan repeated. "With who? The tongs? The triads?" Yukio simply stared at him while he worked it out for himself. *Who else uses ninjas?* He frowned. "The Hand," he said.

She tossed the *shaken* on his pillow. "And they're in bed with the *yakuza.* In other words, a nightmare waiting to happen."

He broke the seal on his minibar and fished out a fistful of tiny Jack Daniel's bottles. "I'm having a drink," he said while he unscrewed one of the caps. "Want one?"

"No, thank you." He felt her watching him as he emptied five shots of sour-mash whiskey into a tumbler and cut it with a splash of seltzer. He was using the tip of one of his claws to stir his drink when Yukio said, "She's fine, by the way."

There was no need for her to elaborate. He knew that she was talking about Amiko. "You saw her? Recently?"

"Yes," Yukio said. "She's learning fast. Mana says she's impressed with Amiko's progress."

Logan swelled momentarily with pride. *That's my girl.* Then he remembered that the burden young Amiko had chosen to take on might one day put her on the front line against horrors unlike any found in this dimension. *She knew what she was doing. We all take risks. Have to respect that.* "That's good," he said.

"I know she'd love to see you," Yukio said, trying not to push or pry but failing miserably.

Logan tilted his head back and drank his whiskey and soda in a few large gulps. The sour bite of the whiskey in his throat sharpened his focus on the moment. "I wish I could," he said, putting down the empty glass and picking up his blue jeans from the floor. "But if the Hand's part of this, I have to move fast—because they always do."

"By the way," Yukio said, "there are a couple dozen *yakuza* ninjas downstairs, waiting for you."

"Pathetic," Logan said, stepping into his jeans. "In the old days, they'd have come upstairs and attacked me in my sleep."

Yukio pointed into the living-room area of his spacious suite. Only now did he notice a few pairs of *tabi*-shod feet protruding from behind the sofa. "Thank me later," Yukio said with a playful smile, and she tossed him his shirt.

"You're getting better," he admitted. "Normally, I'd say let's team up and shred the ones downstairs—"

"But you're traveling with baggage," she said. "I saw her. She's pretty, but a little bit corporate for you, isn't she?"

"It's not like that," he said, putting his shirt on.

"Mm-hm," Yukio said, then grinned. "Yet."

"We just need a quiet exit from the lobby, and then we're gone," he said. "Can you keep the boys in black off my back?"

"Maybe," Yukio said. "Think you can make it to the airport without pissing anybody else off?"

He sat down and started pulling on his boots. "I ain't making any promises."

"Of course not," she said. "You never do."

She stalked swiftly across the living room toward an open window. As she planted her hands to propel herself through it and out into the night fifty stories above ground, Logan spoke.

"Tell her I said hello?"

"Of course," Yukio said. "I always do."

And in a dark blur of muscles and motion, she was gone.

Keenly aware of time slipping away, Logan moved around the bedroom, packed his bag, and got ready

to make another fly-by-night departure from the
Land of the Rising Sun.

Wai Ying was barely out of the elevator before Logan
grabbed her arm and started pulling her at a quick
step through the lobby of the Park Hyatt Tokyo toward the main entrance. His rucksack was strapped
across his back; a lit cigar dangled from his jaw. He
looked grimly focused.

Her laptop computer, slung in its soft case behind
her back, bounced on her hip as she hurried with
him past the front desk. She was grateful that she had
laid out khaki casual wear and broad-heeled hiking
shoes before going to bed a few short hours ago. It
had made transitioning from a dead sleep to a dead
run that much easier when he had rung her room at
quarter to five in the morning.

"Shake a leg, lady," Logan said, as their limousine
emerged from behind the center island of the traffic
circle outside.

She pulled free of his grasp. "What's the rush?"

In a flash, he regained hold of her arm and kept going.

From somewhere off to her right, in the deeply
shadowed recesses of the closed and darkened hotel
restaurant, Wai Ying heard the clang of steel on steel,
followed by a soft thump.

"A friend's got our back," Logan said, quickening
his pace, "but we have to go. Now." The doorman
tipped his hat at them as they walked past.

Something moved with a hiss in the air between her and the doorman. Logan's claws swept past her head, alarmingly close, and she heard the small *plinks* of tiny projectiles deflecting off his claws. Then a rustle of polyester and the meaty *thunk* of metal piercing flesh, and she saw the doorman impaled on the claws of Logan's other hand. Where the blades sank into the man's chest, Wai Ying caught sight of a dull black garment beneath his bright red uniform overcoat.

Logan pulled his claws free and retracted them. He reached the limousine ahead of her and pulled open the rear door. With a move that was half push, half throw, he propelled her into the back of the stretch Mercedes and followed her in. Through the open partition, Hattoro the chauffeur looked back for instructions. "Airport," Logan barked. "Punch it."

The car lurched into motion.

"Wait!" she cried. "My bags are—"

"Anything you can't live without?"

She clutched at her laptop case and remembered that she kept her cell phone and a limited makeup kit in there, as a precaution against luggage-handling errors when she flew on commercial airlines. Abandoning her wardrobe was an annoyance, but nothing that couldn't be corrected in whatever city they stopped in next. She settled back into her seat and massaged her temples. "Can you tell me now what's going on?"

He exhaled a puff of sharply pungent smoke. "The welcoming committee back there was courtesy of the Hand," he said, as if that was supposed to mean something to her.

"I'll need a little more to work with here," she said.

"They're an organization of mystical ninjas," he explained. "Part supernatural, part martial arts, and a hundred percent trouble. Their motive is simple: power for its own sake."

"Delightful," she said. "And they're the ones who stole the Panacea sample? And kidnapped Dr. Falco?"

"Looks that way," Logan said. He opened the minibar in front of the door and began poking through the liquor.

"I thought you didn't drink this early in the morning," she said, gently chiding him.

"Sun ain't up yet," he said. "Far as I'm concerned, it's still last night." He settled on a previously unopened bottle of Yukon Jack and cut away its plastic seal with the tip of one barely extended claw. After filling a shot glass, he hesitated; then he offered it to Wai Ying. "Ladies first."

At a loss for words, she satisfied herself with a scornfully lifted eyebrow. He shrugged, then knocked back the pale golden spirits in one throw.

"So," Wai Ying said, steering the conversation back on track, "if the Hand was responsible for the burglary in Osaka, what would they do with the Panacea formula?"

"Jesus," Logan said, shaking his head and pouring

another shot. "What wouldn't they do with it? Blackmail, extortion, terrorism. There's no telling how they'd deploy it; they could spike the water, cut it into street drugs." He knocked back his second measure of whiskey, clenched his jaw, and exhaled through his teeth. "Hell, they could aerosolize it, take entire cities hostage." He put away the bottle and the shot glass. "Tell me something," he said. "Is this drug ready to go? How much time do you think we have on the shot clock?"

"That depends on the Hand's technological resources," Wai Ying said. "Because of the drug's unique molecular and atomic properties, we weren't able to start decoding its structure until we invented the multiphase electron chromatograph cellular analyzer."

"Don't tell me—let me guess," Logan said, rolling his eyes in her direction. "You call it MECCA for short."

"Made the grant proposals easier to write," she replied. "To the best of our knowledge, the electron chromatograph is unique. The only other piece of hardware that's even similar is owned by the Fantastic Four."

"Hrm," Logan grunted. "This ain't their MO."

She was about to take the bait and say something dumb when she realized that he was joking. "Anyway," she said, "the good news is, without MECCA, it'll be impossible for the Hand to finish Falco's work—or mass-produce the drug."

The limousine merged onto the freeway, headed toward the airport. Even at this ungodly hour, traffic was already beginning to thicken within the Tokyo city limits. Hattoro did a masterful job of weaving the long vehicle back and forth through seemingly impassable gaps in the other lanes of cars. For several minutes, Logan sat quietly next to Wai Ying. He stared out the window at the blur of the thinning cityscape and puffed idly on his cigar. Finally, he asked, "What if someone built their own electron chromatograph?"

"Impossible," she said. "The schematics are top-secret."

"So was Panacea," Logan said. "But someone found out about that, didn't they?" He turned his head and looked at her, resolute in his convictions. "Someone inside your company is a mole who told the Hand about Panacea, and it's a good bet they smuggled out the design for MECCA while they were at it."

She shook her head; the urge to refute his hypothesis was irresistible. "It wouldn't be enough," she insisted. "Even if they have the plans, some of the components are impossible to buy or fabricate—they're classified hardware that we designed for the American military. Burglarizing an Osaka office tower is one thing; robbing hardened U.S. military installations—"

"Isn't their style," Logan interrupted. "Taking on the U.S. government would get messy, fast. That's the kind of attention they don't need or want right now."

She nodded, following his reasoning. "So, if they can't build it, buy it, or steal it—"

"Who says they can't buy it?"

It took her a second to catch up to him once again. "The black market," she said. "That's where they'll get the parts."

"Exactly," Logan said. "They'll let money do their dirty work." He grinned and puffed his cigar again. "And if it's Yankee hardware they're looking for, I got a good hunch I know where they'll be shopping."

6

SIXTEEN HOURS AFTER GOING WHEELS-UP from Tokyo, Logan was sick of looking at the inside of TBC's corporate jet, which he had at first mistaken for a Cessna Citation X. "Right make," Wai Ying had corrected him, "wrong model." It was, she had explained, a Citation Thunderstar, the next generation of Cessna aircraft, capable of supersonic travel and boasting an operational range of more than 3,600 nautical miles. Its interior was comfortably appointed, with leather-upholstered seats, a well-stocked galley, and a host of high-tech satellite communications equipment. It even had a lavatory large enough not to induce bouts of claustrophobia.

But after more than thirteen hours in the air and three refueling stops of just under an hour each—in Calcutta, India; Addis Ababa, Ethiopia; and Dakar, Senegal—he'd had enough of being hurtled through the air in a metal tube. The only part of the trip he'd found bearable had been the time he'd spent flying the aircraft, taking over for Wai Ying while she'd used the jet's communications suite to buy a new wardrobe, which would be ready and waiting for her when they arrived in Foz do Iguaçu, Brazil.

"We just got our landing clearance," she said from the cockpit. "We should be on the ground in about twenty minutes."

"Great," he deadpanned. "I'll try to return myself to an upright position by then."

He tried to figure the local time in his head, but between changing time zones and the fact that he had never got the hang of the International Date Line, he gave up. Checking the local weather with the computer, he watched a Doppler radar image take shape on the wide-screen plasma monitor mounted on the forward wall behind the cockpit. It was just before seven A.M. in eastern Brazil, and already the day was shaping up hot and muggy. He shrugged off his leather jacket and pulled off his long-sleeved pullover. His patience thinned while he dug inside his rucksack, looking for the blue Mayan-print tropical short-sleeve shirt that he was certain he remembered packing. *Dammit, where is it?* Its fabric felt familiar as his fingertips brushed it, and he pulled it free of his jumble of wrinkled clothes.

Outside the window, past the sharp sweep of the wing, the green chaos of the South American junglescape began to thin. A few minutes later, the snaking lines of dirt roads mutated swiftly into the deliberate grid of paved streets, and they passed over Ciudad del Este, Paraguay, just across the Río Paraná from Foz do Iguaçu. The jet made a gentle, banking turn above Lago de Itaipu and then passed over the packed crescent of high-rise buildings that constituted the heart of Foz do Iguaçu. Everything came into sharper focus as the Cessna descended and cut through the pollution haze that lay like a shroud over the city. As they neared Cataratas International Airport, he saw the awesome spectacle of the Cataratas do Iguaçu—a 2.7-kilometer-long region of the Rio Iguaçu that contained nearly three hundred majestic waterfalls, with heights of up to seventy meters. From the air, Logan was able to distinguish plumes of mist rising from the Garganta del Diablo—the Devil's Throat—a U-shaped waterfall nearly 150 meters wide and 700 meters long. Then the hard black line of the tarmac appeared beneath them, and Wai Ying guided the plane to a soft and perfect landing.

It took a few minutes for her to taxi the plane to its assigned hangar. As the aircraft rolled to a stop, Logan noted two cars pulling up outside. One was a nondescript, midnight-blue town car with dark-tinted windows. The other looked as if it had started life as a Jeep but had fallen victim to a mechanic with a lot of orange automotive paint and an adolescent fixation on flame decals. The driving bass and heavy beat of American hip-hop blared from the Jeep's oversized rear woofers.

There was no sign of who was in the town car, but riding in the open-top Jeep from Hell was a mismatched trio: a tanned, blond, beach-bum type; a brown-skinned man who looked to be a mix of Hispanic and local Indian; and a shaved-headed black man, who was driving. The three things that they all had in common were exaggerated muscles; abominable, *Miami Vice*–style vintage clothes; and broad, jungle-clearing machetes in leather sheaths strapped across their backs.

Logan snicked the end off a fresh Corojo and walked forward to the main exit hatch. He leaned into the cockpit. "Finish the postflight and get our customs clearance," he said. "I'll be right back."

Wai Ying was looking suspiciously out at the two cars that had stopped beside the Cessna. "Friends of yours?"

"Not exactly," he said as he unlocked the hatch.

She turned back to face him. "What are you going to do?"

He couldn't help but grin. "What I do best."

The flame of Logan's Zippo touched his cigar as his boot touched the tarmac.

All three of the Jeep boys were already in motion, moving to intercept him. The bald black man took the lead. Pointing his machete at Logan's head, he declared, "You're not welcome here."

The front half of the man's machete spun away into the air and clattered to the pavement a few meters away. Logan doubted that the man had even seen him make the cut. For a moment, he almost felt bad for the three morons standing in front of him. These weren't professionals, just conspicuous muscle better suited to working as bar bouncers than as bodyguards or hit men.

In a rare moment of charity, Logan decided not to kill them. While the leader was still staring at the stump of his machete blade, Logan gut-punched him. The man doubled over, and Logan elbowed him at the base of his skull, knocking him unconscious, facedown on the ground.

Blondie and the Indian attacked together, hacking clumsily with their machetes. Extending both sets of claws, Logan let their blades fall between his middle and outer talons, then he turned his wrists one hundred eighty degrees and disarmed each man. Retracting his claws, he lunged forward with a roar and tackled them. One punch was enough to break the blond's jaw. Before Logan could finish off the Indian, the man had sprung back to his feet and was making a classroom-perfect kick at Logan's head. *Too bad for you this ain't a classroom.* Logan caught the man's foot at its point of greatest extension and twisted it until the ankle gave a sharp, meaty snap. He kicked the Indian in the groin, then dropped him in a groaning, whimpering heap next to his pals.

Through it all, Logan's cigar had stayed securely between his teeth; its burn remained even and its flavor was smooth.

The rear passenger-side window of the town car lowered with a mechanical hum, revealing a gaunt, smartly dressed man sitting inside. At the end of his slender cigarette holder smoldered a pungent, dark brown Gauloise.

The passenger's name was Bouchard. He was a black-market arms dealer from the south of France. Logan had crossed his path once a number of years back, in the course of recovering some stolen Soviet nuclear warheads that Bouchard had been trying to sell to a well-funded doomsday cult.

Despite having watched Logan thrash his underlings half to death, he didn't seem intimidated as Logan sidled up to his car.

"Well done," Bouchard said, his accent as thick as ever. "I was warned you'd be coming. You might want to cut your visit short, though. I think you'll find that Foz do Iguaçu can be rather . . . *inhospitable* to people like you."

"People like me?" He blew a plume of smoke at the Frenchman. "You mean mutants?"

"No, Mr. Logan," he replied. "Heroes."

Logan chuckled. "Me? A hero? I don't think so, bub."

"What would you call yourself, then?"

"I'm just a guy doing a job," Logan said. "Besides, if I was a hero, I wouldn't be stealing your boys' hot-rod."

Bouchard glanced at his incapacitated enforcers and *tsk-tsk*ed. "They aren't going to like that," he said.

"Too bad," Logan replied. "Tell your neighbors, Bouchard: I ain't here to bust heads. This is a *friendly* visit. And as long as nobody makes me feel unwelcome, that's how it'll stay."

"And if my neighbors don't feel friendly?"

"Well," Logan said, "then you and your pals better start stocking up on bandages." He tapped the ash from the tip of his cigar into Bouchard's lap. "Have a nice day."

The car window climbed slowly. Bouchard met Logan's stare with his own unblinking gaze, until the window was closed and all Logan had to look at was his own reflection. As the town car pulled away, Logan ambled over to the Jeep and grinned as he noted that the keys were still in the ignition. He vaulted over the welded-shut door into the driver's seat.

Behind him, Wai Ying descended the steps from the plane and signaled the ground crew to go ahead and tow it into the hangar. She joined Logan at the Jeep. He turned the key. The vehicle's engine growled to life and purred richly.

Wai Ying eyed the Jeep skeptically, then climbed over the passenger-side door into the seat next to Logan's. She cast a glance back at the three hoodlums huddled in agonized curls on the ground a few meters away, then looked sidelong at Logan.

"Fancy," she said.

"I have moments," he said, then he stepped on the gas and sped off the tarmac, turning up the music as he accelerated.

Wai Ying's hair whipped behind her as the Jeep flew down the highway. The wind noise was almost enough to drown out the grinding, relentless sonic assault of the stereo.

Foz do Iguaçu seemed to her like a city of contrasts. As they cruised away from the airport toward the city proper, on the Avenidos des Cataratas, the land on either side of the road had the naked look of a jungle beaten into submission. Then, past a minute's worth of blurred exurban squalor, the city rose up ahead of them, a dense cluster of ultramodern glass and steel towers. From a distance, it had the architectural profile of a major city, yet its streets looked all but unpopulated, even on a weekday morning. Traffic was light in the center of town, and few pedestrians were anywhere in sight.

"There are lots of black markets in the world," she said over the music and the wind roar. "What makes you so sure the Hand came here?"

"Two things," Logan replied as he swerved through some slow-moving traffic. "First, thanks to the 'war on drugs,' there's a lot more high-tech here than other places. Some of it was used for barter by the CIA when they were setting up their own drug cartel back home. Second, Foz do Iguaçu has one thing a lot of other black-market towns don't: nearly sixty international banks competing for the world's money-laundering business. The kind of stuff the Hand needs to buy costs more money than you can fit in a suitcase, which means they need a seller who can handle wire transfers. This town washes at least twelve billion dollars a year in black-market cash."

She shook her head in disbelief. "If this place is so notorious, why don't the authorities do something about it?"

"What? And give up their piece of the profits? Dream on." He was completely serious. Rather than contemplate the scope of the world's corruption, Wai Ying let herself admire the various storefronts that passed by in a blur as Logan sped up again.

Just as she was starting to feel at home among the broad avenues lined with posh boutiques and international banks, the city transformed itself in the turn of a corner. Heading northwest on a gravel road beside the Río Paraná, she and Logan cruised through a series of shantytown slums. Lean-to shelters were propped against run-down buildings that looked as if they had been imported from another era.

The Jeep lurched to a halt in a cloud of dust.

When the beige cloud dissipated, Wai Ying squinted against the low-angle glare of early morning sunlight. Logan had driven them to a bar. Above the bar's door was a neon sign that looked as though it probably hadn't worked in close to a decade; it read, *"A Terceira Axila."* She had seen a lot of dive bars. This one looked ready to be condemned.

Masking her distaste with an air of boredom, she drummed her fingertips on the outside of the car door as she looked at Logan. "And we're here because . . . ?"

"Because this is the first place I always look for Nando," he replied, then turned off the engine.

"Nando? . . . Don't tell me—the local micro-brew?"

"The local fixer," Logan said as he climbed out of the Jeep and walked around the front to the pas-senger door. "I know some of the players around here, but Nando knows all of them." He offered Wai Ying a helping hand out of the Jeep, and she ac-cepted it. "If anyone's gonna know who the Hand would've gone to for spare parts, it'll be him." As Logan assisted her, she felt a slight surge of excite-ment at how strong he was; in his hands she felt light as a feather. Once her feet touched the ground, he let go and walked ahead of her toward the front door of the bar. "And if I know him, this is where he'll be."

"At seven-thirty in the morning?" she asked,

checking her watch. "Kind of early to start drinking, isn't it?"

"Or kind of late for last call," Logan replied, pushing open the door. She followed him inside.

There were too many types of stink for her to count them all. Old cigarette smoke mingled with the stale ammonia smell of urine; the half-rotten wooden floorboards were dark with spilled beer, with vomit and bloodstains, with burn marks and bullet holes. Every one of the few liquor bottles lined up on the shelf behind the bar was of a cheap brand that she had never heard of. Booths steeped in shadow lined the wall opposite the bar counter. A half dozen tables occupied the floor space between the two; every table was unoccupied and littered with filthy, dreg-bottomed glasses, overflowing ashtrays, and dozens of beer bottles all bearing the same nondescript local label. In the back of the room there was a neon-lit jukebox that looked as if it had been stolen from a strip club.

Most of the bar stools were empty, except for the ones occupied by the snoozing bouncer at the end near the entrance and the decrepit, smoke-swaddled whore perched in front of the door to the lone toilet. The bartender, a paunchy and balding man in his forties, stood behind the bar and counted cash; a long-barreled .45-caliber Colt revolver lay on the bartop in front of him. He looked up at the new arrivals, squinted into the morning light, then nodded to Logan. "*A quanto tempo não o vejo,*" he said.

"Sim," Logan replied. *"Onde está Nando?"*

The bartender lifted his chin toward the booths. Wai Ying followed his gesture, and then she saw a pair of trousered legs splayed horizontally across one booth seat, knees folded over the corner, feet touching the floor. Logan walked over to the booth and sat down in the empty seat. She followed him to the booth but remained standing at his side. From the other side of the booth came the soft, regular rasp of a snore.

Logan spent a minute enjoying his cigar, puffing steadily until a thick head of ash formed on its tip. He blew a few smoke rings. Then he reached across the table and tapped off his ash in the far corner of the other seat.

A snort led to a gagging cough, then a mumbled curse was followed by the wooden *thump* of someone sitting up quickly and knocking his head into the underside of the table. After a few more grumbled epithets, a slim, fair-skinned man in his thirties sat up across from Logan and Wai Ying. His dark hair was slightly tousled, and his white silk designer shirt was mildly wrinkled. Dark circles under his eyes branded him as the kind of man who routinely pushed himself too far—perhaps for work, or for play, or for both. After he blinked away his confusion and recognized Logan, he flashed a smile of perfect teeth. "Hey, buddy," he said, extending a hand across the table. "Great to see you."

"Likewise," Logan said, grinning warmly as he shook Nando's hand. Gesturing in Wai Ying's direction, he made the introductions. "Nando, this is Tse Wai Ying; we work together. Wai Ying, meet Nando Velasquez, an old buddy of mine."

She and Nando traded half-smiles and nodded politely at each other. Then he had to go and ruin the moment. *"Enchanté,"* he said with an atrocious French accent that made her wince.

"The pleasure's all yours," she said.

Half a second later he got the message and turned back toward Logan. "What're you doing back in town, man? Last time I saw you, you were off to help some freedom fighter up in . . . what was it? El Salvador?"

"Nicaragua," Logan said.

Nando nodded. "Right, right. What was his name?"

"De la Rocha," Logan said.

"Yeah. De la Rocha." He shook his head slowly. "I don't know what got into you, man. You had to know that was a lost cause. Why'd you get involved?"

Logan shrugged. "What can I say? I got a soft spot for underdogs. Speaking of which, how's life treating you?"

"Can't complain," Nando said. "I get around, I get over, I get by. It's a living." Smiling at Wai Ying, he added, "Of course, my coworkers aren't quite so beautiful as yours."

"You're too kind," she said sweetly, then turned her tone sour. "Comb your hair."

The handsome young Latino's flirtatious grin faltered. Logan cleared his throat and regained his friend's attention.

"I need you to make some inquiries for me," Logan said. "See who might be able to scare up a few hard-to-find items."

Nando subtly checked the room for eavesdroppers. Eyeing Logan with caution, he prompted him: "Such as . . . ?"

Logan reached into his jeans pocket and took out a folded slip of paper. He pushed it across the table to Nando, who lifted it like the hole card in a game of seven-card stud. His expression was perfectly neutral as he read it and pushed it back to Logan. "Hard-core," he said. "You here to buy?"

"No," Logan said. "I want to know who already has."

"Not sure I can get you that," Nando said. "Best I can do is tell you who might've been in a position to sell."

"That'll do."

Nando nodded. "Okay. I'll need a few hours."

"Fine," Logan said, then gestured with his thumb over his shoulder at Wai Ying. "America's next top model here has to go pick up a new wardrobe, and I could use a nap."

"Do you have a place to stay yet?" Nando asked. "If you don't, you can crash at my place. It's not

much, but I have a spare room and a clean couch."
He glanced back and forth between them, trying to
determine if he'd just committed a *faux pas.* "I mean,
assuming the two of you aren't . . . *y'know* . . ."

"No," Wai Ying said, maybe a little too emphati-
cally. "We're definitely *not*—"

"The couch'll be fine for me," Logan cut in.

"All right, then," Nando said. "*Meu repouso é seu
repouso.*"

7

LOGAN'S SENSITIVE HEARING MADE THE INCESSANT
hum of the high-voltage power lines above Nando's
house difficult to block out. After an hour tossing
and turning on the couch, he'd learned to think of it
as white noise, but there was no such easy remedy
to help mask the chain-saw growl of Nando's snor-
ing. From two rooms away, and through two closed
doors, it had shaken the walls like a force of nature.
If not for the fact that Logan needed a favor from
Nando, he might have strangled him in his sleep.

Wai Ying had returned to the house around noon
and promptly begun complaining about how far
Nando lived from the center of town, before segue-

ing into her criticisms of his neighborhood, a low-income housing development off Brazil Highway 277. Logan, without bothering to open his eyes—since that would only have encouraged her to continue talking—had extended one set of claws, which pierced the floor. To his relief, she had taken his meaning clearly and retired to bed.

Now it was dark out, and he was rising to face the night. Nando was long since up and out of the house; Logan had heard him leave around three or four in the afternoon. Until the fixer returned, Logan and Wai Ying would have to wait for him in his slovenly sanctum.

Logan went looking for something to eat. It proved more difficult than he had expected. The kitchen was a shrine to dirty dishes, which were stacked in an unstable pyramid, filling and obstructing the sink. Logan considered throwing them away so he could make coffee, but he couldn't be certain Nando owned a coffeepot. He opened the fridge and grabbed a beer instead.

He walked back into the living room as Wai Ying emerged from the spare room, dressed in simple, dark casual clothes. She carefully plucked a sweatshirt off a chair and sat down. "I love what he's done with the place," she said.

"It's easy to do," Logan said. "Just drop all your stuff out of a helicopter. It'll look like this."

She chuckled slightly. He liked the sound of her laugh.

"So what's the story with you and Nando?" she asked. "It's hard to believe you two ever moved in the same circles."

He tilted his head and gave a wan smirk. "You'd be surprised some of the circles I move in," he said. "As for Nando and me, we met in Rio about twelve years ago during Carnaval. I staggered into a bar looking for a fresh bottle of beer, and I found him getting his ass kicked by four guys built like gorillas. Turns out the lead gorilla had a wife who Nando'd had the pleasure of knowing biblically, and the other three apes were the guy's brothers. Since I hadn't been in a fight for the last few hours, I stepped in and settled their hash. Then Nando and I went bar crawling the rest of the night, and we've been buds ever since."

"Touching story," Wai Ying said. "Toss in a trip to a brothel and you can sell the movie rights to Cinemax."

"Too late," Logan said. "Fox already optioned it."

From down the hall came the sound of the front door opening, then footsteps, and the closing of the door. Nando walked into the living room and waved at his guests. "Good, you're both up," he said. "I think I've got the lead you're looking for. Ready to go?"

"We could use something to eat first," Logan said.

Motioning for them to follow, Nando replied, "I figured you'd be hungry. There's burritos in the

Jeep. Let's go." Nando was two steps down the hall before he realized that neither Logan nor Wai Ying was following him. He turned back, eyes wide with impatience. "Come on," he insisted.

"All right," Logan said, forcing himself off the sofa. "But these better be damned good burritos."

An hour's drive and two damned good burritos later, the trio arrived at a darkened intersection just a few short blocks from the Ponte da Amizade—a.k.a. the Bridge of Friendship, the principal crossing point for smugglers moving between Brazil and Paraguay.

The Jeep rolled to a quiet stop in the darkness beneath the drooping branches of a tree on the corner. Diagonally across the street was a dilapidated warehouse surrounded by a parking lot of fissured, uneven pavement. Logan stubbed out his cigar on the outside of the passenger door as Nando turned off the headlights and the ignition. Pointing at the warehouse, Nando said, "That's the base of operations for a guy the locals call Cavalo. He's the only smuggler in town with enough juice to get the kind of stuff you had on your list."

Logan studied the exterior of the warehouse, looking for fire escapes, ladders to the roof, skylights, or other potential covert points of entry, as well as for vantage points from which lookouts or snipers might be guarding the building. "How do I get in to see him?"

"I could call him," Nando joked. "Ask for an appointment."

"Do it," Logan said.

"I don't think that's a good idea," Nando said, running his fingers anxiously through his hair. "I mean, he's not gonna want to answer the kind of questions I think you'll be asking, and trying to push him around on his own turf . . . let's just say I don't think he'll go for it."

"It's not up to him," Logan said, still surveying the warehouse. There seemed to be a rear entrance, but it was likely to be defended by alarms, surveillance cameras, and maybe even booby traps. That left the front door.

Nando sounded worried. "Look, man, I know you're a badass and all, but he's got a lotta guys on his payroll. Pros—not jagoffs like those guys you whupped at the airport. Cavalo's the kind of guy you absolutely *do not* cross. *Compreenda?*"

"I know what I'm doing," Logan said. "Make the call."

With obvious reluctance, Nando fished his cell phone from his jacket pocket. He covered its keypad with his cupped hand while he dialed with the other.

While Nando carried on his whispered phone conversation, Logan looked back at Wai Ying, who was barely able to conceal her annoyance with the entire situation. When she met Logan's stare, he asked, "Problem?"

"You shouldn't go in there alone," she said.

"It's safer this way," Logan said. "Trust me."

"Don't be a fool," she said. "I can help you."

"No offense, doll, but I don't think you can scare these guys with your stunning fashion sense and your no-limit charge card. Just leave this to me."

"God, you're an idiot," she said, then sat back and looked away, ending the discussion.

Nando folded his phone closed and looked at Logan. "Cavalo's agreed to meet you," he said. "Didn't even ask why."

Logan nodded. "When?"

"Now," Nando said. "I think it might be a trap."

"Of course it's a trap," Logan said. He climbed out of the Jeep and started walking toward the warehouse.

"What're you gonna do, man? Walk in the front door? You'll be surrounded before you get three steps inside."

"That's what I'm counting on," Logan said with a grin. "If I'm not back in an hour . . . I don't know, blow the place up or something."

The warehouse doors slid apart as Logan approached them. They were tall enough to permit entry by a large cargo trailer and were pulled open by what sounded like a simple chain motor. Inside the warehouse, areas of shadow dominated the few pools of dim, yellow incandescent light. Four large and street-toughened men greeted Logan at the doorway. Each man carried a Heckler and Koch MP5K submachine gun and wore Kevlar body armor.

The one in charge, an ugly brute with a face that looked to Logan as if it had been lit on fire and put out with sandpaper, held up his hand, signaling Logan to halt. "Raise your hands and turn around," he commanded in Portuguese. Logan did as he was told. Sandpaper-face said, "Search him."

One of the other men patted Logan down, then reported, "He's clean. No weapons."

"Turn around," Sandpaper-face said. "Two steps forward."

Logan did an about-face and walked inside the warehouse. Sandpaper-face and one of his buddies moved aside to Logan's left. The other two who had met him stepped to the right.

Dead ahead of him, two more men, armed with submachine guns, stood in the middle of the rectangular building's open middle area. Behind them, lurking between a forklift and three barrels marked with red rings at the top and bottom, was another thug, carrying an Uzi machine pistol. Another gunman stood on top of a small mountain of wooden packing crates.

The view to Logan's left was blocked by a parked forklift, a row of four huge beer vats, and a one-row stack of fifty-five-gallon drum containers. On his right, at floor level, three more shooters crouched behind large wooden boxes. Above them, on top of another mound of wooden boxes, were two more guys with guns.

In the rear right corner, an electrified-fence cage surrounded the stairs to the balcony, which ringed the left, right, and rear walls of the warehouse's interior. Nine more men with MP5Ks looked down from there—three on the left, five on the right, and one at the back, next to the only person in the place, other than Logan, who wasn't sporting a weapon.

"You must be Senhor Logan," said the man with no gun.

Before Logan could reply, Cavalo walked back into his office, and a flurry of bullets slammed into Logan's chest.

Nine-millimeter rounds ripped into his body, ricocheted off his adamantium-coated skeleton, tore though his internal organs. The angry stutter of automatic gunfire at point-blank range was deafening, but it couldn't drown out his howls of pain.

Just as quickly as the barrage had begun, it ceased. Blood sheeted down Logan's torso, arms, and legs. His legs buckled. He dropped to his knees and doubled over. The four guards closest to him pressed in, weapons still aimed and ready. As he stared at the pool of his own blood that surrounded him, his second wave of agony began. His mutant healing factor began mending him, knitting together shredded muscles, closing severed arteries, rebuilding liquefied organs—all of it happening sub rosa, beneath his blood-soaked, bullet-torn clothing.

Then his rage kicked in. And his claws came out.

He sliced through the knees of the two men closest to him. They fell forward, blood fountaining from their severed limbs. Logan finished each man with an upward thrust into the heart, then retracted his claws and grabbed a submachine gun.

He head-shot Sandpaper-face and the other advance man.

The other gunmen to his left resumed shooting at him.

Dodging left toward the nearby forklift, he fired at the two men directly ahead of him, in the middle of the warehouse.

As they fell, he strafed his shots left, across the red-ringed barrels behind them. As Logan had hoped, the barrels exploded, sending orange flames and metal debris in all directions—and eliminating the shooter behind the far forklift and the one on top of the crates behind him.

Firearms weren't Logan's preferred weapon, but he'd fought in enough wars to know when and how to use them.

Gunshots *zing*ed off the forklift chassis as he ducked behind it. Despite the acrid bite of gunpowder that filled the air, he caught the cologne-heavy scent of someone else ahead of him, concealed behind a ten-foot-tall stack of bulky metal containers. At a full run he shoulder-checked the stack, which collapsed backward onto the man who'd been using it for cover. A short buzz of gunfire—probably a reflexive squeeze of the trigger, Logan guessed—was muffled by the falling cargo.

Logan saw no one else at floor level on the left side of the building. The beer vats and pyramid of oil drums would give him decent cover, but not for long. He heard the men shouting conflicting orders at one another. As soon as they got organized, this was going to get a lot harder. He had to move before the gunmen came at him from both sides.

He extended one set of claws and slashed through the first support beam holding up the left-side balcony. Then he sprinted the length of the building, staying low and in the shadows, cutting through all the other support beams, one after another. By the time he reached the back of the building, the creaking of wood under stress turned into a groan, and then into a roar as the left-side balcony collapsed and fell flat against the wall, dropping the three men from up above to the concrete floor.

While the three fallen men were still sorting out what had happened, Logan used his claws to cut the steel bands holding the oil-drum pyramid together, then gave the stack a swift kick. Black barrels rolled like wheels and pummeled the three hired thugs. A quick burst from Logan's weapon punctured the first barrel, which erupted in a fiery blast, then belched out a dense wall of greasy black smoke.

A burst of gunfire raked Logan's back from above. He ducked under the rear balcony and cursed himself for getting careless and forgetting about the man at the back of the warehouse.

Gritting his teeth against the searing pain of his healing factor kicking into overdrive, he literally stumbled over an open box of fragmentation grenades. He reached down, picked one up, clutched the safety lever, and removed the pull pin. Leaning half a step out from under the balcony, he lobbed the grenade up and over in a shallow arc, then dodged to his left as he heard it *thunk* onto the balcony above.

Two seconds later, an explosion turned the left third of the rear balcony into smoldering toothpicks.

Wooden debris rained down around Logan, and the gunman who had just shot him landed hard on the floor, dazed but still clutching his assault rifle.

Logan's first slash cut the weapon in half.

His second strike gutted his would-be assassin.

Multiple footfalls thumped across the balcony on the right side of the building and snapped across the concrete floor, on the other side of the stacked boxes that he had set on fire when he'd detonated the barrels twenty seconds earlier.

Screw this, Logan decided. He kneeled next to the box of grenades. One by one, he began pulling pins and hurling them. The first few he tossed over the burning boxes, to slow down the gunmen trying to

flank him. The next four he hurled long, across the
length of the right-side balcony, which quickly was
torn apart, killing two of its five shooters and bringing the other three down to his level.

He was out of grenades. By his count, and judging
from the voices and footsteps that he heard, there
were still seven men taking concealed positions and
making flanking maneuvers. A disturbing thought
nagged at him: *There's got to be another box of grenades in
here . . . and they know exactly where it is.*

Not willing to risk one of these guys scoring a
lucky shot that would enable them to peg him with a
grenade, Logan decided it was time to rearrange the
battlefield to his advantage.

With a dozen short, pinpoint bursts, he destroyed
every lightbulb in the warehouse. Shattered glass and
fading sparks rained down to the floor. The only light
came from isolated, crackling patches of burning
crude oil and the smoldering debris that now littered
the floor. It had exactly the desired effect: every one
of his opponents came to a halt.

He put down his now-empty submachine gun.
Moving with speed and feral grace, he skulked
around the box mountain and ambushed one of the
gunmen, covering the man's mouth with one hand
while impaling him on the claws of the other.

Six little Indians, Logan counted.

He stepped over the body of a man he'd killed
with one of his grenades and reached the second

stack of boxes. Scaling it was easy; they had been stacked in a step pattern, probably to make it easier to recover goods from the upper sections.

Crawling to its rear edge, he found two more gunmen, one at each corner, their backs to each other. Lowering himself over the edge, he touched down silently. Snuck up on the one facing the rear of the building. Grabbed him in a choke hold and broke his neck. The snap was loud and wet. Logan spun around with the dead man in his grip, using him as a shield. His compatriot at the other end of the stack spun and fired, riddling his ally's corpse with bullets. Logan drew the dead man's sidearm and snapped off a shot, hitting the other man in the throat.

Four little Indians.

Logan dropped the dead man and tucked the pistol in his waistband. Then he heard the patter of running footsteps, moving away from him. Climbing back atop the stack of boxes, he spied the last four henchmen scrambling out the front door of the warehouse and sprinting for their lives into the night.

Guess they aren't as stupid as they look.

He jumped down to the floor and walked back to the forklift near the front entrance. It powered up with a rumble and a foul belch of diesel smoke. Logan stepped on its accelerator and steered it through the maze of wreckage he'd left in his wake, toward the electrified fence that surrounded the stairs to the upper level, where Cavalo's office was located. He pushed the forklift to its maximum speed, waited until it was a couple of meters from the fence, then jumped out. The lifter plowed through the fence in a shower of sparks and crashed into the rear wall.

Walking up the stairs, Logan considered the possibility that Cavalo might have already fled his office through the back door. *If he's still there, he could be waiting for me with anything,* Logan knew. *A Gatling minigun; a flamethrower; hell, a rocket launcher, for all I know.*

Logan reached the top of the stairs and stepped into the doorway of Cavalo's office. The black marketeer sat at his desk, facing the door.

In front of him was something Logan definitely had not expected: a bottle of twenty-one-year-old Balvenie single-malt scotch, with two shot glasses.

"Come in, Senhor Logan," Cavalo said. "You've done me a great service. Now let's talk about what I can do for you."

"Mighty civilized of you," Logan said. He walked slowly toward the chair in front of Cavalo's desk. "But if we're such good buds all of a sudden, what was with all the fireworks?"

"A calculated risk," Cavalo said. "My apologies, but it was necessary. I had to let them provoke you so that I could be reasonably sure you'd kill them."

"You *wanted* me to kill them?"

"Oh, absolutely," Cavalo said. "Half of them had already made deals with my competitors, and the other half were trying to. It was only a matter of time before they turned on me." He picked up the bottle and poured two shots of scotch into the glasses. "Your arrival happened to come at a fortuitous moment, so I took advantage of it. I hope you're not too offended."

"That'll depend on whether I get what I came for, bub."

"And that would be?" Cavalo offered one of the shot glasses to Logan, who picked it up and knocked it back in one swallow.

The scotch was smooth and complex, faintly sweet with a hint of port. Logan set the empty glass back on the desk, then retrieved his list of high-tech parts from his pocket.

He handed the list to Cavalo. "Did you recently acquire any of the items on this list for one of your clients?"

Cavalo studied the list for a moment, then said simply, "Yes. All of them."

"Who was the client?"

"No idea," Cavalo replied. "I don't meet most of my clients face-to-face. Most of the time I deal with cutouts, middlemen. The only thing I know about the client is the number of their Cayman Islands bank account, from which they transferred their payment to my Luxembourg account."

"That'll do," Logan said. "Give me their account number, and we'll call this deal done."

Cavalo nodded and pulled a small handheld communications device from his jacket's inside pocket. He tapped a few buttons, then jotted down the bank name and account number on a piece of scrap paper, which he handed to Logan.

"Thanks," Logan said. He got up from his chair to leave, then paused. "Good luck hiring a new goon squad."

"I don't think I'll need them where I'm going," Cavalo said, reclining in his chair. "Thanks to you, I can finally retire. . . . *Adeus,* Senhor Logan."

"All I'm saying," Gregor complained, "is that it wouldn't have cost that much more to let us fly business class."

"You have to let this go," Oskar said, then he returned to the task at hand. The twin brothers stood with their backs to an alley wall. Their motorcycles were parked behind them. Oskar leaned around the corner and watched the warehouse through a pair of binoculars.

"It's just so damned petty," Gregor said. "It's not like they're hurting for cash, so why go cheap on us?"

"Security, remember?" Oskar lowered the binoculars and shot an evil look back at Gregor. "We stood out like crazy. Besides, you got a lot of nerve calling them petty when you're the one bitching because you had to pay for your own drinks."

"Easy for you to say, you had a direct flight. I had four connections, and they lost my fucking luggage."

"Shh," Oskar hissed as he watched Logan through the binoculars, leaving the warehouse. "He just came out the front." Logan got into the Jeep with his two associates. "He's back in the Jeep." Moments later, it pulled away from the curb, made a U-turn, and sped away. "And they're out of here."

"Shouldn't we follow them?" Gregor asked.

"No," Oskar said as he broke cover and walked toward the warehouse's rear entrance. "We know where to find them. Let's go check on Cavalo." Gregor followed him through a jagged gap in the chain-link fence that ran the length of the warehouse's parking lot. As they neared the stairs, Oskar held up a closed fist.

Gregor halted and waited while Oskar checked ahead of them for traps. He reached out with one hand and closed his eyes. Patterns and currents of energy flow tingled his mutant senses. Different colors and textures of energies began to distinguish themselves as his senses focused. The glassy perfection of infrared sensor beams; the violet waves of an active motion sensor; the hot-and-cold nodes of an open circuit waiting to be closed and either sound an alarm or set off a trap.

He looked back at Gregor. "We're going in the front."

They circled the building and strolled inside. The place looked as if it had been hit by a bomb. They knew Wolverine only by his reputation, but he seemed to be everything that they had heard, and no doubt more. Bodies and wreckage, fire and smoke; the inside of the warehouse was a killing field.

At the top of the stairs, they found the door to Cavalo's office wide open. His back was to them. A .44-caliber Desert Eagle semiautomatic pistol was holstered under his left arm. He was hunched over an open safe and busily stuffing shrink-wrapped bricks of cash into a black duffel.

On a table just inside the door stood a simple lamp. Oskar held it in place and yanked its power cord free of its base. The snap turned Cavalo about-face; he reached for his pistol, then froze as he recognized the twins.

Oskar twisted the ragged end of the exposed electrical wire around his index finger. Sweet power flooded through his body. "He's all yours," he said to Gregor, whose grin made it clear he, too, was savoring the sudden influx of fresh energy.

"We're very disappointed in you," Gregor said to Cavalo. "You went mano a mano with Logan. . . . You had the chance to do the honorable thing, and you blew it."

Cavalo put down the duffel and stood tall. "Honorable?" His mien was defiant and his tenor scornful as he faced his executioners. "You know nothing of honor," he said.

"I know that we trusted you to repect our employer's privacy," Gregor said. "And I know that

Logan's one of the least forgiving people in the world. So if he was here and let you live, it's because he got what he came for." Gregor stepped forward and raised his open palm toward Cavalo. "Because you told him what he wanted to know."

"Foda-se," Cavalo cursed. *"Filho da puta."*

A continuous ray of white-hot energy leaped from Gregor's hand and engulfed Cavalo in a crackling shroud. The gangster's screams were momentary, cut short as his body disintegrated. Gregor ceased fire. A ghost of atomized gray ash dissipated in a slow wafting breeze. Gregor folded his hand into a finger gun, lifted it to his face, and comically puffed across his index finger, like a child playing at being a gunslinger.

"Nice shot," Oskar said. "Let's get out of here."

"Sure thing," Gregor said, then he stepped forward and picked up Cavalo's duffel full of money. He zipped it shut. "This time we fly first class."

"Deal," Oskar said. "Once we frag Logan, we'll have earned it." He led Gregor out of the office, back onto the balcony outside. Looking down at the devastation that Logan had wrought, Oskar entertained a moment of caution. "Call me crazy," he said, "but I think we should call for backup."

"Dinner is served," Nando called from the kitchen.

Logan pulled on a gray T-shirt and let it hang untucked above the waist of the second—and last—pair of blue jeans he had brought along for his visit to Japan. It occurred to him that he might want to add a few more pieces to his wardrobe soon if he was going to keep getting into fights in his street clothes.

He stepped out of the bedroom into the living room. Wai Ying sat on the couch with her satellite phone cradled against her ear. He gestured toward the kitchen, trying to indicate that she should end her call and join him and Nando, but she adamantly refused to pay attention to him.

"Read it back to me," she said, then nodded as she listened and compared what she was hearing to what was written on the slip of paper Logan had received from Cavalo. "Yes," she said. "That's the one. Find out who owns that bank account." She listened again, this time growing annoyed. "I know it's illegal, do it anyway. We've got hackers on the payroll for a reason, use them. I need that—hang on, I have another call."

Logan waved again. "Dinner's rea—"

She pressed a button on her phone. "Hello? Yes, I want the Citation Thunderstar fueled and ready to fly ASAP. . . . I don't care, bill us. . . . Just have the plane ready. Good-bye." Another tap on the phone. "I need that name, Hiro, and an address to go with it. Get it done. *Sayonara.*" She hung up with a petulant stab of her fingertip on the phone's keypad and threw a flustered glare at Logan. "What?"

"Dinner," he said.

"Fine," she said, then pushed herself up from the sofa.

They joined Nando in the kitchen and sat down. In the center of the table was a platter of piping-hot pancakes. A bright yellow stick of real butter and a jar of Canadian maple syrup stood next to it.

"They smell great," Logan said.

"Dig in," Nando said proudly.

Wai Ying surveyed the repast with a bemused grimace. "Pancakes? For dinner?"

"They're my specialty," Nando said.

"They're also the only thing he knows how to make from scratch," Logan said, spearing a short stack of four flapjacks with his fork and dropping them onto his plate. He cut off a slab of butter and spread it liberally across the pancakes, then doused them thoroughly with syrup. Nando and Wai Ying helped themselves and went through the same motions. Logan waited until they had buttered and slathered their own pancakes before taking a bite of his.

From the moment they hit his tongue, he knew something was seriously wrong with the pancakes. He noticed only then that they were much too thin. They had a rubbery resistance when he cut through them with his fork. It was like chewing on a Frisbee made of paste. Across the table, Wai Ying and Nando were experiencing much the same reaction.

"Not to be rude," Logan said, "but these pancakes suck."

Nando nodded his agreement. "Um . . . yeah."

Wai Ying quietly disposed of her half-masticated mouthful in her napkin. "Excuse me," she said.

Logan pushed his plate away. "What the hell happened, Nando? You used to have these things down to a science."

"I don't know, I can't explain it," he said. He got up from the table and walked over to the counter. Picking up the box of bake mix, he looked flummoxed. "I followed all the directions. Used all the right ingredients." He carried the box over to the table and put it down as he slumped back into his seat. "It just doesn't make sense."

"Maybe your skillet wasn't hot enough," Wai Ying said. "Or maybe the milk was sour."

"It's not sour," Logan said. "I can smell it from here. It's fine." He picked up the box and sniffed its powdery contents. Then he read the text on the box. "I think I've found your problem," he said, handing the box to Nando. "Have a look at the cookbook offer on the side panel."

Nando read the side panel and shook his head. "So? It's a cookbook offer. What about it?"

"Look at the entry deadline," Logan said. "It's *fifteen years ago*." He watched Nando wince as understanding dawned. "Nando, how long has that box of bake mix been sitting in your cupboard?"

With a sheepish look and an apologetic shrug, Nando replied, "I don't get many visitors, *amigo*."

"At least none who stay for breakfast," Wai Ying quipped.

The shot to Nando's pride was so brutal that Logan felt it. He gently chided Wai Ying, "Was that really necessary?" As she opened her mouth to respond, they all heard a muffled explosion from outside. "Get down!" Logan shouted as he hit the deck.

And the house exploded.

Gregor's first shot severed the electrical transmission line that ran above and behind the row of slum houses.

As soon as the HVDC—high-voltage, direct-current—line touched ground, Oskar removed his hand from the housing of his motorcycle's idling engine. He sprinted over to the fallen electrical wire and picked it up.

It was a 9.7-millimeter, seven-strand galvanized steel cable. Its six-hundred-kilovolt current, the most powerful of its kind in the world, originated from the Itaipu hydroelectric plant several miles west, at the head of the Río Paraná. Buzzing in the palm of his hand, it felt like a permission slip to play God. He let the raw power flood into and through him.

Gregor waited several dozen meters away, next to the SUV, in which he and Oskar had traveled with their Hand-provided backup. Oskar watched his brother's posture change, from an anxious hunching to a regal looming, as the wave of energy coursed into his hands.

Gregor pressed his wrists together and pointed his palms at one of the houses. A bright, golden corona formed instantly around him, a halo of excess electrical fury.

Then a flash of light and heat engulfed the house. The attack had moved at the speed of light, too fast to be observed. Fire and sparks erupted high into the hazy night, lighting up the sparsely built ghetto for half a kilometer around. Chunks of the building flew apart in a storm of splintered, burning wood. Then a geyser of fire swallowed the house into its foundation.

Despite the distance and the cacophony of destruction, Oskar heard his brother laughing, like a dark god triumphant.

The fires retreated into themselves as the initial blast faded away, and a tower of inky smoke climbed into the sky. Gregor pointed with a hand ringed in dancing lightning at the charred remains of the house. He looked back at the SUV and commanded its occupants, "Go find the bodies."

Instantly, the SUV's two rear doors and hatchback opened. Six ninjas tumbled out of the vehicle and dashed into the aftermath of Gregor's attack. Firelight glinted on the blades of their swords and, from Oskar's vantage point below the HVDC tower, turned them all into silhouettes.

Mopping up wasn't the exciting part of the job, but

being a professional meant being thorough and remaining on-site until the mission was confirmed as
done.

For several seconds the ninjas stabbed and poked
their way through the jumbled wreckage. Then a
pile of dusty debris heaved upward and obscured the
smoldering pit in a dense, dusty cloud.

The sounds of metal clashing against metal and the
screams of dying men made it clear to Oskar that this
fight wasn't over—it was only just getting started.

Wai Ying told herself repeatedly that the weight of the
house was an illusion, that its burden was all in her mind.

It still felt like it weighed a ton.

She huddled beneath her dome-shaped force field
with Logan and the surprisingly sanguine Nando.
She'd followed Logan's directions to get down, but
when the house erupted into fire and fury, her
instincts had taken over. She'd crossed her arms,
ducked her head, and projected an invisible shield
around herself and the men.

Crimson flames and broken rock had swirled
around them like an apocalyptic tornado. Splintered
wood and household items, scouring blasts of super-
heated sand, clouds of shattered glass, billows of
toxic smoke, all of it had buffeted her shield—and
not one bit of it had passed through. Then the floor
had collapsed and they had fallen into the basement,
followed by the rest of the ranch-style house.

Now it was all piled on top of them; if her concentration slipped, this basement would become their shared grave. As the sounds of shifting earth and settling debris faded and stopped, Logan calmly took stock of the situation.

"Nice talent you got there," he whispered. "Wish I'd known about that before Cavalo's boys shot me full of holes."

Wai Ying muttered through a clenched jaw, "I offered."

"That's right," Nando said softly. "She did."

"We can play the blame game later," Logan said. "Wai Ying, you're doin' great. Can you expand that force field?"

She winced as she nodded. "I think so," she said, even though she wasn't certain it was true.

"How fast? Just a little at a time? Or all at once?"

Her sensei's words came back to her: *Effort is an illusion.*

"Any way you want it," she said, willing herself to believe that she could deliver on her promise. *There is no burden.*

"Then I'm gonna need one big push," Logan said. "Only when I tell you." He sounded worried about her. "You sure you're up to this?"

For a moment she almost felt as if the load had grown lighter. She met Logan's concerned stare. "Give the word."

He cast his eyes upward and listened, apparently

detecting subtle vibrations that neither she nor Nando could pick up. All she could hear was her own labored breathing, but Logan appeared to be shifting his gaze from one spot to another, following targets that only he could sense. "Get ready," he whispered, then held up three fingers and started folding them down. *Three, two, one.* He pointed at her, and she took that as her cue.

All things are equal. In her mind's eye her force field swelled instantly, like a blowfish inflating itself against a predator. Above her, the layers of dirt and debris exploded away, ejecting a massive crater's worth of thick, sooty dust.

"Let it go!" Logan shouted as he sprang away, and Wai Ying terminated her force field. Her entire body sagged with relief—then she realized that the dark cloud of dust was raining back down on her and Nando. The pair covered their faces as the heaviest particles fell and coated them in ash and soil.

Then came the metallic ringing of blades clashing with adamantium claws and being broken in twain. Two heavy *thump*s followed right away, then two more. Several seconds later the dust started to settle, and Wai Ying saw the dim outlines of Logan and two ninjas, locked in combat. His opponents lunged at him from the front and rear simultaneously, blades swinging in lethal arcs—and yet, when the flurry of action was done, it was the ninjas who collapsed, in pieces, to the ground.

Logan prowled forward, out of the pit of what was once Nando's house. Wai Ying grabbed Nando's arm. "Come on." She yanked him up and pulled him along as she hurried after Logan. As they neared the top of the crater, she peeked over the edge and saw Logan advancing toward a fair-haired man who held fiery spheres of energy in both hands. She wanted to tell Logan to fall back, take cover—but then she reminded herself that he was a professional; he knew what he was doing.

Then he hollered a war cry and charged at the blond man.

Twin bolts of lightning leaped from the man's hands. They blasted Logan into the air and sent him flying clear over the crater. He left a grayish trail of smoke along his trajectory and crashed down hard on the rocky ground.

The blond man wound up to fire another blast.

Wai Ying lunged up and out of the pit as he fired. She projected a concave force field in front of him. His attack rebounded off it and blasted away part of the roof on a house across the street, then continued on the same angle and blasted apart a large insulator coil on one of the distant high-voltage electrical towers, dropping a cascade of sparks.

The blond man's fistful of power seemed to flicker for half a second, and he looked anxiously in a different direction. Tracking his line of sight, Wai Ying spotted another man—the fireballer's identical twin—standing beneath the closest electrical tower, hands clenched around a fallen power line.

That one must be the power plug, she realized, even as the one tossing the blasts recharged to maximum capacity and took aim squarely at her. *Have to do this right.* She didn't even want to think about what would happen if her force field didn't hold.

She didn't wait for the blast to come; when it did, her force field was already in place, curved and angled as precisely as she could in the fraction of a second she had been given to do it. Needles of heat stung her face as the attack rolled off her invisible shield. And at almost the exact same moment, the base of the nearby electrical tower disintegrated in a flash of fire and lightning.

The blast threw the second twin away from the tower, toward the houses. He tumbled through the air and landed hard, facedown in the dirt.

Wai Ying braced herself for another attack, but the blond blaster was already climbing into the seat of the idling SUV. Seconds later, it kicked up a dusty spew of gravel as it sped out to the fallen twin and stopped. The driver got out, picked up his brother, and put him in the back of the truck. Then he climbed back behind the wheel, and the SUV disappeared down a backcountry trail into the night.

Nando climbed out of the crater and took a few halting steps into the street. He turned and looked back. Trudging around the perimeter of the hole was

Logan, whose clothes were tattered and singed. Wisps of smoke rose from his charred but swiftly healing body.

He and Wai Ying joined Nando, flanking him as he stared into the pit. The trio stood together in silence for a moment.

"So," Nando muttered, half in shock, "*that* happened."

"Everybody all right?" Logan asked. Wai Ying and Nando both nodded. Logan grinned at Wai Ying. "I like your style." More thoughtfully, he added, "You saved my ass tonight. I owe you."

She gave a small, single nod of appreciation. "What about you? Are *you* all right?"

"I've been crispier," he said. "Nothing a few beers and a loofah won't fix." He slapped Nando's shoulder in what, between men, passed for a comforting gesture. "Sorry 'bout the house."

"What? This?" Nando dismissed the situation with a wag of his head and an ironic grimace. "Don't worry about it. I have a cleaning lady, it'll be fine."

"Come on, buddy," Logan said, as he and Wai Ying guided Nando away from the smoking rubble and toward the Jeep. "We'll give you a lift into town, and Miss Corporate Card'll get you a suite at the Bourbon Cataratas on our way to the airport."

"You're leaving?" Nando asked.

"No choice, *irmão*," Logan said, glancing at Wai Ying. "We have to follow the money."

8

GUNSHOTS CRACKED IN THE DARKNESS, FROM the edge of the village.

Nishan awoke before the first echo faded. Then came the hoofbeats and distant, panicked screams. She sprang from the floor, between the beds in the clinic where her gravely ill children lay. Fear gave her strength; she lifted Nadif and Kanika, one in each arm, and carried them out of their shared tent of mosquito netting as quickly as she was able. They barely awoke as she hobbled toward the rear exit of the clinic. Around her, the other patients were either too ill or too disoriented to react, but they were not her concern.

She opened the door by colliding with it. It squawked on its rusty hinges, rattled as it rebounded off the outside of the building. Bearing the weight of both her children made her unsteady. She stumbled down the short stairs to the rocky ground. Ahead of her, past the few meters of clearing that ran behind the elevated structure, there was nothing but flatland.

Fleeing into the open would be pointless. She could barely survive alone out on the barren, difficult terrain. With her children in tow it would be impossible.

The hoofbeats and gunfire drew closer.

Men were shouting and women were screaming.

Nishan dropped to one knee and looked under the clinic building. It was a tight space, no more than half a meter off the ground, and it was thick with weeds, spiderwebs, and garbage. On all fours she backed herself into the crawl space, then dragged her children in after her—Nadif first, then Kanika.

She moved away from the edge. Too much chance of being seen there. She pushed with her heels while hanging on to her children's forearms. Rocks gouged into Nishan's back. Weeds tickled her limbs, and webs stuck to her face. A few inches at a time, she and her children moved toward the center of the clinic building, directly beneath the middle aisle. Faint lines of light broke through the gaps in the floorboards above. When she had reached the center of the building, she let go of her children and rolled onto her belly, the better to hide her eyes.

Then the hoofbeats and angry voices were in the street in front of the clinic. Automatic gunfire stuttered several times. Heavy stomping footfalls climbed the clinic steps and spread out inside the building. Nishan heard the men speaking above her, and she understood little of what they were saying—most of the Tanjawar militiamen were Arabic and spoke a different dialect from the one she and other black Zibarans used. It sounded as if they were stealing medical supplies, including patients' intravenous tubes and their mosquito netting.

There was some kind of argument. It ended with several long bursts of gunfire that sent bullets screaming through the floorboards on either side of the building, directly below where the patients' beds would have been. Where Nadif and Kanika and Nishan had been less than two minutes earlier.

Then the gunfire ceased, and Nishan wished that it hadn't. With the shouting and shooting past, there was nothing to drown out the anguished screams of women—and young girls, Nishan realized with horror as she recognized several of the voices. Pleas for mercy that became desperate begging for freedom, and then nothing but heartbreaking wails of terror and pain.

It was a sound Nishan had heard more times than she could count, and she was certain it was the same in any land and in every language: the sound of rape.

She pressed her hands to her face and buried her

weeping in the ground, grateful only that her children were too deathly ill to cry out in fear and betray their hiding place. Desperate to block out the agonized screams of girls and women being brutalized, Nishan focused on anything else—the sweltering heat and suffocating humidity that drenched her with sweat; the creeping itch of bugs traveling across her skin; the taste of dust in her mouth and the sting of tears in her eyes.

But nothing could muffle that awful sound, and nothing could erase her own horrible memories.

It had been more than a year since her own rape, but every Tanjawar raid resurrected that night in her thoughts, as vivid and terrifying as it had been the first time. She still felt the men holding her wrists and ankles; the hot welts rising on her back, where the men had beaten her with leather belts because she had struggled; the pain and shame of being violated while the men laughed and drank whiskey and took turns. But none of that had been the worst part of their crime.

The Tanjawar thugs had made her children watch.

Now the thugs were out in the street, once more laughing like drunkards while they took turns with someone else's mother, someone else's sister, someone else's daughter. And there was nothing that Nishan could do except hide.

She lost track of time, and in the blink of an eye the light seemed to change. Dawn broke, and the Tanjawar, like roaches, scurried to vanish from sight. Hoofbeats and rallying cries resounded through the village, followed by more gunshots.

Then something made of glass shattered inside the clinic, followed by another, and another.

Nishan caught the odor of kerosene moments before a low rush of ignition rumbled over her head. The space beneath the clinic rapidly grew hotter, like an oven. Frozen by fear, Nishan knew that she had to get herself and her children away from the fire, but revealing herself while the Tanjawar were near was too dangerous. She couldn't risk it. To stay put was to die by fire, to run was to die by the sword.

Fear stretched the seconds as she listened to the hoofbeats rise to a gallop, then fade slowly into the distance. Taking hold of Nadif and Kanika once more by their forearms, she scrambled on her back as quickly as she could toward the edge of the building. Above her the floorboards were disintegrating, turning to red embers, stinging her face with dropping sparks, blinding her with hot ash.

A few meters away, a large chunk of the floor collapsed, hastening the implosion of the entire building. Nishan struggled not to lose speed as she neared the edge. Her face broke free first, into the musky but open air. Kicking her way free, she was half out when Kanika and Nadif's soot-smeared faces were clear of the building. She tugged them the last of the way out, then carried them again, one in each arm, as she limped from the blaze of the clinic, which at last crumbled into a massive funeral pyre. As soon as she had moved far enough away that its heat was no longer a threat, she let herself collapse, exhausted, to the ground next to her children.

Most of the village was on fire.

The streets were littered with the dead—all of them men and boys. Some were villagers; others were Médecins sans Frontières doctors or technicians. Among them was white-haired Dr. Maguire.

Crawling atop the carnage, in search of kith and kin, were scores of women and girls, all of them bloodied, bruised, and ravaged. One young girl, perhaps no more than ten years of age, lay alone in the middle of the street, her eyes wide and blank, her thin dark body trembling in a fetal curl, her arms wrapped around her blood-soaked legs. All around her, the other women and girls wore the same numb expression. No one cried any tears, because they would have been wasted—there was no one left who could offer comfort. This was a place without salvation.

Mountains of greasy smoke rose from the burning buildings, announcing the village's victimhood to every other town for miles around. Come tomorrow, Nishan knew, the smoke would rise from somewhere else, and people in every other place who could see it would pray that their homes and families would not be next. But sooner or later, everyone was next.

Nishan drifted up and down the main street, covering her nose and mouth with a damp cloth to block out the charnel odor of burnt flesh and the stench of dead bodies decomposing beneath the merciless African sun. She was desperate to find any of the MSF doctors alive, to find anyone who could help continue treating her children. Around every corner and in every shadow she searched for Dr. Charoenying, but there was no sign of the Thai physician. Just more bodies, more pits of smoking ashes, more examples of this place's endless privations and suffering.

Soon enough, the dead were accounted for, and names were attached to the bodies. One by one the corpses were added to the fire where the clinic building had stood, and it claimed each new cadaver like the devil's maw, ever hungry for souls. This place had become Hell on Earth, and the crackling flames rising from a pool of rendered human fat were the proof.

By midday three cars full of officials arrived from the capital, along with a truck carrying an unarmed platoon of UN peacekeepers. They all proved equally useless. When Nishan begged them for medicine for her children, they told her that they didn't have any, and that the Tanjawar had stolen the MSF's supplies and emptied the pharmacy.

All the doctors except for Dr. Charoenying had been murdered. Charoenying, witnesses said, had been taken by the Tanjawar, though whether it was because they'd demanded her medical services or because they had other plans for her, no one knew—and no one cared to speculate.

All that Nishan would ever know for certain about Dr. Charoenying was that she never saw her again.

9

DR. NIKOLAI FALCO ATTACHED ANOTHER bundle of data connections to the electron chromatograph scanners, then paused to verify his work against the detailed schematic on the floor at his feet. He had been provided with an extremely accurate set of plans for reconstructing the MECCA system, and all the necessary tools and equipment. Well, almost all of the equipment; several key components of the system remained unavailable to him, so he had worked around their absence as best as he had been able.

He had yet to see his captor's face. Miyoko, the woman who had driven him out of Osaka, had later drugged him unconscious. When he awoke several hours ago, feeling distinctly queasy, he was here. As for where "here" was, he couldn't really say.

There were no windows. The walls, floor, and ceiling were made of dull gray metal. He was being housed in a small anteroom next to the spacious lab whose systems he had been ordered to assemble. His "quarters" consisted of a cot, a bare electric lightbulb dangling on a frayed wire, and an industrial portable toilet wedged into the corner. A sliding panel near the floor was used to deliver food and take away refuse. A bottled-water dispenser stood beside his cot.

The doors were another curiosity. They were similar to the kind of airtight portals used in labs that worked with hazardous biotoxins, but these looked even more formidable, as if they had been armored to withstand a sizable explosion.

A constant thrumming pulsed under Falco's feet. He wondered if it was the rumble of generators, or perhaps the drone of a large-scale ventilation system. The air was warm but also noticeably well filtered in his quarters and in the new lab he was constructing. Based on the specs that he was working from, the lab would eventually have to be dust- and contaminant-free, just like the one he'd been taken from in Japan.

The work would normally have been slow and tedious for one person, but many of the larger components were being delivered preassembled, and entire bundles of cables had been set in place to provide power distribution, grounding, and data transfer even before he'd begun his assigned task. Now he was at the final step, which required the integration of several components that everyone working at Tanaka Biotechnology had been repeatedly assured were unique and impossible for a competitor to acquire. If what he had been told was true, this project for which he had been conscripted would be over right now.

But when the access panel on the wall beside the main portal lifted open, a wheeled pallet rolled through, bearing every single one of the items that were supposed to be impossible to get. The panel dropped closed once the items were safely inside. Falco walked over to the pallet and checked each of the high-tech items that rested on it. He knew right away that these hadn't been stolen from the TBC lab; all the original components had been marked with hidden serial numbers and booby-trapped so that their removal from MECCA would result in their immediate destruction. Yet here they were.

The main portal opened, unlocked from the other side. Backlit in the doorway was the silhouette of a tall, powerfully built man. He stood with his hands folded behind his back and spoke English with a Japanese accent. "Dr. Falco," he said. "I trust you have everything you'll need to finish?"

"Looks that way," the German scientist replied.

His own accent was slight in comparison to that of his visitor. "You're quite resourceful."

"I command significant resources," said the silhouette. "It is not exactly the same thing." The visitor took a half-step forward. Light spilled across his trousers and the bottom edge of his matching suit jacket, both of which were silvery gray and smartly tailored. "Please answer my original question: Do you have everything you need to finish the lab?"

Looking around, Falco answered, "Yes."

"How long until it is operational? Be specific."

"I will need at least ten hours to complete assembly and run diagnostics from the mainframe," Falco said.

"Once your equipment is functioning, how long will it take you to refine your formula for mass production?"

"I cannot really say," Falco admitted. "I am close to isolating the drug's curative compounds, but its side effects—"

"The side effects do not concern me," the visitor said. "I want a formula for mass-producing the drug in its current form."

Falco hesitated to answer; he had no idea what this man intended to do with a mass-producible version of raw Panacea. *Whatever he's planning,* Falco reminded himself, *you're his prisoner, so you don't get any say. Just play along and don't provoke him.* Composing his face into a mask of calm, he replied, "I can finish the formula in approximately twelve hours."

"How much of that is labor, and how much is computer processing time?"

"About half and half," Falco said. "Once I finish my tests and put in the data, the mainframe will complete the formula."

"Excellent," the man in the suit said. "How portable will the drug be? Will it require strict temperature control? Limited illumination?"

"Refrigeration," Falco said. "It's a very durable compound, as long as it's kept cold."

"Understood," the visitor said. He turned as if to leave, then pivoted back. "Is there anything—within reason—that we can provide to make your stay more comfortable?"

Falco frowned. "Not unless you can teach your cook to make a proper bratwurst with sauerkraut, or get me a decent beer."

"I'll see what can be done," the silhouette said. "I will return tomorrow. Please have the formula ready for production."

This time the man walked away into the darkness, and the heavy portal swung closed. The pneumatic hiss of an airtight seal was followed by the dull, heavy thud of security dead bolts moving solidly into place.

Falco had not been harboring any illusions about his status, but there now could be no doubt that he was a prisoner. He surveyed the scope of the task ahead of him and realized that he felt severely fatigued. *Maybe I should rest before I continue,* he decided. The same dizzy, nauseated sensation that had assailed him when he'd first awoken returned as he plodded back toward his anteroom. He eased himself onto his cot and lay back slowly, until his weight was off his feet.

Many deep, calming breaths later, he felt more relaxed and more centered, but his low-grade vertigo continued. Then he noticed the lightbulb on its long, frayed wire. It was swaying. Only very slightly, and by small degrees, but it was swaying.

Falco realized where he was: *I'm on a ship.*

10

THE RUSSIAN CUSTOMS OFFICER EYED THE PASS-
port that Logan had handed him, moved it aside to
take another look at Logan himself, then went back
to staring at the passport. *"Nyet,"* the man grumbled,
even though no one had said anything or asked any
questions. He was exactly what Logan had long ago
learned to expect of any career civil servant: literal-
minded and stubborn.

Clearing customs at Pulkovo Airport in St. Petersburg, Russia, was proving a great deal more difficult
than it had in Brazil. For one thing, the Russian customs officers actually had computers that worked, and
showed that neither Logan nor Wai Ying had received

a tourist invitation or a proper visa for entry. For another, Logan felt that the officers had been suspicious of him from the moment he'd stepped out of the Cessna jet—no doubt because he was still wearing the same charred and shredded clothing that he'd had on when he was getting barbecued by the twin mutants.

He'd meant to have some new clothes delivered to the plane during its second refueling stop, in Vienna, but all the garments that had been waiting at the hangar had proved to be the wrong size, and there had been no time to exchange them. So now he found himself looking as if he'd gone ten rounds with a flame-breathing wheat thresher. It wasn't exactly the best first impression he'd ever made, but it wasn't the worst, either.

Wai Ying paced back and forth along an imaginary straight line behind him, chattering rapid-fire Japanese into her cell phone. She was trying to find some way to leverage Setsuko Tanaka's connections to persuade the Japanese government to intervene and extricate herself and Logan from this mess before it escalated into an international incident.

The automatic sliding-glass doors behind them opened. Logan turned and nodded to his old friend and Cold War–era Soviet contact, Alexander Zivojinovich—or Ziv, as Logan had always called him. It had been almost fifteen years since he'd last seen Ziv. He was pushing sixty now, he had put on weight, and his blond hair was thinning on top and starting to look more silvery gray.

Ziv's smile hadn't changed at all, though. He chortled as he surveyed Logan's shredded shirt and pants. Logan's only intact pieces of attire were his leather jacket, because he'd left it in the plane during the trip to Brazil, and a pair of snakeskin boots that had proved to be damned near indestructible, no matter what he'd done to them.

"Logan, *moi stariy droog*," Ziv said as he crushed him in a bear hug. "I see you're as sartorially challenged as ever."

"Good to see you, too, Ziv," Logan replied. He made gestures of introduction. "Wai Ying, this is an old buddy of mine: Alexander Zivojinovich. Ziv, for short."

"A pleasure," Ziv said with a courteous nod of his head. Wai Ying said nothing in reply; she just nodded at Ziv.

The customs officer shouted, "Who are you? These people—"

"These people are guests of the state," Ziv snapped. He marched to the counter, reached inside his trench coat, and produced a vinyl flip-fold, which opened to reveal a Russian government ID. "Issue their visas immediately and have them delivered to the Grand Hotel Europe on Nevsky Prospekt." Then Ziv plucked both their passports from the officer's hand, turned on his heel, and stalked swiftly back to Logan and Wai Ying.

Jaw agape with surprise, Wai Ying slowly folded

her cell phone closed and tucked it back into her purse. She glared at Logan. Ziv walked past them and said, "My driver picked up your bags from the hangar. He's waiting for us outside." He passed through the sliding-glass doors and led them out of the office, then through the modern-looking terminal to the exit.

Logan followed his friend outside to the ground transport area. It was just after sunset. Instantly Logan's breath became visible in the frigid air, white plumes vanishing before him as he moved. Wai Ying walked beside Logan. They strolled toward a black limousine that idled several meters away. In an aggrieved whisper, she asked him, "You knew he was coming?"

"I called him from Dakar," he replied. "Figured we'd need the help."

"Any special reason you didn't tell me?"

He flashed a shit-eating grin in her direction. "'Cause I like the way you look when you get riled up."

Her eyes narrowed, her lips pursed with tension, and Logan was almost certain that he saw the tiniest hint of steam emerge from her ears. He blamed it on the weather.

They crouched and stepped into the back of the limousine with Ziv. As soon as the door closed, the car was in motion, racing away from the airport toward St. Petersburg city center. Logan reached inside his leather jacket and pulled out his last two Punch Rare Corojo cigars. He offered one to Ziv, who happily accepted it. While Logan snipped the end of his cigar with one of his claws, Ziv produced a sterling silver cigar cutter from his overcoat's side pocket and clipped his own. Logan snapped open his Zippo and lit his Corojo, then held the flame steady while Ziv puffed his cigar to life. Flipping the lighter closed, Logan settled back into his seat. He savored a few rich puffs while enjoying the discomfited look on Wai Ying's face as the off-white tendrils of smoke snaked around her.

"So, Ziv," Logan remarked, "I thought you retired from the KGB."

"The KGB doesn't exist anymore," Ziv said with a sly grin. "You know that."

"Fine, call it the FSB if it makes you happy," Logan said. "I still thought you were retired."

"Section chiefs don't retire," Ziv said. "They just become 'inactive.' Fortunately, it doesn't say that on my credentials." He closed his eyes and took another long pull on the Corojo. Exhaling, he said, "I know a place in town that can get you excellent Cubans, if you'd like."

"I would," Logan said.

Wai Ying cleared her throat a bit overdramatically. Logan felt his eyebrow arch with annoyance, by pure reflex.

Ziv's reaction was a far more dignified, urbane

smirk. "To business, then," he said. "Your message was rather cryptic. What brings you here?"

"A few days ago, some classified materials were stolen from a private laboratory in Japan," Logan began.

"The specifics aren't important," Wai Ying interjected, apparently worried that Logan didn't know how to be discreet. "Let's just say that whoever took them could use them to commit genocide and engage in blackmail on a global scale."

"To do that," Logan said, continuing the briefing, "they needed some gear that they got on the black market in Brazil. We've linked the Cayman Islands account that paid for the gear to a Russian citizen, a man named Alexei Pritikin."

Ziv nodded. "Anbaric Petroleum," he said. "The oil mogul."

"That's our boy," Logan said.

"We already have reason to believe that the *yakuza* are involved, and possibly another organization, known as the Hand," Wai Ying said.

"*Svyataya Maria,*" Ziv mumbled. Logan recalled that Ziv had helped thwart several attempts by operatives of the Hand to establish a foothold in the former Eastern Bloc nations. The Russians had expended so many resources combating groups like the Hand that they'd eventually bankrupted themselves, which had been a major factor in the Soviet Union's 1989 collapse.

Ziv's countenance was grim. "These materials they stole," he said to Logan, "are they as dangerous as Ms. Tse claims?"

"Worse," Logan said. "A lot worse."

"We need to investigate Pritikin, up close and personal," Wai Ying said. "I think he's using his company for more than just financing, but we'll have to data-mine his entire life before we can connect the dots."

"And we have to do it now," Logan added. "He and his pals have a head start, and they're moving fast; we have to be faster."

"First things first," Ziv said. He nodded to Logan. "Before we can do anything, we need to get you some new clothes." Then, in a dark and deadly earnest tone, he said, "As for Mr. Pritikin . . . I know exactly how to proceed."

Despite Wai Ying's insistence during the ride to the hotel that there was no time to delay in pursuing the Pritikin lead, Ziv had made it clear that the opportunity to act would have to wait until the following night. He didn't even want to divulge the details; Logan guessed that Ziv was probably concerned that Wai Ying would let her impatience get the best of her.

Logan had done his part by telling Wai Ying to trust Ziv's judgment; the man was a professional, and he'd brief them when he finished planning the op. It wasn't what Wai Ying had wanted to hear, but Logan had been relieved to have the night to recover his equilibrium; hopping back and forth through time zones had left him feeling dragged out. *Nearly getting blown up and then spending more than ten hours helping fly a jet nearly ten thousand miles will do that to a guy,* he'd reminded himself.

As usual, Wai Ying had spared no expense at the hotel. She'd booked herself into one of its terrace rooms and Logan into another. He had been too tired to appreciate its style when he'd first arrived; all his attention had been captured by the pleasantly strong water pressure in the stinging-hot shower and the fact that the bathroom's marble floor was electrically heated from below. After toweling himself dry, he'd crawled onto the king-sized bed, where he'd fallen asleep before he could finish untucking the corner of the duvet.

He awoke late in the morning to the glow of daylight, warm and diffused by the pastel orange draperies in front of the French doors to the terrace. Scratching a few wandering itches across his torso and ribs, he sat up and took in his surroundings. Most of the furniture appeared to be antique. Two slender padded armchairs faced the bed, which was flanked by two fragile-looking nightstands. A small end table sat between the armchairs; on top of the table was a crystal bowl filled with fruit. In the corner of the room was a small writing desk, above which hung a wide, gilded wall mirror. The overall décor of the room was evocative of the tsarist era.

Logan stepped over to the desk, picked up the phone receiver, and pressed the button for room service. The operator answered immediately. "*Gornichnaya,*" she said, and he figured that was Russian for "room service." He cobbled together what little Russian he remembered from his Cold War days working behind the Iron Curtain and made a halting attempt to order eggs Florentine, a rare steak, well-done potatoes, and a pot of black coffee. By the time he hung up, he wasn't sure what would be coming for breakfast; he just hoped that it would be hot and untainted by borscht.

Noticing in the mirror that he was naked, he grabbed one of the white terry-cloth bathrobes off the back of the bathroom door and tied it loosely shut at his waist. Then he picked up the phone again and this time dialed the concierge. He was greeted by another pleasant-sounding voice, male this time.

"Do you speak English?" Logan asked.

"Yes, sir," the concierge said. "What can we do for you?"

"I need a personal shopper to get me some new clothes."

"Very good," said the man on the phone. "Do you need anything in particular?"

"Nothing fancy," Logan said. "Just a basic wardrobe. T-shirts, underwear, shirts, some blue jeans—"

"American-style blue jeans are very expensive in Russia."

"Just charge it to my room." He decided that, as expenses went, this was one that Tanaka Biotechnology owed him right now. He gave the concierge his size information, then hung up the phone and flipped channels on the satellite television while waiting for his breakfast to arrive.

The meal that eventually was delivered (after an interminable, hour-long wait) consisted of a broccoli omelette, a bowl of potato soup, and a side of steak sauce. *Guess I'll have to work on my Russian,* Logan mused as he signed the room check. *At least these bozos got the coffee right.* He wheeled the rolling tray table out onto his terrace and wolfed down his meal while admiring the view of Arts Square, whose most notable structure was the Church of the Spilt Blood. *Sounds like my kind of church. If I went to church, that is.*

It was early afternoon when the personal shopper dropped off Logan's new clothes. He got dressed quickly, pulled on his boots and his jacket, and finally left his room to find Wai Ying. There was no answer at her door, and he didn't hear any activity from inside her room. *Probably out setting a world record for buying shoes,* he figured. Turning back toward his room, he toyed with the notion of stealing a nap and testing his Russian again; he was fairly certain he'd just remembered how to say "champagne," "caviar," and "Swedish massage."

Before he got more than three steps back to his room, however, the elevator doors opened down the hallway, and Wai Ying stepped out, followed closely by Ziv. She was carrying a pair of garment bags; he toted a polished-aluminum briefcase. Three more people, hefting large plastic toolboxes, exited the elevator behind them and appeared to be following them.

"Ah, good," Ziv exclaimed to Logan. "You're up. Come with us, there's a lot to do."

Logan eyed the approaching procession with mounting suspicion. "What's goin' on?"

"The plan," Wai Ying said. "Ziv and I worked out the details over breakfast."

"Hang on," Logan said. "There's a plan?" He watched Ziv with an accusing stare. "Ziv, you made the plan without me?"

Ziv shrugged. "Your own fault for sleeping all day and then stuffing your face out on your terrace." He tilted his head in Wai Ying's direction. "She was up at daybreak. Caught up to her running laps around Arts Square." With an extra touch of teasing sarcasm, he added, "If only you had her discipline, you might've made something of yourself by now."

Though Wai Ying wasn't looking in Logan's direction, he thought he noticed the slightest hint of a self-satisfied smirk on her face as she opened the door to her room. Ziv and his three-person entourage followed her in, and Logan entered last.

Wai Ying laid the garment bags flat on the bed. Taking a closer look, Logan noticed that both bags bore the logo of the Gostiniy Dvor department store, which was located directly across Nevsky Prospekt from the hotel.

Ziv sat down at the writing table and opened his briefcase. From it he removed a slender-profile laptop computer, which he opened and activated. Meanwhile, the anonymous trio had split up to different corners of the room and opened their bait-and-tackle-style toolboxes. One of them had a collection of sewing needles, threads, fabric swatches, cutting implements, and measuring tools. The other two were packing an impressive array of sprays, gels, dyes, combs, miniature hair dryers, and assorted hair-care and manicure products.

Logan didn't like where this was going at all.

"Somebody want to fill me in?" he asked.

"You're going undercover," Ziv said.

"Correction," Wai Ying interrupted. Looking at Logan, she continued, "*We're* going undercover."

"Undercover where?"

Ziv answered while typing rapidly at his computer. "The mansion of Alexei Pritikin, owner and president of Anbaric Petroleum." He swiveled the laptop around so that Logan could see the floor plan now displayed on its screen. "He's got a lakeside estate in Vaskelovo, about forty minutes from here."

Eyeing the tailor, hairdresser, and manicurist,

Logan inquired, "And that has what to do with them?"

"They're here to make you presentable," Wai Ying said.

"For . . . ?"

"Pritikin's hosting a fund-raising dinner tonight, filling his war chest so he can challenge Oleg Shumeyko for his seat in the Duma. The FSB bought tickets for the party, with guest names to be declared later. Two of them are now yours."

"Gee," Logan said, "I'm honored."

"You should be," Ziv said. "But we have a lot to do before tonight. I have to create new passports for you two and send your aliases on to the event planner for the guest list. But before we get to that, there's a much more serious issue to contend with."

Logan become keenly aware that everyone in the room was looking at him. "And that issue would be . . . ?"

In as serious a tone as Logan had ever heard him use, Ziv replied simply, "Your hair."

Six miserable, odor-filled hours later, Logan's wild coif continued to defy all attempts to tame it. The stylists had tried mousse to no effect. Hairspray had only made it stiffer and more difficult to work with. Straightening chemicals and relaxers had produced only short-term gains, because his mutant healing factor seemed programmed to rebel against even the most basic cosmetic alterations. Now they had moved on to a mixture of maximum-hold gels, which bought them enough obedience from his dark, feral mane to set it in place. Spying his reflection in the wall mirror, he had to admit he looked almost respectable.

By comparison, his manicure had gone off without a hitch. Logan had never known until this afternoon that he had "exquisite cuticles" or that a man's fingernails could be described with the term "scrumptious." He still had his doubts on the second point. For a moment, he'd considered extending his claws and seeing whether the manicure included a buff-and-polish, but Ziv—ostensibly having intuited Logan's intentions from his grin—had simply shaken his head no and left his warning at that.

There was a knock at the door. Ziv answered it, accepted a padded envelope from someone on the other side, then shut the door. He walked over to Logan, opened the envelope, and handed him a new Canadian passport. Logan flipped it open and grimaced at the photo, which he'd always hated. The name next to it read "James Howlett III." Nodding, he looked up at Ziv. "Nice work."

"Glad you like it," he said. "In case Pritikin checks up on you, we've set up a cover background for you, complete with dummy phones, business cards, a Web site, the works."

"I almost dread to ask," Logan said. "Who am I?"

"A high-end wine-and-spirits importer," Ziv said. "Specializing in rare European wines and fine liquors."

"You just want to see me squirm in there, don't ya?"

"Don't worry, you'll have all the help you need." He handed Logan a translucent plastic device that resembled a small kidney bean. "Put this in your ear. It's a subaural transceiver."

"Who's gonna be listening in?"

"I will," Ziv said. "While you and Ms. Tse are inside, I'll be running the op from a surveillance van a few kilometers away." He held up a maple-leaf-shaped lapel pin with what looked like a ruby set in its center. "Mini-camera. I'll see what you see. Try not to get it wet."

"Yes, Dad," Logan said, rolling his eyes. "What's our objective once we get in?"

"Break into Pritikin's private home office," Ziv said. He pointed to the floor plan of the mansion, which he had printed out on several sheets of letter-sized paper and taped together on the wall for Logan to study while the stylists fought with his hair. "It'll be on the top floor, in the north wing. The reception is being held in the south wing."

"That's a lot of open space in there," Logan observed. "How much do we know about Pritikin's internal security?"

"Not much," Ziv said. "He has armed guards

inside and outside the house. And his office is probably wired."

"Count on it," Logan said. "After I'm in the office, what then?"

"Power up the computer," Ziv said. "It has a secure hard-line connection to Anbaric Petroleum's internal network." Ziv reached in his pants pocket and took out a tiny, flat piece of plastic that had a slender connection interface at one end. "This is a flash memory stick," he explained. "On Pritikin's computer, you'll find a port on the side of his keyboard. Once you've started the machine, attach this. It'll run a program that'll help me hack into his machine from the van. Once I'm in, I'll clone his drives and any encrypted files I can find on the network. When I'm done, you pull the flash stick, shut down the machine, and go back to the party."

"Sounds too easy," Logan said.

"For you, sure," Ziv said. "I'm doing all the hard work."

"Just keep tellin' yourself that, bub," Logan said. He hooked a thumb toward the lounge, where Wai Ying was changing her clothes. "If my job's so easy, why's she taggin' along?"

"She'll be posing as your wife. When you excuse yourself from the reception, she'll cover for you till you get back."

"My *wife*? That's rich. Who's gonna believe that?"

Another knock at the door pulled Ziv away. When

he returned, the tailor followed him inside, holding two more garment bags and a shoebox from the posh department store across the street. "Your disguise," Ziv said, as the tailor laid the bags down on the bed and unzipped them. Logan followed Ziv's curling-finger summons and stepped over to the bed to examine the clothes.

It was a classic black-tie ensemble: a two-button Ralph Lauren black tuxedo jacket and pants, a white formal shirt with an off-white herringbone pattern and French cuffs, a charcoal-colored vest, and a black bow tie, of the variety that actually had to be knotted by hand. Secured in a small plastic bag were the accessories: gold cuff links and studs and an ivory-hued silk square for the jacket's breast pocket. Inside the shoebox were a fresh pair of black wool socks and a pair of Gucci shoes that had been polished to perfection.

"Sharp threads," Logan said.

"We started with the best and made some improvements," Ziv said. He reached under the jacket's collar and detached a black flap that had been secured with Velcro tabs. It was wide enough to cover the space between the two lapels of his suit-coat. "For those moments when you'd prefer to be incognito," Ziv said.

"Very thoughtful," Logan said. "Anything else? Magnets in the shoes? Lasers in the cuff links?"

"If we'd had a few more days to prepare, maybe. But no."

"Too bad."

Ziv handed Logan a platinum wedding band. "Put this on and go get dressed. The valet has your car ready downstairs."

Logan was heading toward the bathroom when the door to the suite's lounge opened and Wai Ying stepped into the bedroom. She had her hair up, revealing the soft-ruffled straps of her red scoop-neck Valentino dress, which had been matched perfectly to her crimson Manolo Blahnik spike heels. On her left hand she wore a sapphire-and-diamond engagement ring and a diamond-crusted wedding band. An Arctic white fox stole was draped over her shoulders, giving a decidedly Russian flair to her ensemble.

She scowled and snapped at Logan, "Aren't you dressed yet?"

Logan tossed a sullen look Ziv's way. "I take it back," he said. "She sounds *exactly* like a wife."

11

NO OTHER CAR IN THE WORLD THAT LOGAN
had ever heard sounded quite so perfect as a 1985
Ferrari 308GTS Quattrovalvole.

The one he was driving tonight was red, as mint as
the day it had rolled off the assembly line, and blessed
with enhanced carburetor performance. Idling, it
purred; in motion, it roared. He'd protested at first
that it was too flashy for his cover story, but Ziv had
merely waved away Logan's concerns. "It'll be fine,"
he'd said. "Trust me."

Bringing the Italian sports car to a stop in the cul-
de-sac in front of Pritikin's mansion, Logan realized
that Ziv had been correct: the car didn't stand out at

all. He and Wai Ying were surrounded by other guests exiting rare and exotic vehicles of every kind. An emerald-green Lamborghini Countach was stopped directly in front of Logan's Ferrari. Behind him a Jaguar XJ220 went from a silver blur to a halt less than a foot from his rear bumper. A clean-cut valet drove past in a white Mercedes-Benz SLR, followed a moment later by another uniformed young man driving a gleaming black Aston Martin Vanquish. Pritikin's benefactors, it seemed, were both rich and inclined toward conspicuous displays of wealth.

Logan turned off the engine and left the keys in the ignition. He got out of the car, walked around the front to the passenger side, and opened the door for Wai Ying. She accepted his outstretched hand, and he helped her out of the car. A fair-haired young man in a valet's uniform caught Logan's eye as he and Wai Ying climbed the wide, white marble stairs to the mansion's main entrance. Logan nodded to the valet, who hurried into the Ferrari and accelerated away to a distant parking area.

The night was damp and cold, and the air smelled heavy to Logan; there was a snowstorm moving in. Ahead of and behind him and Wai Ying, men in tuxedos and trench coats guided women in evening gowns and furs up the stairs. Most of the guests entered the party as couples, but a few small clusters of friends or business associates had formed where the crowd grew denser, near the mansion's broad, wide-open double doors.

A small flock of coat-check girls weaved through the arriving guests, handing out claim tickets while spiriting away countless fur coats, wraps, and stoles to a spacious wardrobe somewhere just off the main foyer. One of the women relieved Wai Ying of her fox stole and handed the claim ticket to Logan, who tucked it in his jacket's front pocket. He jutted out his elbow slightly toward Wai Ying, and she daintily slipped her own arm through it. Moving along with a small knot of other guests, they drifted upstairs into the palatial estate.

Marble and mahogany were the materials of choice. Arched doorways led to long hallways lined with rooms. Most of the passages were blocked by velvet ropes on brass stands. Man-sized white marble statues lined the main hallway. Logan didn't know if any of them were famous, or even if they were authentic. Most looked Asian, but a few were clearly of Central American origin. Behind them, the walls were decorated with broad tapestries and enormous oil paintings. Overhead, suspended at regular intervals from the high, vaulted ceiling, were cut-crystal chandeliers.

The rhythmic melody of a waltz resounded from the ballroom directly ahead. Several men and women stood in front of the doors, checking guests' invitations. Logan and Wai Ying stepped into a line of guests. When they reached the front of the line, he handed a man an envelope containing his and Wai Ying's invitation. The usher checked the intricately milled and embossed document by scanning it with a dim red laser beam from a small device in his hand. An indicator light on the back of the device turned green. "Welcome, Mr. Howlett," he said as he handed the invitation back to Logan.

"Thank you," Logan said, tucking the card back into his pocket. He led Wai Ying past the ushers, into the main ballroom. Couples twirled and turned in perfect form on the parquet dance floor. A legion of serving staff dodged through the room, dispensing wine and champagne and collecting empty glasses. Logan plucked two flutes of Dom Perignon from a passing server's tray and handed one to Wai Ying. They clinked their glasses and sipped slowly while walking a slow circuit of the room. He quickly lost count of the number of different perfumes and colognes his mutant senses picked up.

As Logan had expected, the music was provided by a few dozen live musicians. Behind the music, a low murmur of conversation and clinking glasses filled the room like white noise. When he focused, he was able to eavesdrop on any of several conversations near him. To his chagrin, they were all in Russian, so most of the nuances were lost to him. He caught enough, however, to realize who most of Pritikin's guests were.

"This room is full of Russian mobsters," he muttered, as much to Wai Ying as to Ziv. He knew that both of them heard him, because Wai Ying also had been given a transceiver, and they all shared the same continuous, digitally encrypted signal.

"Of course it is," Ziv said via the earpiece. "There isn't a business or a politician in Russia today that isn't in bed with the mob. Call it the price of capitalism."

A waitress offered them their choice from a selection of phyllo pastry shells stuffed with pesto and brie. Wai Ying took two of the appetizers and handed one to Logan, who popped it whole into his maw. Only after he'd swallowed it did he notice Wai Ying's icy stare and realize that a less enthusiastic response to the food might be in order.

Wai Ying studied the room and said, "No sign of Pritikin."

"He's the kind who likes to make an impression," Ziv said. "Look for him to enter the ballroom by walking down the east staircase, right behind you."

Logan turned and looked up the mountainous, curving stone staircase. He admired its intricately carved marble railings, banisters, and balusters. Heavy scarlet curtains blocked the view of the hall beyond the archway at the top. There was a slight flutter in the curtains, caused by some motion behind it. "I think he's about to make his big entrance," Logan observed.

"Move away from the staircase," Ziv said. "Try to blend in with the crowd."

"Screw that," Logan said. "I want to get a good look at the sonofabitch."

"Logan, don't be a fool. You're supposed to be undercover. Just lay low and stick to the plan."

"He's a player, Ziv," Logan said. "It's time to size him up. Now stop yakkin', you're distracting me."

Ziv's muttered Russian curses buzzed inside Logan's ear as the scarlet curtains parted. A trim, tall Russian man in his late forties emerged. Walking arm-in-arm with him was a striking Japanese woman in a modern kimono, one that Logan could see had been styled to afford her a greater freedom of movement. From an overhead speaker, a man's voice announced, first in Russian, then in English, "Ladies and gentlemen, please welcome your host, Alexei Pritikin, and Ms. Miyoko Takagi." The announcement was repeated in several more languages as the couple gracefully descended the staircase to thunderous applause. Pritikin waved graciously to his supporters and flashed a politician's calculating smile.

With every step that Miyoko took, her preternatural grace and poise made Logan more suspicious. Everything about her was precise and controlled; her economy of movement was superbly disciplined. It was rare to find such a quality of focus in even the most gifted martial-arts masters. Whoever she was, Miyoko was a factor that Logan knew not to underestimate.

She and Pritikin reached the bottom of the stairs

and began working their way through the crowd. Pritikin did the talking. He shook hands and doled out promises and nicknames as he went. Miyoko remained silent, but Logan noted the way she eyed every person within several meters of Pritikin. She was trained for combat, for assassination.

"Okay, Logan," Ziv said, unable to hide his agitation. "You got your close-up look, now back off."

Ignoring the tinny voice in his ear, Logan side-stepped through a gap in the crowd and put himself directly in Pritikin's path. Wai Ying stayed with him, staring down a man who tried to block her from reaching the front of Pritikin's receiving line. Logan mustered his least frightening smile as Pritikin stepped forward and extended his hand. The smooth, practiced manner he had displayed with his other guests faltered as he came face-to-face with Logan, but only for a moment. He shook Logan's hand firmly as he stole a glance at the maple-leaf pin on Logan's lapel. "Thank you for coming," he said in flawless, uninflected English. "So glad you could make it."

Playing along, Logan maintained eye contact with Pritikin while nodding sideways in Wai Ying's direction. "I'm sure you remember my wife, Wai Ying."

"Of course," Pritikin said, lying with aplomb. "Wonderful to see you again."

Just as Logan had expected, Wai Ying took the wind out of Pritikin's sails. "We've never met, Mr.

Pritikin," she said. "Nor has my husband made your acquaintance before today."

Another half-breath of hesitation. Then Pritikin heaved a sigh and smiled broadly. "Yes, you've caught me. I'm relieved, actually. I thought my memory had failed me." He reached out and shook Logan's hand again. "Alexei Pritikin."

"James Howlett the Third," Logan replied. Then he turned to Miyoko and scrutinized the details of her kimono. "Ms. Takagi," he continued. "It's an honor to meet someone who has such exquisite taste in kimonos."

Her expression was unreadable. "You admire it?"

"Very much," Logan said. "Correct me if I'm wrong, but I'd say it's hand-painted, in the traditional *yuzen* style—by master Kunihiko Moriguchi himself, if I'm not mistaken."

"You have a trained eye," she said, her tone neutral.

"Just an eye for beauty," Logan said, pulling Wai Ying gently to his side.

Miyoko whispered something in Pritikin's ear. His smile didn't falter as he listened, but his eyes darted quickly, his gaze falling on everything except Logan and Wai Ying. Then his face brightened and he looked at Logan. "It's rare to meet someone of such refined tastes," he said. "Miyoko and I would be honored if you'd both dine with us at our table this evening."

"We'd be delighted," Logan said, nodding his assent.

"Excellent," Pritikin said. "I have a few more guests to greet, Mr. Howlett, but we'll look forward to seeing you in the banquet room shortly."

"Absolutely," Logan said. Then Pritikin and Miyoko moved away, continuing to press the flesh with his campaign contributors and would-be allies and benefactors.

Once they were out of earshot, Wai Ying glared at Logan. "Are you out of your mind?"

Ziv immediately joined in over the transceiver: "What the hell are you doing, Logan?"

"I needed a closer look at her kimono to be sure," Logan said. "It's subtle; if you don't look closely, you'll miss it."

Wai Ying was beyond flustered now. "Miss *what?*"

"The repeated pattern in its design," Logan said, pulling a Cuban cigar from inside his jacket. "It's the same Fu symbol that's on the *shaken* we found in Osaka. She's a member of the Hand. Which means they're either using Pritikin, or they're in business with him." Using the silver clipper he'd borrowed from Ziv, he trimmed the end of his cigar while he let his report sink in with his partners. He lit the cigar with his Zippo.

"All right," Ziv said. "That's a good lead. But you nearly blew your cover getting it."

"Almost," Logan said, exhaling a puff of smoke. "Didn't."

"Regardless," Ziv said. "No more stunts, Logan. This is a recon, not a showdown."

Escorting Wai Ying toward the banquet room for dinner, Logan replied, "You do it your way, Ziv. I'll do it mine."

"Idiot, eto ne moya zhena," boomed Russian oil minister Yassev Soltsin, the fat man sitting two seats to Logan's left. *"Eto sobaka!"*

Six of the eight people at Alexei Pritikin's table guffawed heartily—everyone, in other words, except for Logan and Wai Ying, neither of whom possessed a sufficient grasp of Russian to get the joke. Soltsin's wife, Mariska, sat beside Logan and tried unsuccessfully to mask her embarrassment; her husband had been cracking jokes ever since they all had been seated for dinner. On the opposite side of the circular table from Logan sat Pritikin. Miyoko sat to Pritikin's right, opposite Wai Ying. The other couple at the table, Logan had learned during the curt preprandial introductions, were Ukrainian-born media baron Darius Mikalunas and his Croatian wife, Angelika Digorizia.

Logan feigned interest in the small talk but kept his attention on Miyoko. The ravishing Hand assassin had whispered in Pritikin's ear repeatedly. Every time she'd done so, Pritikin had glanced at Logan and Wai Ying. Logan tried to discern what she was telling the oil mogul now, but he found it difficult to hear her over the jabbering that filled the room.

Wai Ying pointed at Logan's plate with her fork. "Have you tried the escargots?"

Half grimacing, half smiling, he said, "I'm waiting for dessert." They were up to the fourth course of dinner, and Logan couldn't name half the foods that were on the table. The soup was a thin broth clouded with miso and tangled with filament-thin green tendrils. As delicate and sculptural as the appetizer had been, Logan had deemed it fundamentally inedible. Now he was staring at an entree whose overabundance of butter made him fairly certain that the chef had been trained in France.

To the best of his ability to tell, the only part of his meal that had so far met with his satisfaction had been the draft Guinness, which had been poured from a keg imported directly from Dublin. It was like a tower of creamy black velvet in a glass. As a result, the four glasses of wine that had been poured so far for each guest—a different varietal with each course of the meal—sat untouched in front of him while he sipped his beer.

The tenor of the conversation among Pritikin and his guests was not what Logan expected. Instead of Pritikin playing the part of a supplicant looking for funding, Yassev and Mikalunas seemed to be courting his favor, heaping praise and making vague promises all through dinner. Wai Ying leaned over to Logan and whispered, "The way they talk, you'd think he'd already won the election."

Talking softly, Logan replied, "Knowing the way voting machines work these days, he probably already has."

Mikalunas was waxing ecstatic about the entree, then he detoured into a halting appreciation of the wine. "They're all quite remarkable, Alexei," he said. "Especially the red with the entree. Truly first-rate. What did you say the label was?"

Before Pritikin could answer, Miyoko cut him off and gestured in Logan's direction. "Perhaps you should ask Mr. Howlett," she said. "I'm made to understand that rare wines and liquors are his area of special expertise." She lifted her own glass of red wine in a toasting gesture toward Logan. "Mr. Howlett, would you honor us with your thoughts about the red?"

Silence fell over the table as everyone looked at Logan with varying degrees of interest and expectation. Wai Ying's demeanor betrayed nothing, but Logan could almost hear the increase in her heart rate.

Ziv sounded a bit flummoxed, too. "Hang on," he said over a rapid flurry of tapping and clicking noises. "I'm checking the feed from your lapel cam, maybe I can see the label on the bottle from when it was poured."

Wai Ying made an admirable attempt at running interference. "I'm certain my husband wouldn't want to bore you all with his—"

"It'd be my pleasure," Logan said, offering a polite smile to Miyoko and Pritikin. "Just let me cleanse my palate first." He took a swig of water, swished it liberally, then swallowed.

Pulling his glass of red wine to a patch of open space on the white linen tablecloth, he rested his fingertips on the base and jogged it gently in a tiny circle, creating a steady, high swirl inside the half-filled glass. "Lovely color," he remarked. "Almost purple. . . . Remarkable body." He stopped swirling the wine, satisfied that it was sufficiently aerated, and picked up the glass by its stem. "Long legs," he observed. "And smooth." Tilting it forward, he closed his eyes, leaned his nose fully inside the voluminous Bordeaux glass, inhaled deeply. The aroma was like lying on his back in a field of Alpine strawberries.

Scents mingled in his memory, triggering visions of years gone by, of mountainside villas and simpler times, of the Second World War and friends long dead and buried. Recollections of tastes and textures and long Mediterranean afternoons . . .

"The Gros Vien grape," he said finally. "High-altitude varietal, very rare." He imbibed a large mouthful, held it, and savored it for many seconds before he swallowed it. "The fruit has tremendous character," he said. "Youthful, richly acidic." He leaned into the glass and breathed in its perfume once more, just to be certain. "I had no idea you were so decadent,

Mr. Pritikin. So few bottles of the '61 Chambave Rouge left in the world, and you're serving one to people who don't even recognize it." Rising from his chair, he continued, "To be honest, I'm appalled that your sommelier would allow it to be served with this kind of entree, instead of the rustic northern Italian cuisine it was meant to accompany."

Logan took a cigar from his pocket and snipped its end, then put away the clipper and picked up his glass of Chambave Rouge. "Now—with your leave, Mr. Pritikin—I'd like to find some place I can enjoy the rest of my wine with a good cigar." Nodding to the other couples, he added, "Gentlemen; ladies."

Leaving the table of stunned faces, he walked quickly toward the banquet room's exit. As he left the room and began searching for a way out to one of the terraces or balconies, he heard Ziv's amused chuckle in the earpiece. "Sounds like you've learned a few things since the eighties."

"I've been at school," Logan retorted.

The Chambave Rouge proved more compatible with Logan's cigar than he'd expected. It was a pleasant surprise.

He'd found a quiet place to smoke: a balcony at the rear of the building, facing the mansion's sprawling grounds. A light snowfall had begun during dinner. Flakes wafted down into the estate's halo of light and alighted upon the expanse below and everything in it.

The scene glowed bluish-gray beneath dozens of pale lamps mounted on nineteenth-century antique posts. Topiary sculptures stood silent vigils amid the property's slumbering fountains and icicle-draped benches. Several hundred meters away to either side, obscured by the slow-moving curtain of snow, solid walls of pine trees flanked the estate like dark battlements. Directly ahead, past the manicured gardens, was a frozen lake. Its far side appeared undeveloped, an unspoiled stretch of virgin coastline backed by more of the same dense pine forest. *Put a glass dome over it and label it "Welcome to Russia," and you can sell it in a gift shop,* Logan thought as he watched the snow fall.

Below him, at ground level, a man in a dark suit walked silently along the perimeter of the house; his overcoat bulged under the arm, exactly where a shoulder holster would be. Logan waited for the guard to pass by; when the man rounded the corner, Logan decided it was time to go to work. Abandoning a fine Cuban cigar only half smoked went against his nature, but, with regret, he snuffed the robusto in a few centimeters of freshly fallen snow heaped on the wide stone railing in front of him.

Logan turned his back on the winterscape. One quick tug freed the black flap hidden beneath his lapel from its Velcro tabs. He secured it in place beneath the other lapel, concealing his shirt. Then he began climbing.

Handholds were easy to come by, thanks to the

building's intricate trellises and window frames. In a few easy moves, Logan pulled himself onto the part of the roof that overhung the balcony. He was one level away from the topmost section of the roof, which reached the entirety of both wings of the mansion. The ice on this level was thick, and the new snow made the curved roofing tiles especially slippery.

Moving with caution, he sidestepped to a corner and took hold of a drainpipe. Testing it to make certain its fittings were solid, he scaled it. His hands slipped once, then again; the pipe was also slick with ice, which melted beneath his hands. He sought out the roughest patches of its surface and fixed his grip.

A few awkward moments later, he was on top of the mansion, surrounded by the aimless drift of snowflakes weaving drunken paths to the ground. Immediately he dropped to a low crouch, to improve his balance on the frozen, flurry-dusted surface. Keeping one foot on either side of the roof's peak, he swiftly traversed the length of the mansion. In less than a minute, he'd passed an enormous skylight that dominated the center of the roof and reached the north wing.

Edging down the slope, he was uncertain whether he was on target for Pritikin's office window ledge.

"Ziv, position check."

"Close," Ziv answered. "One meter to your left."

"You're sure?"

"Your GPS is reading five-by-five," Ziv said. "Once you're over the edge, it'll be a three-meter drop to the ledge below." Now it was Ziv's turn to sound uncertain. "You're positive you can stick that landing?"

"What are you, a gymnastics coach? I'll be fine." Logan descended the roof in half-steps, using the tips of his claws like climbing spikes in the roof tiles. At the edge he dug in one claw a bit deeper, pivoted around it, then sank his other claws in for additional support. He lowered himself over the edge and dangled for a moment. It was only three meters from the soles of his shoes to the ledge outside Pritikin's office window, but that ledge was icy and coated with fresh, powdery snow. If Logan missed it, or if he lost his footing, it would be a sixty-foot drop to a concrete walkway at the rear of the house. Not enough to kill him, but it would hurt like hell and be a damned inconvenience. *Better nail the landing, then, canucklehead.*

He retracted his claws and let gravity take him.

His feet hit the ledge and slipped. He reflexively stabbed his claws into the sandstone façade of the mansion, arresting his fall. A second or two later he steadied himself and wedged his toes into the corners, against the window frame. He pulled his right claws free of the wall and retracted them; the left set he kept in place, as a precaution.

"Okay, I'm at the window."

"What kind of security does he have on it?"

"I'm checking," Logan said, as he peered past his reflection to study the inside of the window frame. He paid special attention to the middle, where the top and bottom halves of the window met. "I don't see any magnetic contacts. He might be using a glass-break sensor."

"Cutting through the glass without tripping the circuit will be tricky," Ziv said. "If we'd thought to prepare for—"

Logan opened the bottom half of the window. "It ain't locked, Ziv." Hanging on to the window, he retracted his left claws and crouched to look inside the room. "Checkin' the corners. No passive infrared, that's good." Closing his eyes, he listened for a few moments. "I could be wrong, but I can almost pick up a tone inside the room."

"Ultrasonic?"

"Probably," Logan said. "Looks like he's runnin' a motion sensor in there. Ain't in the corners; betcha it's disguised."

"If it's tied in to the mansion's primary security grid, it might look like an electrical outlet."

Another long look at the room, including a slow, careful peek over the edge at the wall below the window, didn't help. "All the exposed outlets are in use. Gotta be something else." In front of the window was Pritikin's desk and high-backed leather chair. The desktop was mostly bare, except for a wide flat-screen monitor on a sleek pedestal, a phone, and a

Tiffany lamp with an octagonal shade. The desk faced the door to the office. On the left wall hung a flat-screen plasma television; the wall to the right was dominated by a tall bookshelf crowded with leather-bound volumes. One orderly row stood above another, the uniformity only rarely interrupted by small objets d'art.

Then Logan found what he was looking for: a single book that didn't look as if it belonged. It was three times thicker than any other tome in the room, and its spine had two matching circles—one at the top, one at the bottom. Most suspicious of all, it bore no title or author's name.

"Got it," Logan said as he climbed through the window and walked directly toward the faux book.

Ziv sounded apoplectic. "Are you insane?"

"Trust me," Logan said calmly. He was banking on the fifteen-to-twenty-second delay built into most motion-sensor alarms—a feature intended to allow an owner to enter a room and deactivate the sensor manually before the alert sounded.

"Abort, abort, abort!"

"Don't get yer panties in a bunch," Logan said. He lifted the "book" from the shelf; it was made of lightweight plastic. The back of it, opposite the spine, was recessed. Inside the nook was a numeric keypad and a few other controls, none of which was adjustable while the device was active. Below the keypad was a simple red toggle switch—confirming that this motion sensor was exactly the kind of cheap-knock-off, eastern European piece of crap that he'd thought it was. Logan flipped it from on to off, then put the book back on the shelf. "Five-by-five, Ziv. You can breathe again if you want."

"Too kind," Ziv grumbled.

Logan sat down at Pritikin's desk, pulled out the keyboard shelf, and powered up the computer. As expected, there was a port on the side of the black keyboard for the flash memory stick Ziv had given him. He retrieved it from inside his wallet and inserted it into the slot. "Stick's in," he muttered.

"I'm on it," Ziv replied. "And . . . we're in. I'm cloning his drive now and patching in to the Anbaric Petroleum server."

On the computer monitor, nothing seemed to be happening. At the moment, Logan felt slightly . . . superfluous. "Mind if I poke around his office?"

"Do as you like. Just don't touch the computer."

As offices went, Pritikin's was tidy and free of anything that even remotely resembled a sentimental touch. There were no photographs. All the small decorative pieces seemed to have been chosen for their aesthetic qualities; nothing had the quirky or idiosyncratic feel of a memento or keepsake. The books were mostly in Russian, including several by Tolstoy and Dostoyevsky. Taken in its entirety, it presented the appearance of a man who took life—and himself—all too seriously.

"I'm done," said Ziv, interrupting Logan's appraisal of the room's contents. "Wrap up and get back to the party."

"On it," Logan said, crossing to the desk. He removed the flash stick from the keyboard and shut down the machine. Tucking the slender digital device back inside his wallet, he returned to the fake book on the shelf and rearmed its sensors. Aware of the short time delay, he hurried to the window. The snow was falling more quickly now, and it pelted against him as he climbed out onto the ledge and pulled the window shut behind him. Using his claws, he scaled the stone wall of the mansion, then found his handholds on the roof's edge. With one muscular pull, he vaulted himself back up onto the roof.

Standing there, waiting for him with a *ninja-to* in one hand and three *shuriken* between the fingers of the other, was Miyoko.

"Lies do not become you, Logan-san," she said. "Or should I call you Wolverine?"

"Call me whatever you want," he said. "Your funeral."

Snowflakes, ethereal and silent, dipped and swirled and stalled in their descents around and between Logan and Miyoko, each regarding the other with an unblinking stare—a battle of wills, a test of nerve. She had him at a disadvantage; not only did she hold the high ground, near the roof's peak, but her *ninja-to* could strike from a greater range than his claws could reach. He would have to breach her defensive circle or else face a slow battle of attrition, a death by a thousand cuts.

Then her three *shuriken* cut through the curtain of snow, gleams of black and silver blurring through the flakes. By the time Logan's reflexes impelled him to motion, the metal stars had already struck him—one in his throat, another in his cheek, the third deep in the meat of his left shoulder. The bite of impact lasted for a fraction of a second, but by the time Logan regained his focus, Miyoko was lunging at him with her sword.

Her first slice he deflected with his claws.

He charged at her, his battle roar more of a blood-frothed gurgle. As he'd hoped, she sidestepped his attack, enabling him to move farther up the roof, away from the edge.

Her blade severed the Achilles tendon above his right heel. A second blade—shorter, probably a dagger—plunged between his unbreakable ribs and shredded part of his right lung. He stumbled forward and broke his fall with his elbows, since his claws made it hard to land on his palms.

Logan plucked the throwing stars from his throat and face; they were identical to the one that he had found in Osaka. He scrambled back to his feet. Miyoko was circling him, taunting him with feints. A breeze snapped the billowing fabric of her kimono, which Logan remembered had been tailored in a

unique manner, to afford her total freedom of movement—an attribute that his tuxedo didn't share.

Logan felt his slashed tendon repair itself even as
he pivoted on the icy tiles, tracking Miyoko. Her
flowing black hair danced and twisted in the teasing
wind, a dark halo framing her emotionless face. He
swung his claws in a wide slash at her, but he found
only empty air, falling snow, and darkness.

Then came another brutal cut, gouging deep into
his back.

Miyoko was supernaturally fast, more agile and
dexterous than even a ninja's training could account
for. The Hand had been known to use magic to
enhance the abilities of its most senior members. He
surmised that Miyoko was one of those whom the
organization had gifted with its most potent charms.

He turned toward the attack, squared his stance,
and raised his arms, one in front of the other, to
defend his throat and head. Her sword sliced across
his left forearm, adding another trail of blood speck-
les to the thin sheet of snow on the roof.

As she brought the blade around for another slash
in the opposite direction, Logan stepped into the hit,
blocking it with his left claws. He punched forward
with his right toward Miyoko's center of mass. She
turned her torso clear of his lunging attack and with
her free hand grabbed his wrist. Her right foot shot
up, struck his groin, then bent quickly back from the
knee, lifted, and snap-kicked him in the face.

A torquing pull spun Logan through the air, pointed his feet toward the sky, rotated his whole body around his shoulder. He landed hard on his back.

Miyoko's knife swung fast, in a tight arc toward the underside of his jaw, looking to pierce the soft flesh behind his chin and drive up into his brain for a quick death blow.

He rolled to his left and pushed himself back to his feet.

Explosions of pain flared across his body—a burning slash through his left ear, a deep gash in his right flank, a *shuriken* suddenly wedged between his shoulder blades. Miyoko was moving so quickly that Logan could barely see her.

Then he heard her laugh. *She's toying with me,* he realized. *She thinks this is funny.*

He backpedaled toward the middle of the mansion, weathering Miyoko's harrying blows. His healing factor struggled to keep up as the ninja shredded his clothes and his flesh, one vicious slice at a time. As he reached a broad, flat section of the roof near the central skylight, he had begun to sense a pattern to her assaults, a rhythm. *Like a ballet,* he told himself. *You just have to learn your part of the dance.*

Little was left of his tuxedo except for loose, blood-soaked tatters. His hair was wet and heavy with melting snow. Miyoko dealt out cuts faster than his body could heal. Sheets of his blood soaked his chest and back, his arms and legs. Another *shuriken* slammed into his temple, in front of his right ear.

Here it comes, he thought, imagining the next step in Miyoko's invisible dance of steel and darkness. Then, even though he couldn't see more than a blur of her in the corner of his eye, he pivoted and thrust his claws into the night—

—and they found flesh and bone, blood and sinew, a body pliant and warm and fragile.

Miyoko dropped her sword. She writhed and struggled, impaled on the claws of Logan's right hand. Then her training reasserted itself and she attacked once again with her knife, thrusting up at Logan's chin. He caught her left hand by the wrist, but she pressed upward. Her strength was superhuman. She added her right hand to her efforts, forcing the blade up until it broke the flesh under Logan's jaw. Misting gales from her ragged breaths teased his face.

Thrown off-balance by the burden of her weight and the ferocity of her struggle, he stumbled backward. Miyoko growled like an animal as she fought to push her blade just a few more inches, into his head. Logan felt his feet slip. He didn't want to let Miyoko get him onto his back. The additional leverage of being on top of him while they fell would likely be all she needed to finish him.

He twisted his right hand, ground Miyoko's internal organs into paste, ruptured her thoracic aorta . . . but something—maybe rage, maybe magic—wouldn't let her die.

Logan's foot landed on something angled upward behind him. Before he could adjust his footing, the surface he'd stepped on gave way under his and Miyoko's combined weight.

They were falling. For the first half-second, it seemed to happen in slow motion: the delicate crunch of breaking glass, followed by the musical screech of a windowpane fracturing.

As they dropped backward through the skylight, his claws finally pierced Miyoko's heart, which trembled and then seized. His memory flashed on the final moments of his beloved Mariko, expiring on his claws . . . then he clutched the ninja's dead body as they plummeted like stones inside a storm of shattered glass, ten meters down, into the mansion's natatorium. Undulating ribbons of dark blue light danced on the surface of the water below. He retracted his claws and let go of Miyoko's body a moment before they splashed into the heated indoor swimming pool.

The water embraced Logan, then it smothered him. His feet touched the bottom, and he pushed himself upward. Breaking the surface with a grateful gasp of air, he checked to make certain that Miyoko was really dead. Her lifeless eyes stared into the pool as a deep scarlet cloud of her own blood spread around her.

Ziv's voice crackled over the earpiece. "Guys, we are now officially screwed. Get out of there, both of you."

Wai Ying's voice followed. "How do we get back to the car?"

"We don't," Logan said, wading toward the edge. "Leave through the kitchen and meet me out back, near the cottages."

"All right," Wai Ying replied. "See you there."

He was climbing out of the pool as he heard the approach of running footsteps and the clacking of automatic weapons being primed for action. There were men coming from every entrance.

The rear wall of the natatorium was an enormous, floor-to-ceiling grid of windows. It looked out on the gardens behind the mansion and the lakeshore down below. Logan decided that since his clothes had already been turned to confetti and his body was still fighting to heal the wounds that Miyoko had dealt him, he had nothing to lose by taking the easy way out.

He sprinted toward the glass wall, shielded his face and throat with his arms, and hurled himself through it, out into the garden and the cover of darkness.

And, just as he expected, it hurt like a sonofabitch.

Keeping a straight face hadn't been easy.

Wai Ying had remained seated at the dinner table with Pritikin and his VIP guests while Logan had left on his covert mission to tap the computer in Pritikin's office. She'd been listening to the exchanges between Ziv and Logan as Miyoko rose from the table and left the banquet room. She'd considered warning them that Miyoko was no longer at dinner, but that would have required her to excuse herself from the table, and Pritikin had chosen exactly that moment to engage her in small talk.

"I've cut your channel to Logan," Ziv had whispered in her ear while Pritikin rambled. "I don't want him distracted."

Nodding absently at Pritikin, she masked her response by grinning at some upbeat remark of his and then muttering, "Delightful."

Then had come the fighting words between Logan and Miyoko, followed by the alarming sounds of cold steel whistling through thick winter air and striking fabric and flesh. She'd responded by plastering an insincere grin on her face and taking another sip of the rich, fruity Chambave Rouge. Even as she'd been forced to listen to Logan's grunts and roars of pain, she'd picked halfheartedly at her dessert, a towering chocolate concoction whose curving, swooshing architecture looked more ambitious than Frank Gehry's museum in Bilbao.

Shattering glass, a splash of water, and a sputter of static rasped in her ear. She winced and reflexively reached a hand toward the side of her head before she caught herself.

Pritikin abandoned his anecdote and leaned forward, looking concerned. "Are you all right?"

"Yes," Wai Ying said. "Fine. Just a headache."

"Nothing too serious, I hope," he said.

"I do sometimes get migraines," she lied.

He nodded, then motioned to someone across the room. "Let me have one of my people bring you something for the pain."

As she glanced over her shoulder, she noticed men in dark suits moving discreetly toward all the guest exits from the banquet room. Two more men were crossing the room from behind her, taking long strides as they detoured around tables. This wasn't a first-aid call. She got up from her chair.

Ziv's voice squawked again in her ear and told her what she'd already figured out for herself. "Guys, we are now officially screwed. Get out of there, both of you."

Her cover was blown. Subtlety was no longer necessary.

A sweep of her hand sent a wave of repulsor force surging away from her, overturning tables and flinging people like rag dolls to the floor. "How do we get back to the car?" she asked, hurling another half-dozen tables and nearly fifty people into the air. Behind her, Pritikin and his VIPs were already running for cover.

"We don't," Logan replied over the transceiver. "Leave through the kitchen and meet me out back, near the cottages."

"All right," she said, kicking off her shoes and jogging backward inside a protective hemispherical force field toward the kitchen doors. "See you there." Bullets ricocheted off her invisible shell and tore dusty divots from the banquet room's marble pillars. She reshaped her defensive screen as she neared the door, reducing it to a curved wall in front of her as she backed through the swinging portal into the hustle and bustle of the kitchen.

A shout like a bulldog's bark rattled her nerves. *"Stoy! Ruki vverkh!"*

She turned her head and saw a beefy, sandy-haired man in his thirties. He was pointing an assault rifle at her. Smiling sweetly, she turned slowly to face him. "Sorry," she said, "I don't speak Russian."

"Put up your hands," he said with a heavy Russian accent. He braced his rifle against his shoulder and aimed at her. Calming her nerves, she focused her concentration on the narrow space inside the muzzle of his weapon.

"I lied," she said. "I do speak Russian. And I know you won't shoot, because you're too much of a *pider* to kill a woman." Then she flashed an evil grin and walked right at him.

He pulled his trigger, and the barrel of his rifle exploded as multiple rounds struck the force field she had projected inside the weapon's muzzle. The flash of ignited gunpowder was blinding, and the sharp crack of detonation drowned out his instantly silenced howl of pain. He collapsed to the floor, his face burned, bloody, and studded with metallic debris.

The kitchen doors slammed open behind her. She ducked to cover behind a stainless-steel counter, projecting a clumsy shield around herself as she dropped to the floor. Above her, two large and nearly full soup terrines simmered over gas flames. With a thought, she launched the terrines at the guards pursuing her. Heavy thuds of impact mingled with shrieks of agony.

Back on her feet again, she dashed sideways out of the kitchen, hurling a storm of cooking utensils and pans of hot grease at anyone who tried to walk through the door from the banquet room. It was only a few more meters to the back door. The heavier outer door had been propped open, to allow cool air to ventilate the steamy kitchen. Wai Ying pushed through the closed screen door, out into the night, to freedom—

Directly into one of Pritikin's guards. The man's hand clamped around her throat and started crushing her windpipe. Suddenly, her ability to focus kinetic fields betrayed her. The panic flooding her mind was too great, too immediate. All she could think of was her desperate need for air denied, the vertiginous spin of swirling snow flurries cocooning her. Her hands flailed futilely against the man's viselike grip. Any second now her cervical vertebrae would snap, she knew it—

Logan's adamantium claws erupted out of the man's chest. His grip slackened and released. The claws vanished back inside him, and he buckled and fell straight down like a marionette severed from its master. Wai Ying was still swooning from asphyxia as Logan clutched her shoulders and steadied her. "Ace! You all right? Say something."

Giving him a blurry-eyed once-over, she said, "You look terrible."

"You're all right." Logan pulled her away from the mansion, toward a set of what looked like guest cottages along the lakeshore. Wai Ying felt light-headed as she stumble-sprinted away from the mansion with Logan. The snow numbed her feet.

"Logan?" Ziv sounded nervous. "Where are you going?"

"The sat-recon you showed me—it was recent?"

"Taken yesterday."

"Then get the van runnin', bub. We're comin' in hot."

They rounded the corner of the nearest cottage, and suddenly Logan's exit strategy made sense to her. Parked behind the cottages were several snowmobiles. He jumped on the nearest one, jabbed one claw into its ignition, and twisted. It growled to life. "Get on," he said, "in front of me."

"You'd like that," she said.

"The bullets will be coming from behind us," he said.

She mounted the snowmobile and hunched down in front of him. Just as he'd predicted, the gunshots started seconds later, as he accelerated away from the mansion, out onto the frozen lake. She shouted over the wind roar and engine noise, "You sure the lake is solid?"

"Nope," he shouted back, twisting the throttle to maximum.

Riding on a snowmobile, in Wai Ying's opinion, was a lot like riding on a motorcycle. A really fat motorcycle. With skis. On ice. Actually, about all they had in common were the handgrip controls for the brake and throttle and the bitter sting of cold air in one's face.

She hunkered down behind the windshield and guarded her face from the screaming wind with her arms. Glancing backward, beneath Logan's arm, she saw three snowmobiles, each manned by two of Pritikin's guards, pursuing them into the snowy night.

Bullets *zing*ed past her and Logan and *ping*ed off the ice. Several more shots slammed hard into Logan's back, jerking him forward with each impact. Wai Ying could barely hear the shots above the buzzing drone of the snowmobile engine. A fresh hail of gunfire strafed the ice to either side of their snowmobile, then a single shot struck home into its engine with a deep metallic *thunk*. Immediately, they began losing speed, and the engine belched grimy black smoke. *At least it'll make it harder for them to see what they're shooting at,* she figured.

Logan quickly zigzagged his course, no doubt to muddy his pursuers' aim just a little more. "Nice smoke screen," Wai Ying shouted over the now-grinding engine. "That'll buy us about ten seconds."

Cocking one eyebrow at her, he said, "You got a plan?"

"Actually, yes." She rested her palms on the center of the handlebars and lifted herself off the saddle. Gracefully, she twisted at her hips, steadied herself by placing her hands on Logan's shoulders, and turned herself to face him. Then she straddled him on the seat, gripped his torso with her left arm, and leaned over his left shoulder. "Punch it."

She kept her eyes on the drifting curtain of oil smoke they'd left behind them, and she gathered her strength and focus. Extending her hand toward the black cloud, her breath caught in her throat, which clenched in anticipation.

The pursuing snowmobiles emerged from the inky darkness, and Wai Ying unleashed a single, massive cone of force at the ice in front of them. The invisible wave struck with a deafening boom. One of the pursuing snowmobiles veered wide to safety as an enormous swath of the lake's ice sheet disintegrated into froth and swallowed the other two vehicles.

Logan steered their own snowmobile off the lake and up into the forest on the far side, dodging at unsafe speeds between thick-trunked pine trees, lurching and slaloming over the uneven ground. About fifteen meters away through the trees, the last pursuing snowmobile was closing the gap, having found a less challenging path through the woods. "Get closer to them," Wai Ying said. "Before they cut us off."

Logan didn't debate her, he just did as she'd asked. Weaving and scraping past stumps and rotting logs from dead trees, he blazed a diagonal trail back toward the clear path to their right. They tore past a drooping bough, scattering pine needles and twigs, and emerged ahead of their pursuers.

The timing would have to be just right, because the element of surprise was everything. Pointing her palms outward and slightly behind her—which was in front of her and Logan's snowmobile—she unleashed two wide but flat planes of pure kinetic force. Splintering cracks gave way to the shriek and groan of green wood bending, and then the rifle-shot snap of that same wood breaking. By the time gravity finished what she had started, she and Logan were safely away. Their pursuers at least had the good sense to abandon their speeding snowmobile and take a rough tumble into the snow, rather than ride their machine into the sudden collapse of a dozen massive pine trees.

Less than a minute later, Logan and Wai Ying were clear of the woods and cruising downhill toward Ziv's waiting van.

She noticed that Logan was grinning and chuckling to himself. "What's so funny?" she asked.

He smiled. "I knew there was a reason I married you."

A pale, narrow ladder of snowflakes reached down through the shattered skylight and dissolved on contact with the surface of the heated swimming pool. Alexei Pritikin sat at the pool's edge, numb. Floating in the water was the body of his lover, surrounded by a slowly roiling cloud of her own blood. Shock, horror, and disbelief smothered his thoughts. He was furious and paralyzed, raging at his own helplessness to defy fate.

Footsteps echoed as they approached. He looked up at Mikhail, who was in charge of the mansion's security detail. The aquiline-featured bodyguard wore an expression of a kind that Pritikin had never before seen on his face: contrition.

"They escaped," Mikhail said. "On a snowmobile, across the lake. We have six dead and three seriously wounded."

"Have Piotr talk to Mikalunas—not a word of this gets in tomorrow's papers. Then take your things and leave."

Mikhail started to nod in confirmation, then he wrinkled his brow in confusion. "Sir?"

"You're fired," Pritikin explained. "Get out."

By necessity, Pritikin had been ruthless in his ascent to power. Subordinates who'd failed him had been dispatched without pity. Competitors had been crushed without mercy or hesitation. When the law had stood in his way, he'd bent it, broken it, or defied it; when there'd been no other way, he'd simply had the laws changed to suit his needs. His business was oil. What he provided everyone needed—and if the only way for him to give it to them was for the government to rewrite the law, then so be it. A criminal, some had called him; a gangster. He hadn't argued. They were probably right. Hell, he knew they were right. But what did it matter? So he'd profited from wars; someone was going to, it might as well be him. He'd lied, blackmailed people in positions of power, even had a few politicians killed.

Nothing he'd done made him a monster. Opportunity had conspired with desire to send him down those paths. Anyone in his position, knowing the stakes as he did, would have done the same. What was the alternative? Allow the world's oil supply to dwindle? Give free rein to chaos when the Western world was finally made to understand what "peak oil" really meant? Unthinkable. The world needed time to plan its transition to a new form of energy; in the interim, barring any kind of socialistic governmental interference, someone was going to make a profit. Pritikin had decided decades ago that the someone in that equation would be him.

He knew that he was a criminal; he'd never denied it. But he was also a man, and he'd loved Miyoko, more than any other woman he'd ever known. It hadn't mattered to him that she did not love him in return, or that she likely never would. Her beauty had been without equal, and his heart had been lost to her from the moment he'd seen her. Now she floated facedown in the water, disemboweled, her viscera dangling loosely below her. The bloodstained fabric of her kimono undulated around her, tendrils reaching out in a futile effort to anchor her to the physical world, though her spirit was obviously long departed.

Vengeance was in order. "I'll kill him," Pritikin muttered to no one. Having dismissed Mikhail, he thought himself alone now with Miyoko's body. "I'll eat his heart," he grumbled, quaking with anger. "If it takes my entire fortune, if it takes the rest of my life. I'll kill him for this."

The man behind Pritikin sounded smug and condescending. "Take care when making curses against Wolverine," he said. "I've yet to meet anyone who didn't come to regret it."

Pritikin took a deep breath and slowly counted to ten. He stood, straightened his jacket, and composed his face into a mask of sophisticated disinterest. Then he turned to face his unexpected visitor, Keniuchio Harada.

Harada looked exactly as he had every other time Pritikin had met with him: trim, focused, and attired in a silvery gray business suit. His shirt was an off-white with silvery pinstripes. The only splash of color in his ensemble was a silver-hued silk necktie emblazoned with a bold red Japanese rising sun design. On the index finger of his left hand, an ornately engraved silver band gleamed as it caught the light.

"You know I hate when you drop in with that teleportation ring of yours," Pritikin said. "It's damned rude."

"Exigent circumstances," Harada said, nodding toward Miyoko's body. "I told her not to face Wolverine alone, but you know how she was: stubborn."

Recoiling with indignation, Pritikin said, "You knew who he was? And you let him walk into my house without warning me?"

"I warned *her*," Harada said, nodding at Miyoko. "Defending you was her responsibility."

"And avenging her will be mine," Pritikin said.

Harada shook his head. "That would be unwise." The Japanese *yakuza* overlord walked to the edge of the pool and gazed forlornly upon his fallen assassin. "Wolverine is not just any mutant; he's one of the oldest, and one of the toughest. Your resources are formidable, Alexei, but they aren't equal to the task you've set for yourself. I would suggest you leave Miyoko's retribution to more capable hands."

Pacing behind Harada, Pritikin retorted, "I don't give a damn what you'd *suggest*. I'm not *yakuza*, and I'm not part of the Hand. I'm your *partner* in this operation, not your flunky."

"You aren't thinking clearly," Harada replied, shaking his head. "I admit, Miyoko's death is a terrible loss; she was a great assassin. And I know that you cared for her deeply. But our venture is at a critical stage; you mustn't let your emotions trump your judgment. This is a time not for rash action, but for a calculated response."

Pritikin stepped up and put himself face-to-face with Harada, who towered over him. "*Calculated response?* Such as?"

"When the operation is irrevocably engaged," Harada said, "then we can satisfy our debt of honor against Wolverine."

"Not good enough," Pritikin replied. "He had enough time to reach my office. If he accessed my computer, he might know about the *Pandora*."

Harada said calmly, "I've already assumed that he does. Steps have been taken."

"I'm sure," Pritikin said with a frown. He turned his back on Harada and walked toward the natatorium's closest exit.

"Where are you going?" Harada asked.

"To do us both a favor," Pritikin said.

He was halfway to the doors when Harada's off-hand comment brought him to a halt. "Ah, yes—your vaunted Red Star team." As Pritikin turned slowly back toward Harada, the *yakuza oyabun* added, "I was wondering when you'd deploy them."

Paranoia colored Pritikin's tone as he walked

slowly back to face Harada. "How do you know about them?"

"Some secrets are harder to keep than others," Harada said with a grin. "Three suits of powered battle armor, each one manned by a former Spetsnaz trooper. Impressive, really. Though I'd expected you to save them for something of a . . . *less precise* nature than fighting Wolverine."

Naturally, Harada was right. Pritikin's research team had developed the three suits of mechanized battle armor as prototypes for an eventual battalion of powered-armor soldiers. The long-term purpose for such a force was to be ready to secure his claims to oil fields in the Caspian Sea region, as well as in the deserts of Zibara. It was a necessary precaution; if and when the reality of the globe's rapidly diminishing supply of crude oil became commonly understood, riots and then war would follow in rapid succession. Nations would aim to follow America's lead in Iraq and start seizing petroleum and natural-gas resources while there were still some to be exploited. The only private entities that would be able to retain control of their assets would be those, such as Halliburton, that had made themselves indispensable to their government, or those like Pritikin's company, Anbaric Petroleum, that had armed themselves and were prepared to hold on to their property by force.

"I will employ my resources as I see fit," Pritikin

said. "And I don't give a damn what your code of honor says about it."

Harada loomed over Pritikin and said in a grave tone, "I will tolerate your wrathful behavior only so long as it does not put our operation at risk. We are each other's means to an end, Mr. Pritikin—but I have already obtained what I need from our arrangement. Only my word of honor compels me to repay my debt to you." Harada's beatific expression became a murderous glare. "I *suggest* you remember that."

12

ZIV DROVE LIKE A MANIAC. THE VAN LURCHED
from side to side as he veered around what few other
cars were out on the snow-swept, forest-lined highway. Every tight turn hurled Wai Ying and Logan back
and forth in the van's cramped rear compartment,
which was packed with high-tech equipment. Wai
Ying stayed near the front, while Logan huddled near
the back doors, glancing occasionally out the windows
into the speed-blurred nightscape.

They were already an hour away from Pritikin's
mansion and clear of the snowstorm, but Ziv hadn't
slowed down, not once. Wai Ying clutched a padded
seat mounted on a glide track in front of the com-

puters and monitors and glanced forward to see where they were going. They were skirting the St. Petersburg city limits, taking a less traveled route to Pulkovo Airport. Unable to hide her surprise, she said to Ziv, "Aren't we going back to the hotel?"

"*Nyet,*" Ziv snapped. "Too dangerous."

"But our clothes," she protested. "Our passports—"

"Already on the plane," Ziv said, swerving around a slow-moving, boxy-looking economy car.

Wai Ying leaned into the van's rocking motion, then turned her accusatory glower on Logan. "Your idea?"

Logan shrugged. "Didn't want to wear out our welcome. Figured no matter how it went, we'd better get on the road."

"Good point," she said. "Ziv, whatever intel you downloaded, I'll need to copy it to my laptop before we leave."

"Already done," he said. "Your computer's back in its case, near the rear door. Once we get to the airport, we'll frag the van and analyze the data in the air."

It took Wai Ying a second to parse that. "We?"

"That's right," Ziv said. "I can't stay here after this fiasco. This was supposed to be a low-profile recon. I guess I ought to be grateful you didn't torch the place."

From the back, Logan quipped, "If I'd had more time—"

"Shut up," Ziv said. "I called in favors to get you into that party. Now my contacts are as good as burned—and my pension along with them."

"I'd almost feel sorry for ya if I didn't know you had four tons of gold bullion stashed in Zurich."

Ziv laughed. "It's not worth much to me if I'm not alive to spend it, comrade. So wherever the wind takes you next, it takes me as well."

"The more the merrier," Logan said. "Speaking of which, we're being followed."

Checking the rearview, Ziv replied, "I don't see anyone."

"Neither do I," Wai Ying said, looking past Logan out the rear windows. "There's no one behind us."

"I didn't say it was a car," Logan replied. "There's a tunnel up ahead. Stop in there and kill the lights."

The van passed into a dark, two-lane tunnel carved through a jutting mound of gray mountainside. In the middle of the tunnel, Ziv brought the van to a halt and turned off its lights, as Logan had instructed. Logan picked up Wai Ying's laptop case and handed it to Ziv. "Get clear of the van and take cover past the far end of the tunnel, just in case."

"What are you going to do?" he asked.

"What I do best," Logan said. He took Wai Ying by the hand, opened the van's rear doors, and led her into the darkness. "With a little help from my friend."

Two hundred meters above the ground, Vadim Ilyanov guided his battlesuit in a tight circle above the lonely stretch of rural highway where he and his two compatriots had last seen the van, less than two minutes earlier. "Still no sign of it," Roman, his second-in-command, reported over the secure comm.

Kiril, the third man in the team, added, "They must have stopped inside the tunnel."

"Of course they did," Vadim said. "Cut the chatter and pick up your infrared." He turned off the night-vision settings and activated the infrared filter on his own holographic head-up display. The HUD rerendered the wooded hillside below in washes of cool green and pale blue, superimposed over a topographical wireframe of the surrounding terrain.

His suit's vertical takeoff and landing thrusters gave off a high-pitched hum but little other sound. From the ground, he and the other members of Red Star were essentially inaudible. Even more important, they were nearly invisible, thanks to their battlesuits' combination of stealth features, ranging from radar-dampening composites to active-mode optical cloaking.

"I've got something," Kiril said. "One bogey, exiting the north end of the tunnel." A tiny but bright red figure appeared on Vadim's HUD as well. Over the comm, Roman confirmed the sighting. "Roger that. Orders, sir?"

Vadim primed his suit's arm-mounted .50-millimeter cannons. "Weapons hot," he declared. "Kiril, flush him out and drive him uphill, it'll slow him down. Roman, drop in behind him, don't let him

retreat. I'll go for high ground, and we'll box him in."
Both men acknowledged their orders and initiated a
swift descent to engage the target on the ground.

Less than a hundred meters up the mountainside
was a clearing wide enough for Vadim to set down
without disturbing the surrounding trees. He accelerated to it, then hovered while the suit reoriented
itself into a standing position. From his vantage point
in the cockpit it was fluid and not at all disorienting,
thanks to the battle armor's gyroscopically stabilized
cockpit. His HUD confirmed that he was solidly on
the ground and set to advance "on foot" to engage
his target. Through the thick forest, there was no
sign of the target's infrared signature. Soon enough,
however, all Vadim would have to do would be to
target any explosions he detected in the forest and
fire at will.

Sending three battlesuits after one unarmed man
seemed wasteful to Vadim, but orders were orders.
Mr. Pritikin had provided the satellite intelligence
identifying the van that had fled from an attack at his
estate, and he had made it clear that he wanted
Vadim and his men to find that van, destroy it, and
kill its occupants. *If only all my assignments were so easy,*
Vadim mused ruefully.

As if on cue, that's when the explosions started.

The glare filters on his HUD engaged as incendiary plumes lit up the night and stripped bare broad
swaths of the forest. *"Got him!"* Kiril crowed over the

comm. "He's toast!" Vadim patched in the tactical display from Kiril's system and replayed the last several seconds from his battle camera. Kiril had locked his targeting crosshairs on the running humanoid figure they'd flushed out of the tunnel, then fired a volley of RPG-7 high-explosive rockets from his suit's shoulder-mounted launchers. The recording indicated a direct hit.

"Nice work, Kiril," Vadim said, switching back to a real-time link with Kiril's tactical monitor.

"*Da,* Kiril," Roman added. "Good shot."

"Thanks," Kiril said. "Should we—" He paused abruptly, and Vadim saw why in the sudden jumble of data from Kiril's onboard computer. Hydraulic pressure was dropping quickly in the legs of the younger man's suit.

"Kiril," Vadim cut in, "did you get hit by shrapnel from your own ordnance? Your hydraulics are damaged."

"They—they were fine a second ago," Kiril stammered. "I don't . . . I don't understand. I just lost my left hip actuator." His voice grew more alarmed as he continued. "Right hip actuator offline. Guys, I'm stuck."

"Dammit, Kiril, lift off," Vadim said, propelling his battlesuit through the forest at a run. Using the cybernetic link between his arms and those of the gigantic armored exoskeleton, he swatted trees out of his path. Inside the suit he couldn't hear them snap, but he felt their feeble resistance as they broke apart and fell away with each sweep of his arms. His running steps shook the entire battlesuit, and he remembered the thunderous impacts and ground-shaking tremors these massive war machines caused when accelerated to a full sprint.

"Wing mechanism's jammed," Kiril said. "Guys, I'm FUBAR over here, and I'm starting—" His transmission stopped there.

"Roman," Vadim shouted, "converge on Kiril's position! He's under attack! Kiril, activate your IC!" It was only another twenty meters to Kiril's position. A few more seconds running. Roman's transponder was closing from the opposite direction. Vadim didn't know what kind of mutant fiend Kiril had met on the battlefield, but if the battlesuit's infantry countermeasures could slow its attack for a few more moments . . .

After catapulting forward through the last thick tree trunks, Vadim's battlesuit landed squarely, weapons armed. In front of him was Kiril's battlesuit; its exterior was scratched and gouged, and it smoldered from the recent activation of its fiery antipersonnel self-defense system. The left side of its cockpit canopy had been shattered and torn apart.

Roman's battlesuit broke through the trees behind Kiril's crippled unit. As he had been trained to do, he dropped to a more stable defensive posture and waited for new orders.

Through the gray veils of smoke, Vadim saw

Kiril's silhouette waving to him from inside the damaged battlesuit's exposed cockpit. Then Kiril pointed down, below his machine. Vadim checked his ventral scanners and noted the scorched humanoid form on the ground. "Kiril, are you all right?"

From the other battlesuit's cockpit came Kiril's "out of action" hand signal, followed by a tapping against the side of his helmet.

"Roman, his comm's out," Vadim said. "Go frag the van. I'll evac Kiril and get a recovery team for his suit."

"Yes, sir," Roman replied, then he guided his battlesuit back to its upright position, turned it back downhill, and proceeded toward the south end of the tunnel.

Vadim guided his own armored titan in slow steps until it was nose-to-nose with Kiril's. He released his canopy lock; it detached from the armored chassis with a hydraulic hiss. As he reached under his seat and retrieved his first-aid kit, a blast of cool, pine-scented winter air surged into the temperature-controlled cockpit. Then he stood up to see a rocket-propelled grenade scream into his cockpit and turn his world to fire.

Logan rolled out of his long fall to the ground. Above, the RPG warhead ripped through the exposed cockpit of the second battlesuit he'd destroyed in as many minutes. Burning fuel and twisted black hunks of machinery slammed to the ground as Logan sprinted clear, in pursuit of the third and final walking tank, which was now going after Ziv and Wai Ying.

Wrecking the first machine had been easy for Logan. Wai Ying had provided him with an invisible, undetectable force field for cover from its missile attack. Jumping through the fire cloud that had lingered after the blast had hurt a lot, but only for a minute, and the pain had spurred his climb up the metal marauder's legs to its torso. He'd cut through every servo, wire, tube, and circuit board on his way to the top. By the time he'd scaled its back to sever its transmission antenna, the steel walker had been all but paralyzed. Cutting into its cockpit had been like ripping open a present; the pilot had even been kind enough to arm an exterior antipersonnel system that Logan was able to use to dispose of the man's body.

Following the third giant exoskeleton through the forest was easy; keeping up with it wasn't. Despite its size, it was fast and agile. In addition, it also didn't have to navigate the obstacle course of fallen pine trees that it left in its tracks.

Tremors rocked the cold, hard ground. Booming thundersteps echoed in the night. Leaping from one fallen tree trunk to another, Logan raced to catch up with the last armored cybersuit, his gusts of breath voluminous and white in the frigid air. Then he stopped, perched in a low crouch atop a sheared-off stump. Listening, he realized that he didn't have to chase the titanic war machine anymore. It was coming back, directly at him.

Logan turned downhill and ran like hell.

Rockets lit up the night. Flashes of light and thunder rained cordite brimstone into the forest. An infernal chain-saw roar of .50-caliber guns droned beneath the blasts. The barrage sheared off treetops and turned them to sawdust before they hit the ground. Sharp reports from a dozen grenades were barely pops in the nightmarish din that swelled around Logan.

A blast hurled him forward, a leaf in a firestorm. Heavy bullets raked his back as he fell, ripping away large chunks of his flesh. Another explosion scoured him with burning shrapnel. He struck the ground in agony, his body torn and seared, his skin flayed. Screams of rage lay trapped inside his chest, unable to escape his bloody, shredded throat. His fingers clawed the carpet of dried pine needles, dug at the cold black dirt underneath. Instinct told him to get up, keep moving, but his leg muscles were still knitting themselves back together, magnifying his suffering.

The hum of engines and servos counterpointed a regular cadence of deafening booms, the thunderous herald of several tons of metal striding at a quickstep. Determined not to meet death with his back turned, Logan fought against his ravaged body, forced himself to roll over onto his back. The metal colossus came to a halt towering above him, an iron god gazing with contempt at a mere insect.

Logan gathered the phlegm from his throat and spat it at the weathered, gray foot of the beast. "Go on, you bastard," he said in a voice like a cougar's growl. "Bring it."

A ruby-red flash of laser light danced over Logan's eyes. The machine's targeting system was locked.

Its autocannons blazed—sending a stream of crimson tracers arcing away into the trees, deflected as if by providence.

The last two rockets in its shoulder-mounted launchers leaped forward with a deep *whoosh*—then detonated, nova bright, less than three meters from the battlesuit.

Rocked by the point-blank explosions, the metallic behemoth stumbled backward, its torso spun off-center. When the smoke and fire dissipated seconds later, it had righted itself, but Logan could see that its cockpit canopy had been badly fractured, and the armor on its chassis had been cracked open. For a moment, it didn't move at all, suggesting that its pilot had been stunned.

Logan tilted his head backward. At the edge of the glade, huddled under a fallen tree, was Wai Ying. Her open palm and unblinking stare were trained steadily on the giant machine. The operator of the walking tank swiveled the machine's torso to aim its autocannons at her. A moment later, the gun barrels cracked and ballooned out, then exploded into pieces as misfires touched off conflagrations in their ordnance packages. *Plugged up the barrel,* Logan realized. *Damn, she's good.*

His muscles had repaired themselves enough that he could move again. Scrambling onto all fours, he crawled for cover beneath a stack of overlapping toppled trees.

Behind him, the iron goliath charged forward, on a straight path for Wai Ying. Instead of running, Wai Ying moved into the open, kneeled, and raised her open palms above her head.

Logan grinned with admiration. *Meeting it head-on. Good for her.* He picked himself up. Rolled a painful crick out of his neck. Extended his claws. Grinned. *Can't keep a lady waiting.*

He charged into battle with a roar. The thirty-foot-tall battlesuit was stomping down at Wai Ying, but every crushing blow of its enormous steel foot glanced off her unseen defensive force field. Building up speed, Logan sprinted the final steps, pushed off his right foot, and leaped at the monstrosity's back.

The machine's torso pivoted in a blur and swatted Logan with its mangled right autocannon, which was still effective as a blunt-force weapon. On impact, Logan's vision became faint and spotty. A sensation of weightlessness lasted until a tree halted his lateral flight. None of his bones broke—thanks to the adamantium, they were unbreakable—but he could have sworn they compressed and collapsed into a new and wholly unnatural shape. He bounced off the tree and fell in a dazed heap to the ground.

Swinging its disabled left-side autocannon like a golf club at Wai Ying, it launched her into the air. In midair she adjusted her pose, spreading her arms and legs into an X shape. She ricocheted off trees without seeming to hit them and then cartwheeled away downhill, safe inside her unseen sphere of protection.

This time, Logan chose stealth rather than a head-on assault. He kept low to the ground, dodged beneath and between precariously piled trees, then darted out toward the hulking walker's left flank. Its left foot lifted up, then crashed back down with such speed that Logan was barely able to roll clear and avoid getting turned into salsa. Rather than wait for it to take another stomp at him, he sprang forward onto its foot.

His first blow sank his left claws deep inside the foot's main structural support. Slashing with his right at its principal pivot point, he reveled in the fountain of viscous hydrocarbon lubricant that sprayed outward.

He ducked behind the ankle assembly as the machine's left autocannon swung down to swat him away. As he'd hoped, the machines had not been designed to be able to hit themselves. *Now I just have to get to the cockpit before—*

A fine mist of burning fumes stung his eyes. He

scrambled blind up the machine's leg and was less than halfway over its knee when its antipersonnel system doused its left leg in caustic acid. His already tattered clothes now smoldered where a few drops made contact, and the soles of his shoes slagged as he pushed off an acid-smeared edge for leverage.

Ignoring his half-melted footwear, Logan pulled himself up as quickly as possible. He'd barely reached the hip actuator when blue-white arcs of electricity skipped across the battlesuit's exterior. All he could do was grit his teeth and hang on as every muscle in his body convulsed. White-hot bolts of artificial lightning scorched his back and singed his hair.

The electrical assault ended. Smoke snaked off him in long, wispy coils. He could barely breathe. Reddish haze clouded his vision. His entire body quaked; he couldn't unclench his white-knuckle grasp on the machine's hull. Two deep breaths gave him strength. Nothing was left in him now but battle rage, the primal drive of the animal that owned his soul.

Hand over hand, he climbed and clawed his way up the machine's back. Stabbing at the rounded surfaces, he was rewarded with the pungent fumes of high-octane fuel. One hard swipe of his claws made a hash of the shielded communications bundle behind the cockpit.

Clicking noises came from either side of him. Survival instinct propelled him from a crouch to a superhuman vertical leap, high above the walking tank's head. Twin flamethrowers mounted on its shoulders bathed the back of the machine's chassis in napalm. Streams of burning jellied gasoline drizzled off the steel behemoth, setting fire to the ground below.

The flames were still spewing like the breath of Hell when Logan made a solid landing on the cockpit canopy and tore it apart with three easy hits. Metal and glass scattered like confetti, stinging his exposed chest. Then there was nothing between Logan and the battlesuit operator except the man's nine-millimeter sidearm. Flashes of fire pulsed from its muzzle.

Bullets slammed into Logan's gut and chest. They only hurt. After the fourth shot, Logan tore the weapon from the man's grasp, chucked it into the air, and cut it to pieces with his claws. Metal fragments and gunpowder dusted the inside of the cockpit. Logan retracted his claws and pummeled the battlesuit pilot. Ribs cracked like toothpicks, a collarbone snapped with a wet popping noise, bloody sputum flew in long streams with each sledgehammer hit. The man's nose flattened from a single jab and dumped bright red blood down the front of his jumpsuit.

He'd stopped fighting back and lifted his open hands instead. *"Perestan!"* he cried through broken teeth. *"Ya sdayus!* . . . I surrender!" Logan ceased his attack and backed off.

The rational part of Logan's mind came slowly back into focus between heaving breaths. The adrenaline rush subsided, leaving only enervation and trembling limbs. Making eye contact with the battered Russian, he asked, "You work for Pritikin, right?" The man nodded weakly. "I figured. I'm gonna let you live so you can give him a message." He leaned into the cockpit and poked the man's chest as he spoke. "What happened at the mansion was business. But this"—he gestured at the battlesuit—"this makes it personal." Yanking the man by his collar until he was halfway out of his seat, Logan snarled and lowered his voice to a menacing whisper. "You tell that sonofabitch I know who he is—and now I'm *pissed off.*"

He head-butted the man unconscious, dropped him back into his seat, then used his claws to destroy what was left of the cockpit. The machine's internal power plant shut down with a pathetic, falling whine.

The walk back to the van was long, cold, and painful. By the time Logan rejoined Wai Ying and Ziv, the van was idling at the south end of the tunnel, ready to resume its journey to Pulkovo Airport. He climbed in through the open back doors and shut them behind him. Then he sagged to the floor, exhausted.

"Are you all right?" Wai Ying asked.

Logan sighed. "Just tell me there's beer on the plane."

Cool and slick with condensation, the unopened bottle of Molson Golden pressed against Logan's temple was the perfect remedy to the pounding headache that lingered in his skull.

As soon as he, Wai Ying, and Ziv had reached the plane, he had grabbed the beer from the fridge and collapsed onto one of the luxurious padded seats in the passenger cabin. He'd sunk into the deep embrace of the broad seat and savored the frosty relief of the beer bottle on his brow. After a minute, he'd twisted off the cap and guzzled the brew, then asked Ziv to fetch him another. The two old friends had repeated that scenario several times in the past hour, to the point that Logan had lost count of how many beers he'd had, not that it really mattered, since his mutant healing factor made it impossible for him to get drunk—much to his chagrin.

Logan put down the beer bottle and opened his eyes. Ziv sat on the other side of the fold-out table between their facing seats, which were near the front of the cabin. The Russian tapped and clicked at Wai Ying's laptop computer. His brow was creased with fervent concentration. Yawning, Logan rubbed the fatigue from his eyes, then he opened the beer. "Where are we?" he asked, and took a long swig.

"Making our descent into Vienna," Ziv said without looking up from the computer screen.

"Whadda we got? Anything interesting?"

"Perhaps," Ziv said. "Pritikin's security was really quite good—kind of a new twist on visual matrix encryption—"

"Can we skip the gee-whiz crap and get to what I need to know?" Logan's headache was still bothering him, and he was in no mood to sit through one of Ziv's jargon rants.

Ziv, clearly annoyed, grunted and turned the laptop toward Logan. "Aside from the garden-variety money laundering that goes with paying off politicians, most of Pritikin's business and personal finances are fairly ordinary."

One of Ziv's bad habits that had worsened with age, in Logan's opinion, was his tendency to withhold information for dramatic effect until someone asked for it. Since the only other person in the cabin with Ziv was Logan, that task had unavoidably fallen to him. "Most are ordinary? Which ones ain't?"

Reaching over the top of the screen, Ziv pointed at a highlighted line on a complicated-looking spreadsheet. "This one. Six months ago, Anbaric Petroleum bought a six-thousand-TEU container ship, the *Pandora,* Liberian registry."

The numbers were nothing but a jumble to Logan. He shrugged. "What's so odd about that?"

"His company operates nearly four hundred oil tankers, but until six months ago they'd *never* owned a freighter."

"Maybe he's expanding his business," Logan said.

Leaning across the table, Ziv tapped a couple of keys on the laptop. Two new windows crammed with data opened on the already crowded screen. "In the six months since the ship has belonged to Anbaric Petroleum, it hasn't delivered even one piece of cargo, anywhere. It's made three refueling stops, but until a few days ago it'd never taken aboard even one piece of freight. Yet a satellite photo shows its deck fully loaded."

"Okay," Logan said. He pointed at the screen. "What else?"

"The *Pandora*'s last port of call was Pôrto Alegre, Brazil—easy trucking distance from the site of your little dust-up in Foz do Iguaçu. She made port the day after your Osaka robbery, received a sealed, forty-foot 'hi-cube' shipping container, and weighed anchor as soon as it was aboard."

"And where was it heading?"

"Next port of call," Ziv said, "Cape Town, South Africa."

Shaking his head in disbelief, Logan said, "You came up with all this in just an hour?"

"What can I say?" Ziv replied with a faux-humble shrug. "I'm a professional. I also checked on your playmates from Brazil." He tapped a key on the laptop. Pictures of the fair-haired twins who'd attacked Nando's house appeared on the screen. "Oskar and Gregor Golovanov, a.k.a. Slake and Surge. Part of the Soviet mutant-research program in the late eighties." It was hard for Logan to tell, but he felt as if his headache was getting worse the longer Ziv kept talking. "Oskar's a power siphon, has a gift for absorbing electrical current. Gregor's the blaster, releases energy as heat, magnetic pulses, lightning, you name it." Another key tap called up old KGB dossiers about the brothers.

"They're symbiotically linked," Ziv continued. "Without Oskar, Gregor's got no power. And if the KGB's tests are right, without Gregor, Oskar is a walking time bomb." He closed the laptop. "They escaped Soviet custody a couple decades ago, went rogue."

Giving free rein to his rotten mood, Logan replied, "Is this gonna be on the test? 'Cause I forgot to take notes."

"Have another beer," Ziv shot back, rolling his eyes.

Outside, the nighttime lights of Vienna rose to meet the Cessna jet. With a mechanical whining and grinding, the landing gear unfolded from the aircraft's nose and belly.

Wai Ying called back through the open cockpit door, "Buckle up, boys, we're about to land."

While Ziv put away the laptop, Logan shifted his half-empty bottle of beer to the drink holder on the narrow maple-wood shelf beside their seats. The high, melodic hum of wing flaps adjusting to a landing configuration sent sympathetic vibrations through the deck. Ziv opened the wall panel, folded down the hinged tabletop into the bulkhead, and secured the panel in its closed position. Then both men fastened their seat belts and settled back to await wheels-down in Austria's capital.

"So what do you think?" asked Ziv.

Logan downed another swallow of beer. "I think we have to find that ship."

13

NISHAN CARRIED HER BARELY CONSCIOUS daughter along a dirt road choked with charred debris, festering excrement, rotting bodies, and a horrifying array of living human wreckage.

Entire families lay collapsed together from exhaustion and dehydration. Peering through the honeyed light of a drifting dust cloud, Nishan tried to find the end of the line for food and water; a Red Cross truck had arrived just minutes earlier with fresh supplies. As the dust curtain passed, her already meager hopes diminished again. The bedraggled parade of the sick and the dying that had packed this road *was* the line.

"Hang on, my angel," she whispered to Kanika, whose fragile body sagged limply in her arms. The girl's eyes were dull and unfocused, as if staring into another world—or perhaps into the next world, the land beyond life's border. Breaths came slowly to her now, and her chest barely rose with each feeble gasp.

Wary of anyone and everyone, Nishan looked back and made certain that no one had disturbed the threadbare lean-to shelter she had built for the children. It had taken her most of the day yesterday to scrounge unburned wood and mosquito netting from the lost buildings. Nadif, who was faring as poorly as his sister, lay there now, alone and awaiting Nishan's return, which seemed much longer delayed than she had expected. The choice to carry Kanika had been motivated by practicality as much as by precaution; even though both children were frighteningly emaciated, Nadif was still taller and heavier than Kanika. And since Nadif was a boy, Nishan did not have to fear that he might be raped while she left him to fetch water and food.

"Maybe they'll have medicine," Nishan whispered to her daughter, even though experience had taught her the folly of hope. Kanika continued staring at nothing; she no longer responded to the sound of Nishan's voice, and her skin felt radiantly overheated all the time now, even in the deep watches of the night. Dr. Charoenying's grim diagnosis had haunted Nishan for several days. Now she knew the truth, felt it in her soul: her children were going to die. It was no longer a question of if, but of when and how painfully.

Up ahead, nearly fifty meters away, the crowd surrounded the Red Cross truck like ants swarming on a fallen morsel. Fear and desperation twisted through everyone, binding them like a chain, shackling them with misery. It had been less than five minutes since the volunteers on the truck had begun dispensing clean water and bags of grain, but already the crowd susurrated with fearful whispers: *What if there's not enough food for everyone? What if they run out of water? I need medicine—do they have medicine? Shouldn't the old people go first? Shouldn't the children go first? Why can't pregnant women go first?*

From the sky overhead came the steady *whup-whup-whup* of a circling black helicopter with American markings. Its thumping rotor noise was like a demon's drumbeat. Inside the helicopter, men who looked well fed and bored slouched against their mounted machine guns. Once, many months ago, Nishan had asked Dr. Maguire if there was a risk that the helicopter men might fire on the villagers. The white-haired Irishman had responded with a mirthless laugh and ruthless honesty: "The Americans don't think you're worth the cost of a bullet."

The crowd's murmured worries turned suddenly into an electric current of panic. Women grabbed up their infants and struggled to push free of the clutch of pressed bodies. Children on the fringe of the mob scattered. The men nearly trampled them all in their haste to save themselves. Everyone fled from the Red Cross truck. Then a new sound drew closer, and Nishan was finally able to discern it from the helicopter's incessant, thundering tempo: hoofbeats.

All around Nishan people were frantic, looking for anyplace to hide. Some crawled beneath the maggot-ridden corpses in the road and pretended to be dead. Others ran out toward the plains, hoping to take cover in the parched brown stands of tall grass. Nishan stood her ground in the middle of the road. There was no place she could run to while carrying Kanika, so she decided not to waste the effort.

Dozens of dust-covered men on camelback rode past Nishan, all of them firing short bursts from their assault rifles and whooping in some Arabic dialect. Quickly they surrounded the Red Cross truck. Angry words flew back and forth between the men on the truck and the Tanjawar militiamen. The argument came to a quick end when the unarmed Red Cross volunteers found themselves looking into the muzzles of a dozen Kalashnikov rifles. Seconds later, with strict military efficiency, the Tanjawar commander directed the off-loading of all the truck's supplies, which were packed into the militiamen's mostly empty saddlebags and backpacks.

It was a routine that Nishan had seen before. First the Tanjawar would devastate a village and make cer-

tain that word of the pillaging reached the government in Kaltoum. Then the government—which
made only the most superficial effort to pretend that
it didn't, in fact, endorse and sometimes direct the
Tanjawar's rampages—would dispatch a fresh shipment of aid supplies, under the watchful gaze of one
Western peacekeeping force or another. Then the
Tanjawar, always in need of fresh supplies for their
troops, would steal the aid shipment. The peacekeepers, Nishan had been told, were not allowed to
intervene unless the Tanjawar fired upon them
directly. If some civilians were killed, or if some
homes were reduced to cinders, the peacekeepers
dismissed it as an "internal Zibarese matter." In other
words, they did absolutely nothing.

The militiamen finished loading the truck's cargo
onto their camels. A rallying cry from the leader
sparked wild stutters of gunfire and a chorus of
prideful yells. Then they galloped their camels away
toward the nearby hills.

The angry chatter of their battle rifles lingered in
Nishan's memory like the sulfurous bite of gunpowder in the air. She stood in the middle of the road,
staring at an empty truck and a future that held nothing but broken promises.

Part of her was grateful; the Tanjawar had been so
intent on raiding the supplies that they had paid no
mind to her or Kanika. Then she looked down at her
dying child's face—and cursed the Tanjawar for not

being more generous than the Americans with their bullets and sparing her and her children from the dark promise of slow death that now circled them.

Nishan turned and walked slowly back toward the shelter where Nadif lay, silent and expiring by degrees. The fresh supplies were gone. There was nothing left to do now but conserve the few drops of water that they had left and try to make it through another night. For a moment, she considered praying for a miracle.

Then she remembered: *This is Africa. There are no miracles here.*

14

EXITS TICKED BY WHILE LOGAN STARED OUT
the window at the blur of the landscape, happy just
to be back on the ground after a long night in the
air. He'd flown the Cessna jet from Vienna to Addis
Ababa, Ethiopia, and then on to Cape Town, while
Wai Ying had slept. They'd touched down just before dawn, local time, at Cape Town International
Airport and had cleared customs just after seven
o'clock. At Ziv's suggestion, Wai Ying had agreed to
keep a low profile as they left the airport; she'd hired
a privately operated minivan to take them to a hotel.

Tinny pop music warbled from the minivan's dashboard speakers as it raced up the N2 highway, past

seemingly endless clusters of shantytown shacks. The sprawling squalor grew sparse, then surrendered to the rising gleam of the city, which glittered in the long morning light. Summer was in full force in the southern hemisphere, and the air was humid and strangely alive with the promise of a scorching afternoon to come.

From a distance, the city looked like a clumsy patchwork, a hastily assembled grid with random patches of forest breaking up the brown slopes of sun-parched hillsides. It reminded Logan of the fur of a dog afflicted with mange.

Twenty minutes after leaving the airport, they had switched from the N2 to the N1, which skirted the waterfront near Duncan Dock. A few minutes later the driver followed Wai Ying's directions and got off the highway at the Coen Steytler exit, which he followed out toward the Victoria & Alfred Waterfront hotels. To the right of the minivan, the turquoise waters of Table Bay rippled and shimmered beneath a pale sky. Brightly colored sails unfurled as a handful of private boats navigated gracefully out of Victoria Basin into the bay, toward Robben Island and the open sea.

The minivan followed the edge of the waterfront and began heading northeast on Breakwater Boulevard. The eastern view was dominated by the rough-hewn slopes of Table Mountain, which, along with Signal Hill, gave the city an almost mythical quality.

Soon the driver turned the minivan onto East Pier Road, then slowed and came to a halt at one of the largest and most opulent accommodations in all of Cape Town: the Table Bay Hotel.

Wai Ying thanked the driver in Afrikaans and paid him in a fistful of South African rands that Logan hadn't even realized she'd been carrying. By the time he and Ziv exited the minivan, she was already directing the hotel's porters to unload their luggage and summoning the concierge to expedite her check-in, which she'd reserved the night before from Vienna.

Ziv and Logan stood together, hands in pockets, staring up at the magnificent white palace of a hotel that towered before them. Finally, Ziv just shook his head. "She has to be kidding."

"I'll give her this much," Logan said as he took two Cuban cigars from his pocket. "She knows how to pamper herself." He handed one of the cigars to Ziv. "Can I borrow your cutter? I'd rather not make a scene with the claws."

Nodding, Ziv found his cutter, trimmed the edge from his own robusto, then handed the miniature guillotine to Logan. "It's extravagant," Ziv said, gesturing at the hotel. "But it makes sense. As long as we get rooms facing east, we'll have an unobstructed view of both Duncan and Schoeman docks."

Logan clipped the end of his own cigar. "We could've had that from the Holiday Inn," he said, handing back the cutter. Fishing out his lighter, he added, "Instead, we're running our stakeout from a five-star hotel with a sailboat marina." He flicked open his Zippo and ignited his cigar, then held the flame steady for Ziv while he lit his.

After savoring a few puffs, Ziv exhaled a mouthful of sweet smoke. "And the problem with that would be what, exactly?"

"Never said it was a problem," Logan replied. "I'm just worried, that's all."

Concern colored Ziv's expression. "Worried? Why?"

Logan grinned. "Because I'm startin' to get used to it."

Just as Logan had expected, Wai Ying had set herself up in the best accommodations the hotel had been able to offer and declared her luxury suite to be their new base of operations.

He wasn't complaining, by any means. Throughout the many decades of his life, he had stayed in some miserable places: a roach-infested cold-water flat in Madripoor, a hostel in East Germany whose cots all had been rife with lice, a thatched-roof hut in Sri Lanka that had only served to slow down the rain rather than keep it out. He wasn't even counting the numerous hard nights he'd spent in the wilderness, whether it had been the frigid, knifing cold of a Canadian winter in the Rockies or even just the banal misery of hud-

dling among the homeless beneath a highway under-
pass during an Arizona summer.

Now, courtesy of Wai Ying's seemingly unfettered
expense account, he and Ziv had been booked into
their own luxury rooms. Rarely had he ever lived so
lavishly. Even at the Xavier Institute, his accommodations had been modest; he'd stayed in a private dorm
room like most of the other adults. Now he found
himself in a bright, airy, expansive space. With a king
bed. And a big-screen, high-definition, satellite-signal
television, unlimited access to a minibar, and round-
the-clock services of every kind, from food and laundry to anything else he could ask of the concierge. All
he could think of was to request more cigars.

Though he considered his room extravagant, it
was nothing compared to the accommodations Wai
Ying had arranged for herself. She was comfortably
ensconced in the Lion's Head presidential suite. It
boasted an entrance hall, a lounge, a fully equipped
kitchen, a dining room, a dressing room, and a spa
bath with scenic views, all in addition to a bedroom
that, by itself, was more than twice the size of Logan's
room.

More important to their mission, however, its balcony offered a commanding view of the Victoria &
Albert Waterfront, including the entirety of the commercial docks to the east. Beyond the orderly grid-
work of the city jutted Table Mountain, the defining
feature of Cape Town's landscape.

Logan and Ziv stood on the balcony, observing the activity below. At the moment, it was Ziv's turn to look through the binoculars that had been purchased for them by the concierge, at Wai Ying's request. Logan asked, "Anything coming in?"

"*Nyet,*" Ziv said as he scanned the horizon.

Logan didn't need binoculars to examine the container ships that were currently in port being serviced by the row of cranes. Even from several kilometers away, he could discern the names painted on the ships' hulls. None of them was the *Pandora.*

"I'm getting hungry," Logan said. "Are you hungry yet?"

Ziv lowered the binoculars. "It's only been an hour since breakfast."

"Boredom gives me an appetite," Logan said.

Inside the suite's lounge, Wai Ying's cell phone rang. Ziv and Logan both looked back at it. Wai Ying strode in from the bedroom, attired in a new, dark burgundy variation of the same suit she'd been wearing when Logan had first met her, several days ago in the cemetery. She picked up the ringing phone and answered it, then paced away toward the dining room.

"Slave to fashion, that one," Ziv remarked.

With a shrug, Logan replied, "I've seen worse."

"Let me guess," Ziv shot back with a grin. "That girl in Prague?"

"For one," Logan said, remembering the alluring

female spy from the Eastern Bloc who had tried to seduce him on Ziv's orders, back when they were still competitors in the Cold War. "I was thinking more of that Hungarian girl you strung along by promising to help her become a supermodel."

Ziv feigned indignation. "I thought she had potential."

"You thought a five-foot-three twenty-six-year-old with a chipped front tooth was gonna be a super-model? Gimme a break."

"What can I say? I'm an optimist." He lifted the binoculars and made another slow pan of the horizon. "You're right, I'm bored and hungry. Are they still serving breakfast?"

Logan checked his watch. "No."

"Damn," Ziv said. "I could've gone for more eggs Benedict."

"Yeah, what a shame," Logan said. "Your life is so hard."

An updraft carried the scent of chlorine from the hotel's Jacuzzi and the brine of the harbor. Seagulls floated on the noonday air, wings glowing with reflected sunlight. From the marina and boardwalk came the sounds of music and laughter, people talking, the ringing of a dock bell. Aromas from several varieties of food teased Logan's hyperattenuated olfactory sense. Yet, with such a rich spectrum of sensory delights to hold his interest, he found himself focused on the sound of Wai Ying's hushed voice from two rooms away. He couldn't hear what she was saying, but he could sense the extremely agitated way that she was saying it. As she returned to the lounge, she shot a look of exasperation toward Logan, who nudged Ziv.

Walking toward the two men, she flung away her cell phone onto the couch. "You can stop watching the harbor," she said.

"What happened?" Logan asked.

She rolled her eyes. "The official story? Twenty-four hours ago, a freak storm sank the *Pandora* in the South Atlantic."

Ziv groaned. "Where did she go down?"

"No one knows," Wai Ying said. "Lost without a trace, no survivors. Just gone."

"Hang on," Ziv said. "What about its GPS system?"

Wai Ying shook her head. "They lost the signal from its transponder about an hour before they lost radio contact."

"Convenient," Logan interjected. "The most reliable part of the entire navigation system failed, but the radio still worked so they could tell us about it—for the record."

"Exactly," Ziv said, nodding. "It's still out there."

Wai Ying shook her head. "Not likely. Setsuko called in a favor with a friend at the NRO. They came up with nothing."

"Doesn't make sense," said Logan, whose years of

work for the intelligence community had acquainted him with the abilities of the U.S. National Reconnaissance Office. "I don't care where that ship is—on the water or under it—they can find it."

"The Classic Wizard network?" Ziv asked.

"Exactly," Logan said. "They could find a rowboat in the middle of the Pacific if they wanted to. No way they'd miss a container ship."

"Not if someone found a way to hide it from them," Ziv said. "You saw that optical-cloaking tech Pritikin's walking tanks were using. What if he figured out how to put it on a ship? It might be invisible to radar, sonar, and satellites."

"Well, get ready for bad piece of news number two," Wai Ying said. "Pritikin himself vanished yesterday. We had four satellites tracking his every move; there's no record of him leaving Russia, but the next thing we knew he was gone."

"First his ship sinks, then he goes missing," Ziv said. "Forgive me if I don't send lilies to his memorial just yet."

"After everything he and the Hand went through to get their hands on Panacea," Logan said, "no way they're gonna let it get lost at sea. Betcha ten to one Pritikin's on that ship."

Wai Ying folded her arms and looked back and forth between Ziv and Logan. "Gentlemen, we have to find that ship. *Now*."

"Then what are we waiting for?" Ziv asked sarcastically. "Let's get to work. I'll take the Atlantic. Logan, you take the Pacific. Miss Tse, be a dear and check the Indian Ocean. After all, it's just an invisible ship, floating somewhere on the continuous body of water that covers three-quarters of the planet's surface. How hard could it be?" Wai Ying's eyes narrowed as she fumed silently in Ziv's direction.

Logan walked away. "I'll be in the bar."

A neon-orange X marked the spot. Despite the bulky headphones that protected Alexei Pritikin's ears, the rotor noise drowned out every other sound as the sleek EC-135 passenger helicopter descended toward the landing pad on the container ship's aft deck. The struts touched down with a wobbling bump, then the helicopter settled to rest. Ground crewmen crouched as they jogged to Pritikin's door and opened it for him. He unfastened his safety harness, removed his headphones, and climbed out of the chopper into the painfully loud clamor and swirling winds of the rotors' downwash.

Although the vessel was at anchor in a secluded harbor, the horizon still rocked in a manner that made him queasy. Pritikin had never liked the sea; he'd bought a yacht strictly for entertaining clients, but he had yet to unmoor it from its slip in Odesa; feeling a tide of nausea churn in his stomach and vertigo spinning in his head, he doubted he ever would. It took a great effort to hide his seasickness as he crouched and hurried away from the chopper and down a few short flights of stairs to a lower deck, where Keniuchio Harada waited for him, attired as ever in his impeccable silver-gray business suit.

Harada nodded to greet Pritikin and yelled over the rotor noise, "You made good time."

"What the hell am I doing here?" Pritikin shouted back, skipping the pleasantries and cutting to business.

With a tilt of his head, Harada invited Pritikin to follow him. He guided him away from the landing pad toward a starboard hatch that led to an interior passageway. Once the heavy metal hatch closed behind them, the noise from the helicopter was gone, replaced by the low hum of the ship's internal ventilation and plumbing systems. The passage was claustrophobically close; its low overhead was packed with thick pipes and steam-hissing valves.

"Sorry to tear you away from your business in Russia," Harada said. "It's just a precaution."

"A precaution?" Pritikin had been unhappy at being summoned by Harada. If it turned out to be for nothing, or for something trivial, he was going to be furious. "Against what?"

They turned left and descended a steep, narrow stair-ladder toward the main deck, several flights down. Their shoes clanked loudly on the gray steel steps. "Wolverine learned more than we thought during his visit to your home," Harada said. "He and his friends are in Cape Town right now."

"So what?" Pritikin said, following Harada as he circled back to another ladder nestled directly behind the one they'd just descended. "The *Pandora*'s not going to Cape Town."

"And by now Wolverine knows that," Harada said, gracefully gliding down the ladder to the next deck and landing with perfect poise. "The problem, of course, is that he's looking for this ship at all. Clearly, he already knows too much."

Clambering down the ladder to rejoin Harada, Pritikin felt slow and clumsy—an unusual sensation for him, since he'd always enjoyed both excellent health and good coordination. Compared to Harada, however, he was a weakling, a doddering fool. The fact that Harada was more than two meters tall made the Japanese crime lord intimidating enough, but the clearly phenomenal strength and grace that he possessed made it obvious to Pritikin that Harada was something more than human.

Catching his breath, Pritikin said, "Let him look. No one's going to find this ship unless we want them to."

A wan smile conveyed Harada's derision. "Your cloaking system might fool the eye, Mr. Pritikin; it might even fool machines. But there are greater forces at work in this world. And against those, I fear it will be of little help."

Harada opened another hatch and stepped through onto the main deck. Noise from the helicopter and the ocean washed over them once more. An unbroken wall of multicolored steel shipping containers, stacked four high, stretched across the width of the ship. Ushered by Harada, Pritikin stepped through the hatch, then waited while Harada sealed it behind them. The deck had been freshly mopped; it was still streaked with rapidly evaporating, ammonia-scented liquid.

They walked toward the far left corner of the container mountain. "You still haven't explained why I need to be out here in the middle of nowhere," Pritikin said, hoping that bravado would mask his unease at being seasick.

"You are here, Mr. Pritikin, because you are currently the weak link in our security." Harada stopped at the padlocked doors of one of the bottom containers. The lock had a digital keypad rather than a numbered wheel or keyhole. Harada tapped in a lengthy sequence of numbers as he continued. "Though Wolverine knows the Hand is involved, his ability to identify our members is extremely limited. My role in our operation remains unknown to him. You, on the other hand, are an exposed asset." The lock's bolt released with a sharp *click,* and Harada removed it. "Wolverine and his allies could use you to compromise the security of the *Pandora*—if they knew where to find you." He opened the container doors, revealing a dimly lit corridor that stretched far longer than any one container's length and was intersected by other corridors. "The only place I can be certain they don't know how to find you . . . is here."

"I can't stay here forever," Pritikin said as he trailed behind Harada, who led him into the secret passages. "I have to be in Kaltoum tomorrow to meet with the Zibarese oil minister."

"And you will," Harada said. "As soon as my people handle the Wolverine problem."

"And when will that be?"

"Soon," Harada said.

They turned a corner into an intersecting corridor and arrived at a pressure lock. Harada opened the hatch, stepped through, and motioned for Pritikin to follow him. "This is the first decontamination phase," he said. "In the next compartment, we'll put on protective gear over our clothes." As soon as Harada sealed the hatch behind Pritikin, the lights changed to a ruddy crimson, then an electric blue. A hiss of rushing gas preceded a painful popping sensation in Pritikin's ears.

The next hatch opened automatically. They stepped through into a room with several baggy bio-hazard outfits hanging in open lockers. The hatch at the far end of the compartment was marked in several languages, warning that the area on the other side was a sterile environment. Pritikin put on one of the hazmat suits, helped Harada secure his own gear, then remained still while Harada returned the favor. Once their suits registered secure, Harada led him through into a small pressure lock. All the air was removed from the chamber, then the final hatch rolled open to reveal a masterpiece in chrome and steel.

Bathed in flat white light, two dozen stainless-steel fermenters stood in three rows of eight. The high-pressure, airtight bioreactors were linked by a complex series of pipes, valves, and wiring surrounded by temperature and pressure gauges and complex chemical analyzers. Each one was more than three meters tall and just as wide.

"It's all working properly?" Pritikin asked.

"Perfectly," Harada said. "Dr. Falco has done an admirable job under less than ideal conditions." He rested his right hand on the surface of one of the fermenters, as if stroking a beloved pet. "Every one of these is brewing five million doses of Panacea right now."

"How soon until they're ready?"

"The test batch will be ready for your meeting with the oil minister," Harada said. "The first full batch will be ready later that day. As soon as we can crate it, we'll send it on to the mainland."

"Excellent," Pritikin said. Nodding with his chin toward a window of one-way glass that looked in on Dr. Falco and his laboratory at the far end of the production plant, he asked, "When are we done with him?"

"As soon as the process is automated," Harada

said. "Then we can shift production to the plant in Yangon."

"Good, good," Pritikin said. He started walking back toward the pressure lock. Harada followed him without complaint.

They didn't talk again until after they had navigated the complex process of removing the suits and decontaminating. Harada led Pritikin back out to the main deck. By now, Pritikin's seasickness had abated slightly, and he was able to appreciate the briny smell of the sea—for about five seconds, until he got a good whiff of diesel exhaust and felt a surge of bile climbing up his throat.

Harada looked amused. "Are you all right, Mr. Pritikin?"

"Fine," he lied. It took a moment before he could continue. "I'm glad your operation is running so smoothly. Now that I've completed my part of our agreement, when can I expect you to fulfill yours?"

Motioning for Pritikin to keep pace with him as they walked aft and back inside the superstructure that housed the ship's command center, Harada replied, "Steps are already being taken."

"Such as?"

"The foreign minister in Aschabad who blocked your pipeline request is being persuaded to change his mind," Harada said. "The mullah in Afghanistan who took your money and then reneged on the deal is being . . . replaced." He opened a door for Pritikin, then followed him through, pointing ahead and to the right, toward the officers' mess. "As for your former partner in Karachi, who cut his own deal with the Americans—we'll deal with him by tonight." They entered the officers' mess and were greeted by the mingled aromas of beef stew and fresh-baked rolls. "You needn't worry that I've forgotten our agreement. Your long-delayed Caspian pipeline will be approved within the week, and the funding for it will be in place as soon as Panacea makes its global debut."

Pritikin's face was warm with embarrassment. "I shouldn't have doubted you, Mr. Harada." He bowed his head. "I apologize."

"Not necessary," Harada said. "I should have kept you better apprised of our efforts."

With a wave, he summoned over a steward, then motioned to Pritikin to sit down with him. As soon as he and Harada were seated, the steward stood at attention beside their table. "What can I get for you, Mr. Harada?"

"Two bowls of stew," Harada said, "two Tsing Taos, a basket of rolls, and some steamed vegetables." He glanced at Pritikin, then added, "And a glass of water for my guest."

The steward nodded and walked briskly toward the galley. Pritikin looked askance at Harada. "A glass of water?"

"To wash these down," Harada said, handing him

a pair of motion-sickness pills. "No offense, Alexei, but if you vomit on my suit, I will kill you."

That'd be funny, Pritikin realized, *if he wasn't completely serious.* "Hurry up with that water," he yelled to the steward.

Oskar Golovanov climbed the dark gray concrete stairs two at a time. He was in a hurry to reach his brother's room, which was on the ninth floor of the seediest dive hotel in São Paulo.

Walking up the back emergency-exit stairwell hadn't been Oskar's first choice; he had planned to take the lift. When it had finally arrived, however, after a delay of several minutes, its doors had opened to reveal an indigent man lying half-conscious and doubled over on its floor. A reek of body odor, wine-scented breath, and stale urine had wafted out of the lift car into the lobby. The stench was then further compounded by the man's sudden loss of bowel control.

And so, Oskar was climbing eight flights of stairs.

For the sake of keeping a low profile—and also for Oskar's peace of mind—he and Gregor had checked into separate hotels, under aliases. As always, Oskar had remained the principal contact for their orders from Mr. Harada. Less than twenty minutes ago, his cell phone had rung, and he had answered it promptly, to receive Mr. Harada's latest instructions.

Now his task was to relay those orders to Gregor,

get him packed, and extricate him from whatever squalid catastrophe he'd wrought this time. True to form, of course, Gregor hadn't answered his cell phone or his hotel-room line when Oskar called to rouse him. Having no other choice, Oskar had accepted that he would have to collect Gregor in person, but he resented it all the same. He feared that his twin brother would likely be in no better condition than the man in the elevator.

Ever since their forced retreat from the fight in Foz do Iguaçu, Gregor had been even more sullen and violent than usual. Before Foz he had been grouchy, but now his temper had turned volcanic, and the liter bottles of alcohol that seemed never to leave his hand proved unable to drown his black moods.

At the eighth floor, Oskar pulled open the already ajar fire door and stepped into the corridor. Cigarette burns freckled the stain-blotched carpeting, and the bitter smell of old tobacco smoke seemed to cling to the tacky, yellowing wallpaper. He noted the ripped upholstery on an armchair that had been evicted from one of the rooms. Sickly greenish light oozed from the bare fluorescent fixtures overhead. Loose-cornered wooden frames hung just shy of right angles around art prints so boring that their selection had to have been the work of a committee.

As Oskar neared the end of the hallway, he heard the shattering of something fragile, followed by a feminine-sounding whimper of either fear or pain.

Business as usual for Gregor, then, he brooded as he arrived at the door to his brother's room. Reluctantly, he knocked, then waited. Several seconds dragged by and became half a minute. Then came his brother's inebriated drawl from the other side of the door.

"Who ish it? Whaddayawant?"

"It's me, Gregor. It's Oskar."

He heard coughing through the door. "Go away, I'm fine."

"Open the door, Gregor. We have new orders, we have to go."

A groan turned into a growl behind the door, then came the *clack* and *thunk* and scrape of bolts and chains being unlocked.

The door swung open. Gregor hung off it like a monkey with no bones. He looked up with drooplidded, bloodshot eyes and slurred, "Wherewegoing?"

"Cape Town," Oskar said. "Let me in. You have to pack."

Oskar gently pushed past his brother into the hotel room. Even by Gregor's standards, the level of damage was impressive. Enormous cavities had been punched or kicked or otherwise smashed through the drywall; every piece of furniture was broken to one degree or another. Broken glass sparkled on the floor, bathed in the hazy afternoon light that slanted steeply in through the shattered fragments of the window.

Oskar took a few cautious steps farther inside, mindful of what was crunching under his shoes. Amid the fragmented ruins of countless cocktail glasses, he found the pulverized remains of Gregor's cell phone. The room's phone and its television, he noticed, were both conspicuously absent.

Looking to the left, he eyed the bathroom. Water drizzled from the broken toilet bowl and cascaded over lethal-looking shards from the savaged mirror. Jagged-edged halves of bottles lay jumbled together in one far corner of the bathroom; in the other huddled a trembling, half-naked, bloodied woman.

Studying her face, Oskar felt pity for her. In all likelihood, she had been quite beautiful before she'd stepped inside this hotel room; she never would be again. Her face had been battered, her teeth broken, her lip slashed or possibly even bitten. Oskar couldn't tell, and he didn't want to know.

He sensed his brother lurking behind him, looking over his shoulder, eyeing his handiwork with false contrition. A sick glee that Gregor could barely suppress tainted his words with insincerity. "I got carried away," he mumbled.

"Go pack your things," Oskar said, burying his disgust in the cold baritone of professionalism.

Gregor shambled away and awkwardly retrieved various articles of clothing from the debris of his room. In the bathroom, Oskar tried to comfort Gregor's traumatized whore. "It's over," he said in a soothing, low voice. "Whatever he did to you, it's done. He's not going to kill you. I won't let him."

The prostitute said nothing, she just hugged her legs and tucked most of her face behind her knees, until all that he could see were her two eyes, wide and dark and frightened. She was so slight, so fragile-looking . . . against his better judgment, he let himself really look at her. She wasn't a woman; she was just a girl, probably not much more than fifteen years old. *Another of Gregor's appetites I wish I knew nothing about,* he realized. Revulsion churned hot bile into his throat, and he finally turned away, surrendering to the utter hopelessness of the situation. The best he could hope to do now would be to get Gregor out of this room as quickly as possible, before the local authorities caught wind of what Gregor had done.

A few minutes later, Gregor stood off-kilter in the middle of the room and clutched a lumpy, dark green canvas duffel. "I'm ready to go," he said, his breath rank with tequila fumes.

Oskar kept a grip on the back of Gregor's shirt, partly to propel his brother out the door and partly to keep him upright. Gregor weaved sloppily down the hallway.

When it came time to descend the stairs to the ground floor, it became obvious to Oskar that Gregor was not up to the challenge. To save time, he dropped Gregor's duffel of clothes down the meter-wide gap between the two sides of the switchback staircase. The canvas bag bounced its way down and struck the concrete floor far below with a heavy slap.

Then Oskar hefted his brother over his shoulder in a fireman's carry and portered him down the stairs, out the hotel's rear entrance, and across the street, where he dumped him unceremoniously into the backseat of their rented car—to which Oskar had wisely kept the keys. With Gregor safely in the car, Oskar returned to the hotel, retrieved Gregor's duffel, and brought it back to the car, where he tossed it into the trunk beside his own bags.

All the way to Guarulhos International Airport, Gregor mumbled in a drunken stupor. As they neared the rental-car return lot, Gregor sat up in the backseat, possessed of a sudden clarity. "Where the hell are we going?"

"I told you this at the hotel," Oskar said patiently. "We have new orders from Mr. Harada. We're going to Cape Town, South Africa, to kill Wolverine."

"Yeah!" Gregor roared, as if he'd just won the lottery. He interlaced his fingers and cracked his knuckles. "Payback time."

For the next three hours, until they boarded their flight to Cape Town, Gregor was a bundle of energy and nerves, like a boxer before a prizefight. Oskar knew that what he was seeing in Gregor was a classic bipolar mood swing. *He probably doesn't even remember what he did to that poor kid back at the hotel,* Oskar realized. *Probably doesn't remember she even exists. . . . He's coming unglued.*

The prospect of Gregor going mad terrified Oskar, and not just because they were brothers. Even when Oskar wasn't trying to absorb energy, he did. There was almost no place on earth he could go without being exposed to some kind of directed energy; microwaves had become ubiquitous. It was a low-grade effect, enough that his presence could dim a lightbulb or garble a cell-phone call, but the gain was cumulative. Sooner or later, he would build up too much charge to hold on to.

If Gregor went insane, there was no predicting what kind of damage he might do with a full charge from Oskar. But an even more troubling scenario now kept Oskar awake at night: *What if he dies? What'll happen if I can't release the energy I absorb?*

Oskar didn't know the answer to that question. He didn't want to know.

15

LOGAN TOOK A BREATH, FIXED HIS EYES ON the TV above the bar, and counted to ten as Ziv waved a cell phone in front of him.

"Just make the call, Logan," Ziv said. He slammed the phone down next to Logan's plate, rippling the cocoa-dark surface of his pint of Castle stout. "The *Pandora*'s not coming to us, and we're out of leads. He's the only one who can help us."

Logan didn't know how Ziv and Wai Ying had tracked him to this local pub, nearly a mile from the hotel. It had taken him half a day to find a place that had decent food, good beer, Johnny Cash in the jukebox, and a bartender who was always ready with a light for his cigar. But in they'd walked, before he'd had more than two bites of his swordfish steak.

A sip of the stout and a puff of his Cuban, and Logan collected himself enough to look at Ziv and say, "I ain't talkin' to him, and you damn well know why."

Wai Ying leaned in from the other side and met Logan's glare with her own unrelenting gaze. "I don't. Tell me."

He took another swig of his beer. "No."

Even thinking about Xavier's betrayal made Logan angry, and he wasn't going to discuss it.

Ziv sighed and signaled Eddie, the bartender, to bring two more pints of stout. Looking past Logan at Wai Ying, he said, "Logan's the kind of man who holds a grudge."

"I never would have guessed," Wai Ying said flatly.

"This is none of her business," Logan cut in.

Ignoring him, Ziv continued, "A few years back, a mutant named Magneto tore out all of Logan's super-duper adamantium, nearly killed him."

"Grudge-worthy," Wai Ying admitted with a half-nod.

"Ziv, I'm warning you," Logan said, low and hostile.

"Skip ahead a few years," Ziv went on. "Everyone thought Logan'd hacked off Magneto's head. Xavier took Magneto's body back to Genosha for burial. Smiley here objected."

"He didn't deserve to be buried," Logan said, unable to hold the reins of his bitterness. "Shoulda left him rotting in the street, where dogs could piss on him."

In the mirror behind the bar, Logan noticed Wai Ying's urbanely arched eyebrow. Eddie set down the two pints of stout. Ziv picked his up, took a long sip, then continued his narrative. "So, bad enough that Xavier goes to show Magneto the respect of a funeral, but here's the funny part: it wasn't really Magneto that Logan iced. Some impostor or something. Anyway, make a long story short—"

"Too late," Logan grumbled.

"—Xavier and Magneto are working together, rebuilding the parts of Genosha that got leveled by the Sentinels."

An awkward silence fell over the trio. Everyone sipped their beer, and Logan savored a few rich mouthfuls of his robusto. The blue-gray smoke curled away in serpentine coils toward the slow-turning ceiling fan.

Logan's thoughts turned inward, to a part of himself that he didn't like to face. For years he had looked up to Professor Charles Xavier, had almost thought of him as a mentor. At a time when Logan had been convinced that he was coming to the end of himself, Xavier had offered him a chance to be something more than a living weapon, more than an animal prowling the fringe of the world: he had

offered Logan a chance to live like a man. Then
Charles had befriended the man who'd tortured
Logan in ways more terrible than any he had ever
known. Thinking of Xavier calling that monster a
friend felt like the metal being rent from his bones all
over again.

Wai Ying set down her beer and leaned her back
against the bar so she could face Logan. "I've never
met these people, but if what Ziv said is true, I think
you're right to hate them," she said. "But I'm not
asking you to invite them to dinner. This isn't a social
call. We're talking about the lives and freedom of
millions of people. Maybe billions."

He knew she was right. Servicing his grudge at the
expense of innocent lives was an evil he couldn't live
with. Glowering at his reflection in the mirror, he
picked up the cell phone.

"This might take a few minutes," he said. "I don't
exactly have him on speed dial."

He dialed the mansion in Salem Center, New
York, identified himself to the switchboard operator,
and asked to be connected to Xavier. Then he walked
away to the most secluded corner of the bar, behind
the jukebox, while the operator put him on hold.

About five minutes later, there was a click on the
line, followed by Xavier's hesitant, cautious saluta-
tion: "Logan?"

Hearing the older man's voice provoked deeply
conflicted feelings inside Logan. In many ways, Xavier

had filled a paternal role in Logan's life; he had been all the things that Logan's father never was: patient, wise, and encouraging. But there was no forgetting where Xavier was, or why he was there.

That's not what this is about. Suck it up and do this.

"Yes, Charles, it's me." Acid crept up Logan's esophagus as he fought to keep his tone civil.

"The switchboard said this is an emergency," Xavier said.

"Sit down and get comfortable," Logan said. "It's kind of a long story." As quickly as he was able, he told Xavier about Panacea, the black-market deal and its link to Alexei Pritikin, and the missing ship and oil mogul. "So we need to find Pritikin," he finished, "before he and his pals start dolin' out Panacea around the globe."

"I'm not really sure I can find him, Logan," Xavier said. "You're asking me to seek out one mind among billions—a mind that I've never met before."

"C'mon," Logan said, incredulous. "I've seen you pull off harder tricks than this."

"Back when I had Cerebro, certainly," Xavier said. "But I don't have anything even remotely comparable here. I would have to reach out and try to isolate one unfamiliar voice from the noise of all the other human psyches on earth."

Logan hated when people avoided coming to the point. "Are you saying you can't do it?"

"I'm saying I can't make any promises," Xavier said.

"You don't have to. You're the best there is, Charles. And right now, you're the only chance we've got."

From the other end of the phone line came Xavier's tired sigh. "I'll do everything I can."

"Good enough," Logan said. He was about to say good-bye when Xavier cut him off.

"Logan . . . I know you resent my decision to stay in—"

"Don't apologize," Logan shot back. "You did what you did. Let's leave it at that."

"I wasn't apologizing."

Logan closed his eyes for a few seconds while he raged in silence. "The switchboard has my number," he said. "Call me when you know where Pritikin is."

"And if I can't find him?"

"Then a few billion people are gonna become slaves."

Alexander Zivojinovich paced in front of his hotel-room window. Outside, sunrise had turned to early morning, and the long rays reaching through the streets of Cape Town felt new, as yet unspoiled by the disappointments of a day squandered. He hadn't slept well the night before. After goading Logan into calling Charles Xavier for help, Zivojinovich and Wai Ying had joined Logan for dinner at the pub before returning to the hotel. At that point, there hadn't been much else to do, and everyone had said a muted good night.

Bad dreams had fueled his restlessness, but now he knew that the real source of his anxiety was simply a lack of forward motion. *We've been at this hotel too long,* he chastened himself. *The ship's not coming, we know that. Staying in a place this flashy just draws attention. We should have moved to a less visible hotel yesterday.*

In the distance outside his window, Table Bay glittered, an azure canvas dotted with the colorful triangles of sails, which captured the warm breezes and propelled sleek boats through the gently rolling waves. Duncan Dock and Schoeman Dock both teemed with activity: forklifts and cranes shifted cargo; stevedores loaded and unloaded pallets; shipping containers were hooked to trailer trucks and hauled away.

It's another perfect summer morning in Cape Town, and I'm pacing my room like an inmate.

A glance at the clock confirmed what he already knew: it was slightly after half-past seven. *Time for breakfast,* he decided. *Then maybe I'll catch up to Wai Ying at the spa.* He slipped on a pair of shoes and a clean shirt, then left his room and took the elevator downstairs to the lobby.

As he'd hoped, the Atlantic Restaurant was open and not too crowded. On the way to a nearby open table, he stopped a waiter and ordered some coffee. For a moment he considered ordering the eggs Benedict again from the à la carte menu, but then a twinge of psychosomatic pain tugged inside his chest and he steered himself toward the buffet. Eyeing his options, he helped himself to a plate of fresh fruit, a bran muffin, and a pair of hard-boiled eggs. Temptation called to him again in the form of a chef's offer to prepare a fresh Belgian waffle with Canadian maple syrup, but a peek down at his own burgeoning waistline gave Zivojinovich the fortitude to refuse. Minutes later, however, the idea of "the waffle that might have been" made his low-fat, low-carb breakfast seem less than satisfying.

He finished his meal shortly before eight o'clock and charged it to his room. Upstairs, the health spa was moderately busy with guests exercising, getting massages, or swimming in the heated saltwater pool. Though Wai Ying had gone directly to the spa after checking in the morning before, and had made a point of boasting how she almost never missed her morning workout, she was nowhere in sight. Neither was she in the pool, or in the steam rooms or the Jacuzzi.

It's a wonder she doesn't already have me running errands, he mused with a grin. Wai Ying had made quite an impression on him in St. Petersburg; clearly the woman was a personality to be reckoned with and not inclined to leave things to chance. That trait was what he liked best about her, even if he found her personal style to be extravagant to the point of imprudence.

A short while later he stepped off the elevator and walked toward the Lion's Head suite. The door was propped open by a housekeeper's cart. He slipped inside past the cart and nodded to the maid cleaning the bathroom. The rest of the suite was quiet. "Wai Ying?" he called, and was answered only by the faint echo of his own voice. Walking quickly, he made a quick survey of the suite; her things were still there, but she wasn't. He took his cell phone from his pocket and dialed her number. The call dumped directly to voice mail; her phone was either off, out of signal range . . . or no longer functional.

More than forty years of service in the spy business had made Zivojinovich paranoid, and that paranoia had saved his life many times over. He flipped his cell phone closed, picked up the receiver of a phone in the suite's foyer, and pressed O. The front desk operator answered, and at his request connected him to Logan's room.

The phone rang four times, then it, too, went to voice mail.

His next stop was his own room, where he retrieved his SIG-Sauer P226 pistol and shoulder holster from the room's safe. He covered the weapon by donning a black sports blazer, so as not to draw attention in public. Then he proceeded directly to Logan's room, taking the stairs rather than the elevator. He emerged from the stairwell, one hand resting on the grip of his sidearm. There was no one in the hallway, no sign of trouble. He unholstered his pistol and stepped briskly down the hall to Logan's door. Fixing both his hands on his weapon, he held it in front of him and pressed his ear to the door. All seemed quiet.

He stepped to the hinge side of the door and put his back to the wall. With his foot, he tapped three times on the door.

Inside the room, a shuffling sound was followed by a grunt. Soft footfalls drew closer, and the bright pinpoint of light through the peephole was eclipsed. Then he heard Logan's voice through the door: "Ziv? Is that you?"

"Yes," he replied. "Let me in."

Metal *clack*s accompanied the release of the door's multiple bolts and latches, then it cracked open to reveal Logan's bleary stare and hairy bare chest. "Ziv, it's too damn early for—"

"Wai Ying's missing," Zivojinovich said. Logan didn't respond right away, so the Russian continued, "I checked her room. All her things are there, but she's not. She doesn't answer her phone, and it dumps right to voice mail. Considering the kind of people we've been pissing off lately, I think we—"

The bathroom door inside Logan's room opened, and Wai Ying padded out, sleepy-eyed and barefoot and attired only in one of the hotel's complimentary white terry-cloth bathrobes.

Suddenly, Zivojinovich felt monumentally stupid.

He looked at Logan and struggled to find some way to backtrack or otherwise extricate himself from the situation with even a modicum of grace. Logan, for his part, said nothing, but his stare was enough to keep Zivojinovich silent as Logan let go of the door, which closed with a frame-rattling thud.

Zivojinovich holstered his weapon, straightened his jacket, and grimaced with embarrassment as he walked to the elevator. "Well," he said to himself, "at least that wasn't awkward."

Lunch later that day was exceptionally awkward.

Logan sat between Wai Ying and Ziv, who both kept their attention on the plates of food they'd barely touched. Not more than half a dozen sentences had passed between them since they met in front of the restaurant. Skipping breakfast had given Logan an appetite, however, and he was devouring a rare filet mignon and washing it down with neat whiskey.

Wai Ying sipped her water.

Ziv took a small bite of his lunch. "Good conch fritters," he muttered. Logan and Wai Ying both nodded mutely.

If I'd known everyone was gonna be this weird, Logan brooded, *I never woulda slept with her.*

Resting in the center of the table was Wai Ying's cell phone. A few times each minute, Wai Ying stared at it. Just as often, Ziv also eyed the phone. They were fixated on the small flip-top device, as if they could simply will it to ring.

Logan swallowed a large bite of meat, sipped his Maker's Mark, and set down the glass forcefully enough to get their attention. "Knock it off, will ya? You're makin' me edgy."

Wai Ying abashedly averted her eyes from the phone.

"Sorry," Ziv said.

It was a start. Logan returned to sawing off another chunk of his steak.

"We might want to switch hotels," Ziv said offhandedly. When he noticed Wai Ying's surprised glare, he added, "We don't need to watch the docks anymore, and this is a bit too high-profile to be safe."

Shaking her head, Wai Ying speared a forkful of salad. "We won't be here much longer. As soon as Xavier calls, we're gone."

"If he calls," Ziv grumbled.

"He'll call," Logan cut in, surprised at how quick he'd just been to defend Xavier, considering all that had happened.

Silence fell back over their table. Wai Ying picked through her salad, extracting the black olives and setting them aside. Ziv pushed a few pieces of his conch fritter to one side of his plate, then nudged them back to the other side. And they both kept trying to sneak glances at the cell phone.

"For Pete's sake," Logan said. "You look like you're

waiting for someone to ask you to the prom. Just eat your damn lunch." He picked up the phone and stretched in his seat so he could tuck it into his pocket. "When it's gonna ring, it'll—"

The phone rang.

He scowled at it then glanced at his companions as he flipped it open. "Hello?"

Xavier sounded weak, out of breath. "Pritikin's in Zibara," he said. "In Kaltoum, the capital."

Logan couldn't hide his concern. "Charles, are you okay?"

"It wasn't easy finding him, Logan. Keeping track of him now is difficult. Someone or something is trying to hide him."

The Hand, Logan surmised. Their magical abilities sometimes extended to shielding their thoughts. They were probably helping Pritikin remain incognito while he aided them in whatever plan they'd set in motion for Panacea.

Logan asked, "Where is he now, specifically?"

"In motion," Xavier said. "He just got off a private jet, at Kaltoum Airport. He'll be leaving Zibara later today."

"And going where?"

"I don't know," Xavier said. "His mind is masked." His voice faltered as he added, "I can't track him much longer."

"You don't have to," Logan said. "We'll take it from here." His next words were not as difficult to say as he'd expected them to be. "Thanks, Charles. I owe you."

"Good luck, Logan," Xavier said, then he hung up.

Logan closed the phone and lobbed it across the table to Wai Ying, who caught it in one hand. "Call your people in Osaka," Logan said. "We need tracking satellites pointed at Kaltoum Airport. We're looking for a private jet that arrived in the last hour. The professor says it'll be leaving later today."

"When? Going where?" she asked, as she flipped open the phone and pressed the speed dial.

"No idea," Logan said. "But once the satellites have a lock, we can run this op from upstairs."

Ziv looked as if he felt left out. "Can I do anything?"

"Sure," Logan said, as he pushed away his plate and stood up. "Get the check."

Back in the Lion's Head presidential suite, Logan watched over Ziv's shoulder as the older man clicked through scads of satellite data, which had been routed from the NRO to Wai Ying's laptop in less than an hour. On the one hand, Logan marveled at the amount of pull that she and Tanaka Biotechnology seemed to wield in the global intelligence community; on the other, he wondered just how many U.S. federal laws had been violated acquiring this intel.

"I've got Pritikin's plane," Ziv announced. With a click, he magnified the image on the screen. It was a sleek, gleaming white twin-turbofan jet. "Looks like they're refueling."

"Let's get the Cessna ready to go wheels-up ASAP," Logan said. "We're not losing this guy again."

"He's not getting away," Ziv said. "We've got a tracking network in place now. Wherever that plane goes, we'll see it."

"Not good enough," Logan said. "I want to be right behind that sonofabitch wherever he lands next."

Ziv looked over his shoulder at Logan. "What for? We can track him in the air and on the ground. We can let him lead us to the *Pandora*. Even if it's cloaked, we'll be able to see where he goes dark and pinpoint the coordinates."

Shaking his head, Logan replied, "Waiting's too risky. If we try to reach it after Pritikin's aboard, they'll see us coming long before we see them. Besides, there's no guarantee the ship won't move before we get there. If I'm gonna take it out, I have to strike as soon as we find it."

With a dubious expression, Ziv folded his arms and swiveled his chair in Logan's direction. "And how will you get aboard the ship? Hide in Pritikin's luggage? FedEx yourself? Trojan fish?"

"Trojan fish," Logan repeated. "That's a good one. I'll add it to my list of possibilities."

"In other words, you don't actually have a plan."

"Sure I do." He snicked off the end of a cigar with one claw. "Same plan as always."

"You mean you're making it up as you go," Ziv said.

Logan flipped open his Zippo and lit his cigar. "Exactly."

Wai Ying stepped out of the bedroom and set down her last two suitcases against the wall. "I just talked to the bell captain," she said. "The hotel staff is packing your bags for you. They'll be downstairs when we're ready to go." She walked over and joined them at the laptop. "Where's Pritikin now?"

"Somewhere in the Zibaran capital," Ziv said. "We couldn't get a fix on his ground transport, so we have to wait for him to come back to his plane before we pick up his trail."

Logan waited for Wai Ying to respond, but after several seconds of silence, he noticed that she was staring intently at the screen, her mien pensive. Finally, she looked at him and said, "It can't be a coincidence that he's in Zibara. Not now."

Logan didn't know what she was driving at. "How so?"

"He's an oil man," she said. "Geologists have been saying for years that they think there's an untapped reservoir of crude under Zibara, but no one's been able to find it. Meanwhile, Zibara has epidemic infection rates for both AIDS and malaria."

Now Logan understood. "And what better way to seal a deal for Zibara's oil than to take its people hostage with Panacea?" He frowned. "Ziv, set up a signal intercept on the land lines from the control tower at Kaltoum Airport. Pritikin's plane has to file a flight plan before it lifts off. As soon as we know where it's going, I want to be wheels-up inside the hour."

"You got it," Ziv said. He turned to the laptop and went immediately to work on the wiretaps. Logan gave him a fraternal pat on the shoulder, then turned and made for the door.

"Where are you going?" Wai Ying said.

"Down to the gift shop," Logan said with a dour look at Ziv. "I want to see if they have any Trojan fish."

16

KHALEED AL-RASHAD WAS NOT AN UNREASON-
able man. A lifelong civil servant, he had built his
entire career in government on the art of compromise, and on knowing which battles were worth
fighting. It had been three months since Prime Minister Qamran el-Fatah had named him to Zibara's
newest cabinet position, minister of petroleum resources. At the time, al-Rashad had thought it to be
the most fortunate promotion he had ever received.
Today, however, he was having the distinct misfor-
tune of making the acquaintance of Alexei Pritikin, a
Russian thug in an Armani suit.

"Bullshit," Pritikin said with a sneer as he flung

the folder of economic projections back across the negotiating table. "I'm not spending billions to build your pipeline. First you want to tax me to death for *finding* your oil, now you want me to subsidize your national infrastructure, too?"

"With all respect, Mr. Pritikin," al-Rashad replied, "as Zibara's sole oil contractor, you would be reaping the greatest profit from that pipeline. It's only fair that—"

"Screw you," Pritikin interrupted. "I'm not paying for your pipeline. You are. And while you're at it, you can cut the export tariff in half. I'm running a business, not a charity."

Pritikin was the owner and chief executive of Anbaric Petroleum, which had pinpointed the locations of Zibara's once elusive reservoirs of easily recoverable, high-grade crude oil. If Anbaric Petroleum was accurate in its estimate of the reserves' volume—just over 109 billion barrels' worth—Zibara was the third-most oil-rich nation on earth, behind only Saudi Arabia and Iraq.

Apparently, Pritikin believed that his geologists' fateful discovery somehow afforded him immunity from Zibara's laws. Minister al-Rashad was finding it extremely difficult to disabuse Pritikin of this flawed assumption.

"Mr. Pritikin," al-Rashad began in a carefully practiced, diplomatically neutral tone of voice. "I am aware that your oil-exploration contract with Zibara grants you unique privileges with regard to drilling rights, as well as substantial financial incentives. But I am also certain that it does not exempt you from taxation, nor does it restrict our authority to levy new taxes. In addition, it obligates you to absorb up to fifteen percent of costs related to—"

"I've read the damned contract," Pritikin said. "Hell, I wrote half of it. But that was then. The situation has changed, and our deal is changing with it."

Civility was becoming increasingly difficult for al-Rashad. "Perhaps this is how one conducts business in Russia, Mr. Pritikin, but in Zibara, men are decapitated for lesser offenses than the breaking of a national contract."

"Save your threats for someone who's afraid of you," Pritikin said as he rose from his chair. His retinue of lawyers and junior executives did likewise. "You're reducing the export tariff by half, and you'll finance the pipeline without my money." He closed his brushed-aluminum briefcase. "Furthermore, Anbaric Petroleum will be deducting its exploratory costs from its revenues until our investment is recouped." Pritikin marched out the door, trailed by his entourage.

Determined not to let the arrogant Russian have the last word, al-Rashad followed him. As he elbowed his way forward through the crowd of young men in dark gray suits, al-Rashad became fatigued; his forty-eight-year-old body felt older than its years. By the time he caught up to Pritikin, they were outside in the afternoon swelter, descending the broad stairs of the Interior Ministry toward Pritikin's waiting black limousine and its SUV escorts. Prismatic flares of sunlight reflected off all the vehicles' immaculately buffed exteriors.

"You arrogant bastard!" al-Rashad shouted at Pritikin's retreating back. "By tomorrow, your competitors will be making us rich! Can you outbid ExxonMobil? Or ChevronTexaco? How much do you think BP will pay for exclusive drilling rights? You'll never take one drop of oil from my country! That's a promise!"

Pritikin stopped at the back door of his limo and turned to face al-Rashad. Squinting into the glare of the sunlight, Pritikin smirked. "Spare me your threats," he said. "You're going to agree to every one of my demands."

Al-Rashad pushed himself nose-to-nose with the smug Russian. "And why would I do that?"

The oil mogul almost chuckled as he opened the car door. Out of the car leaped al-Rashad's ten-year-old son, Mustaf. "Father!" the boy cried with joy as he pushed past Pritikin and hugged al-Rashad around his legs. The youth's eyes were bright with hope, his embrace strong, his footing rock-solid.

Al-Rashad rested his hand on his son's head and tried to conceal his horror that Mustaf was walking at all.

Sixteen months ago the boy had been diagnosed with osteosarcoma—bone cancer, the doctor had explained to al-Rashad and his weeping wife, Parveen—in both femurs. Every protocol had failed to halt the progression of the disease, which had metastasized into the blood vessels and surrounding tissues of Mustaf's legs. Radiation therapy was not helping. Last night the doctors had suggested to al-Rashad that they consider amputating both legs while there was still a chance to save Mustaf's life.

Breaking the news to Parveen had been heart-rending. "Allah have mercy, Khaleed," she'd cried. "Allah have mercy on our son!" Now al-Rashad was staring at his healthy, smiling boy.

He looked accusingly at Pritikin. "Explain."

"It's called Panacea," Pritikin said. "It cures anything, as long as you keep taking it every day for the rest of your life. Fortunately, I have access to an unlimited supply." Pritikin motioned to his entourage to begin getting into their vehicles. Engines roared to life, and the humid summer air grew heavy with exhaust fumes. "Your son is now in perfect health," he continued, lowering his voice. "But if you don't meet my every demand before my plane leaves the ground in ninety minutes, the boy will never get another dose—and he'll be dead in less than seventy-two hours." He patted al-Rashad's cheek. "That's a *promise.*"

Pritikin tousled Mustaf's black hair, then got into

his limousine. As soon as the door slammed shut,
the car lurched from the curb and accelerated away
in a dusty nimbus, followed by its gleaming black
convoy of SUVs.

Watching the procession of vehicles race away, al-
Rashad clutched his son and wept in silence. He
knew that he had no choice; he would have to
endorse all of Pritikin's insane demands and con-
vince the prime minister to accept them.

He knew that he ought to thank Allah for his
son's life, but he couldn't . . . because that which had
made Mustaf whole had also made him into a slave.

17

EDDIE THE BARTENDER SET DOWN LOGAN'S braised lamb shank and crispy *pommes frites,* handed him a set of utensils wrapped in a napkin, then whisked away Logan's empty pint glass to refill it. With a flick of his wrist, Logan unfurled the napkin and caught the utensils with his free hand. Eddie had just brought back the refilled glass, and Logan had just begun cutting through a hunk of succulently tender meat, when Ziv barreled through the front door and halted at the threshold.

"We're rolling," he said.

Logan dropped his fork and knife on top of the bar as he stood up. He pulled a few hundred South

African rands from his pocket and slapped it down. "Keep the change, Eddie."

Eddie waved farewell to Logan, who followed Ziv out the door.

Ziv made a beeline to an idling, black-sapphire BMW Z4 convertible and vaulted over the door into the driver's seat. Not feeling quite so dramatic, Logan circled around to the passenger side and opened the door to get in. Before he finished closing the door, the two-seat sports car shot like a rocket down the busy city street.

"So I'm guessing we're in a hurry," Logan said over the growl of the engine and the roar of the wind.

"*Da,*" Ziv said.

The leather interior of the car smelled brand-new. A glance at the odometer confirmed that the car had less than six thousand kilometers on it. "Nice ride," Logan said. "Please don't tell me she put this on the corporate card."

"*Nyet,*" Ziv said. "Borrowed it from the hotel parking lot." Ziv yanked the wheel hard and whipped the roadster through a wild turn onto Eastern Boulevard, cutting off at least four other cars. Unlike most people Logan had ever met, Ziv tended to accelerate through turns instead of slowing down.

Logan pushed in the dashboard lighter and fished a robusto from his jacket's inside pocket. "What's going on?"

"Wai Ying's already at the airport," Ziv said as he swerved through a slow-moving knot of traffic. "Pritikin's plane filed a flight plan—they're en route to Murtala Airport in Lagos." A cacophony of car horns blared behind the Z4 as Ziv blew through a red light. "Customs'll clear our passports at the gate."

"Good to know," Logan said. The lighter popped out from the dash. He lit his cigar. "Can we catch up to Pritikin?"

Ziv whipped through a U-turn and cut off a line of cars on the N2 highway on-ramp. "*Nyet*. We can make Lagos in one hop, but we'll be about an hour behind him."

With the melodious precision of an opera singer, the Z4's engine changed its tune, rising and falling and climbing again, as Ziv pushed the car to its maximum speed on the highway. The risks that came with moving at that velocity didn't bother Logan, but he was irked that the gusting wind was rapidly devouring his cigar. He tapped a few centimeters of gray ash from its end and watched it scatter into the car's airstream.

Although the day had started out sunny, the sky was now growing overcast. The soot-dark bellies of storm clouds hung low overhead, promising a downpour. Logan exhaled a puff from his cigar. "Great flying weather," he said.

"This?" Ziv flashed a broad grin. "Try landing a Piper Comanche at José Martí International in the middle of a Category Four, while drunk on Two Fingers tequila." He waved dismissively at the leaden sky. "This is *nothing*."

Logan shook his head and almost laughed. "Whatever you say, Ziv. Whatever you say."

Oskar watched through his binoculars as the ground crew prepared the Tanaka corporate jet for takeoff at the East Hangar of Cape Town International. The fuel lines had been disconnected and put away, the wheel chocks were being removed, and the Asian woman who had thwarted them in Brazil was pacing beside the jet, talking on her phone, and checking her watch every ten seconds.

He and Gregor were concealed in an ancillary hangar that was part of the Aviation Center, across a taxiway from the East Hangar. While Oskar stood in the narrow gap between the towering hangar doors, peeking out through the field glasses, Gregor sat behind him on a Ducati motorcycle, slumped forward onto the handlebars, moaning through his hangover.

Though Oskar had pleaded with the flight attendants on the flight from São Paulo not to serve Gregor alcohol, his request had been ignored. Gregor had waited until Oskar went to the lavatory; during that brief interval Gregor had bribed the attendants into selling him more than twenty shots of vodka, which he'd promptly imbibed, knocking himself unconscious. Oskar had smelled the cheap spirits on Gregor's breath when he'd returned to his seat. Hours later, Gregor had awoken violently ill and vomiting into his own lap when the plane touched down in Cape Town. Oskar had not shown him the least degree of pity.

Gregor sat up, belched, and spit a thick wad of milky saliva onto the hangar's concrete floor. His voice was hoarse from vomiting. "Let's just frag the plane now," he said.

"No," Oskar said. "We wait for Wolverine to get on the plane. Take it out during liftoff."

"That's the dumbest thing I've ever heard," Gregor said. "I can barely see it standing still, and you want me to hit it when it's going over three hundred kilometers an hour? *Tvoyu mat.*"

"Takeoff is when they'll be most vulnerable," Oskar said.

Gregor fished one last tiny bottle of airplane vodka from his pants pocket and twisted off the cap. "Doesn't matter how vulnerable they are if I can't hit them." He downed the shot. "As soon as Wolverine shows up, I'm frying them."

Oskar frowned at his disheveled mess of a brother. "Are you sure you can hit them from here?"

"Give me enough juice and I'll just have to be close."

"That's not encouraging," Oskar groused.

Another glob of spit hit the floor behind Oskar's

feet. "So much for my career in motivational speaking," Gregor said.

The sound of a sports-car engine echoed off the clustered buildings of the Aviation Center. A black BMW Z4 roadster turned off Beechcraft Road and veered toward the East Hangar. It screeched to a halt in front of the Cessna Thunderstar. Two men clambered out and walked toward the Asian woman. One of the men was Wolverine; the other Oskar had never seen before.

Lowering the binoculars, Oskar looked back at his twin. "They're here," he said. He stepped over to the circuit-breaker station. As soon as the wire cutters were in place to put him in touch with the electrical main, he nodded to Gregor, who turned the ignition key of the Ducati. It purred to life; then, with a twist of its throttle, it roared like a steel tiger.

Gregor put on his helmet and flashed an evil grin. "Juice me up, Oskar. It's showtime."

Logan was out of the BMW the moment it came to a halt. Ziv followed a half-second behind him, and together they walked quickly toward Wai Ying. She flipped her cell phone closed and raised her voice above the whine of the Cessna's engines. "That was Setsuko," she said. "They've identified the mole: a senior chemist named Jiro Kazaki."

Ziv asked, "Will he talk?"

"Not likely," Wai Ying said. "They found him in his apartment with his head cut off."

Logan frowned. "That's the Hand's idea of a retirement program." He nodded with his chin toward the Cessna. "Ready to fly?"

"We will be," Wai Ying said, "as soon as Ziv moves his midlife-crisis-mobile out of the way." She turned and started climbing the jet's fold-down stairs.

With a long-suffering shake of his head and a roll of his eyes, Ziv turned around and jogged back toward the Z4. Logan glanced in Ziv's direction as he moved to follow Wai Ying into the jet—then he saw a man on a motorcycle on the far side of the taxiway. The motorcyclist's hand was pointed in their direction and surrounded by a crackling halo of electricity.

Ziv's pistol was clearing its holster as Logan shouted to Wai Ying, "Shield!"

The BMW exploded in a yellowish-white fireball. Ziv's body disintegrated in the flash. Burning gasoline and glowing-hot debris slammed into Logan. His shirt shriveled and turned to ash. Airborne from the force of the blast, he tumbled wildly, then slammed facedown and slid hard across the tarmac. Fire cooked his skin and vaporized his hair, leaving behind only a sickening, acrid stench.

Nothing was left of his world but shadows and agony.

Waves of noise pounded in his head, like the crash of the ocean inside his skull. From somewhere far beyond the wall of sound came the crackle of flames and the shrill timbre of a panicked voice shouting his name. He tried to turn his head and get his bearings, only to discover that his eyelids had been cooked shut. His fingers curled in on his palms like dead spiders. A million blistering needles stabbed across his body, belatedly delivering the news that he had been burned alive. His face was pulled taut in a death's mask rictus of pain.

There was only rage now. Fury and darkness. The animal urge to survive, to pull free of a trap, to retaliate.

Brittle skin cracked and flaked and bled as he forced himself to crawl. The odor of his own flesh was sickly sweet in his nostrils. His mutant healing factor was sluggish, overtaxed.

All he wanted was to scream, to howl, to roar. Instead, hot air hissed in his throat—dry and soundless, wordless, empty and hollow, as primal and as inchoate as his suffering.

High-pitched and louder now, the voice of panic was bright in his mind, but words were too much, too difficult. His skin was on fire; his muscles twitched with violent spasms as he pulled himself over the unyielding ground.

Thunderclaps and flashes of lightning. The wrath of the gods was close now, so close.

As he dragged his charred body across the tarmac, he felt bloody pieces of himself being left behind, chunks of flesh cooked off his bones.

His left eye cracked open, and he forced it wide. Through a milky-red haze he recognized the familiar shape of the plane above him and, inside it, the watery outline of a woman beckoning frantically for him to come to her.

She was the one shouting. She was afraid.

Blinding light, like the sun pulled down from the heavens, surrounded the plane with a terrible booming. Heat washed over Logan's body, renewing the torture of his broiled flesh. The clarity of pain resurrected his voice in disjointed grunts and splutters as he clawed his way up the short staircase into the jet. A groan became a snarl and then a howl, and then swelled into a battle roar.

His right eye pulled open, just as watery and bloody as the left one had been half a minute ago. Coherence forced its way back into his thoughts, self-awareness reasserted itself.

Christ, I'm growing new eyes.

Wai Ying's voice was both strident and fearful. "Logan, do you understand what I'm saying? Answer me!"

He coughed out a mouthful of blood and phlegm. "I . . . hear you."

A nerve-rattling blast rocked the plane, and Wai Ying's composure with it. She stood with her arms out to her sides, palms open and facing out, obviously fighting to shield the plane from the energy assault. "You have to fly the plane," she said, then gasped in pain and exhaustion. "I can't shield it and fly at the same time."

Lying on the deck of the passenger cabin, skin

scorched into charcoal, his face and head and body all burned clean of hair, his clothes reduced to sooty rags . . . Logan almost laughed. "You've gotta be—"

"On your feet, soldier!" she snapped at him. "Get off the deck and close that goddamn hatch! *Now!*"

Hearing the order was like having a switch flipped inside his brain. Suddenly he was back in boot camp, all those decades ago, being conditioned by a Canadian Army drill sergeant, being infused with military discipline. An order was an order.

Red pulses of agony darkened his vision as he pushed himself onto his knees and then pulled himself to his feet. He found the automatic closing mechanism for the hatch and pressed it. With a hydraulic whine, it lifted shut.

"Get this bird in the air, soldier! Do it!"

Stumbling and weaving like a drunk, he caromed off the thickly padded seats, leaving dark blood smears as he went. He lumbered forward into the cockpit, where he fell backward into the pilot seat and landed heavily and off-center. His hands found the yoke by instinct, but he couldn't read the bright screens of instrument data. *Doesn't matter,* he decided. He shoved the throttle forward. The jet rolled toward the taxiway.

Another explosion of light and heat rebounded from the unseen barrier in front of the plane. Logan shielded his eyes with his forearm, which he now saw was still smoldering.

The jet reached the taxiway. Logan steered it to the right, toward the approach to the airport's main runway. Outside, the man on the motorcycle was accelerating forward in pursuit. Logan turned and looked back at Wai Ying. "Behind us."

She nodded feebly. Logan's vision had cleared enough that he could see she was weakened and bleeding from her nose. Each energy blast took a gruesome toll on her. Their only hope was to lift off and get above the cloud cover, where they could evade the fireballer's line-of-sight attacks.

The deafening percussion of multiple impacts followed the plane down the long taxiway. The safe taxi speed was posted at twelve knots; Logan pushed the Cessna to twenty knots and hoped no one pulled out in front of him. He crossed three taxiway intersections at full speed without incident and guided the jet through a slight right turn—against posted directions for aircraft movement—toward the main runway.

The Cessna jerked forward, jolted by the increasingly powerful blasts from their attacker. Logan closed his leathery, cracked, bleeding hand on the throttle. He increased the aircraft's ground speed to forty knots as he steered it left onto the main runway, then he pushed its turbofans to full thrust as he aligned the nose of the jet with the runway's center line for takeoff.

Fifty knots. Sixty. Seventy. The center line became a blur.

A jarring impact hammered the plane from behind. Logan fought to keep from losing control. His skin and muscles were knitting back together even now, and it felt as if his body were squirming with barbed fishing hooks. He winced against the pain.

When he opened his eyes again a second later, his vision was clear—and so was his view of the Boeing 767 cargo aircraft descending toward the runway ahead of him.

The Cessna hit a hundred and twenty knots. It was too late to stop. Logan's only hope was to increase his speed and try to slip under the 767 before it touched down, and pray that its pilots were able to see him and pull up.

A hundred and thirty knots: thirty-five more for the Cessna to reach takeoff velocity. He pushed the jet to its limit.

The hulking mass of the 767 loomed large outside the windshield. Tracking its descent against his acceleration, Logan realized that he wasn't going to make it. The Cessna was at a hundred and sixty knots; he suddenly regretted all the times he'd said he'd rather be cremated than buried, because it looked as if he was about to get his wish.

Then the massive cargo aircraft's nose lifted. Wavy curtains of heat distortion shimmered behind it as its pilots struggled to climb over the Cessna Thunderstar.

Logan was about to call himself the luckiest canucklehead on earth when a massive red pulse of energy sliced over the Cessna and obliterated the 767.

A mountain of blazing wreckage and tons of decimated cargo dropped onto the runway in front of him. He pulled back hard on the yoke. The nose of the Cessna lifted, and the sleek business jet lanced through the bloom of orange flames and roiling black smoke. Its twin turbofans sputtered and whined in the heart of the fire cloud, then surged back to life as the jet broke through into open air. Its airspeed climbed rapidly—two hundred knots, then two hundred fifty. Numbers ticked swiftly higher on the digital altimeter. A few more blasts trembled the aircraft as it neared the low-lying clouds. As soon as the gray vapors embraced the plane, Logan banked left while continuing to climb. After a minute without more hits from below, he leveled their flight.

"We're clear," he said to Wai Ying, whose arms fell slack at her sides. She slumped forward and collapsed to the deck, drained of every last bit of strength and willpower.

Clutching the Cessna's yoke like a life preserver, Logan knew exactly how she felt.

Oskar sat on his idling motorcycle and waited for his brother.

Crooked pillars of smoke drifted and twisted away

from the Aviation Center, toward the runway. Across the taxiway, small gasoline fires burned amid the car debris and black, carbonized soot. The humid air was heavy with fumes.

Sirens wailed, bleated, shrilled in the distance, grew louder. People were evacuating the Aviation Center and the East Hangar. Fire alarms rang steadily inside both buildings.

To the west, a couple of kilometers away, a gargantuan black mushroom cloud bled upward and spread across the dreary gray canvas of the sky. Oskar had felt his brother unleash a massive burst of energy a moment before the explosion that had spawned that terrifying plume of darkness.

The soft buzz of Gregor's motorcycle echoed ahead of him, off the walls of the hangar buildings, before he emerged from behind a corner and rejoined Oskar on the taxiway near the East Hangar. Gregor slowed quickly and rolled to a stop beside him.

Oskar noted his brother's scowl and knew the news wasn't going to be good. "They got away?"

"Lost them in the clouds," Gregor muttered as the shrieks of police sirens closed in.

"Then that explosion—"

"Cargo plane," Gregor said. "Tried to block the runway."

So much for making it look like an accident, Oskar brooded. "All the exits are closed," he said. "First responders are moving in."

Gregor was openly sarcastic. "Really? I was wondering what all those sirens were for. Thanks for the tip."

"The police are looking for us," Oskar said, waving his pocket-sized police radio scanner at Gregor. "Apparently, a few thousand people inside the airport saw a man on a motorcycle shooting at the planes." He tucked the radio back in his pocket. "The helicopters will arrive shortly, followed by every anti-terrorist commando in Cape Town."

"What the hell was I supposed to do, Oskar? The girl with the force shields is tougher than I thought." His fists balled with frustration. "If I'd just had one more shot—"

"It's too late," Oskar said. "We're burned in Cape Town. I've called the daimyo for an extraction."

That brought Gregor up short. "You did *what?* Are you out of your goddamn mind? He'll kill us."

"Probably," Oskar replied, knowing that it was true. He revved the throttle of his Ducati and moved it into gear. "We're meeting him inside the auxiliary hangar in two minutes. Let's go." With a twist of his hand, he accelerated away. A moment later he heard the drone of Gregor's motorcycle following him.

They slipped through the narrowly open doors of the auxiliary hangar and veered left to a stop in the shadows. Both cycles' engines went quiet in a breath as they disengaged the ignitions. Oskar got off his bike and abandoned his helmet on the concrete hangar floor. He sat down on a crate and checked his watch; roughly thirty seconds remained until Mr. Harada would appear courtesy of his teleportation ring and pluck the twin mutants out of harm's way.

Looking back, he saw Gregor casting his eyes around the cavernous space, as if seeking something.

"What are you looking for?" Oskar inquired.

"A power source," Gregor said. "You'd better juice me up in case the boss is in a bad mood."

Oskar checked his watch: ten seconds to extraction. "If the boss is in a bad mood," he said, "it won't make any difference."

Within an hour after leaving Cape Town, Logan's body had repaired and rebuilt enough of his flesh for him to be in constant, torturous pain. Dry, desiccated hunks of skin sloughed off his forearms as rapidly regenerating dermis displaced it from below. The hair on his chest and arms grew so quickly that he could watch it get longer. And he knew that his facial and cranial hair was reëmerging because of the persistent, maddening itch that crawled over his scalp and the nape of his neck.

Reaching back to scratch, his hand separated from the plane's controls with a wet sucking noise. The handles of the Cessna's yoke were sticky with his dried blood and partially liquefied fatty tissue. A charnel odor hung thick and disgusting inside the confines of the jet. *Cleaning this up will be fun.*

The pain that burned across the entire surface of his body, though it was scathing and omnipresent, was almost manageable now. It added fire to his rage, and venom to his vow of revenge on the men who'd killed Ziv. He hadn't seen the second twin on the ground at the airport, but he remembered how Wai Ying had said they'd worked together in Foz do Iguaçu. The second man had been there somewhere. Logan was certain of it.

Ahead of the Cessna, puffy banks of clouds were stacked miles high, like organic sculptures of dirty cotton. The sapphire dome of the sky darkened to indigo high overhead. Forty thousand feet below, fleetingly glimpsed through mist-smeared gaps in the white skyscape, were the greenish-brown smudges of central Africa, creeping slowly under the Cessna's nose.

Wai Ying entered the cockpit in halting, unsteady steps. Resting her hand on the back of the copilot's seat for balance, she eased herself into it with the gingerly caution of the recently injured. Her nose had stopped bleeding. A patina of dried blood covered her upper lip and chin—dark brown, caked, and cracking like a thirsty riverbed. With bloodshot eyes she checked the instrument dashboard, then, apparently satisfied, slumped back into her seat. "You look messed up," she said.

"You've looked better, too."

She half smiled, then lowered her eyes as sadness dimmed her countenance. "I'm sorry about Ziv."

"Don't be," Logan said. "He lived like a soldier, and he died like one—on his feet."

She brushed a few stray locks of her tousled black hair from her face. "It just seems like a horrible way to die."

"Worse than some," Logan said. "Better than others. It was fast." He felt his own jaw tighten with anger. "What pisses me off is that he got iced by a couple of scumbags. Ambushed, like a punk in the street."

Conversation was scarce for a little while. Silence suited Logan just fine. Wai Ying busied herself checking their position and plugging numbers into the onboard computer. Logan focused on keeping the jet steady and true to its course. Finally, she sighed, with what sounded like both exhaustion and frustration. "We're losing time," she said. "Pritikin'll be on the ground at Murtala almost two hours ahead of us."

"I was afraid of that," Logan said. He looked up and around at the cockpit. "We've been feeling a bit weak on thrust ever since boom boy lit us up in Cape Town."

Wai Ying nodded. "That's part of it. I also usually project a conical force field ahead of the plane to reduce wind resistance and improve our fuel efficiency." Wiping some of the dried blood from her lip, she added, "I really don't feel up to it right now, though."

"We can't risk losing him in Lagos," Logan said. "If he pulls another vanishing act before I pick up his scent—"

She cut in, "I know, Logan. With the parts they acquired in Brazil, and the time they've had since then, there's no telling how much Panacea they've manufactured by now." After a momentary hesitation, she asked, "When you said 'pick up his scent,' you were speaking figuratively, right?"

"Take it any way you like," Logan replied. "But we have to catch up to Pritikin on the ground."

A devilish gleam enlivened her eyes. "Then we'll just have to make sure we know where to find him when we get there." She reached forward and picked up the copilot's headset from the second yoke. As she put it on, she was punching numbers into the radio communications interface.

He started to ask, "What are you—"

She silenced him with a show of her palm. A moment later, she was speaking into her headset mic, to someone on the ground.

"Operator? Patch me through to the NDLEA in Lagos, please." After a short delay, she continued. "Hello? I'd like to report a shipment of sixty-one kilos of Afghan heroin that will be trafficked through Murtala Airport in approximately ninety minutes. . . . Yes, I'll hold. Thank you."

Logan cocked a half-regenerated eyebrow at her. "Heroin?"

She shrugged. " 'Go with what works,' my dad always said." Looking away, she switched back to her conversation with the authorities on the ground. "Yes, that's right. . . . It's a Gulfstream G550, registry Roger Alpha 4573 Kilo. . . . The heroin is hidden in the passenger compartment. . . . There's also forty-six million dollars in laundered U.S. currency notes in the hold." The person on the other end peppered her with questions, to which she rolled her eyes, then replied simply, "They're not planning on staying in Murtala for more than an hour. I suggest you get moving." Then she cut the channel.

"You do realize that Nigeria's one of the most corrupt countries on earth," Logan said. "They don't give a damn about drug smuggling."

Wai Ying took off her headset. "I know." She rested the headset back on the yoke in front of her. "But they *will* give a damn if a rich white foreigner— who *hasn't* paid them a bribe—lands in their country with sixty keys of smack and a brick of cash big enough to build a boat."

"You fight dirty," Logan said. "I approve."

"It's an art." Reclining her seat, she added, "That'll keep him busy in Lagos long enough for you to 'pick up his scent.' "

Logan smirked with appreciation. "You keep this up, I might just marry you all over again."

"Promises, promises," she said, and drifted off to sleep.

18

THOUGH THE NIGERIAN OFFICERS SOUNDED to Pritikin as if they were speaking English, they didn't seem capable of understanding a single word that came out of his mouth. "How many times do I have to tell you? There are no drugs on my plane!"

His jet had been allowed to land without incident or warning, and a towing car had arrived promptly to guide it into the refueling area near the short-term hangars. The moment his pilot had powered down the Gulfstream's turbofans, however, a wall of blinding halogen floodlamps had snapped on, bathing the jet in white light so intense that it seemed to have physical substance. Then fists had begun pounding on the outside of the hatch, and angry voices repeated the same phrase, over and over: "Federal police! Open up!"

Pritikin's first assumption was that this was all just a misunderstanding, or a case of mistaken identity. He had kept on thinking that until the officer in charge, a man by the name of Colonel Mfume, addressed him by name. "Alexei Pritikin!" Mfume had bellowed. "You are under arrest!" Pritikin had been forced to his knees with his hands on his head, and from there he'd been pushed facedown on the deck of his own private jet by a boot on his neck and the muzzle of a submachine gun at his head.

He and his entourage—pilots, bodyguards, prostitutes—had then been escorted off the plane one at a time and "processed"—a polite way of saying they'd been photographed and fingerprinted. Separated from the others, each passenger on the plane had his or her very own interrogator. Pritikin wondered if the other investigators were as dense as the one he was stuck talking to.

"Why don't you just tell us where the drugs are?" Mfume asked him, as though this was the most reasonable thing in the world. "The sooner we find what we're looking for, the easier this will be for you."

"There are no drugs on my damn plane," Pritikin said, unable to hold his temper in check. "No laundered cash, no drugs. Get it?" He'd been repeating this for nearly two hours. He clung to the slim hope that Mfume might begin to grasp what he was telling him any moment now.

Mfume, still doing a very good impersonation of a calm and reasonable man, nodded at Pritikin's statement, then summoned over one of his subordinates. "Start opening up the fuselage," he instructed the younger man.

Pritikin just couldn't stand it any longer. "Have you lost your mind?" He bolted up from his chair and was swiftly confronted by a line of large, brutish-looking Nigerian federal policemen. "You can't just rip holes in my plane!"

"Of course we can," Mfume explained. "We're the police."

He heard the sound of people descending the stairs of his jet. Hoping that the search might be over, he looked back—and saw that the uniformed men leaving his jet were carrying cardboard boxes that they'd loaded with every bit of loose personal property inside the plane. Jackets, dishware, electronic devices like phones and cameras, even the booze and mixers from his wet bar.

"You *yebani v rot,*" Pritikin muttered. "You don't know who you're pissing off here. When I get done with you, you'll—"

"Threatening a police officer?" Mfume looked amused. "I didn't give you enough credit. You're braver than I thought."

A stunning blow hit Pritikin square in the center of his upper back, between his shoulder blades. The wind was knocked out of his lungs, and his legs abandoned him to gravity. In a hazy swish-pan of motion he was on the ground. Handcuffs closed with an icy click around his wrists and bit into his skin.

From a few meters away, he heard bottles smash. It was all so Kafkaesque that he began to laugh. He couldn't help it.

Mfume looked curious. "Is something funny, Mr. Pritikin?"

"Yes," Pritikin replied between huffs of laughter. "I'm going to have you killed, you ignorant *sko-tolozhets.*"

The Nigerians probably didn't understand what he'd called them, but one of them kicked him in the back of the head anyway. Pritikin was almost grateful to be relieved of consciousness.

Even from the air, Pritikin's jet had been easy for Logan to spot amid the sprawl of Murtala Airport. It was the one surrounded by a few dozen uniformed Nigerian federal police, a squad of drug-sniffing German shepherds, and a phalanx of floodlights. The entire scene was as bright as high noon in the Sahara, a white-hot beacon demanding attention in the otherwise unbroken curtain of night that had descended, humid and oppressive, upon Lagos.

Logan and Wai Ying observed the chaos around Pritikin's plane as their Cessna Thunderstar was towed slowly into a short-term hangar. Through their cockpit windshield they could still see Pritikin himself for a few more moments; he was on the tarmac and shouting, red-faced, at the Nigerian officer in charge. Pritikin seemed to pay no heed to the officers facing him in a skirmish line, hands resting on their submachine guns.

"He looks unhappy," Logan quipped.

"Very," agreed Wai Ying.

As their plane entered its hangar, they left the cockpit and moved back into the passenger cabin. They sat down across from each other and watched the fracas through the windows.

A procession of Nigerian police exited Pritikin's Gulfstream. Each officer carried a box of assorted loose items from inside the plane. Since none of it was likely to be the fictitious heroin that Wai Ying had reported, Logan could only assume that they were using the search as an excuse to loot the plane of anything that wasn't bolted to the fuselage. Not surprisingly, Pritikin seemed rather irate about their behavior. One of the uniformed officers responded by using his nightstick to club Pritikin on the back, between his shoulder blades.

Wai Ying winced in sympathy. "That had to hurt."

"Not nearly as much as it should've," Logan said.

Pritikin dropped to his knees, then pitched forward onto his hands. The officer who had struck him down handcuffed him.

"Well, that's a shame," Wai Ying deadpanned.

The last officer leaving Pritikin's plane tripped and dropped a box filled with bottles of scotch, which shattered on the tarmac. "No," Logan corrected her, "*that* was a shame."

One of the Nigerians kicked Pritikin in the head, knocking him unconscious. "Looks like he's out of action for a while," Wai Ying said.

Logan shook his head and got up. "Don't count on it. If I know the Hand, they already know he's running late. I bet he'll be free in less than fifteen minutes."

She followed him to the hatch. "A rescue op?"

"No, a legal one," Logan said. "Like most criminals, the Hand has a lot of lawyers on the payroll."

The hatch opened with a soft hiss and lowered with a hydraulic whine. "What's our next move?" Wai Ying asked.

"Get our plane refueled," Logan said. "Depending on how I do tailing Pritikin to the *Pandora*, we might need to move again in a hurry."

"Hold on," she said. "How *you* do?"

"No offense, ace," Logan said. "You're good in a stand-and-fight, but this is a different ball game. I have to go alone."

He braced himself for her counterargument, which he figured would be particularly vitriolic.

Instead, she handed him a cell phone. "It's my spare," she said. "Speed-dial five to call me."

Logan closed his hand around the phone and nodded to her. "I will." He tried to tuck the phone in his pants pocket, then he realized he was wearing a tattered, fire-shriveled set of rags. He motioned toward the outside. "I'll grab some new clothes on my way out." Eager to avoid excess sentiment, he descended the stairs into the dimly lit hangar.

He ducked under the wing to the baggage compartment hatch and opened it. After shuffling aside a few bags, he found his duffel, opened it, and retrieved a pair of jeans and a pullover sweater, both black. He dressed quickly, choosing to forgo shoes. Stepping back as he closed the baggage hatch, his foot landed on a slick patch. From the odor, Logan knew that it was old motor oil. *That'll do,* he decided. He reached down and ran his fingers through it, then smeared the black greasy liquid over the tops of his feet; he finished with a broad, four-finger diagonal pull across his face, which he knew would make for a fine, organic-looking camouflage pattern. The excess he rubbed over his hands. As for the smell . . . where he was going, it would likely fit right in. *Time to go to work.*

On his way out he passed the Cessna's open hatch, where Wai Ying still stood, watching him. "Be careful," she said.

Logan turned back and permitted himself a wan half-smile in her direction. "Not really my style."

•   •   •

Motion was a blessing for Logan, a sacrament under cover of darkness. Set free from the measured caution of human behavior, he trod silently on the borderline between the human and the animal, summoning the darker aspect of his soul, the core of his being that owed its allegiance to the primeval hunter within.

He kept his claws hidden. Stealth was the order of the moment. Concealed behind the stacks of cheap wooden crates, he was on the hunt. His blood rose with the moon as he circled closer to his prey. As he'd expected, lawyers—sent by either the Hand or the *yakuza*—had extricated Pritikin from the Nigerian federal police with stunning alacrity. Whatever threats had been made had been sufficient to scare the cops into giving Pritikin a wide berth as he walked tall out of their custody.

Trailing him back to the hangars was invigorating. Pritikin's scent was fresh and lingering, a blend of musk cologne and sweat laced with the perfume of metabolized scotch, Italian wool and leather, a hint of blood on his breath from the beating he'd taken a short time ago.

It was so very raw. So tangible.

He followed Pritikin into the cargo warehouse. While his prey walked right up the broad central aisle, Logan slipped into the stacks and scaled one to watch from the shadows above.

Inside the cargo facility Pritikin moved purposefully, trailed by his retinue and attended by men who wore coveralls and carried clipboards. The Russian strode quickly from crate to crate, tapping those he desired, and squads of cargo workers rushed to haul them onto a pallet or mark them with ink for future pickup.

His instructions to the foreman were quick and curt.

"A hundred more liters of this.

"Get five more of these.

"Pack this last.

"Cover those markings.

"Put this in storage.

"Destroy that manifest when you're done. No copies."

Through it all, the foreman nodded, his expression serious and his mouth pressed resolutely shut, as if he feared letting even a stray sound escape. Pritikin waved him away and beckoned over a pilot, who dutifully jogged to him. "Yes, sir?"

"As soon as the Chinook's loaded, we're going," Pritikin said. "Get the EC ready." The pilot nodded and jogged away.

Logan shifted his position so he could better reconnoiter the scene. From his new vantage point, he espied a Chinook CH-47F cargo helicopter hovering outside the warehouse, beyond the stack of crates opposite his position. The enormous chopper appeared to be a military-surplus bird modified for civilian use. Its rotors were already turning at near full speed, primed to depart at any moment. A small forklift was loading pine crates onto a pallet inside a slack cargo net beneath the Chinook.

A few dozen meters away from the Chinook's net was another helicopter; it was smaller, a passenger chopper. Based on the design of the airframe around the tail rotor, Logan surmised that it was a Eurocopter EC-135. The pilot to whom Pritikin had spoken returned to this bird, clambered into the pilot's seat, and started throwing switches. Seconds later its rotors turned sluggishly, then gradually gained speed as the Eurocopter's engine warmed up. Apparently, Pritikin planned to leave soon.

Taking a moment to think, Logan became painfully aware of his body still adjusting itself to his demands. Regenerating this much muscle tissue always left him feeling stiff. Growing back all his hair at once meant enduring a pervasive, relentless itching, especially on his scalp and face, and in his groin. Rather than ignore it, he made every effort to funnel the constant irritation into his growing reservoir of rage.

Options looked to be scarce at the moment. He couldn't really hope to blend in with the Nigerian ground crew, which ruled out walking up to the helicopters to stow away. Getting too close would get him noticed by Pritikin, who certainly knew Logan's face by now. Head-on was definitely the wrong approach.

As soon as Pritikin left the warehouse, the mood became palpably less tense. Lurking atop one of the stacks, Logan noticed that three of the cargo handlers immediately abandoned their duties and slipped away to a secluded nook in the mountain of boxes. The tallest one produced a pair of dice from one of his pockets and a fistful of cash from the other. His two compatriots also fished rolls of cash from their coveralls and flanked the man with the dice as he gave a puff of breath on the ivories and prepared to make his throw. Logan climbed down behind them.

A flick of the wrist sent the cubes tumbling across the pitted gray concrete floor. They bounced off Logan's oil-blackened foot and came to rest, a pair of lonely dots faceup. "Snake eyes," Logan said with a grin. "Tough luck."

If any one of the three saw the hits that knocked them unconscious, they gave no sign of it. Logan scooped up their cash and climbed back atop the crates, liberated to the shadows.

Surveying the warehouse, Logan saw just what he'd expected: the one guy who hadn't been invited to the craps game, doing all the work, moving crates to the Chinook. The skinny young man—he couldn't have been much older than nineteen, Logan guessed—drove the forklift clumsily, like someone who was teaching himself by trial and error. The man set down the pallet, already heavy with four crates, near one of the last two boxes to be shipped. Struggling with a crowbar to lift it enough to kick a wedge underneath, he grunted and groaned in frustration and pain.

At last he got the wedge under the crate, propping up its edge so that he could get the forks under it to put it on the pallet. He heaved a tired breath, rested the crowbar on his shoulder, and stepped backward—and halted as Logan's claws pressed against his back. "Please don't kill me," the kid whispered. "Natubo sent you, right? You came for the Semtex? It's in the janitor's closet, under—"

Logan shushed him. With terrifying slowness, he extended another lone claw in front of the man's bare, dark throat. He kept his voice low and menacing. "What's your name, kid?"

Shaking with fear, the man said, "Wathiongo."

"Pay attention, Wathiongo. You can get paid, or you can get killed. Your call. Choose."

One fear-shaken breath later, Wathiongo replied, "Paid."

"Smart choice." Logan removed his claw from the man's throat. "Here's what's gonna happen. You're gonna put me in this box, then you're gonna put this box in the Chinook's net. Follow me so far, kid?" The man nodded. "As soon as you do that, I'll cut myself an air hole and pass you this wad of cash." He reached over Wathiongo's shoulder and showed him the massive roll of money he'd taken from the gamblers. Then he put it back in his pocket. "Rat me out—" He plucked the crowbar from Wathiongo's grasp and tossed it straight up. As it fell, he lashed out with his free set of claws and sliced the iron tool into four pieces—two long and two short. The metal pieces clanged brightly across the cement floor. "And I'll cut your head off. Get the picture?"

Wathiongo nodded quickly.

"All right," Logan said. He retracted his claws and slapped Wathiongo fraternally on the back. "Let's get to work."

The inside of the pine shipping crate was cramped and left Logan almost no room to move, not even to shift his weight. Every bump and wobble of the imbalanced and overloaded forklift felt like a tectonic shift inside the box, which bobbled on the forks as it was moved out to the Chinook's cargo net.

Barely audible over the Chinook's rotor noise, the forklift's hydraulic motor whined as it deposited the crate with the rest of the shipment. A jarring bump heralded the crate's touchdown on the pallet. Voices overlapped outside, and he heard someone say, "What are you doing?"

Wathiongo answered, "Securing the crates."

"All right, make it fast," the first voice said.

Chains clanked over and around the box, followed quickly by the dull *thwap* of elastic cargo netting being pulled taut around the stack of cargo. Then came a soft knocking on the outside of the box—two short taps, a pause, then two more. It was Wathiongo signaling the all-clear.

Logan partially extended one claw, pressed it against the center pine board on one side, and rotated his wrist back and forth until, seconds later, he'd drilled through. Without a word, he pushed the roll of cash through the hole and felt it plucked away. Then receding footsteps, and the rumble of the fork-lift motor growing quieter with distance.

The Chinook's rotors increased speed; the pounding noise was deafening. Logan peeked through the hole he'd drilled. He had a clear view, facing in the direction of flight. Ahead of them, the Eurocopter made its steady vertical ascent. The horizon dipped and wavered as the Chinook hefted its load into the air, then steadied itself. Moments later, the Chinook fell in directly behind the Eurocopter, which was all but invisible in the darkness, nothing more than a set of flashing lights against the curtain of night.

Away we go, Logan mused, trying not to dwell on the thought that delivering himself to his enemies in a pine box might prove to be a bad omen.

19

Salt air. Briny and primal, the scent had
reached Logan within minutes of the Chinook's departure from Murtala Airport. By his best estimate,
the Chinook and the Eurocopter that it was following were roughly two hundred miles out of Lagos,
hugging the Nigerian coastline. They were flying
extremely close to the water—low enough to evade
radar. The weather was clear; the moon was full and
so bright that its features were washed out. Looking
down, Logan saw the pale shimmer of moonlight on
the crests of slow-rolling waves and the dappled forest canopy.

Ahead of the cargo helicopter, the EC-135's flickering lights beckoned like sprites in the darkness, luring the bigger, tandem-rotor aircraft on its secret journey.

Then the blinking lights of the Eurocopter went dark—vanished without a trace.

The Chinook slowed, hovered a moment, then continued slowly forward, steady and level. Moments later, a bizarre visual distortion rippled over the chopper and its cargo, twisting and warping the starlight and the dancing points of light on the water. Like a wall of heat radiation it swept through the inside of the crate. It tingled Logan's skin as it pushed over and through him. Hairs on the nape of his neck stood at attention, roused by a sensation of electric potential in the air.

When the effect retreated behind him, his vision cleared—and through his hastily drilled aperture he saw a massive container ship at anchor in a small harbor. Mounted on the forward deck was a small loading crane. On its aft deck was a small helipad, where the EC-135 had already touched down.

Inside the perimeter of the cloaking field, the stars and moonlight were distorted. The Chinook hovered above the stack of multicolored shipping containers and began lowering its net of cargo. Peeking through a sliver of space between the boards at his feet, he realized that the tops of several shipping containers were retracting, rolling back to reveal a spacious compartment hidden within. *Camouflage,* he realized. *Those aren't shipping containers—it's a structure disguised as shipping containers.*

The net full of crates descended slowly into the broad, poorly lit space, lowered by the Chinook's winch into the custody of a half dozen cargo workers, two of whom were operating forklifts. Working quickly, they pulled away the now-slackened netting and began unloading the crates from the pallet. Logan heard the deep thunder of the Chinook's rotors continuing overhead. His surveillance of the activity inside the hidden storage area was interrupted as a forklift moved his crate off the pallet and into the stacks.

Logan's crate fortuitously was deposited in a shadowy corner. Prying open the narrow crack between two boards with one of his claws, he watched as the ground crew removed the empty pallet from the netting. The Chinook retracted its net. As soon as it was clear, the ground team maneuvered a massive, rectangular shipping container mounted on a rolling dolly platform onto the same spot. Seconds later, the Chinook lowered a set of heavy-duty steel cables that clanked onto the deck. The ground crew set to work attaching the cables to the corners of the slingable metal box, which, to Logan's eye, looked like an ordinary, twenty-foot refrigerated shipping container—exactly what one would need for delivering perishable medicine to a remote location.

The steel cables snapped taut, then the refrigerated container was hoisted off the dolly and out of the storage area. Seconds later, it cleared the edge of the camouflaged roof, which began to creep shut with a resonant, mechanical hum. Before it closed fully, Logan saw the Chinook pivot one hundred eighty degrees and begin its journey back to Lagos.

Have to catch up to it later, he decided. *Job one is free Dr. Falco. Job two is sink this boat.*

He slipped one claw sideways in the gap between the pine crate's lid and its sides. Slowly, he sliced through the nails holding the lid in place. In less than a minute, he eased the lid up and away, then put it gently off to one side. He climbed out of the box and snuck deeper into the shadows, until his back was pressed against a bulkhead. He began moving aft.

As soon as the overhead doors had closed, four of the six cargo workers exited aft through a broad loading and unloading passageway. Thick steel doors pushed inward and barricaded the opening behind them. The last two workers moved lethargically amid the stacks, checking inventory.

Unlike many industrial ships Logan had traveled on, this one smelled almost antiseptically clean, as if it had been sanitized every day. As he passed by a ventilation duct, the cool air gently flowing from it smelled of ammonia mingled with the medicinal odors of alcohol and iodine. Even here, in a cargo area, the decks were immaculate.

Logan slipped behind a very neat and symmetrical

stack of refrigerated containers like the one that had just been flown away. None of these seemed to be active; their compressors were off, and all their gauges were zeroed. The sheer number of them, however—forty in this stack alone, and two more stacks like it elsewhere in the compartment—alluded to the scope of the Hand's plans for Panacea.

In the corner he found an unsecured door. He cracked it open and listened. There were no voices, no footsteps, not even the soft tides of breathing. Just the low hum of air in the vents and the hiss of water and vapor in the pipes. He slipped through the door into a flatly lit passageway. Its bulkheads were of the same widely ribbed metal as the shipping containers that its exterior had been made to resemble. He checked the corners. No surveillance cameras. The deck looked uniform, nothing to suggest pressure pads or motion sensors. Featureless walls left no place for the installation of infrared sensor beams. His bare feet made almost no sound as he stole quickly through the passageway toward its less well-illuminated far end.

The throb and thrum of the ship's engine room was louder here, deeper. Around the corner was a shorter passage. Three doors were spaced at regular intervals along its aft bulkhead. Still no sign of surveillance. Logan moved swiftly and checked all three doors: in order, they were marked "Exit," "Ladder," and "Lab." The last door was the only one that was secured, with a numeric keypad and magnetic dead bolts. He considered just slicing through the bolts, but he knew from lessons learned the hard way that doing so would probably trigger an alert. If he was going to keep his promise to Setsuko and make every effort to save Dr. Falco, discretion would have to be the order of the day.

He checked the ventilation gratings along the top of the bulkhead and confirmed that they were all too short and too narrow for anyone larger than a toddler to move through. Cutting through the bulkhead itself was problematic; if he hit a major electrical bundle, he might fry himself to death.

After weighing his options, he listened at the door to the ladder. There was no sound of movement or human presence from the other side, and the door was unlocked. He inched it open and sniffed the air. More of the same disinfectant-tinged, purified air, cool and dry, no human or animal scents. Through the door. Up the steep metal steps, fast and light-footed. Another door, one level up, unlocked. All quiet again. A peek through confirmed a dark passageway with hints of blue light to one side and reflected white light from the other. Closing the door, he reached up over his head and unscrewed the blistering-hot bulb dangling from a black wire above the ladder landing. Cloaked in shadow, he reopened the door, crouched, and stole through.

The blue light was a caged bulb above a watertight

door to his right. White light poured through an angled observation window that began five meters to his left and continued for twenty meters, taking up most of the passage's far wall. Skulking forward on all fours, Logan approached the corner and peeked down into the space below.

Arranged in three long rows were enormous stainless-steel machines, bulbous in shape, gleaming brightly under the flat, omnipresent flood of white light from scores of hanging fixtures high overhead. A seemingly endless labyrinth of pipes and tubes and wires connected the machines to huge vats and compressors. Entire bulkheads were covered with gauges and digital flat-screen displays. Four freestanding banks of computers were situated in the corners, each one inside its own Plexiglas safety barrier. Along the bulkhead to Logan's right was a pressure door.

Directly below Logan was the end of what appeared to be a fully automated production line. Robotic arms worked in tandem with precisely calibrated nozzles and a timed conveyor belt to fill sixty bottles at a time with a golden fluid that Logan could only assume was Panacea. He counted the seconds as the small glass bottles filled and the case in which they were packed was moved on to the next stage. Six seconds. Six hundred bottles per minute, with as many as ten doses per bottle. Three hundred sixty thousand doses an hour. Then he considered the size of the cases and quickly estimated that more than a thousand could have been loaded inside the refrigerated shipping container. More than half a million doses of instant slavery were already airborne and on their way to Africa.

At the far end of the production facility he caught sight of motion. Through a dark-tinted window, he saw a lone man walking across a lab, lit only by the pale blue glow of his computer screens. Even from this distance he recognized him from his Tanaka dossier photo as Dr. Nikolai Falco. He was relieved that the man wasn't dead yet.

Logan crawled below the edge of the observation window, to the door at the far end. Beyond it was another untrafficked set of steps. He descended the ladder quickly, found the door to the next level, and checked it before continuing on through another dull gray passage, toward what he hoped might be another entrance to Falco's laboratory.

At the end of the corridor was a watertight door. He looked through its circular view port; on the right, at the head of a T-shaped intersection, was another door marked "Lab." Unlike the other lab entrance, this one had no security keypad next to it.

A spin of the door's wheel released its bolts. The heavy metal portal swung open. An overpowering blast of ammonia and diesel fumes flooded Logan's senses. It was stronger than any routine shipboard operation could account for; in Logan's experience, whenever he encountered an odor so profound, it was because someone was expecting him and was using a powerful stench to mask their scent.

He extended his claws. Stepped through the door, ready and looking for a fight. Turned the corner at the intersection and met his foes head-on. Four people stood looking back at him.

Pritikin was safely at the back of the group. His hatred for Logan was obvious and fiery. The honesty of it was the only thing about Pritikin that Logan found even remotely admirable.

Standing in front of the Russian were the fireball twins.

At the head of their diamond formation was the man who clearly was in charge. Majestically tall, his powerful frame was expertly attired in a silvery gray business suit and a chrome-colored necktie. His shoes matched his suit and were polished to such perfection that they reflected the tip of his *katana*, which he had drawn and held casually in front of him. The weapon's scabbard was slung diagonally across his back, crisscrossed with the scabbard for a shorter sword, a matching *wakizashi*.

Logan eyed the *katana* carefully: in this man's hands, it was one of the few things on earth that his own adamantium claws couldn't cut through. He nodded at Silver Samurai.

"*Konnichiwa*, Keniuchio."

"*Konnichiwa*, Logan-san," Harada replied.

One of the twins had his hand against a junction

box. The other had small sparks dancing off his fingertips.

"So," Logan said, "you've signed up with the
Hand, eh?"

"Signed up?" Harada smirked. "No. I've taken
command of a joint effort, adding their power to that
of the *yakuza*."

"So it's true," Logan said, disappointed. Though
Harada had started out years ago as Logan's rival in
Japan, Logan had come to think of him almost as a
friend. Shaking his head, he added, "Blindspot really
did a number on you, didn't he?"

"Don't delude yourself, Logan," Harada said. "I've
simply awoken to the truth, embraced what I really am.
I put aside the childish fantasy of a hero I never was."

The twin with the crackling fingers took a step
forward. "Let me frag him, boss." He lifted his hand.
"I could fry his—"

Harada's sword slapped flat and hard against the
energy thrower's chest. "No," Harada said. "If Logan
dies, it will be at my hand, in honorable combat."

"Like hell it will," Logan said.

Now the hotheaded twin strained against
Harada's blade. "Come on, let me finish this! I already made a crispy critter out of him once at—"
His mouth snapped shut as the flat of Harada's
sword slammed into the underside of his jaw, with
its razor edge a hair's breadth from cutting his
throat.

Cold and unforgiving was Harada's tone. "You will speak to Logan as your better, youngling. He is my fellow *ronin,* a warrior without a master. Even in defeat, he deserves respect."

"Can't say the same for you," Logan interjected. Seeing that he had Harada's full attention, he continued. "Using a drug with the world's worst side effect to enslave billions of people? That's the most gutless thing I ever heard of. And until right now, I'd never have believed you could do something so sick."

With a quizzical look, Harada asked, "What, exactly, do you think my ultimate objective is, Logan? Do you think I would undertake such a massive change in the global status quo for a mere blackmail scheme? Or some simple power grab?"

"Let me guess," Logan shot back. "You're doing it for world peace."

"Exactly," Harada said with a sly grin.

It wasn't the answer that Logan had expected. "Want to run that by me again?"

"What I am accomplishing here, Logan, is nothing less than everything that the combined wealth and effort of the entire Western world has failed to do in more than three decades of trying: I am going to bring peace, health, prosperity, and stability to the Third World—starting with Africa."

"For a price," Logan replied, keeping an eye on the twitching blasting finger of the anxious twin behind Harada.

Harada nodded. He made a sweeping arc with his sword as he spoke. "Nothing is free, Logan. You know that." The tip of the blade cut through the air between them in a figure eight. "The difference is that I'm prepared to offer something of value in exchange for the fealty of those I help—an end to poverty, to hunger, to pandemic disease. I shall set them free from need and want and suffering."

"Your generosity is touching," Logan said. "Hell, I bet you didn't even think about all the uranium and other mineral resources you'd score on this deal. And I'm sure Africa's gold, diamonds, and oil had nothing to do with your decision to enslave its people."

A disappointed sigh, then Harada replied, "What an ugly way of thinking about such a boon to humanity."

"Half a billion people working for their daily dose? Dissent becoming a death sentence? That don't sound like a boon to me. Sounds more like I shoulda killed your ass in Tokyo when I had the chance."

Logan lurched half a step forward, then halted as the fireballer's fingertips turned white-hot with energy.

"I can take him out right here, daimyo," the twin said.

The other twin shouted, "Don't be stupid, Gregor!"

"Shut up, Oskar." Fire-fingers looked to Harada for his orders. "Give the word."

"Your brother's right," Harada said. "A blast strong enough to kill Logan would sink the ship."

A sick smirk darkened Gregor's face. "I'll go easy on him."

Forks of lightning jumped from the man's fingers and snared Logan. Spasms racked Logan's body; his jaw clenched painfully and against his will. Stabbing bolts of hot pain skewered him from every direction. Writhing and growling, he felt himself slip away amid a blinding ring of fire. Then the circle of light and heat raced away as his mind plummeted into the darkness.

Consciousness returned with a shudder. It was pitch dark.

Logan's entire body twitched and jerked. A nervous flutter in his eyelid was followed by a yanking muscle spasm in his cheek. He felt like a fish with a hook in its mouth.

Ringing in his ears rose and fell like a Doppler effect. He felt groggy, disoriented. Despite the perfect darkness, multihued spots danced in his vision.

Under his palms and bare feet was cold, naked metal. Smooth and icy, it had the same perfectly sanitized odor as the cargo hold of the *Pandora*. He shifted his balance. Stood up, staggered to one side. His steps echoed in the empty space around him.

"Echo," he said, to test the acoustics. His own voice came back to him, close and resonant.

Vertigo, another stumble to his left. He became aware that he was in motion, rocking in a shallow arc, like a slow-swinging pendulum. Muffled by the metal walls around him, he could barely hear the hum and grind of motors, the buzz and clatter of coiling cables. He pressed his ear against the wall.

The machine noise was louder, clearer. Outside were voices, shouting, overlapping. *Easy. More to starboard.*

Focusing, he picked out distinct voices.

Pritikin. "Get it over with."

Harada. "Be patient, Alexei. It's almost done."

Gregor the fireballer: "Back a little, over the edge. A little higher. . . . Keep it steady, dammit! Dump the chum."

Over the edge? Logan dropped and flattened his ear to the floor, like an Indian in an old western. Below him he heard the scrape of steel, then the slap of waves lapping against the hull of the ship. In a flash, he realized that he was in one of the shipping containers, and that Gregor was about to use him for target practice. Then Gregor's last instruction repeated itself in Logan's thoughts: *Dump the chum.*

Sharks, Logan realized. *Sonofabitch.*

Extending his claws, he moved to the side of the box that was facing away from the man with hands of fire. He punched forward, through the steel wall, to start cutting his way out.

Everything exploded.

The blast at the airport had been nothing. Like a welder's flame, a massive pulse of white heat disintegrated the shipping container into a swirling fire cloud of shrapnel. Flames and chunks of steel ripped flesh from Logan's bones. He felt himself screaming, but there was no sound other than the consuming roar of the blast. He was the soft target in a volcanic blender filled with brimstone and razor blades.

Born again of fire, he fell from the burning womb into darkness—numb, stunned, blind.

Impact came hard, like landing on a bed of frozen nails.

Seawater paralyzed him with its icy bite, pulled him down like quicksand, surrounded him like a shroud. He gasped and it poured into his throat and lungs. Mixed with the water was the coppery tang of blood. Some of it was from the remains of bait fish; some of it was his own.

Watery darkness drew him down like iron to a magnet. Burned and torn, he was dead weight in its irresistible embrace.

Then came the first strike. A viselike pressure around his lower left leg. His sense of motion through the water increased. Another attack, seizing on his right arm, halted his movement. In less than a second he was caught in a tug of war between two sharks, their sawtooth jaws clamped through his flesh down to his unbreakable bones.

Crushing pressure bore down on him. He was sinking fast. Then another hit, a bump against the left side of his lower back, and a fresh cloud of his own blood stained the water.

Nausea and asphyxia fogged his thoughts with panic.

In a flash the pain hit, and pure rage took over.

He struck with his left hand at the shark tugging on his right arm. His claws tore into the beast's head with no effort. Instantly it released its fierce grip on him. Bending at the knee, he pulled his upper body to his trapped left foot, then slashed savagely at the first shark that had assaulted him. He felt chunks of the aquatic predator rip loose, then he was floating free. Behind him, a near-silent rush of displaced water. Twisting like a corkscrew, he struck as he turned, and severed the front of the third shark's snout.

Logan was still all but blind in the lightless night-time sea, and his lungs were screaming for air. Red jolts of pain surged through him, made it hard to think, but instinct was not enough now. He was floating, deprived of any reference point, and his adamantium-laced skeleton made him too heavy to float to the surface. *Don't panic,* he commanded himself. *Think.*

There was less than half a breath still held in his

lungs, and his only chance of surviving hinged on letting it go. He retracted his claws, cupped his hand a few centimeters above his mouth, and exhaled slowly, then felt which way the bubbles moved. They crept backward over his face, and he turned himself so that they rose directly from his mouth and over his fingers. *That's up,* he told himself. *Swim, canucklehead.*

His strength was fading, and he had only one arm and one leg able to kick and pull and fight against the leaden weight of the water above. There was no light, no sense of where the surface might be. The ocean yawned around him, its watery voice deeper and more ancient than life itself. Seawater burned inside his windpipe. As fast as his arm and leg fought against the sea, he felt as if he wasn't moving, as if he were fighting merely to keep from being pulled back into the depths.

At any moment more sharks could appear, and he'd have no air, no strength left to fight, no hope of breaking free.

A rippling gray shadow. Hallucination or salvation?

His hand found no resistance. It reached into the nether realm above. Then his head broke the surface, and the crash of air against his waterlogged eardrums was like a hurricane wind. The ocean pitched and rolled, and he bobbed passively on its surface, gulping down air and coughing out filthy brine. He lifted his right hand from the water and was satisfied to see that it was already well on its way to being mended. With effort, he rotated his left foot from the ankle. The rends in his flesh were almost healed; if he could get away quickly, he might avoid further attention from sharks.

Pivoting in slow, careful turns, he scanned the harbor, which shimmered beneath the full moon. No matter what direction he looked, he didn't see the *Pandora*. He closed his eyes, and he heard it—the voices of men working on its deck, the creak of its anchor chain, the slap of waves against its hull. A sniff of the night air brought diesel fumes from close by. For a moment, Logan was surprised not only that the ship was close enough for him to swim to but that it wasn't moving at all. Then he recalled that when he'd first seen it from his hiding place in the crate, it had been lying at anchor.

It made sense, he realized. With its cloak up, the only way for the *Pandora* to be an effective base of operations was for it to remain anchored at a precise set of coordinates. Logan, however, was just glad that he wasn't facing a several-kilometer swim to shore with the sharks.

He took slow, easy strokes as he swam toward the diesel fumes. It was important not to draw attention from the deckhands. The sound of waves lapping the hull was intimately close when he encountered the distorting effect of the cloaking field. He took a deep breath, submerged, and swam underwater until he reached the ship's hull.

Surfacing against the side of the massive container ship, he was able to get his bearings. He was at the starboard bow of the vessel. Above him, two massive anchor chains descended from the hull into the ocean. Both chains were pulled taut on long angles away from the ship.

A deep breath, and he slipped back beneath the dark water. With a powerful breaststroke, he propelled himself under the water toward the anchor cable. Half a minute later, his hand closed on the rough steel. He cautiously surfaced and glanced up at the ship's main deck. No one was looking in his direction.

Gripping the cable with both hands, he locked his ankles around it further down, then began pulling himself upward. Hand over hand, foot over foot, he climbed with smooth, easy motions toward the top of the cable. He worried that the water dripping from his sodden, shredded trousers would give him away, but between the wind and the waves and the hubbub on deck, a few drops of water that far overboard were inaudible.

At the top of the cable, he clambered through the circular aperture into the anchor winch compartment. Everything smelled like machine oil. The space was dark and unoccupied. He checked the door; it was unsecured. The passageway on the other

side was empty. Using some oily rags that he found
next to the winch, he wiped away most of the water
from his body, replacing it with smeared black
instant camouflage. He took off his pants long
enough to wring them dry, then put them back on.
He checked the passageway again. Still clear.

His list of objectives was growing. He counted
five now.

Rescue the scientist.

Recover a sample of Panacea for Setsuko Tanaka.

Destroy the ship.

Stop the Chinook.

And kill Pritikin, Harada, and the twin mutant
thugs.

Not necessarily in that order, he decided as he opened
the door to continue his mission.

20

MURTALA AIRPORT WAS A GRIMY, FRIGHTENING place by daylight. At night, it was among the most intimidating locales Wai Ying had ever seen. Sequestered inside the locked confines of the Cessna, she huddled under a blanket in the passenger cabin, curled into the plush embrace of the jet's luxurious seats.

She had been drifting in and out of sleep, pursued by bad dreams, nightmares of falling, of running to stand still. In a few she'd watched Ziv vanish again, consumed by fire. Too edgy now to sleep, too exhausted to stay awake, part of her anxiety was a fear of being alone in this dangerous, sinister place.

Even more poignant was her admission to herself

that she missed Logan. They'd known each other for less than a week, but already he'd become important to her, in a way that few men had since her father died nearly a decade earlier. Certainly, Logan could be brusque, sarcastic, and uncommunicative. The rawness of his anger and pain, which he wore outwardly like a badge of honor, made her nervous, scared her a little. But from the first moment she had seen him in the cemetery, she'd known he was more than he appeared—soulful, conflicted, complicated. And the rose he'd brought to Mariko's grave had spoken of a romantic's soul.

She wasn't going to kid herself. Men like Logan weren't good candidates for long-term relationships. They didn't like to stick around. Always off to the next crisis, another adventure, the wide horizon, the lure of the unknown. It was a testament to what a remarkable woman Mariko must have been that she had inspired such lasting devotion in a wanderer like Wolverine. *Her death must have been a defining moment for him,* she concluded. *What would it take for a man to risk falling in love again after losing someone who meant so much?* It seemed like the kind of loss that would make a loner of anyone.

Then, like a taunt from her subconscious, she remembered a line from Oscar Wilde's *Picture of Dorian Gray*: "When a man marries again it is because he adored his first wife." Wai Ying shook her head and laughed at her own irrepressible optimism. *Hope springs eternal.*

Tucking her head onto the pillow she'd propped against the wall, she closed her eyes and tried to relax herself enough to drift off once more to sleep. Like the blanket, the pillow smelled freshly laundered—cool and crisp and laced with the vaguely floral scent of detergent. Then a low murmur, like a weak heartbeat, vibrated up through the body of the plane, through her seat, shook her awake. Minute by minute it grew stronger, deeper, more distinct. Soon she recognized it—the pounding *fwup-fwup-fwup* of a Chinook helicopter's tandem rotors.

She tossed aside the blanket. Stepping quickly to the cockpit, she found the binoculars and scanned the airfield for signs of ground crew activity. A cluster of men, including one with lighted signal batons, surrounded a low, flatbed dolly.

Rapid and powerful enough to shiver her teeth, the noise of the Chinook passed directly overhead. The baton man waved and coached the Chinook into position. Roiling plumes of dust kicked up from the rotor wash as the massive aircraft hovered above the flatbed. Wai Ying craned her neck and saw a twenty-foot-long metallic shipping container slowly descending from the Chinook, whose markings matched the one that had departed a little more than two hours ago. With help from the ground crew, the container was planted squarely on the wide, low dolly.

Four men climbed on top of the container and

detached the sling cables, which were hoisted back into the air. The rotor noise faded as the Chinook departed. A small towing car drove up and hitched itself to the dolly. After a few lurching false starts, the car pulled its payload to a slow crawl across the tarmac, out of Wai Ying's sight.

Cursing softly, she lowered the jet's hatch ladder and snuck out, alone into the night. She slipped under the plane and stayed in the shadows as she jogged to catch up with the towed container. Dodging between low, dilapidated buildings and scampering across wide avenues of cracked asphalt whose fractures were packed with cigarette butts smoked down to their crumpled filters, she managed to get ahead of it. She pressed herself flat against a wall. The towing car and the container crept past, traveling a floodlit path.

They turned onto a wide taxiway that led directly to the main runway. Waiting there was an enormous C-130 Hercules cargo aircraft. Its four engines were warming up, the propellers filling the air with a chainsaw-like buzz. The towing car halted at the massive aircraft's lowered rear ramp. The metal container was unhitched from the towing car, which drove away. Four men, attired in the black uniforms of ninjas, exited the plane and attached cables to the container, which was then hoisted slowly inside the C-130. Three teams of men removed the chocks from beneath the C-130's broad wheels. Another signalman directed the plane's pilots to bring their engines to full power.

Wai Ying ducked back behind the corner and considered her next move. Letting the plane get away with what she suspected was a massive shipment of Panacea was unacceptable, but she wasn't in a position to halt its departure by herself. When Logan returned, he would be the better person to handle this.

If he returns, warned her inner pessimist.

Shaking off her fears for Logan's safety, she pondered trying to follow the C-130, then realized that doing so not only wouldn't help her, it would also effectively strand Logan in Nigeria. Another peek at the gargantuan plane brought her to her senses. *It's a propeller plane,* she told herself. *You can give it a head start, as long as you know where it's going.* Carefully, she navigated the shadows and dark corners back to the Cessna Thunderstar.

Safely back inside the jet, she made an encrypted call to TBC headquarters in Osaka. The switchboard operator answered. "Tanaka Biotechnology."

"This is Wai Ying," she said. "Put me through to extension five-five-six-eight."

A click on the line, then a single, deep, buzzing ring. A man's voice answered the extension. "Satellite Recon."

"Hiro, Wai Ying. I need a redirect on the tracking bird."

As always, Hiro Kagehara was a consummate professional, never asking why but simply following orders. "Go ahead."

"Pick up a C-130 Hercules on the main runway at Murtala," she said. "Markings two-alpha-seven. Maintain visual, track its chatter. And Hiro? Do not lose them."

"Roger that," Hiro said. "Tracking bird has the ball."

"Thanks, Hiro, you're a prince." She hung up and reclined in the pilot's seat with a heavy sigh. There was nothing more to do but await Logan's return. Staring at her worried reflection in the windshield, she braced for a long, lonely night.

Harada led the Golovanov twins and Alexei Pritikin through a narrow passageway aboard the *Pandora*, toward a ladder that would bring them back to the aft helipad.

"I still don't see why we have to go with him," Gregor complained. "Logan's toast, and you're in the clear."

"Mr. Pritikin still has enemies and rivals," Harada said. "And there are other potential threats to our operation. Just because you've dealt with Logan, don't make the mistake of thinking success is guaranteed." Looking back over his shoulder at Gregor's anger-knitted brow, he added, "Besides, you're all Russian. You should have lots to talk about."

They passed through a heavy door and ascended a switchback ladder inside the aft superstructure. Their steps clanked and echoed sharply off the blue-gray bulkheads. Slightly winded, Pritikin spoke between heaving breaths as they climbed. "Can I go back to my mansion yet?"

"Soon," Harada said. "My people are making some much-needed improvements to its security. For now you should plan on staying in Istanbul while we lock down the pipeline deal."

Pritikin nodded. "Fair enough." The foursome reached the top landing, and Harada pushed open the outer door to the main deck. A low whistle of wind poured through the open portal, warm and briny and tainted with the odor of aviation fuel. The EC-135 sat idle on the helipad, its pilot apparently still below-decks.

Harada was the first person through the door onto the narrow walkway, and Pritikin followed close behind him. As Gregor stepped through the door, Harada saw the blur of motion half a moment too late to act. An impact bashed the door shut, slamming Gregor between it and the bulkhead.

Pritikin bolted away from the door—only to collide with Harada, who pushed the cowardly Russian aside and over the railing. Flailing and yelping in distress, Pritikin tumbled several meters to the next deck and landed hard.

That left no one between Harada and Wolverine,

who was crouched low, in a battle stance, claws extended and reflecting the moonlight. Harada reached over his shoulder and drew his *katana* from its scabbard. "You're making a mistake, Logan."

"Done talkin'," Logan replied, and he lunged forward.

Harada charged into the first wild swing of Logan's arms. Projecting his mutant power into his blade, he deflected the first swipe, parried an upthrust, then counterattacked, slashing a deep cut across Logan's chest. Undeterred, Logan pressed his assault. Every slash of his claws came faster than the one before, every blow landed with greater power.

Dodging left, Harada took a killing shot at Logan's neck. The *katana* wedged into the muscle behind Logan's right shoulder, then halted as it struck his scapula. In the blink of time it took to pull the sword free, Logan slashed him brutally across the midriff. It felt like razors of fire. A warm stain of blood bloomed instantly across Harada's shredded shirt. Logan jabbed with his right hand. Harada barely twisted clear in time.

I need more room, Harada realized. A single leap and he was over Logan and behind him. He catapulted himself off the narrow catwalk of the superstructure, turned and tumbled in the air, reversing his facing, and landed on the wide-open metal surface of the fake shipping containers.

Logan slammed down in front of him, arriving on

the hollow steel battlefield with a boom like a cannon-ball.

They circled each other for a moment, then Logan barreled straight at him, roaring with fury. Harada feinted right, ducked left, and spun to strike Logan in the throat. Inches shy of contact his blade was blocked—and snared between two of Logan's unbreakable claws. Logan's counterstrike was a blur. Arching his back like a limbo dancer, Harada felt the tips of the claws cut through the air a millimeter from his face.

He used Logan's grip on his sword as an anchor and kicked him under his jaw. Logan stumbled backward, and Harada's sword slipped free.

An explosion, bright and furnace-hot, erupted between them. Concussed by displaced air, Harada tumbled backward, then rolled back to his feet. A smoldering hole had been blasted in the fake shipping containers. On the other side of the charred cavity, Logan was scrambling back up from all fours, shaking off the burns and the gashes from metal debris. Harada looked back up at the superstructure and saw Gregor leaning against the railing, fighting to remain on his feet, the right side of his face lacerated and bruised.

An energy thrower with a concussion, Harada fumed. *He'll destroy everything!* He knew that turning his back on Wolverine would be suicidal, but if he didn't halt Gregor's barrage, the consequences might be far more disastrous. Harada sprinted across the container tops, racing to intercept Gregor before he fired another blast.

Logan chased Harada, closing the distance quickly. He was about to overtake Harada when Gregor unleashed another firebolt.

The blast struck Logan square in the chest, and the report flattened Harada against the steel underfoot. Charred and wrapped in a fetal curl, Logan tumbled wildly across the multicolored steel surface and fell into the gap opened by Gregor's first attack. Smoke, thick and brownish-black, coiled up from inside the ragged hole in the steel.

Moments later came sounds of metal hacking through metal. Logan bounded up from the crater and flung three freshly cut steel wedges through the air. The metal chunks embedded in Gregor's gut, throat, and right eye. The fair-haired young Russian howled in agony and staggered. Then, just as Harada had feared, Gregor started firing wildly. Clutching one hand over his eye even as blood poured from his slashed throat, he hurled one thunderbolt after another, missing Logan and Harada but blasting massive holes through the ship, all the way down into the sea.

Less than two seconds after the insane barrage had started, Harada had scaled the superstructure, back to the catwalk. One stroke of his *katana* removed Gregor's head, which sailed into the open air, over the side, and into the water. His body crumpled to the catwalk, its firestorm quelled, its lifeblood cascading across the rough-textured steel walkway and streaking down the gray bulkhead below.

Logan climbed over the railing in pursuit of Harada, who backpedaled clear of the blood-slicked section of the catwalk. Feral and snarling, Logan was not going to bargain, not even going to waste breath on words. Killing Logan when he was like this would be exceedingly difficult, but not impossible.

Harada drew his *wakizashi* and readied himself for Logan's charge. In a blur it came, raw force and rage, unstoppable, unavoidable. Harada fell backward and let Logan run roughshod over him, risking a split-second of vulnerability for a chance to deliver one perfect, instantly fatal stroke.

Logan pinned him on the catwalk.

Lifted his claws to take Harada's head.

Then Harada struck, driving his *wakizashi* into Logan's gut, behind his sternum, through his heart.

A twitch, then a violent convulsion as Logan rolled off Harada. The *ronin* once known as Silver Samurai snapped back onto his feet and pivoted to jab his *katana* under Logan's chin, up into the brain pan. He lunged for the coup de grace—

And once again his blade was snared in Logan's claws.

With his left hand Logan held Harada's blade hostage, while his right pulled the *wakizashi* free of his torso. All but gutted, Logan looked up at Harada . . . and flashed the bloody grin of a predator.

The *wakizashi* stabbed upward. Its tip sank into Harada's abdomen for a split-second before he thought to let go of his *katana* rather than let himself be run through with his own blade. Now he was unarmed, wounded, and bleeding badly. Logan rose slowly back to his feet, his wild eyes never blinking as they probed Harada for weakness and fear.

Nowhere to fall back to, Harada knew. *No time to regroup.* In a single twist of his teleportation ring, Harada removed himself to a safer location—and abandoned the *Pandora* and its precious cargo as collateral damage. Regret gnawed at him, but then he put that feeling aside. *It doesn't matter,* he consoled himself. *We already have what we need. This battle is lost—but the war is about to be won.*

Fear spun Oskar's thoughts into a flurry.

He'd felt Gregor's death in the form of a massive wave of feedback. Instinct had driven him to try to shut it out, to block it, but it was too raw, too powerful. Never in Oskar's life had he feared electricity until this moment, as his body quaked and collapsed from the onslaught of his brother's expired life force.

Maybe I've gained his powers, he thought optimistically. He extended his hand and tried to release a bolt of energy. Nothing happened. Instead, he felt the familiar flow of ambient energy entering his body, which siphoned it all without trying. Oskar could never stop charging; with Gregor gone, he knew it would be only a matter of time before he overloaded.

The door to the outside catwalk opened, revealing the burned, bloody, half-naked, and still-smoldering form of Logan. His claws were extended, his eyes wide with bloodlust. The pugnacious mutant strode through the door and reached to grab Oskar, who scrambled away toward the ladder and plummeted headfirst to the next deck.

Oskar's only impulse was to flee. He caromed off bulkheads as he ran. His thoughts were bright with panic; they spun inside his mind, whirling faster by the moment, like moths trapped between a burning bulb and a lamp shade, wings banging and burning in a futile struggle for freedom. He ran without having a destination, focused only on escape, on survival. The door ahead of him was ajar. He paused only for a moment to yank it open. Then Wolverine's powerful hand gripped the back of Oskar's neck and slammed his face against the bulkhead.

Darkness fell like a cut circuit.

When he awoke, Oskar felt like a spectator to the slow return of his own consciousness. He watched the passageway's overhead drift through his field of vision for a few moments, until he became coherent enough to know that he was being dragged. Too groggy to struggle, he tried to move his hands and his feet, but they were held fast. His wrists had been secured behind his back, and his feet were bound at the ankles.

Logan was taking him deep into the lower decks of the *Pandora*. Here the diesel fumes and the clattering din of engine noise were overwhelming. As Logan pulled him through a flooded intersection, Oskar saw through an open door that a fire was raging in one of the adjacent compartments. No one seemed to be there to put it out. He wondered if the crew had already abandoned ship.

The floor-level tour of the engineering deck halted at a door marked "Engine Room." Logan opened it. The machines inside were deafening and high-pitched. He reached down and snagged Oskar by his collar again, and pulled him into the compartment.

Oskar felt the raw current that coursed through this area. When he looked at it with his mutant senses, he saw how bright its machines were, how radiant, how robust. All the *Pandora*'s onboard electricity was generated here, including the power for its energy-hungry cloaking field. Just being within a few meters of these systems was flooding his body with power that he couldn't release—at least, not in any way that would be safe. The proximity of such dynamos had him squirming in terror of the inevitable.

Logan picked up Oskar from the floor, gut-punched him harder than he'd ever been hit before in his entire life, and draped him backward over the ship's primary alternator. Raw power flooded into Oskar's body; the overhead lights flickered and dimmed for a moment. The rush of electricity racing through him was like a drug, heady and intoxicating. A sharp tug on his wrists snapped him back into the here-and-now, and he realized that Logan was tying his bound wrists to his ankles with a length of wire stretched beneath the alternator housing.

"Stop!" Oskar blurted. "You don't know what you're doing!"

"Wrong," Logan said, giving the twisted wire lashing one final pull for good measure. "I know exactly what I'm doing."

Then Logan turned and walked away, closing the door behind him. In just a few short minutes, Oskar's body became hot as it flooded with current siphoned from the ship's alternator. Sweat rolled from his brow and soaked his back. His pulse raced and his breaths grew shallow. There wasn't much time left, maybe a few minutes before he'd reach the limit of his ability to hold the charge. Mere minutes until he came to the end of himself.

Just a few minutes till I see you again, Gregor.

In life his twin had been a burden, an embarrassment, the albatross around his neck. Oskar had spent all his free time cleaning up Gregor's disasters, masking his mistakes, providing him alibis. *But at the one moment when he really needed me, I let him die.* Sorrowful and furious at the same time, he cursed himself for not having had the strength to deny Gregor's demand for power. *If I'd held back,* he castigated himself, *forced him to run, he'd still be alive, we'd finally be free . . .*

Oskar's jaw clenched as his muscles coiled with unspent power. The end was close now, so close. There was barely time left for one last, lonely act of contrition. *I'm sorry, Gregor,* he prayed, hoping that his slain brother could hear his apology and see his guilty tears. *I'm sorry.*

His tears ran dry . . . and then it was over.

Logan hurtled forward through passageways choked with smoke from the fires belowdecks. With Harada gone, Surge dead, and Slake on a short fuse to a big finish, there was no longer any reason to worry about setting off alarms. The ship's captain had ordered the crew to abandon ship, and no one had hesitated. *Pritikin was probably the first one off,* Logan figured.

As far as he knew, the last two people left aboard the *Pandora* were himself and Dr. Falco, whom he had seen moments ago through the observation window, struggling against his laboratory's locked door. The man was bloodied and burned, leading Logan to suspect that one of Surge's wayward blasts had been responsible for the scientist's injuries.

Coughing as he ducked under the blanket of

sooty vapor hugging the overhead, Logan scrambled down the ladder and into the T-shaped intersection where he'd been intercepted by Harada. Three hard punches with his claws shredded the lab door's lock mechanism, and a battering push with his shoulder forced the portal open. He let his momentum carry him inside.

Falco was lying on the deck, barely conscious. Toppled equipment trays and shattered computers littered the floor. Several dozen ampoules of amber fluid had spilled from the pocket of Falco's lab coat. Logan kneeled beside him. "I'm here to help you. Can you walk?"

The scientist shook his head. "Too late," he gasped through a pink froth of blood. "Toxic gas. Lungs . . ."

Logan picked up one of the ampoules. "Is this Panacea?"

Nodding, Falco spit to clear his mouth of blood, then he weakly grasped Logan's forearm. "Please . . . stop . . ."

"I know," Logan said. "The chopper left with a shipment. I'll catch up to it."

Falco tightened his grip, shook his head. "No," he said, more forcefully than before. "*You*. . . . Stop . . . interfering."

Is this guy nuts? He pulled free of Falco's grip. "What the hell're you talkin' about, bub?"

"Let . . . the Hand finish . . . its work."

An explosion from below shook the ship, which

groaned like a drowning elephant. Lifting the man by his shirt collar, Logan growled, "Don't you know what that stuff does to people?"

A demented smirk twisted Falco's features. "Better than anyone," he burbled, sputum overflowing the corner of his mouth.

"It'll turn people into slaves!"

The smirk became a grin. "Not for long," Falco said. "Not when my changes take effect."

Logan cocked his fist and twisted Falco's collar into a noose. "What changes?"

"Go on," Falco said. "Kill me. . . . I can't . . . feel it anyway. . . . Nerve damage." His snort of smug laughter made Logan coil with fury. "Too late for me . . . for Kazaki . . ."

"Kazaki?" Logan said, remembering where he'd heard the name. "Jiro Kazaki? The chemist who tipped off the Hand?"

Falco rolled his eyes in Logan's direction. "I did that," he said. "Set up Kazaki . . . to take the blame."

"The Hand murdered him," Logan said.

The dying scientist chuckled. "I figured."

Glaring, Logan demanded, "What have you done?"

"What I had to," Falco said. His voice faded swiftly. "What Tanaka . . . wouldn't let me do." He coughed. "No one knew . . . Changed the drug. Heals for a month . . . then it kills. Kills . . . everyone."

"You sonofabitch," Logan said. "Don't you know where the Hand's gonna use this stuff?"

After a slow nod, Falco's words came out long and dreamlike. "I know."

The crackle of spreading flames drew closer, moving between the bulkheads, raising the temperature rapidly. Logan shook Falco back to half-consciousness and shouted, "Why, goddammit?"

Falco shrugged his eyebrows. "Numbers," he said. "Too many people . . . not enough food . . . not enough oil." A wracking cough spewed dark blood over his lower lip and down his grimy shirt. Through a bloodstained smile, he boasted, "If we're lucky . . . my drug will kill two billion." He gagged on mouthful of blood, sputtered, then continued. "Maybe four."

Numb with shock, Logan mumbled, "Four billion."

A spasm traveled through Falco's body as death began to lay claim to him. It galled Logan that he had been sent to save this fiend's life. He let Falco lie flat on the deck, then reached down and scooped up a handful of the ampoules filled with Panacea. He removed the rubber caps, pulled open Falco's jaw, and poured in the drug. With a push on the man's chin, his mouth closed and his head tilted back. The swallowing reflex did the rest. Logan counted off the seconds while he listened to more eruptions stutter through the ship beneath him.

All at once, Falco shuddered awake, eyes bright and lucid. His surprise was betrayed by his sharp intake of breath. He looked with terror at the empty ampoules on the deck, then at Logan. "The drug? But—why?"

Logan regarded him with all the contempt he could pack into one scowl. "I just wanted to make sure you could feel this."

He punched his claws through Falco's chest, skewering his heart and staking him to the steel deck. He kept Falco pinned and stared into his eyes just long enough to be absolutely certain that he'd suffered, and that he was dead.

Alexei Pritikin stood next to the EC-135 helicopter as its rotors warmed up and filled the air with thumping noise. After being pushed over the catwalk railing by Harada, he'd barely regained consciousness in time to find a submachine gun and shanghai the helicopter pilot off the lifeboat, to take him off the sinking ship by air. "There ain't enough time to do the warm-up," the pilot had protested, but a spray of bullets at his feet had persuaded him to make the effort anyway.

All the lifeboats were away now, bobbing atop the gentle crests of the bay, borne silently away into the night, toward the nearby shore. If the pilot turned out to be right, and the *Pandora* sank before the helicopter was ready to lift off, they would have no other means of escape but to attempt a long swim to shore through shark-infested waters.

An orange fireball erupted from inside the fake mountain of shipping containers, hurling shrapnel and spewing toxic clouds into the night sky. Flames raged across the foredeck. The *Pandora* listed sharply to port. The hull groaned, its death cry deep and mournful, as if the ship itself were aware that it had begun its descent to a watery grave.

When the spiraling plume of smoke drifted starboard with the wind, Pritikin saw a silhouette against the vermilion curtain of fire that was consuming the ship. A single man, leaping from one island of safe footing to another, crossing the inferno, then scaling the ship's superstructure. The long, fearsome claws extending from each of the man's hands left no doubt who it was.

Pritikin leveled his MP5K and opened fire.

Bullets *ping*ed off the deck and bulkheads. A few struck Logan, whose stride flagged but never halted. The weapon clicked empty, and Pritikin removed the spent magazine, tossed it aside, and slammed in the first of his two replacements.

Logan was closer now and moving faster, low to the ground, like a tiger on the attack. Firing on full automatic, Pritikin's weapon chattered angrily beneath the pounding drone of the EC-135's rotors, which were almost at liftoff speed. He raked Logan with a prolonged burst, and the mutant's stride faltered again—but he kept coming, until Pritikin's second clip ran dry.

Pritikin climbed inside the chopper but left the door open. "Go!" he yelled to the pilot. "Let's go! Now!"

The pilot struggled with the controls. Waves lapped over the port half of the *Pandora*'s main deck, which was slipping into the sea. As the helicopter began to slide left across the helipad, the pilot coaxed the aircraft up and off the aft deck of the ship. Then a heavy impact on the helicopter's right strut wobbled them enough that their rotors nicked the tilted deck of the ship, showering both with sparks.

Leaning out the door, Pritikin saw Logan clutching the landing strut. He fired a few short bursts at him, but the quaking of the chopper made it almost impossible to aim. "Shake him loose!" he shouted toward the cockpit. "Get him off of us!"

Then he saw Logan's hand grip the edge of doorway.

Pritikin held his weapon with both hands, steadied his aim. Waited for a clean shot at Logan's chest and head. Seconds later he had it, and he fired.

The bullets shredded Logan's chest, ripped into his face, sprayed blood across the inside of the chopper's passenger cabin. Logan almost fell backward, but he arrested his fall by driving the claws of his left hand through the cabin's deck, anchoring himself in place. And he just hung on and took it as Pritikin continued to fire, pumping every last bullet he had into him, until the weapon ended its barrage with an impotent *click*.

Then the bloody, shredded man in the doorway smiled—and climbed inside. He retracted his claws and advanced with predatory grace, then locked a single hand around Pritikin's throat. "Burning's too good for ya," he said in deep rasp. "Drowning's too good for ya. . . . Sharks're too good for ya." Then he pulled Pritikin away from the wall and held him in front of the open side door. "But all three sound about right."

With one push, Pritikin was plummeting, dropping away from the helicopter. Free fall was both exhilarating and horrifying—then he made impact. His back twisted and his legs snapped under him. Jagged bones gouged through soft flesh. He bounced off the twisted bulkheads and tumbled across the deck of the *Pandora*. Flames licked at his face and crisped his hair. Burning oil and fuel stuck to his clothes. The agony of the fire was like the devil's breath. Then came the shock of immersion as he plunged into the sea and choked on the briny water.

When the first shark bumped against his shattered, bloody leg, he knew that it wouldn't be long before the last part of Logan's death sentence came true as well.

Logan sat down in the copilot's seat, relieved to be off his feet and able to rest for a moment. Next to him, the pilot sat quietly, not moving and clearly watching Logan out of the corner of his eye. Glancing at the pilot, Logan extended a single claw and gestured at the man. "We gonna have a problem?"

"No," said the pilot, and he obviously meant it.

"Good," Logan said. "Take me back to Lagos." Detecting a familiar, pleasant aroma from the inside pocket of the pilot's jacket, he added, "And give me one of your cigars."

Just less than two hours later, the EC-135 set down at Murtala Airport. Its struts settled onto the tarmac with nary a bump, as if the helicopter were as light as air. The pilot powered down the engine, and the pitch of the rotor noise began to fall. "Nice landing," Logan said to him, then he punched him across the jaw, knocking him unconscious.

Out of the helicopter, Logan abandoned stealth and sprinted beside the taxiways, back to the hangar where he'd left Wai Ying and the Cessna Thunderstar several hours ago. It was a few hours before sunrise. Most of the airport was dark and empty as a ghost town. He hoped that Wai Ying had been able to get the jet refueled in the hour since he'd contacted her from the EC-135, en route from the sinking of the *Pandora*.

He remained at a full run until he dashed into the hangar. The jet was there, closed up tight. He knocked on the door and waited. After a few seconds' delay, Wai Ying peered through the door's circular window, then opened it and lowered the ladder.

"Are you all right?" she said.

"Fine," he said, climbing the ladder. "Lost your phone, though. Sorry."

When he got to the top, she embraced him with relief and affection. It caught him off-guard, so he just stood there for a second before he hugged her back. Feeling the silken texture of her hair, the softness of her skin—it brought back memories that he'd fought for years to put behind him. *God, how I've missed this,* he realized. *Like coming home.* His appreciation for the moment was bittersweet, tainted by the specter of a love long lost but never forgotten. He cleared his mind of thoughts and let himself be in the moment for just a few breaths longer . . . then it was time to return to the task at hand.

He broke free of Wai Ying's embrace. "Where's the C-130?"

"On its way to Kaiduguri Airfield in Zibara," she said. "TBC's tracking it now."

"Zibara? That's where we picked up Pritikin's trail yesterday."

Wai Ying nodded. "We're hearing chatter in Kaltoum that a private charity has made a deal with the Zibarese government to take over its relief programs. Care to guess this charity's name?"

Logan held up his open hand and pointed at it. Wai Ying nodded in confirmation. He frowned. "Ready to fly?"

"Ready," she said.

He moved forward into the cockpit and powered up the flight-planning computer. "How big is their head start?"

"About three hours," she said. "But the C-130's a propeller aircraft—maximum speed about three hundred eighty miles per hour. If we go wheels up in the next ten minutes, there's a slim chance we can beat them to Kaiduguri."

"They're never gonna reach Kaiduguri," Logan said. "'Cause we're gonna take 'em out before they get there." He switched off the computer and left the cockpit. Wai Ying followed him.

"Where are you going?" she asked.

Recalling the panicked young cargo handler's accidental confession about a load of Semtex hidden in a janitor's closet, Logan smirked and replied cryptically, "To get some cleaning supplies."

21

KNEELING BENEATH THE LEAN-TO SHELTER AND between her children, Nishan dipped her ragged cloth in the bowl of cloudy water and wrung it half dry. It was Kanika's turn to have the cloth on her forehead. Nishan had been careful to keep track of whose turn it was as she alternated between Kanika and Nadif. Both children lay deathly still, their breathing too shallow to measure. All night, Nishan had kept watch over them, determined to stay awake and maintain her vigil against death's angel. *I won't let their souls be taken while I sleep,* she'd promised herself. *I will be with them every moment. Every moment.*

Dark violet streaks began to stand out in the eastern sky. Insects' nocturnal songs faded, and the birds awoke to fill the predawn hush with chirping melodies as pale sunlight washed slowly over the horizon.

Nishan no longer knew what to do, where to go, or whom to turn to. Not to God; prayer had failed her. Not to the government; it was in league with the men who had sired this evil. She couldn't even take comfort in curses. All the same cruelties had claimed her ancestors for as long as anyone could remember. If they had been powerless against this evil in life, how could she expect them to be of aid from the world beyond? Many of those who'd shared her fate had blamed God, had called him cruel, vicious, merciless. Nishan did not believe such talk, not even now, because the truth was even more painful. All the misery and evils that she had seen done had been the work of men, and all of it had gone unspoken and unavenged. This was not the product of a malicious deity; a cruel God would at least take an interest in human life, if only to inflict misery upon it. Life in Zibara was proof that God was indifferent—blind and uncaring, as distant as the stars and as cold as the grave.

An engine rumbled in the distance and drew closer. Rattling metal shook and banged as the vehicle navigated the uneven land outside the village. As the sound of tires crackling across a dirt road became clear, the vehicle's horn honked.

Though she was reluctant to turn away from

Nadif and Kanika even for a moment, lest the angel
of death take her children in those fleeting seconds,
curiosity compelled her to crawl out from under the
lean-to and see what the ruckus was about. When she
tried to stand, she faltered. She had been kneeling for
so long that her legs had grown weak and cramped.
By the time she steadied herself, an open-top truck
had come to a halt in the middle of the village—or, at
least, amid some cinder piles where the village's center had once been. Its driver and passenger were both
Asian men. The passenger stood up on his seat and
called out to the villagers. "Come closer!" he cried.
"We have important news! Please, gather 'round and
listen, everyone." Following the shambling horde,
Nishan drifted closer to the truck, wondering if they
were being evacuated to one of the refugee camps.
She had seen one of those places as a child; it was just
as miserable as life anywhere else in Zibara, with the
additional indignity of being imprisoned "for your
own safety." If that's what these men were here to
announce, Nishan had already decided to take her
chances and flee toward Ethiopia.

"All right," the Asian passenger said, speaking
loudly and slowly. "Listen now. We are from a new
international relief organization called the Hand.
We're going to be bringing you food, water, and a
new medicine that can cure any illness."

No one believed what they had just heard. A shrill
woman shouted back, "Any illness?"

"Yes," the Asian man said. "Malaria, AIDS, Ebola, cancer, anything. It can heal wounds, repair organs. It can—"

"Lies!" shrieked a scar-faced young woman clutching an infant to her emaciated breast. Her accusation was followed by more angry, disbelieving shouts from the crowd.

"How can we believe you?"

"Their medicine's a poison! They're out to murder us!"

"You're putting us in the camps, aren't you?"

"The Tanjawar will take it all, like they always do!"

Waving his arms for silence, the Asian man replied, "No, the medicine is not a poison! You're not going to the camps, and the Tanjawar will not harm you again—their pact with the government in Kaltoum is over. We will protect you from them."

Now the crowd's cynicism reached a fever pitch. "Like the Americans protected us? Or the British? Or the United Nations?"

Voices overlapped, growing more stridently bitter each moment. No one believed such promises anymore. Too many times had such relief revealed itself as a mirage, as a lure for the unwary or the too-trusting.

"Hear me now!" bellowed the Asian man, in a mighty baritone that silenced the crowd. "If the Tanjawar try to take your food, your water, or your medicine from the Hand, they will be killed. We are not the United Nations. We do not make promises we can't keep. If the Tanjawar interfere with our mission, we will not negotiate with them. I promise you again: we will *kill them*. We will kill them *all*."

Never in her life had Nishan heard someone make a promise so clearly or so forcefully. Whomever these men worked for, they were not the impotent diplomats of the West, or the noble but ultimately powerless doctors and nurses of Médecins sans Frontières, or idealistic but helpless clergymen and nuns. The Hand, whatever it turned out to be, was something different. Could that be reason enough to give hope one last reprieve?

"You talk big," a gnarled old woman croaked at the Asian man. "But *when* will you help us? When do we *eat?*"

This was it, Nishan knew. Always at this stage the promises became vague, the timetables of relief unclear. When it came time for specifics, this was always the moment when all the generous, hopeful pledges were exposed as good ideas bereft of substance, and the villagers' hopes again were dashed.

This time, the Asian man looked the old crone in the eye and answered, "In a few hours. The medicine is being flown in from Lagos now. As soon as it arrives, we're bringing it here."

Excitement passed like a virus from person to person. *Today? Food and water and medicine are coming in a few hours?* It was almost enough to make Nishan believe that she had been wrong about the value of prayer, wrong about the power of her ancestors, wrong about God.

Elation swept through her fellow villagers. Some held each other and wept with joy, praised God, or thanked Allah; some just cried and forgot words altogether.

Then Nishan caught herself. She would not weep or give thanks—not yet. Darkness still lay over the land; sunrise was still in the distance. There was no food yet on her plate, no water in her cup, no medicine in her children's mouths. Until there was, she would not celebrate. In a land of broken promises, only a fool believed in anything he wasn't holding in his hand.

She returned to the lean-to and crawled back beneath it, between her two children. Their chests barely moved now, the spans between their breaths growing longer. Nishan lifted the rag from Kanika's forehead and pushed it gently into the dirty water. Another half-twist, then she unfurled it, folded it half over itself, and laid it tenderly on Nadif's feverish brow.

Nishan wanted to believe that the Hand was telling the truth, that an end to the horror and suffering was at hand. She wanted to believe that a cure was coming in time to save her son and daughter. But she couldn't dare to hope, not now; if the Hand's promises turned out to be a lie, she would soon have nothing left . . . not even the dark comfort of sorrow.

22

LOGAN GREW ANXIOUS. HE STRAINED TO pierce the pale glow of predawn light rising from beyond the distant curve of the horizon. Dense, sculpted mountains of peach-tinted clouds surrounded the Cessna Thunderstar. Somewhere beyond this, or inside it, or below it, the C-130 Hercules was making its initial approach to the landing strip in Zibara. "Come on," Logan muttered to his unseen prey. "Where are you?"

Wai Ying nudged the Cessna into a shallow dive, picking up speed, pushing them well past Mach 1. "We're close," she said, obviously trying to reassure him. "You should get ready."

Like an arrow into cotton, the Cessna plunged through the cloud bank. The world outside vanished into a watery mist. Wai Ying kept her eyes on her instruments, ignoring the hypnotic, featureless gray void outside the cockpit window. Logan got out of his seat and started back toward the passenger cabin. He paused in the cockpit doorway. "You're sure you can do this?"

"No problem," she said. "I've got the easy job. You're the one jumping out of the plane."

"Just get in as close as you can," he said. "And don't try anything fancy."

The Cessna's engines whined as it dived. Logan climbed the slope of its center aisle, fighting against gravity, until he reached his rucksack, which was tucked under one of the seats. From the rucksack he retrieved several long, narrow bricks of Semtex-H plastic explosive and set them on one of the seats. At the bottom of the sack was a detonator and a roll of black gaffer's tape. Using the tape, Logan quickly secured all the bricks together into a single unit, then implanted the detonator leads, taking care to embed them deep and tape them into place. A quick test confirmed that the detonator was ready. He stuffed the entire bundle back inside his rucksack and slung its brown leather straps over his shoulders.

He returned to the cockpit just as the plane burst free of its obscuring veil of mist, revealing the long rays of sunrise reaching swiftly across the dusty landscape. Nearly three hundred meters below them and several kilometers ahead was the C-130 Hercules, barely staying above the gnarled, deadwood treetops as it hurtled toward Kaiduguri Airfield.

"They're only a couple minutes from landing," Logan said. "Get us in there now. And lock the cockpit door—I'm opening the side hatch."

Wai Ying looked over at him, eyed the rucksack, and raised one eyebrow to express her incredulity. "No parachute?"

"It'd just slow me down," Logan said.

She smiled. "Good luck."

"See you on the ground," he said, then closed the door behind him as he left the cockpit.

He stood at the side hatch and waited for the plane to level out of its descent. The engine noise grew louder and deeper as the Cessna reduced speed to match the C-130's velocity. Over the onboard PA, Wai Ying alerted him, "Ten seconds to intercept."

Logan overrode the safety locks and opened the side hatch.

Wind noise and jet roar—louder than a freight train, like an explosion that wouldn't end. Air blasted into his face, watered his eyes, stung his skin. His clothes snapped and fluttered around him like the filthy flags of destitute nations. The Cessna was low enough that explosive decompression hadn't been a problem when opening the hatch, but there was still a definite suction effect near the doorway, and he braced himself with both hands while awaiting his moment to fly.

Under his feet, the African savannah blurred by, a dark wash of sunburned beige and sparse splotches of green. *Only one chance at this,* he knew. *That's a long way down.*

The tail of the C-130 drifted into view. Wai Ying was guiding the Cessna on a diagonal intercept path toward the C-130's right wing. *They've got to see us on radar,* Logan thought. *Why aren't they going evasive?* Only two answers came to him: either the C-130 was on a schedule that it couldn't risk breaking, or someone was already aboard the plane and waiting to greet Logan when he arrived. *Please let it be ninjas,* he thought with a bloodthirsty grin. *Please.*

Seconds later the doorway of the Cessna was aligned with the nose of the C-130, about ten meters above. *That's as good a shot as I'm gonna get,* Logan figured, and he launched himself out the doorway, claws extended and ready. Free fall and wind resistance shot him backward, under the Cessna's wing as he fell. Reaching out with his adamantium talons, he skewered the top of the C-130's rear fuselage as he made impact. Like anchors finding purchase in a soft seabed, his claws brought him to a halt. Keeping his left claws in place, he pulled his right claws free to cut his way inside the plane. On the edge of his vision, he saw that Wai Ying had already guided the Cessna away and accelerated ahead, determined to land at Kaiduguri ahead of the C-130 in case Logan failed.

Time to drop in and say hello. He reached behind himself, plunged his right claws into the metal skin of the cargo plane, and made a broad, arcing cut, using his own position as the center of a circle, which then fell away beneath him, into the plane. He landed on top of it, pulling his left claws free, and came up in a low crouch, ready to meet his welcoming committee.

The Hand didn't disappoint him.

Two dozen ninjas swarmed from every direction. They tumbled, rolled, slashed, hurled projectiles. The first several hits cut the straps of his rucksack, which fell away into the shadows. *Shuriken* buried themselves into Logan's chest and thighs, blades slashed across his back, his shoulders, his arms.

Some of the blades were poisoned, and the toxins burned in his fresh, bloody wounds.

He pulled into himself, tightened his defensive circle. The ninjas, predictably aggressive, pressed their apparent advantage and moved in for the kill. And then Logan went berserk.

No effort, no thought, no conscience, just the primal drive to strike, to kill. Unleashed and uncontrolled, the animal predator in him struck at anything and everyone, reveled in the orgy of violence, the baptismal glory of warm sprays of blood against his face and chest. There were no friends or allies here, only enemies and prey. A target-rich environment. He remained fixed in place, beneath the shaft of daylight pouring in through the hole in the fuselage overhead, eviscerating all who darèd to emerge from the shadows to challenge him. Severed heads and limbs piled up around him, and the scents of burlap and aviation fuel that he'd noticed when he first dropped through the fuselage had now been overpowered by a coppery stench normally not found outside an abattoir.

Then the rush of blades and fists ceased, leaving only the drone of the C-130's massive propellers and the howl of wind flooding in through the hole overhead. Logan stood alone in the massive, open space inside the cargo plane, peering into the darkness toward the front of the aircraft, where he saw the square outline of the shipping container from the *Pandora*—and the ghostly outline of an enormous, armored figure standing in front of it, posed like a statue and watching him.

"Always we return to the old ways, eh, Logan-san?" The words passed through Logan, around him, over him. Harada kept talking. "All you see is the fight, the bloodshed. Someone turns you loose and you go on a killing spree . . . but you never ask why." Silver Samurai took a few slow steps forward. He was fully appointed in his trademark titanium-white battle armor with a red rising sun on the chest, apparently not satisfied this time to trust his reflexes as his sole defense. "The Hand is bringing order to people who live in chaos, life to those who were cursed to die. With Panacea, we can end the genocides, remove the warlords, put an end to centuries of pointless war. We can bring these people peace, Logan." He stopped and smirked. "But I suppose you've never had much use for peace, have you?"

Forcing his thoughts to line up and push through the surging heat of his primitive rage, Logan answered slowly, "You're . . . making a mistake."

"No, I'm correcting one," Harada replied. "I'm fixing the weak, futile policies of the West. Putting an end to hunger, to war, to disease. Decades of promises have yielded nothing here, Logan. Every year, Africans die in greater numbers and America does nothing. Europe does nothing. Japan does nothing."

He was almost within striking distance now. Logan's mutant healing factor stitched his body back together as he watched Harada circle him, just out of arm's reach. "Hate to tell ya this, bub, but yer army of grateful slaves has an expiration date. And a pretty short one, to boot."

That provoked a wrinkled look of concern on Harada's face. "What are you saying, Logan?"

"Falco double-crossed you," he said. "Turned your miracle drug into a slow poison. Works for a month, then it turns toxic. Spread that stuff around and next month the planet's gonna be a lot less crowded."

For a moment, the truth seemed to register with

Harada, but then he shook his head, choosing the easier path of denial. "I don't believe you," he said. "You're just trying to buy time, trying to postpone the inevitable so you can rally your X-Men or call in the Avengers. I can't allow that, Logan."

"I'm tellin' you the truth," Logan said. "Listen to me: Panacea needs to be destroyed. All of it."

"No," Harada said.

Logan rolled out a crick in his neck. He kept one eye on Harada at all times. Steeling himself for battle, he gave his foe one more chance. "I'm fraggin' the drugs, Keni. We can do it the easy way or the hard way. You don't want it the hard way."

Harada raised his blade. "I'll be the judge of that."

He lunged, thrusting his sword in and up. Logan deflected the blow and counterattacked. His claws ripped through Harada's layers of chest armor but only grazed the flesh beneath.

Both fighters' next flurries of lightning-quick strikes missed their targets and hacked long gouges in the metal skin of the plane, permitting long slashes of light to penetrate the C-130's dark interior. They attacked again.

A low block by Harada thwarted Logan's combination strike and left Logan open. Harada's *katana* slashed over Logan's forearms, then his knee cracked into Logan's jaw, knocking him backward. Logan fell hard on his back but rebounded to his feet almost instantly. He saw now that Harada had drawn his *wakizashi* and was employing a two-weapon fighting style. The deck was treacherously slick with blood.

Logan charged, hoping that momentum would carry his attack past Harada's defenses. His attack fell on empty air. He hit the left bulkhead; his shoulder collided with a large red switch that started a hydraulic motor in the rear of the plane. Then he felt the burning slice of steel through his Achilles tendons, and another slash severed his hamstrings. *Biomechanical cutting,* Logan realized. *Smart move.*

Claws retracted, Logan pushed up and away from the wall and tumbled backward through the air. Upside-down, his claws sprang back out in time to catch and trap both of Harada's swords with turns of his wrists. He slammed into Silver Samurai, and the two of them rolled across the deck, against the right bulkhead. Punching and gouging, Logan ripped apart the deck as Harada writhed and struggled to free his blades and himself. Keeping Keniuchio pinned for a few more moments was all that Logan needed for his healing factor to repair his torn ligaments and restore his mobility.

At the rear of the cargo compartment, the C-130's loading ramp was lowering with a groan of hydraulics and a shrieking blast of wind. Outside was a bright blur, the landscape blasted white by the blinding light of a freshly broken dawn.

Harada let go of his blades and used his superhuman strength to flip and throw Logan, who inflicted two horrendous gouges on either side of Harada's torso. Logan landed on the ramp and rolled to his feet just shy of going over the edge. Behind him was a high-velocity fall to an uncertain fate. Ahead of him, Harada recovered his swords and charged. Logan raced to meet him, determined to get some room between himself and the edge of the ramp.

All of Logan's rage and reflexes weren't enough to keep up with Harada, whose already formidable powers had been lethally enhanced with super speed by the Hand. For every three blows that Logan was able to block, two more hit home.

A stabbing thrust skewered Logan's liver. In a flash of silver, a razor edge slammed into his face and severed his upper lip and part of his nose, spewing blood into his mouth and down in sheets over his chest. His left bicep was cleaved in twain. Every hit came from an oblique angle, a blind spot, the one point from which he couldn't defend himself for a split-second. A snap kick in his shredded, bloody face knocked Logan backward, off-balance, and a sweep behind his knees put him on the deck, kneeling and twisted, his right clavicle exposed.

Feel the blade in the air, counseled his old sensei's voice, speaking to him now through the waves of blinding agony. *Hear its point pierce the silence. Know its moment.*

The blade was falling, its point seeking Logan's heart.

Its moment was near, and then it arrived.

Logan's right hand shot up and back, then turned.

The blade of Harada's *katana* was snared, and its samurai wielder stood at Logan's right side, premature in his pose of triumph. With the captured blade, Logan yanked Harada down, doubled him over—then thrust his left claws up and deep through Silver Samurai's armor, through his all-too-human ribs of bone, into the spongy bronchi of his lungs.

Logan gave his embedded claws a half-turn. Harada gurgled, then dark blood frothed inside his mouth even as it ran down Logan's claws and soaked the outside of Harada's armor. Harada lost hold of his *katana*. Logan flung the weapon away, onto the ramp, where it clattered to a stop against the edge.

Then Harada's *wakizashi* gouged into Logan's throat. Logan knocked the weapon from Harada's hand, then retracted his claws as he fell to the deck and applied pressure to his savaged, erupting carotid artery. Harada, meanwhile, staggered forward, one hand covering his eviscerated right side, then fell to his knees and began to crawl toward his *katana*.

Logan turned and fought against vertigo to stand upright. His barely healed tendons screamed in protest, almost too stiff to move. Blood continued to gush from his face and throat. All that he knew was pain. He decided to let his wounds bleed; he wanted both his hands free for what had to come next.

Tattered and baptized in vivid crimson, Logan

hobbled after Harada, who stopped crawling at the edge of the ramp as a jolt of turbulence knocked his sword over the edge, out of the plane, out of reach. As Logan inched up on him, Harada looked back, his eyes dulled with pain, dimmed from blood loss. His *wakizashi* lay on the deck, back where Logan had dealt Harada's mortal wound.

As Logan staggered forward, close enough almost to grab hold of him, Harada draped one leg over the edge of the ramp. He looked up at Logan with a doleful expression. "I could've given these people peace," he rasped through a mouthful of bloody foam. "The Hand could've given them a future."

"As slaves," Logan said. "And when the poison kicked in, you'd have killed them all. The biggest slaughter in history." Another half-step forward, and now Harada had his right leg and his right shoulder over the edge. *No way I can reach him before he lets go,* Logan realized. He raised his claws as a warning. "Don't make this harder than it has to be, Keni. Don't make me come looking for you."

"You won't have to," Harada said. "When it's time . . . I'll find you." Then he pushed himself off the ramp, into free fall, several hundred feet above a dusty plain.

Logan watched Harada plummet, even knowing what he would see. Several seconds later, Harada vanished in mid-fall—just a flash of light and color, then empty air. *Damn teleportation ring,* Logan groused. *Have to cut that off him first next time. Better yet, maybe I'll take the whole damn hand.*

He turned away from the ramp and limped with great effort back toward the front of the plane, leaving the ramp open behind him. There was little clearance around the sides of the shipping container, but it was enough to let him reach the pilot's side ladder to the cockpit. He used his arms to pull himself up, since his legs still weren't cooperating with his desires.

The pilot was sluggish on the draw as Logan entered the cockpit. By the time he had his sidearm drawn and aimed, Logan had already cut its barrel and slide into pieces with one slice of his claws. Bits of metal and a few grains of gunpowder pattered on the deck beside the pilot's seat. Belatedly, the copilot reached for his own holster, but stopped as Logan said, "Don't even try it." Climbing all the way inside the cockpit, he added, "You've both got parachutes. Use 'em."

The two pilots traded fearful glances, then scrambled down the copilot's ladder out of the cockpit and made a run for it. Logan settled into the pilot's seat and kept watch out the side window. Moments later, he saw two white parachutes blossom open and catch the sunlight as they drifted away behind the C-130.

He made a quick review of the gauges and was satisfied that the C-130 had enough fuel left to ensure Panacea's immolation. A gentle nudge of the yoke veered the plane away from Kaiduguri Airfield, out into a desolate stretch of land to the northwest. He opened the throttle and increased the plane's speed. The drone of the engines grew louder and higher-pitched.

Narrow columns of smoke rose along the horizon, just a few kilometers ahead. He aimed the C-130 at them. Then he leveled out the plane's flight at an altitude of just over two hundred feet and set the autopilot.

Logan limped down and out of the cockpit, past the tight clearance of the shipping container. Then he found his rucksack, tucked into a corner behind the protrusion for the left-side wheel well. He opened the sack. All the Semtex was still inside, secured together, the detonator wires in place. He armed the detonator and set the timer for thirty seconds. With a touch, the countdown began.

In halting steps he left the rucksack behind, on the deck next to the shipping container. He paused at the edge of the ramp. Counting the seconds in his head, he knew he didn't have time to think this over, and that was probably for the best.

He stepped off the ramp and pressed his arms to his sides. Tucking his chin to his chest, he fell head-first toward the ground. For several moments stretched by adrenaline, he heard only the low roar of air and felt nothing but the regularly increasing pull of gravity. It was freedom, tranquility, just himself and open air, without burdens, in the light of sunrise.

Then the C-130 exploded above him, closer than he would have expected, but far enough away not to pose any threat. The fireball was a deep reddish orange, like a marigold of flames in bloom amid a cloud-streaked sea of blue. Heavy grayish-black smoke billowed, no doubt thick with incinerated aviation fuel. Burning, smoky debris fell from the cloud, like dark angels cast out of a fiery heaven. Chunks of fuselage and fragments of wing spiraled to earth, leaving corkscrew smoke trails to drift in the humid African breeze. One intact propeller spun as it dropped into gravity's merciless embrace.

Logan turned his eyes from the plane to face his own moment of reckoning. Larger than life and faster than he could have imagined, the ground was rising to meet him, dark and rocky and unforgiving. The landscape was uncommonly, almost unsettlingly beige, and unrelieved by the graces of nature or the touch of human arts. There were no broad-limbed trees to break his fall, no conveniently placed ponds or lakes, not even a deep but slow river toward which he might struggle to direct his fall. Just the ground, simple and brutal and waiting like a reaper with mile-wide arms to greet him on impact.

He used his last few seconds of free fall to do a couple of midair somersaults, just for the heck of it.

Then he flattened out and faced the sky as he fell, arms and legs wide. *Bring it.*

Then the sky turned black.

Logan's eyes fluttered open slowly. Pain hammered inside his skull with diabolical ferocity, turning like a drill that bore holes through all his thoughts.

He didn't remember making impact, but obviously he had. He was sprawled on his back, on a muddy patch of ground. His vision was hazy and tinted red, and no matter how he tried he couldn't move, not even his fingers or toes. An odor of blood was heavy in the air, and he realized that it was his own. The mud in which he lay had been moistened by his pulverized soft tissue. *Musta mashed goddamn near everything,* he reasoned.

His head was lolled to one side, just enough that he could, with effort, look down the length of his body. *Everything still looks like it's attached,* he noted. *So far, so good.* Above him, a cast of vultures circled, slow and patient. He heard a few more on the ground nearby as they stepped cautiously around him, trying to determine whether it was safe yet to eat him.

The sun was low on the horizon; it was still early morning. *Can't have been here long,* he figured. Looking out across the blighted plains, he saw dark smoke rising from the strewn wreckage of the C-130. Between the initial explosion and the incendiary effect of the plane's fuel, he was certain that he'd accomplished his mission: Panacea had been destroyed.

A good day's work, he told himself.

Exhaustion and injury caught up to him at last, and a dark wave of fatigue swept over him. Despite the excruciating throbbing in his skull and the million-twisting-maggots sensation of his flesh slowly reweaving itself from the inside out, one thought nagged at him as he let go and drifted into the comforting shelter of unconsciousness.

Man, I wish I had a cigar right now.

23

KHALEED AL-RASHAD HUNG UP THE PHONE AND looked out the window of his den. His son, Mustaf, splashed joyfully in the swimming pool. All traces of Mustaf's osteosarcoma had been erased, leaving only the bright, curious young boy whom Khaleed had treasured as a gift from Allah every day since he was born.

Also vanished now was any hope for prolonging Mustaf's life. Coastal patrols had just investigated an explosion in a harbor near the border between Nigeria and Cameroon. A freighter registered to Anbaric Petroleum had been found scuttled in a burning slick of fuel. Most of the crew had escaped, but among the unfortunate few whose bodies had been recovered from sharks swarming the wreckage had been Alexei Pritikin.

The first call al-Rashad had made after getting the news was to Kaiduguri Airfield, to see if Pritikin's cargo plane had arrived with its shipment of miracle drugs. *Maybe there's still time to divert it here,* he'd thought. *Time to stockpile the drug for Mustaf.* But then Kaiduguri's tower supervisor reported that the plane had veered off-course just after 0621 hours. Minutes later it had vanished from radar and was believed to have crashed in Tanjawar territory, to the northwest.

There was nothing left to do now but await the inevitable.

Khaleed left his den and walked outside, across the perfectly maintained greensward behind his home, then onto the broad walkway of Spanish tile that surrounded his pool. Parveen, his wife, sat poolside, her eyes brimming with tears as she watched their miraculously healed son submerging and crashing back up through the pool's sparkling azure surface. She swept a thick lock of her black hair from her cheek and squinted against the blazing morning sun as she smiled up at Khaleed, who buried his torment and smiled back at her.

How do I tell her these are his last days? That his future died with Pritikin?

Rationalizing the situation didn't help. He told himself over and over again that even this brief reprieve was a blessing, despite the swift end that was going to follow in less than three days' time. But it felt like a cruel joke, to dangle health and freedom and a future in front of a boy doomed to die, a boy who had never harmed anyone, whose only sin had been to have Khaleed for his father.

Mustaf climbed out of the pool. Dripping wet and giggling, he ran to Parveen and hugged her. She kissed his wet head and clutched him to her. Then the boy pulled away from her and jogged clumsily to Khaleed, who kneeled to greet him. He caught the boy in a bear hug and all but crushed him to his chest, committing to memory the sound of his son's voice, the smell of chlorine in his hair, the solidity of his presence. All too soon he would be gone, and memories of these things, recollections pale and insubstantial, would be all that remained.

He held his son but could not hold back his own tears, which rolled in fast cascades down his face. Parveen watched him and read the truth in his eyes. She could see into his soul with a glance, she always had been able to, so he knew that she could see that his tears were shed not in joy but in mourning.

Pushing away from Khaleed, Mustaf asked, "Father? Why are you crying?"

"I'm just thanking Allah that you're well, Mustaf." He pressed his palm against his son's cheek. "Now that you don't need the medicine anymore, you can eat anything you want," Khaleed said. "Whatever you want, for lunch, for dinner, just ask. And I think we should invite all your friends right away to come celebrate with you."

Excitement filled the boy with energy. "You mean it?"

"Yes, Mustaf, invite them all. We'll make a party of it."

Mustaf embraced him again. "Thank you, Father!" Then he let go and ran inside the house to call everyone he knew.

As soon as Mustaf closed the sliding-glass door behind him, Parveen wiped away a fresh sheen of tears from her own face.

"How long does he have, Khaleed?"

Khaleed hung his head in grief. "Less than three days."

For a long moment, Parveen hid her face in her hands and fought for breath while resisting the desire to collapse into wracking sobs. Khaleed knew exactly how she felt—stunned, helpless, undone. She couldn't look at him or at the house, so she turned away and gazed into the rippled depths of the pool. "Will he suffer?"

"I don't know," Khaleed said, and it was the truth.

He felt cut off, shut out, as if Parveen was blaming him for this tragedy. Keeping silent, he knew that he wasn't to blame, that if Panacea hadn't claimed Mustaf's life three days from now, the metastasized cancer likely would have within a few more months. It was just the insult of an apparent cure that made the reality of the matter so power-fully bitter.

Parveen sighed so deeply that he wondered if there could be even half a breath left within her. "Why has Allah done this to us, Khaleed? Why?"

"He didn't," Khaleed said. "Evil men did this. For oil, for money, for power. This is what man does—not Allah."

Rage swelled in her voice. "Then why does He permit it?"

"Imam Yosef says that Allah made us all free to do as we will, for good or for evil. If He made it impossible for us to do evil, we would be nothing but slaves. We must choose." He walked slowly, cautiously, to her side and took her hand. "I choose to make these last few days with Mustaf ones of joy. If he must be taken from us, let us love him while we can." Parveen squeezed her eyes shut, and Khaleed pulled her to him and cradled her head on his shoulder. "Let him tell Allah how we loved him. Let us love him enough to make Allah proud."

Logan awoke to the blinding flare of the noonday sun. Its blistering heat was a hammer, the earth its anvil, and his body the raw mass trapped between them. He squinted hard and turned his head away from the glare. Several meters to his left, someone sat watching him.

Raising his arm to shield his eyes, he saw that the

watcher was an emaciated black woman. The landscape of her face was etched with deep lines of
tragedy, but her eyes looked lifeless. Flies congre-
gated on her skin and buzzed around her as though
she were already dead. She made no effort to shoo
them away.

He sat up and took stock of himself. Filthy from
top to bottom, attired in nothing except a tattered
pair of pants and some bloodstained rags that used to
be a shirt. His wounds from the battle in the C-130
and the fall had healed. All his muscles were stiff and
his joints almost literally creaked as he turned to face
his visitor and rub the back of his neck.

"Hey there," he said to the woman. "What's your
name?" She didn't respond; she just stared at him.
Affectless. Numb.

Slowly he got to his feet and bent himself backward until he heard a satisfying crack and felt a knot
of pressure unwind in his middle back. The air was
hot and dry, laced with the earthy fragrances of baked
dirt and drought-withered plants.

His eyes swept over the harsh country that surrounded him. Barren plains of parched dust reached
away in all directions and only in the distance gave
way to raw rocky hills. In the middle of one empty
expanse sat an animal's sun-bleached skeleton, picked
clean by predators and scavengers and scoured
smooth by wind-driven sand. Forlorn and stripped of
flesh, it spoke to the ancient beast in Logan's soul,

cried out the bloody truth of the world's endless, eternal violence.

Then his eyes fell upon an off-white cloud of dust kicking up in the distance, drawing closer. He stood and waited, having nowhere to go and nothing to do when he got there. Several minutes later, the Jeep inside the dust cloud became visible as it bounced over the uneven terrain. There were two people in the vehicle. The passenger pointed in Logan's direction.

Meanwhile, the gaunt woman sat nearby, her eyes fixed on Logan. He assumed she had to be aware of the Jeep as it closed to within fifty meters, but she paid it no regard.

The Jeep slowed and then stopped in front of Logan. He nodded to its occupants, both dusted the color of chalk. Wai Ying sat in the passenger seat. "Are you all right?" she said.

Logan shrugged. "You?"

She nodded, then introduced her driver. "This is Gary Lee," she said. "He's a park ranger here in Zibara." Lee nodded to Logan. Wai Ying continued, "He said he can take us as far as Kaltoum. From there, we're on our own."

Suspicion creased Logan's brow. "What about the Cessna?"

Wai Ying averted her eyes, clearly embarrassed. "TBC took back the jet," she said. "We're stranded."

"Because I destroyed the Panacea, right?"

She nodded. "That . . . and they got my expense

report." Unable to suppress a smile, she confessed, "I think I set a company record. And I'm pretty sure I've been fired."

He chortled for a moment. "Good for you. Don't worry about getting home. I'll have some cash wired over when we reach Kaltoum. We'll be fine." Logan was about to climb inside the Jeep when he remembered the Zibarese woman sitting on the ground watching him. He turned and took a few steps toward her. Wary of spooking her, he asked softly, "Miss? You need a ride?"

The woman met his inquiry with a suddenly fiery gaze. "It was you," she said in French-accented English. "I saw you fall from the plane. . . . You destroyed it."

Held by the force of her hatred, Logan nodded. "Yes."

"The miracle drug was on that plane?" she asked.

He wondered how much she knew about Panacea. "Yes," he replied.

"Why?" Grief radiated from her even though she didn't shed a tear or make a sound. Behind her, Logan only now noticed the two short mounds of recently excavated and refilled soil, and the short entrenching tool that lay between the narrow piles of dirt, which was still dark from being freshly turned over.

The mounds were too short to be for adults, he realized. *The graves of children. Her children.*

"I had no choice," he said, immediately regretting that he'd resorted to so trite a verbal defense.

"My children needed that drug," she said, more desperate than angry. She stepped closer, until she was right in front of him. "I needed it. And you destroyed it."

"I had to," he said. "It was a poison."

"The men from the Hand said—"

"They lied," Logan interrupted. "It would have seemed like a cure, but in a month it would've killed you all, and billions of other people."

The woman spit in Logan's face. "I don't care about other people!" She pointed in turn to the two graves. "I cared about Nadif! About Kanika!" Her fists clenched with sorrow and rage. "Some cure is better than no cure."

Logan shook his head. "Not this one," he said. "Even if it could've been fixed, you and your kids would've had to take it for the rest or your lives, or else you would've died. You'd have been slaves of the Hand."

Shock and disbelief contorted her face. "So? So what? We're already slaves—to the warlords and the Tanjawar, to the foreigners who ration our food and water, to the doctors who decide what cures we can have! We live like cattle waiting for slaughter. Is that not slavery? At least we would have been free of disease, free of hunger, safe from the warlords and the rapists. . . . Who were you to choose our fate for us?"

Logan stood before her, stunned and silent, unable to fathom the abyssal depths of her suffering. Despite more than a century of walking the earth and witnessing its evils, he still couldn't wrap his mind around the scope of the tragedy that defined this country and its impoverished, abused people. He wanted to tell her that he understood her sorrow, that he could share in some measure of her pain, but he knew that was a lie. There was no way he could empathize with the millions of people around the world, most of them in Africa, who were destined to die from diseases to which his mutation had made him immune. And there was nothing he could do that would help any of them. Violence was his sole vocation, his only talent. Brute force was of no value here. This was not a battle for men such as himself. Something told Logan that a man like Charles Xavier could do a lot of good in a place like this. He hoped he was right.

Nothing more to do, nothing left to say, Logan turned away from the Zibarese woman and climbed into the back of the Jeep. He gave a small nod to Wai Ying, who signaled the driver to head back to Kaltoum. As the Jeep made a U-turn, Logan watched the grieving mother settle slowly on her knees between the graves of her children, her eyes still piercing his soul with her bitter accusation. He could see the fatigue that plagued her, the sorrow and the hunger and the disease that all had taken their toll and had left her spent and broken, too beaten even to weep for her children. Beneath the white-hot orb of the sun and the pale vault of the sky, her silence was her mourning shroud.

Riding back to Kaltoum, every time Logan closed his eyes, he saw her, flanked by those tiny graves . . . and he knew that her specter would stalk his dreams, reminding him of his impotence in the face of true evil, for as long as he lived.

24

ALONE AT LAST, KENIUCHIO HARADA LAY IN BED,
swathed in bandages and tucked under crisp white-
linen sheets. He was surrounded by medical machines, all beeping or thrumming. A slow drip filled
his arm with painkillers, saline, and nutrients, while a
catheter drained his bladder in a slow, near-constant
trickle. The naso-gastrointestinal tube that wound
through his sinus and down his esophagus into his
stomach was monitored every few hours for signs of
internal bleeding. The morphine was doing its part to
dull his pain, but the massive, rude gouges in his side
throbbed with a deep, relentless ache.

It was fortunate for him that the modern-day

yakuza tended so well to its own. Surgeons and pharmacists were kept on retainer, and private hospital facilities such as this one provided a crucial haven for highly placed *kumicho* during emergencies. When, without warning, Harada had appeared, bloody and all but incapacitated in the doctors' midst, they had snapped into action without hesitation, eager to serve their *oyabun* in his hour of distress.

His armor would be repaired, his swords replaced. With enough medicine, transplants, and money, his wounds would heal. Only his pride, cut down by Logan's claws like autumn wheat before a scythe, would carry a scar from this debacle.

All this work for nothing, he brooded, closing his hand around the one remaining vial of Panacea in the world. He had grabbed it during his first visit to the *Pandora,* without really thinking about it. Now its golden fluid was all that remained of his dreams of worldwide order and power.

The vial had contained ten doses; a team of scientists who worked for one of Japan's more discreet intelligence services had expended all but one running an exhaustive series of tests, trying to unravel its chemical mysteries. In the end, they confirmed what Wolverine had already told Harada on the plane: the miracle drug had been turned into a slow poison. Within a month, it would build up in the brain tissue of anyone who took it and induce fatal strokes, seizures, and aneurysms. Just as Logan had professed, Falco had deceived everyone—his employers at Tanaka Biotechnology, the *yakuza,* even the Hand. He had framed one of his coworkers as the mole, meaning that Harada had ordered the wrong person assassinated after the formula was acquired. And if Logan had not intervened, Harada's orderly world would have ended in the largest slaughter of human beings in history.

And yet . . . the drug still commanded his imagination with its possibilities. If its natural curative and addictive properties could be divorced from its artificially introduced toxic elements, there might still be hope for bringing an end to chaos, disease, famine, and war. But the tiny sample he held in his hand was not enough for research. It was little more than a single-shot, perfect-health death sentence.

So tired, he thought as a timed release of morphine spread warm relief through his body. Lolling his head toward the window, he watched the colorful pinpoints of light in Tokyo's nightscape slowly soften and fuse into a muddy wash of pastel hues. Everything became indistinct, uncertain, and Harada's thoughts drifted to ruminations on missed opportunities.

The alliance between the *yakuza* and the Hand had fallen apart with the loss of Panacea; all their joint plans had been predicated on the unique bargaining power that control of the drug would have given them. Oil resources; gold and silver and diamonds; uranium ore; cheap manual labor. It all had been within their grasp, and as it slipped away Harada was no longer of any use to the ninjas and their secret society. All their lines of communication had suddenly gone dark, vanished into the past like the ninjas themselves into the shadows. The Hand had never really understood Harada's desire for order, for peace. All they had been able to see was the promise of power for its own sake. Where he had espoused a vision, they'd had only an agenda. Now both sides had nothing.

Harada opened his eyes as the door to his room opened and four men entered. They were his *saiko-komon,* his senior advisers, and they all wore serious expressions. Kuhido, the eldest of the four *yakuza* brethren, carried a bottle of sake. His second, Kanashima, carried a porcelain cup. Shinoda and Kokusui followed close behind. All four *kobun* gathered at Harada's bedside.

With a polite nod, Kuhido said only, "Harada-san."

"*Konnichiwa,* Kaziyoshi," Harada rasped, forcing words past the tube in his throat.

Kanashima held the porcelain cup. Kuhido filled it with sake, then handed the bottle to Shinoda. Then Kanashima handed the cup to Kuhido, who drank first.

Kuhido passed the cup to Kanashima, who took a sip. In turn the cup passed to Shinoda and then to Kokusui, who then offered it to Harada. Harada accepted the offer of the cup with a nod. Kokusui tilted the bowl and let a single drop of sake fall on Harada's tongue. As soon as the ritual was done, the four men nodded to Harada; then Shinoda, Kanashima, and Kokusui all bowed to Kuhido. Kanashima collected the sake bottle and handed the cup to Shinoda, and the foursome left Harada's hospital room without speaking another word.

The fact that Kuhido had tasted the sake first had symbolized his ascendance to *oyabun,* the top position. Rank had followed in descending order with the passing of the cup. The fact that they had allowed Harada to drink at all meant that he was still considered a brother, though no longer fit to lead. He would not be killed while lying in bed, and if, when Harada was recovered, he chose not to challenge Kuhido, then the transfer of power would be bloodless and final.

It's for the best, Harada decided.

There would be other opportunities. Even before the Panacea fiasco, he had been contacted by old allies inside the Japanese government. Word on the street was that the new prime minister was looking to pay handsomely for professional protection. Being a bodyguard had seemed to Harada at the time like a retrograde career move; now, the idea of being the right hand to the leader of a growing national power on the world stage held slightly more appeal than it had yesterday.

Harada decided to look into it . . . tomorrow.

Tonight, he would dream of a world that might have been, a global empire of order and harmony, a world-wide hegemony under his authority, its people's fates and actions guided by his wise and beneficent leadership . . . and then he would dream in vivid colors of taking his revenge on Wolverine, for condemning the world to repeat all its worst mistakes for another generation.

If his chemists ever restored Panacea to its original form, he would use it to make his first dream come true. To make his second dream a reality, all he would need would be a sword.

25

TWILIGHT CREPT THROUGH THE SOFTLY CLASH-
ing boughs overhead, and Logan knew that it would
soon be time to leave. His visits to Mariko's grave
often were cut short; not today. He'd spent the afternoon in quiet meditation before the marble mono-
lith devoted to her memory. The red rose that he
had brought last week still lay on the base of the
monument, though the flower was now blackened
and shriveled from desiccation.

In years past, Logan's graveside ruminations had
been about his life that might have been, the possibilities that all had slipped away with Mariko's last
breath. Sometimes, he'd simply questioned fate. Why

had she been taken from him? Why her? Such questions never found answers. The universe was not cruel, but it was arbitrary, and the truest answer to most questions of *Why?* was *Because it happened.*

A low wind hushed between the stones, then dwindled to a whimper. Logan breathed in the approaching night and found it sweet with the scent of freshly cut grass. He reached up and pressed his hand against the cold, glassy marble. *I used to think livin' without you would be the hardest thing I'd ever do,* he confessed to Mariko's unseen spirit. *Turns out I was right.* In a blink of memory, he reflected on all the people who'd ever hurt him, betrayed him, or broken their bond of trust. Despite all the grudges he still carried, none weighed as heavily on him as the one he bore against himself: *I didn't give her the poison, but I was the one who stabbed her in the heart.*

He looked down at his forearms and pictured the adamantium claws that lurked within them. *They can cut through damn near anything, but what good does it do?* Suddenly, his greatest weapons seemed useless. They hadn't been able to cut the poison from Mariko; they could help him destroy a flawed drug, but they were powerless to end the suffering of a billion people dying of hunger, thirst, and disease. He could slay a dozen ninjas, but he couldn't give a grieving mother back her children. His claws held no cures, no promise of a better future, just a faster way to destroy the present, one life at a time.

Lost causes, he brooded. *That's all I seem to fight for these days.* It made sense to him, though—what other battles were really worth fighting? Evil and greed always seemed to trump the better angels of man's nature; cruelty always gained the upper hand in its struggle against mercy. The rich always got their way at the expense of others, and deceived the poor and the weak, like that Zibarese mother, into accepting lives of injustice rather than rebelling against those who had taken advantage of them. Those the rich couldn't fool they bullied.

All over the world, for more than a century, Logan had seen nothing but endless variations on an eternal theme: *The strong prey on the weak.* It was the essence of nature and the primitive instinct that raged in his own heart; it was the animal in him, the feral spark that lived for the hunt, for the kill, pure and honest in its brutality. But it was also the part of him that most needed the civilizing discipline of his human soul—the conscience that could rein in the beast that lurked inside him, feasting and growing strong on his rage and sorrow.

Shadow settled over the graveyard. Logan looked up at the dark mass of marble before him, perhaps hoping for a moment of insight, a glimmer of meaning . . . but he found only the cold reproach of stone.

There's just one thing I'm really good at, he brooded, staring at his clenched fists. *And it doesn't do any good. If I kill a million bad men, a million more'll take their place, just 'cause they can. It never ends. There's always somebody takin' more than they deserve, and six billion morons who let 'em do it. How'm I supposed to fix that with my hands?*

Logan got up from his knees and zipped his leather jacket half closed. It was time to leave; Wai Ying would be waiting for him outside the gate with their motorcycle—which he had bought, since she was now unemployed and broke. They hadn't decided where to go. Maybe to Tokyo, maybe farther north to Sendai, or out of Japan completely. He also didn't know how long they would be together, but what couple ever really did?

What mattered now was simply that, for the first time in years, he was embarking upon a journey for its own sake, just to be on the road, in motion, away and free.

He walked away from Mariko's grave and didn't look back. As he neared the gate he saw Wai Ying. She waved. In her white riding leathers, she was like a pale ghost in the gathering gloom. Riding off with her into the night, their plan unwritten and destination unknown, would be an act of faith: in Wai Ying, in the future, in himself.

I know I can't change the world. Maybe I can't even change myself. But it's worth a try.

He joined Wai Ying at the motorcycle. They climbed on the bike, him in front, her in back, arms around his waist. He turned the key, kicked the starter, twisted the throttle. A buzz-saw growl coursed from its engine, a song of freedom. The bike lurched into motion.

The road of Logan's past was littered with fallen friends and enemies, soaked in the blood of the innocent and the guilty, built on the bones of the just and the unjust. He was leaving that path behind, in search of a better one. In the roar of an engine he was away, on the road to his future.

It was a journey long overdue.

Acknowledgments

PEOPLE OFTEN THINK THAT BEING A WRITER SOUNDS like hard, lonely work. Sometimes it is. But just as lonely—and far less lauded—is the lot of the writer's spouse. My lovely wife, Kara, deals with my reclusive moods, my nights spent brooding behind closed doors, my semipermanent air of mental distraction as I work on my stories inside my head when I'm supposed to be focusing on other things—such as what our dinner guests are saying. For all your seemingly inexhaustible forbearance, my love, thank you.

Next up is my friend Glenn Hauman, who helped me come up with the first germ of an idea for this book. He was the one who suggested a plot based around a miracle drug that kills its users when they try to go cold turkey. Glenn also helped me acquire decades of past issues of *Wolverine* on CD-ROM, so that I could research this book properly. Thanks, my old friend; I could not have done this without your help. You rule.

Some of the story lines to which I made reference in the text of this novel include *Path of the Warlord,* written by Howard Mackie, and *Soultaker,* written by Akira Yoshida. Furthermore, my principal antagonist, Silver Samurai, was the brainchild of writer Steve Gerber, and the Hand would not exist but for the pen of comic-book legend Frank Miller. My thanks go out to all these gifted scribes.

Of course, as long as I'm thanking people for inspiring the story line, I should tip my hat to *New York Times* columnist Nicholas Kristof, whose columns about the genocidal crises in such places as Darfur and Chad helped to inspire this book's central plotline. Thank you, Mr. Kristof, for continuing to make people aware of a tragedy that all too many of us find far too easy to ignore.

My friend Steven Wexler took time to share his martial-arts expertise and suggested a number of sources that I used in my research of sword and knife combat. Thanks for the pointers, Steve. They helped.

Peppered throughout this book are snippets of dialogue in a number of foreign languages. Because I am pathetically monolingual, I needed to enlist the aid of a number of language consultants to pull this off and get it right. Tomoko Kanashima vetted my Japanese; Sonia Kuchuk and her parents translated the various bits of Russian; and Carlos Carranza and his "Brazilian mafia" provided the book's tidbits of Brazilian Portuguese. *Muchas gracias* to all of you, my *amigos,* for all your help.

Keeping watch over the English portions of the book was editor par excellence Marco Palmieri, for whose patient guidance I am always grateful. Thanks also are due to former Pocket Books associate publisher Scott Shannon, who first suggested to me that I should write a *Wolverine* novel. Luckily for me, Ruwan Jayatilleke of Marvel Comics agreed with Scott.

I also feel that I should thank my in-laws—Keith, Donna, and Diana—for being so supportive of all my work. You're probably the only members of my family who will actually pay for a copy of this book.

Last but not least, my heartfelt gratitude goes out to renowned artist David Mack, the critically acclaimed and award-winning creator of the *Kabuki* graphic novels, for agreeing to create this book's cover art. This is the first time that one of my books has had an actual painting for its cover; all my past works have had covers created with digital art or Photoshop-manipulated photographs. This time, a work of singular beauty adorns my words. David, I hope you feel that my book proves worthy of the magnificent cover you've created for it. Thank you.

About the Author

DAVID MACK is the author of numerous *Star Trek* novels, including the *USA Today* bestseller *A Time to Heal* and its companion volume, *A Time to Kill*. Mack's other novels include *Star Trek: Deep Space Nine—Warpath*; *Star Trek Vanguard: Harbinger*, the first volume in a series that he developed with editor Marco Palmieri; *Star Trek: S.C.E.—Wildfire*; and numerous eBooks and short stories.

Before writing books, Mack cowrote two episodes of *Star Trek: Deep Space Nine*. He cowrote the episode "Starship Down" with John J. Ordover. Mack and Ordover teamed up again to pen the story treatment for the episode "It's Only a Paper Moon," for which Ronald D. Moore wrote the teleplay.

Among Mack's upcoming projects are a *Star Trek* alternate-universe tale, *The Sorrows of Empire*; another installment in the *Star Trek Vanguard* saga; and a pair of original novels.

An avid fan of the Canadian progressive-rock trio Rush, Mack has been to all of the band's concert tours since 1982.

Mack currently resides in New York City with his wife, Kara. Learn more about him and his work on his official Web site: www.infinitydog.com.